THE RULE
OF
THREE

THE RULE OF THREE

OF

THREE

a novel

SAM RIPLEY

EMILY BESTLER BOOKS

ATRIA

NEW YORK   LONDON   TORONTO   SYDNEY   NEW DELHI

EMILY
BESTLER
BOOKS

ATRIA

An Imprint of Simon & Schuster, LLC
1230 Avenue of the Americas
New York, NY 10020

First Emily Bestler Books/Atria Books hardcover edition August 2024

EMILY BESTLER BOOKS/ATRIA BOOKS and colophon are trademarks of Simon & Schuster, LLC

Simon & Schuster: Celebrating 100 Years of Publishing in 2024

For information about special discounts for bulk purchases, please contact Simon & Schuster Special Sales at 1-866-506-1949 or business@simonandschuster.com.

The Simon & Schuster Speakers Bureau can bring authors to your live event. For more information or to book an event, contact the Simon & Schuster Speakers Bureau at 1-866-248-3049 or visit our website at www.simonspeakers.com.

Interior design by Kyoko Watanabe

Manufactured in the United States of America

1   3   5   7   9   10   8   6   4   2

Library of Congress Control Number: 2024936162

ISBN 978-1-6680-4769-9
ISBN 978-1-6680-4771-2 (ebook)

For Liz

DON'T FORGET THE RULE OF THREE

IT'S COMING FOR YOU

LIKE IT CAME FOR ME

First thing: take a deep breath.

I can't overstate how important it is to breathe. Do it now. Inhale, long and slow. Hold it in. Exhale even slower. See, you're calmer already, aren't you? I need you calm because you need to listen.

I know you. I know you're terrified and overwhelmed. I know no one believes you and you're desperate and going out of your mind. I know you because I *was* you. I thought I had it all figured out. I thought I knew it all. I was so very, very wrong.

I'll tell you everything that happened. Every little detail. As it happened, how it happened. Because maybe you'll see something I failed to notice. I know the answer is here somewhere. I just couldn't find it myself.

So pay attention. Pay attention to every single detail.

Before we start, you must remember one important fact. What you'll read didn't save me.

But perhaps, together, we can save you.

Good luck,

███

AMY

ONE

I wasn't always crazy, but I was never sane.

I learned this the hard way, of course, and as with all the best lessons, I understood it too late to heed it. What should I have done? Could I have changed things? The questions don't so much swirl around my mind as circle the drain of my sanity. Which leads to another question: Would knowing what I know now have helped me at the beginning?

Maybe by the end you'll be able to answer that.

You better hope you can.

I'm no longer scared, which is a first. I've spent my whole life afraid: of the world, of pain, of fear itself. Fear has been my lifelong companion, the friend I didn't want but who never took the hint. In that way, it was my one true friend, my most loyal friend, yet now even that friend has deserted me.

I can't say I'm at peace—the mad can never rest—but I'm content as the end draws near. I'm content because I now understand what I can do. What I should do. A final good deed. One for the road, so to speak. This, what you're reading now, is that good deed.

You're welcome.

But let's not be any more morose than we need to be so early on when there's plenty of misery to come. Let's start with a celebration instead, a party. They're fun, right? I'll tell you about my birthday.

Not the most recent one. I don't want to overburden you before you're ready. Besides, you don't need to know that I didn't even notice when the clock struck midnight or that I spent the hours that followed lost in my work, in my research. Too busy to see, too determined to listen. Too focused on trying to stay alive. So there's no point starting there.

Stay tuned for more of that fateful day later.

No, I'll begin by telling you about the last birthday I enjoyed, the last birthday that meant something. It meant so much in so many ways.

Ready? Here comes the flashback:

Steve said, "I don't expect you to listen to us."

Jenny said, "But you really should."

I wasn't listening because my heart was racing as I tried to make sure I had everything. The holy trinity: money, makeup, and medication.

My parents were exchanging looks and gestures. A whole silent language at work. I could see them out of the corner of my eye as I checked the contents of my bag. I felt like I was forgetting something, but I was so out of practice socializing I didn't really know what I should be taking with me. My first house party at eighteen years old.

"You're going to be freezing," Steve said.

"I'll be outside for like a minute tops."

"If you take a coat, you can take it off. You can't put one on if you don't have one."

"I have a jacket."

He gave a sort of snorting huff. "If it doesn't cover your behind—"

"Leave it behind," I finish, rolling my eyes. "Yeah, yeah, I know."

"Don't 'yeah, yeah' me. I'm only trying to—"

"I think you look lovely, dear," Jenny interrupted, her soothing hand finding Steve's arm.

I didn't respond because I didn't like all this talk about what I was wearing. I was self-conscious enough as it was and terrified my clothes were just as lame as I thought. Missing so much high school meant I didn't know the rules. There was only so much magazines could teach me about the outside world.

Jenny brushed a stray hair from my shoulder. "Your father doesn't remember what it was like to be your age because he was born a grumpy old man. At the hospital they skipped the neonatal ward and took him straight to geriatrics."

She smiled, pleased with herself. She was on her second glass of wine already. Steve made a throaty grumble of displeasure Jenny's way, which seemed to give her a small measure of extra satisfaction. I guessed the pills were starting to kick in given the glassy sheen to her eyes. I was glad she was feeling upbeat.

In the past they would have laughed, perhaps Jenny continuing the gentle mockery for a few more barbs as Steve stumbled over his words to defend himself. No doubt I would have joined in the fun, and Maya, too, the three girls in his life ganging up and taking turns to tease him, the big cave bear. And he, in response, probably chasing us around the house as we squealed and screamed while he bellowed threats to make us pay by way of raspberries, noogies, or the dreaded wet willies.

I realized they had both fallen silent for a moment like me, as if the three of us were all thinking the same thing at the same time, momentarily lost in the identical, impossible fantasy.

Steve was first to return to reality. "Regardless of what your mother says, I do remember what it was like at your age. I remember the pressure to fit in with my friends." He was speaking in a soft tone because he wanted me to listen to his words as if he were a peer, not a father. "When everyone else is doing something, it's incredibly hard not to go along with it too."

Even before, Steve had been the worrier of the two. Tonight was my first night out in forever, and it was almost like I could hear each of his thundering heartbeats. He knew once I stepped through the front door he could no longer protect me.

Jenny didn't add to his comment, but I knew the D-word was in her thoughts too.

No, not *that* D. Get your mind out of the gutter.

"I'm not going to take drugs," I told them both. "Seriously, it makes like zero sense when I have a nightstand full of them already."

Steve's little speech was because ecstasy was in the headlines again as the go-to tabloid bogeyman. They were concerned because they'd read horror stories of supposedly quiet, ordinary teens suddenly turning into addicts or dying at raves, boiled in their own body heat. I didn't get why anyone would want to go to those things, take pills bought from strangers with crazy eyes, and dance all night to such awful, soulless music.

"The last thing I want to do is swallow even more pills."

There was frustration in my voice, but I couldn't get angry with them. I didn't want to lose them either. I was forever telling Steve to cook with less oil. I was always telling Jenny to slow down with the wine. We were holding on to each other so tightly we didn't realize all three of us were asphyxiating under that unbearable pressure.

I know now they were more scared than I acknowledged at the time. Steve was doing everything possible to resist asking me to please stay home. It wasn't a coincidence that Jenny was on that early second glass of wine. I think they were always scared. I think they were so used to hiding what they really felt that I wonder now if they ever showed me their true selves. I never truly recognized their pain because I was too distracted trying to cope with my own.

Grief is selfish like that.

I'd spent my middle teen years in more hospitals than classrooms, with more doctors than teachers, talking to more therapists than school friends. I could barely recall the time before that, so as I was about to leave the house, it felt like I'd been waiting my entire life to start finally living.

Not my eighteenth birthday, but my first.

"Our daughter is a smart girl," Jenny said to Steve. Then to me, "Aren't you, honey?"

I nodded.

Steve sighed. "I'm just pointing out that even if you say no and they make fun of you, they'll come to respect you more."

"Uh-huh."

"Amy," Jenny then said in a gentle tone, peering over her wineglass at me.

"Yeah?"

She said nothing but made a gesture that I didn't understand for a moment, until I realized she was looking at my left wrist where my sleeve had ridden up a little. I twisted around and tugged the sleeve down over the hard ridge of discolored skin poking out. When I turned back, she'd drifted away so as not to embarrass me. She knew I hated people noticing my scars. I wore only long sleeves and kept several bracelets and bands around that wrist at all times. I had a huge collection of the things, which I wore in different combinations as and when the mood took me. They were handmade in arts-and-crafts treatment sessions. Except one. My lucky bracelet that Maya gave me. It hadn't left my wrist since I first put it on. She'd died the next day.

"I can hear a car pulling up," Steve said, voice full of bubbling fatherly stress. He peered out of the front window. Turned to face me, struggling to keep his expression even. "Why is there a car? Who's driving?"

"It's okay, it's okay," I tell him, rushing closer to take his hands in mine. "My friend's dad, not her. He's driving us all there. It's okay, he's just like you. He's super careful, I promise. I promise."

He swallowed. Tried hard to calm down. I could feel the dampness in his palms. I smiled to ease the panic in his eyes, and Steve managed to nod in return.

"Tell him it's icier than it looks out there," he said, struggling to keep his voice even and rational-sounding. "Temperature has plummeted this evening and it rained all afternoon."

"I will. I swear. It's icier than it looks, I'll say. It rained this afternoon and the temperature's dropped a lot since. Okay?"

He went to say more, to further emphasize the need for care, but he stopped himself. Instead, he forced a little smile for my benefit. He didn't want to lose another daughter, and yet he didn't want me to take his fear out on me.

Jenny came closer. "Back by midnight."

I resisted the urge to argue. Going out was a huge privilege and I was grateful, whatever the curfew attached to it. Besides, Jenny was being the stern one who Steve could not be. He did everything possible not to say no to me, and at my worst I would have gone too far exploiting that. I needed Jenny's unwavering discipline as the authority figure as much as I needed Steve's unquestioning kindness or I wouldn't have survived. It was an excellent system, almost a tag team of sorts, and I bet it had been some strategy from my psychiatrist.

Amy needs a careful touch, I could imagine him saying, *but not a weak one.*

Oh, my parents were careful with me, and they were never weak. They had such resolve, and such unwavering love despite my explosive temper, pendulum mood swings, and relentless crying. I didn't deserve them.

Jenny had already given me the speech about what kind of boys were trouble, to make sure I had my key and could recite our phone number and a thousand other things I didn't care about. I just wanted to get out and have a good time.

I had planned that night with military precision. During the days and weeks leading up to it, I had never slept in, never acted up or argued. I ate all the food given to me, took all my meds, did all my homework, and generally behaved like those perfect kids in commercials. I wouldn't have been allowed out otherwise. I knew I had to fake normalcy like never before, and I was determined as I had never before been. I was ready to have fun again. I was willing to attempt happiness.

And Steve and Jenny were finally prepared to trust me again.

"Promise me one thing," Jenny said as I opened the front door.

Expecting some final lecture, I sighed. "What now?"

"That you'll have a great time."

"You've earned it," Steve added.

It was so sweet, but it made me feel awkward. I hadn't earned anything at all.

"Don't wait up," I said to change the subject, knowing full well they would be awake and anxious until the exact second I returned. But I couldn't have that fun I so desperately needed if I was worried about them worrying.

I stepped outside, smiled and waved at my friends in the car at the end of the driveway, and was about to say goodbye to Steve and Jenny, only I didn't get a chance because Steve suddenly wrapped his arms around me. A big hug because he filled a doorframe. He was like a lumbering giant. Slow and particular. There was a clumsy awkwardness about him that was so endearing. He could lift me up with one hand, yet had me open little bottle tops because he didn't have the necessary dexterity in his massive sausage fingers. We both found such moments hilarious.

I was half crushed by the hug. I knew my friends could see me, and Steve smothered me for so long I could have died of embarrassment. I hated every second of it and wriggled out as fast as possible, pretending I failed to notice how sad that made him.

"I love you," Jenny called after me as I rushed down the drive, so desperate to attempt happiness, to start my new life, that I didn't even look back.

I had THE BEST time. I got drunk. I laughed. I danced. I even had my first proper, heavy breathing teenage make-out session. I mean, I know I had the best time, and yet I can't remember how it felt. I have no emotional recollection of the party. What was the name of the boy who slid his hand into my underwear? Was I too nervous to enjoy it? I can't even picture my friends now. Their watercolor faces are smudged by the thumb of regret; bright memory faded to monochrome.

All withers of that party, that fun, *that* Amy.

All that lingers is Steve's suffocating hug that embarrassed me and Jenny's "I love you" that I didn't reciprocate. Because when I returned home at midnight, truly happy for the first time in years, I found my devoted parents side by side in the garage, hanging from the ceiling by their necks.

TWO

Regrets, I've had *way* more than Sinatra. Like always calling Steve and Jenny Steve and Jenny. It was one of those stupid teenage things. I think I'd seen it in a sitcom, and it seemed rebellious and suited my need to define myself in whatever way I could. We all so badly want to be unique at that age, and yet often the most originality we can achieve is to copy someone else. They hated it, of course, but that only made me more determined to keep doing it. And then it became a habit, and by the time my sister died in the car accident it was too late to change. It still haunts me that I couldn't give them that small kindness of hearing their only remaining daughter call them Mom and Dad.

Did they think of that when they were preparing the nooses?

Maybe I could have taken away a little of their sadness, and perhaps they wouldn't have left me all alone.

Clarity is second only to hindsight of all the things I hate in this world.

After myself, of course.

I'm in an especially self-loathing mood. Having your stomach pumped will do that to a girl.

"I feel like a balloon with all the air forcibly sucked out."

The doctor doesn't look up from his clipboard. "How do you think you should feel at a time like this?"

I'm not sure how much condescension he wants me to infer from his tone, so I don't answer.

Elizabeth is still working on the cover story. "I think one of those frat guys must've spiked your drink when we went for a smoke."

Flipping a page, the doctor shakes his head a little. I'm pretty sure he's annoyed I survived such a cocktail of alcohol, prescription drugs, and illegal narcotics. He shakes his head a lot. His nostrils flare to the point they look like they might fly away. He tuts every chance he can. Naturally, this gives me a small amount of comfort as I recover on the bed, my entire throat pulsing in waves of agony from the tubes they've stuck down there.

Lizzy sees me grimace. "Can't you give her something for the pain?"

The doctor doesn't look up. "I don't think there's enough room in her bloodstream for any more drugs."

I take Lizzy's hand. Squeeze it. "I'm okay. I just want to go home." Seeing the pain and concern in her face hurts more than my deflated insides and raw throat. "I'll be fine by tomorrow."

"Indeed," the doctor says. "Although I can't quite believe you're not in worse shape."

"Why does it sound like you think this is her fault?" Lizzy barks. "She's the victim here. Her drink was spiked."

He finally looks up. "Would you like me to give the police a call on your behalf? I'm sure someone can be here within the hour to take a statement."

I try not to squirm under his scrutinous gaze. "I . . . No, I don't . . . I'm not sure what happened. I don't know who . . ."

Lizzy says, "Can I take her home now or what?"

The doctor sighs. Nods in defeat.

Lizzy doesn't know what happened, but she's backing up my story because she knows I'm a sliver away from being locked up for my own protection. She pretends she was with me almost the entire night, that she willingly took as many drugs as I did, that I was laughing and joking the whole time—until I passed out—and had expressed no desire to kill or harm myself. The doctor doesn't seem convinced, but maybe he's willing to take a chance, to believe. Or perhaps he knows deep down what this was and also knows that with Lizzy backing me up there's nothing he can really do.

Third time should have been the charm, yet I failed again like I had the previous two times. First time: I didn't cut deep enough. Second time: the rope frayed. Now: I threw up all those pills before they could work their magic.

Imitation is the sincerest form of flattery, as I've already mentioned, which was why I tried to copy Steve and Jenny. I figured it would be easy. Seriously, how hard can it be to hang yourself? Rope. Noose. Job done. Ignorance is bliss. I don't weigh much, but turns out most rope isn't all that strong. Should have gone with climbing rope, of course. Or the high-tensile stuff Steve and Jenny used. I just picked up something cheap from the DIY place. I can laugh about it now: buying cheap rope to save pennies when I was trying to kill myself. What was I trying to save the money for? One more flower at my cremation? Still, suicidal thoughts are by definition mental illness, so I try not to give myself too hard a time over the small stuff.

I'm not entirely sure what went wrong with the slit wrists. I bought the most expensive razor blades available. *Closest shave possible*, they claimed. *No razor burn. Kissably smooth legs. Baby-soft cooch.* I cut plenty deep and the right way too. No amateur bisecting cry-for-help grazes for me. No, I went along the tendons. I've never seen so much blood. But I woke up in the hospital. Somehow, I survived. A miracle. Thanks, oh-so-common blood type.

Tonight I can almost understand. The culmination of a prolonged period of weeping and wailing and too hard a comedown. Whatever my mental fragility, my body is pure cavewoman. Its demise requires a more determined effort. I popped everything I could lay my hands on and hoped for the best. Hope failed. Survival through laziness. Darwinism in reverse.

Define *irony*, Amy:

I'm too weak to overcome my own strength.

Lizzy takes me back once the condescending doctor signs the release. I'm silent the entire trip because I know if I open my mouth then all that's going to come out of it will be sobs. I don't want to cry for the whole journey. I don't want her to see me like that. She must already be thinking how pathetic I am, how she wishes she never made friends with me in that first week of college.

Too late now, bitch.

"Are you okay, hun?" she asks me.

I nod and touch my throat to show her it hurts, to explain away my silence. She buys it or doesn't and is polite and kind enough not to challenge me on it. I don't like to be challenged. I tend to lash out. Just don't tell me I overreact a lot or I'll go apeshit.

It's a rocky ride because Lizzy's car is a piece of trash because she's an average person who doesn't have piles of useful cash left behind by dead parents.

I've known her a long time, since we were both wayward teens. Lizzy is everything I wish I could be myself. She's taller, slimmer, smarter, prettier, but above all else she's normal. She had a shitty childhood growing up in care, sure, but she got over her issues and so isn't covered in scars like me. She doesn't have a list of prescribed medication longer than her arm. She's the only family I have left, and oh how I miss her so much in these final weeks.

Where was I? Oh yes, I sleep for sixteen hours straight as my body recovers from all that poison.

My eyes open, and I smile.

I smile because she stands over me. The ceiling light is directly above her and gives her a halo of 60-watt light. She's glorious.

"You look like an angel," I say.

She laughs. "What did they give you again?"

I shrug. "You *are* an angel. You saved me."

"While that's a lovely thing to say I think the doctors should have a little of the credit."

"They just pumped my stomach. Anyone can do that."

"I'm not sure that's true."

"But you saved me. You protected me."

She knows what I mean: she lied for me.

Glorious Lizzy stares down at me, my own personal heavenly

guardian, but she looks sad. She is sad. "You meant it, didn't you?"

I don't answer. I can't meet her gaze. I can't bear this angel to think badly of me.

"Why?" she asks.

She knows why, of course. She knows all about Steve and Jenny and Maya and the hollowed-out husk of a girl they left behind. She doesn't mean that. She means why now, why this time, what pushed me over this particular edge?

"Is it because the anniversaries are coming up?"

She's known me long enough to know this is always a tough time of the year for me with my looming birthday. That means within the space of a few weeks it's the anniversary of Maya's death and the anniversary of Steve and Jenny's suicide. Funnily enough, I didn't feel like celebrating when I turned nineteen, and then twenty. My twenty-first will be no different.

I shrug in response, which isn't an easy thing to do lying down and tucked under a quilt. It feels awkward. I feel awkward. I'm small. I'm nothing.

"Tell me," she says.

There's no insistence in her voice, no order. She wants to know because she needs to know, to know me. How can she help me if she doesn't know me?

I blink. My cheeks dampen.

"Oh no," she says with her soft, heavenly voice. "Don't do that. Don't cry. You don't have to tell me. I'm here for you, regardless."

She reaches down to wipe away my tears with a thumb, first one cheek then the other. Her touch is softer than the pillow. Her touch is warmth and love, and I'm unworthy of it.

"I don't deserve you," I say.

"Don't be silly. Of course you do. I just want to help you, Amy. Let me help you."

I swallow. I nod. I need her help, but I don't want to need it. I don't want to be me at all.

She waits for me to speak in my own time. She doesn't rush me.

"I miss them," I say.

"I know," she says.

She waits again. She has infinite patience for this patient.

I take a breath in an effort to compose myself. A ridiculous notion because I'm so far removed from composure, it's not even funny. But I need a moment to gather myself, to find some courage to speak and some strength to actually get the words out as words and not sobs and more tears.

"I was watching TV," I begin. "Not really watching but it was on, and I was there, so I was watching. Do you know what I mean?"

Of course she knows. She's been there. We've all been there. I continue:

"There was a commercial. I wasn't paying attention, but I could hear the music. I don't know what the music was, but it was classical or opera or something. Lizzy, it was beautiful. It was just so lovely. I looked up at the screen. I saw the ad. It was for a car. I don't even know what kind of car it was, but I started crying because I wondered what kind of music Maya was listening to when she was in her car when she . . ."

My voice cracks. I raise my hand to cover my eyes. Lizzy leans closer to hug me, but she can't hug me while I'm lying down on my back. Instead, she climbs across me and lies down on the bed next to me so she can place an arm over me. She says nothing, but she doesn't need to say anything because no words can change anything. They can't take away my pain and they can't bring Maya back and they can't turn back time and stop Steve and Jenny hanging ropes in the garage. She holds me while I cry, and I don't know how long I cry for because I fall asleep and when I wake she's still lying next to me, still holding me.

"Don't do it again," she says. "Promise me."

I say, "I promise," and I'm glad she can't see my face because she doesn't deserve my lies as much as I don't deserve her.

Of course, I don't have to promise her. I don't need to kill myself when I'm going to die anyway. All I have to do is wait.

The only problem, and it's a significant one, is that I don't want to die like this . . . doomed, cursed. Whatever.

Killing myself is one thing. That's my choice. It's my autonomy as a human being to decide when to end the life that is mine and mine alone. Having it decided for me is unacceptable.

Define irony again:

I want to live so I may die when I choose.

THREE

Y ou don't have to stay with me all day," I say as I hand Lizzy
some breakfast the next morning.

She takes her plate and shrugs as if her kindness is no big deal.
Maybe it isn't to her. Perhaps that's just how ordinary people behave
toward one another.

"I'm here, Amy," she says with a smile. "So get used to it."

She's already missed several classes to look after me and doesn't
so much as mention this fact. I love her for that. Most people are
so desperate for credit whenever they so much as hold open a door
for someone, they can't help themselves but remind you of the favor
they're doing, of their holy sacrifice. Your guilt is their acclaim. Not
Elizabeth. Not my sweet Lizzy.

We're having toast because that's literally all I know how to
make for breakfast besides fixing a bowl of cereal. My toaster has
a whole range of sci-fi–level settings but somehow only seems capable of making hot floppy bread or charcoal. I opt for charcoal and
scrape off so many burnt bread crumbs that the kitchen sink ends
up looking like an ashtray. Lizzy prefers hot limp bread because it's
less work. We both slather on plenty of margarine and munch in
silence, communicating with grunts and eyebrow raises, trying to
outdo one another with increasingly silly expressions. Lizzy laughs
first, so I win.

"Thank you," I say. "For staying, I mean."

Finished eating, I dump my plate and knife into the sink in the hope the dishwashing fairy will come along later and take care of it for me. Said fairy has been somewhat slack in her duties of late because I don't so much as put the plate and knife in the sink as balance them on top of an unstable mountain of pans and crockery.

Lizzy rolls her eyes as she perches her plate on top of mine. "You don't have to thank me."

"I do."

"You don't."

"I did."

"You shouldn't have."

I smile. She smiles. I feel better.

"You can go," I say. "I'm not going to do it again."

She can't hide the skepticism in her eyes, because it's only right to be skeptical.

"I feel like shit," I explain. "My stomach hurts, and my throat is so raw it's like I've sucked off a donkey."

She arches an eyebrow. "I thought you were only into horse dicks."

"I'm trying to be less discriminatory."

She laughs. I laugh. We hug.

I'm not sure what we had for breakfast is incredibly pertinent, but I figure I should tell you everything I remember. I think keeping things as linear as possible is the most logical method. If I start with where I end up, then I don't think it will make sense. I'll have to explain things in reverse, and you'll become fixated on what happens to me instead of why it happens. It's the why that has to be the key. It's the why that can ultimately help you. At least, that's what I think at this moment of the telling. Maybe I'll change my mind later on and start leaping around in time. Throw in some flash-forwards, maybe. Experiment with jump cuts, perhaps. If I'm inconsistent, it's because I don't know what I'm doing. Please don't get annoyed with me, okay? I'm making it up as I go along. I wish I knew what was best, but at this moment I don't. If I did I wouldn't need to write anything down. In fact, although I'm writing a survival guide, if you're reading this then there's a chance that I'm speaking to you from beyond the grave. I could be long dead, couldn't I? Which then means that I'm writing in the now and you are simultaneously reading in the future.

And while I'm alive at the time of writing, I could also be dead in your present.

This is some mind-bending stuff, right?

Anyway, I'll break continuity now to tell you one thing that you mustn't forget, that you need to keep in your thoughts at all times.

It's like a code, a pattern, a puzzle I don't yet understand. Ready? Three.

The number. It's got something to do with the number three. We'll come back to that later, but I want you to be thinking about it from the outset. You see, I might tell you about something that happened, something that didn't seem important as it happened, but perhaps you'll realize it was important, it was significant after all and I just didn't notice.

I'm hoping that by writing this down I'll make sense of it all before the end. But right now I feel like a failure because I can't just give you all the answers.

I'm sorry I failed us both.

But I'm giving you the head start I never had.

Don't waste it.

Don't you fucking dare.

"I can stay as long as you like," Lizzy says. "I can get notes off Cath. She'll be cool with it. She likes to feel needed. Like seriously, bitch, we're just using you. It doesn't mean you're the shit."

I'm shaking my head before she's finished. "It's okay. You really don't have to stay. I didn't actually mean it."

She frowns. Skeptical. She's right to be, of course.

"I did mean it, but maybe I didn't also. Like yin and yang, light and dark. Duality-of-man . . . kind of thing."

"In English, please."

I struggle to find the correct words. I can't speak with any accuracy because I don't know which feelings were real and which were induced, manipulated, or twisted by drugs and alcohol.

I say, "Deep down I'm sure I had to know there weren't enough pills. I was upset. I wasn't thinking. I just wanted the pain to go away. It wasn't like before. I wasn't upset when I cut myself. I had planned it for weeks. I had this ice-cold clarity, this determination. Purpose. Last night wasn't like that."

She wants to believe me but can't quite bring herself to accept my explanation. She thinks I'm lying.

"I swear, Lizzy. I swear it. I wouldn't lie. Not to you. To everyone else in this piss-poor excuse for a world, yes, but not you. Never you. You're the only thing that matters to me."

She raises her eyebrow again, but it's not funny this time.

"I mean it, I wouldn't lie to you. Every other fucker out there, sure. But not you. Never you. Come on. You have to believe that."

"Okay, okay," she says. "I give up. If you swear you didn't mean it, then I believe you. But you really scared me, Amy."

"I'm sorry. I am so sorry. The last thing I want to do is cause you pain."

She gives me a stern look. "If you try again, I'll kill you."

She cracks before she's finished, and we smile and hug again.

I say, "You're crushing me with your balloon tits."

"And I don't even charge."

We release one another. She brushes down some of my unruly hair.

"But please talk to me when you get sad like that. Even if you're not thinking suicidal thoughts. Okay? Just call me. Talk to me. Please. It's not like I have a life beyond studying and chronic masturbation."

"I will," I say, and I want to mean it.

"I thought I'd lost you. I really did."

I don't know what to say. She has a frightened look in her eyes I haven't seen before. It unnerves me just to see it in Lizzy, to see it in this perfect person I wish I were instead of myself.

"What is it?" I ask, yet I don't want an answer.

For a moment it seems as if she won't tell me and I'm relieved, but I don't know why.

The relief doesn't last.

"It's silly," she begins. "Sort of stupid, I know, but I had a kind of premonition. Like a dream, only I wasn't asleep."

"What do you mean? When did you have this *premonition*?"

My tone is mocking and I feel bad instantly, and she bows her head, not wanting to meet my gaze. "I was thinking about your sister, your parents . . . then I had this weird feeling. I can't explain it. But it was like I blinked and you were dead." She looks up. "I got the call from the hospital soon afterward."

She sounds serious, but it's hard to take it seriously. "Were you smoking grass?"

She's shaking her head vigorously before I'm finished. "Obviously I was high, but my mind was clear. That's what's so freaky about it."

"So what?"

I shrug. It doesn't mean anything to me. We all think about weird things all the time. We dwell only on the tiny percentage that happens to sync up with the real world. I call that coincidence, but I've never been remotely superstitious.

She's surprised by my distinct lack of meaningful reaction. "It doesn't bother you?"

I shake my head. "Why would it? You just had a thought. Maybe we were talking about death earlier that day—and let's face it, we do that a lot—and a slice of our conversation popped into your mind. You think it's a premonition, but it's actually just a memory of something you'd forgotten."

It's Lizzy's turn to shake her head. "No, it wasn't that. It really wasn't. Amy, I'm telling you, it was a premonition. I saw you, and you were dead."

I smile. "But I'm here. I'm alive. It wasn't a premonition because it didn't come true."

I can see in her expression that she's sure of what she "saw," but she can hardly fault the logic that I'm alive and standing before her.

I try to clear my throat. I can't. I can't swallow.

I can't breathe.

My eyes widen. My face reddens. I grasp at my throat.

"*Amy*," Lizzy cries out, terrified.

She's punching me in the arm a second later once she sees I'm desperately trying to stop my face breaking into a childish grin.

"That wasn't cool," she says. "And it wasn't funny."

"I think it's pretty funny. Why are you twitchy? It's not like you."

She hesitates, unsure of how best to express it. "You know . . ."

"I don't."

"The expression," she says in answer. "Bad things always happen in threes."

I'm waiting for more because I don't understand what that has to do with me.

"Your sister," she says. "Your parents. You."

"That doesn't make sense. That's four people. If anything, the bad-things-happen-in-threes has already happened. Maya, Steve, and Jenny. Three people."

"I guess," she says, unconvinced. "But your parents died together, didn't they? That's one tragedy."

"Is it?" I ask.

Her eyes flick up, looking over me to the clock on the wall. "*Shit*," she says. "I forgot I have that tutorial with Professor Hot-or-Not. Do you mind? Are you really okay to be on your own for a bit?"

I assure her it's fine. I want to be by myself.

She's gone moments later. I'm alone in my little student abode with nothing but my thoughts for company. These thoughts inevitably form a monstrous dark cloud of sadness and pain and memory that crackles with lightning and booms with thunder. At the center of that maelstrom is the calm eye of the storm, and in that eye, in that calm, is a single inescapable question that will come to define my short life from this point on:

Do bad things always happen in threes?

FOUR

Home is where the heart is. Was. I still have the house I grew up in, not that I've lived in it since my parents decided breathing was an overrated use of their time. It's obvious to say the house feels empty, yet it's cavernous in that emptiness. I step back in time as I walk the rooms and hallways, looking for nothing and everything all at once. The dust sheets over furniture are like spirits trapped in limbo, statue-still yet wailing in a choir of excruciating silence.

In the early days, I tried to sell it—I wanted to be rid of the memories—but word gets around. Not many people want to live in the same house where a couple of ordinary, regular people hanged themselves. An automated rolling garage door seems like a great selling point until you hear that the ropes were attached to the ceiling runners. And even if a potential buyer could get past that, once they found out that the couple had a daughter who died in a car crash, then it's no stretch to imagine that any other house on the market suddenly looks more appealing. Here's a lovely three-bed property with walk-in closets and the haunting stench of violent death, or here's a poky studio with rats in the walls for the same price.

You'd take the rats every time, right?

I don't blame you. I would too.

All that death lingers as poisonous air. I take it in with every breath, and yet I cannot breathe it out again.

I realize I'm toying with the bracelet Maya gave me all those years ago. It's a simple silver band, little more than costume jewelry, but it's the most precious thing I own. I touch it for luck sometimes. I touch it when I'm scared.

A house that isn't lived in has a certain kind of smell. It smells empty. Emptiness has no scent, of course, but it's the absence of all those little odors of a home that is noticeable. There are no delicious aromas of coffee or food drifting from the kitchen. There are no sickly floral scents from air fresheners. There's no whiff of pets. No cleaning chemicals. The reek of nothingness assails my nostrils.

Everywhere is the same.

The living room is lifeless.

The garden won't grow.

This home is a tomb.

I feel the ghosts of my parents following me wherever I go. Every few steps I stop and spin around, hoping to catch them off guard. I fail. Every time they're too fast for me. They want me to know they're there, but they don't want us to connect. Maybe that's for the best. What do you say to a ghost anyway?

Looking a bit pale, Jenny.

Have you lost weight, Steve?

I'm nervous, yet I don't know why. There's a building unease that I cannot rationalize. What do I expect to find? What do I think might happen here?

In my paranoia, I begin lifting up the sheets covering furniture to check no one or nothing is hiding beneath them. Is that a chair beneath that sheet or the crouching shape of a monster?

It's the middle of the day, but I start turning on every light. My heart is racing. My pits are damp.

Lizzy's words echo in my mind. I'm thinking about patterns, about bad things always happening in threes. Just a saying, or is it rooted in something real, something primeval? Something humanity chose to forget for its own sanity?

I'm trying not to look at the door to the garage in case it looks back at me, in case the door opens as I near and pulls me inside.

It was always a nice garage, filled with this, that, and the other, but neat. Steve put up metal shelving units along every wall, floor to ceiling. That way he could give in to his need to collect everything, to throw nothing away, at the same time obeying Jenny's obsession with regimented order. She hated mess. She had lists for everything. No task was performed without a thorough plan. No deviation was ever allowed. We were never late for school.

Steve called her Drill Sergeant Jenny, but never to her face. It was our little game, our little secret. Jenny would bark orders, and Steve would wait until her back was turned and throw me a little salute. She never knew. She never saw. It was just for us. Now I feel awful for making fun of her, for excluding her.

Maybe she was lonely. Maybe deep down, she felt excluded. Maybe I didn't do enough to connect with her.

Maybe . . .

I find myself in Maya's bedroom, now just an empty room. I wasn't allowed in here. She was three years older than me, and our interactions were limited. She could drive and date and didn't have much time for her annoying little sister. I didn't really like her in those last couple of years. All the fun times we used to have were before then, before she became obsessed with makeup and music and boys. At that point, I didn't know her anymore. She was full of hormones and growing up at a much faster rate than me. I may have even hated her at times.

Which is awful to admit. It's the truth, though. I thought she could be a real bitch. Now I know she was just a teenager on the verge of adulthood, and I was still a kid in a teenager's body. I'm sure if she were still alive, we would be the best of friends, talking on the phone for hours every weekend, telling each other everything about our lives: my studies and her new job, our respective dalliances with substances, our relationships, our triumphs and defeats.

In my old bedroom I stand a while looking at the marks left on the walls from old poster tack. It's funny, I can't remember what bands used to look down on me while I slept. That could be for the best, though. I'm sure I would be mortified to know. What did I dream about back then, I wonder? What kind of nightmares woke up that young girl in the middle of the night?

I'm curious because I don't have nightmares these days. Not true nightmares. I have scary dreams now and again, sure, but they're not nightmares, because what could be more horrifying than my real life? The dreams that make me wake up in a cold sweat with a pounding heart, the dreams that make me cry, are the exact opposite of scary dreams. Sometimes I dream Maya is still alive. I dream that Steve and Jenny didn't kill themselves. I dream everything is normal. They're my nightmares. Not because those dreams are horrible—they're not, they're lovely—but because there's this instance, this moment when I first wake up when I don't realize I've been dreaming. There's this semiconscious delusion I dwell within that never lasts long yet lasts just long enough to convince me they're not dead.

Only then do I remember the truth.

Those are the days I don't get out of bed. Those are the days I have to change my pillowcase and leave the pillow outside to dry out. My unconscious is cruel to torture me like that. I can hear its mocking laughter echoing in the deepest recesses of my mind. A sadistic jester shares the same space as I do.

When my cell phone rings, I startle.

It takes me a while to dig it out from my bag because I'm still not used to carrying it. I don't really see the point of it, but it seemed like a fun toy to get when you have money to spare and you're baked out of your tree. And it's kind of cool to walk around and act like a big shot with people staring at you.

I press the rubbery green button, and Lizzy says, "Heya, hun, whatcha doin'?"

"Scaring the shit out of myself, you?"

"Nothin', bored. You finished up with Doc Quiff yet?"

"I'm seeing him in about an hour unless I can think of a decent excuse."

"I'd rather see a shrink than do this assignment. Trying to get my head around the question is a fuckshow. It's like he's trying to drive us insane with these big words and ambiguity."

I say, "Uh-huh," because I haven't even read the question. Studying is the last thing on my mind. Kind of got better things to do, too, only I don't know it quite yet.

"So," Lizzy says, "you about? Can I come over and bother you before he digs around in your subconscious?"

"I'm sorting out some personal crap. Admin of the soul, if you will."

My ambiguity doesn't work, and she understands straightaway. "House stuff?"

I grunt something that could be construed as agreement.

"Potential buyer?"

I don't want to talk about it, but I don't want to dismiss her perfectly reasonable inquiry. It's not her fault I have entirely unreasonable mood swings.

I say, "There might be some interest. It's not at the viewing stage, and probably won't even get close, but I thought I'd come back and take a look around just in case."

"Wise," she says. "Better to know in advance if a gang of cannibal vagrants have taken up residence."

"I was more worried about satanic circus clowns, personally."

"This is why you need me to keep you grounded. You've got your priorities all messed up."

Don't I know it.

We talk about the assignment for a minute and then about whether the lecturer's face is worth sitting on, and for a tiny, sweet moment I forget where I am and what I'm doing.

It's murderously expensive to call a cell, so Lizzy can't talk for long and skips to the point: "Wanna get fucked-up when you're done with Doc Quiff?"

"Do hoes blow for cookie dough?"

She screeches in delight.

"Love ya, bitch," she says before hanging up.

I leave the house, my old home. I didn't find what I was looking for because I don't understand why I came back this time, why I keep coming back.

Maybe I'm hoping this life of mine is a delusion, an extended cruel dream, and one day I'll wake up and run into Maya's bedroom and tell her all about the worst nightmare ever before rushing downstairs to begin calling Jenny and Steve Mom and Dad.

It's cold outside on the porch. Was it cold when I arrived? Were the clouds so dark, so oppressive? When was the sky last blue? When did the sun last feel warm?

I don't need to cry when I'm back in my car because the clouds do so for me, peppering the bodywork and windows. The relentless downpour draws a veil over me, so I decide to exploit this unexpected privacy by rolling a joint. I don't intend to smoke the entire thing before driving—even I'm not that reckless—but I have a few more pulls than I should, my brain becomes fuzzy, and I recline the seat to close my eyes to enjoy better the rhythmic pitter-pattering of rain on metal and glass.

There's a pattern to the pattering.

I can hear the melody: *pat, pat-pat, pat.*

Over and over again, hundreds of raindrops hitting in the car with that exact same pattern.

Pat, pat-pat, pat.

Maya, Steve-Jenny, me.

The rain intensifies into a deluge. Thousands, or tens of thousands, of raindrops falling now, and yet I can still hear the same melody. The reverberations work their way through the seat until I not only hear the relentless *pat, pat-pat, pat* but feel it too.

I'm hyperventilating.

I'm scared.

My eyes snap open, and it's darker now than it was before.

It's dark because there is a shadow lying across the car.

No, a shape blocks the daylight.

Dark and glistening, distorted by the downpour and the raindrops on the glass between us, a hooded figure stands next to the car, next to the driver's door, next to me.

I gasp as a pale hand reaches out.

Death himself has come for me.

FIVE

My gasp becomes a scream of terror and surprise that is muted by the rain hammering the car. If the Grim Reaper hears, he makes no sign. The pale hand, long and thin, forms a fist of skin and bone, and those protruding knuckles rap on the window: *tap, tap-tap, tap.*

My surprise becomes confusion that becomes embarrassment.

The hand belongs to no skeleton. The cold rain has bleached the color from the skin to a ghostly white, but this is no apparition.

Through the relentless rain, a muted voice says, "Amy?"

I sit forward, adjusting the lever to bring the seat with me, so I'm upright again. The voice sounds familiar, and I reach for the handle to wind down the window.

Cold rain splashes through the resulting gap, getting onto my hand, my face.

"Jefferson?" I ask the hooded figure.

A face emerges through the shroud of weather, old and kind with a crooked smile.

"*Jefferson*," I cry out, smiling too as I remember this face, this old man whom in my grief I had forgotten even existed.

"What are you doing here?" he asks.

The stench of marijuana smoke wafting out of the car answers for him.

"It's not good for your mind, you know," he says, disapproving, disappointed.

"Didn't you hear?" I ask, rhetorically. "I lost mine long ago."

The rain sluices from the hood of his black parka. His breath clouds in the frigid air. He's freezing. He's soaked.

"Oh God," I say, "where are my manners? Get in the car, Jefferson, before you catch your death."

He shakes his head. "I have a better idea. Why don't you come inside for some hot tea?"

He gestures back over his shoulder to his house that sits next door to mine. In the rain, the mist, it's barely there. An illusion, almost.

I don't want tea. I don't like tea.

"That sounds lovely," I say, because the guilt I feel at forgetting Jefferson, sweet old Jefferson, is unbearable.

He smiles wider, hearing my agreement. "Get ready to sprint," he says, "otherwise you'll drown."

Jefferson lives alone. He's lived alone as long as I can remember, as long as he's lived next door, which is forever. He was there when we moved in, living alone, keeping to himself, the perfect neighbor, never causing any bother and never complaining about a couple of unruly young girls screeching and screaming all day long on the other side of the fence. Maya had the hots for one of the boys who visited next door, Jefferson's grandkids, only he was at college and not interested in someone still in high school. Jefferson seemed old back then, back when I was a teen, back when I was a child, yet he looks no older. He must be *really* old now, and yet he seems hardy, like an old oak tree that has endured the elements for far longer than the younger trees around him, yet will outlast them all.

He's outlasted Steve and Jenny and Maya.

He might outlast me, too, although neither of us realizes that right now as I sit at his kitchen table and watch him boil up some water to make tea.

We make some small talk, and it's a little awkward. We were never close, and though we lived next door to one another for more years of my life than not, I never knew him. Not really. He must have had a wife at some point. Did she leave before I was born? Did she die?

He asks about my studies and my car and my clothes and everything else that doesn't involve mentioning Maya or my parents. The gaps between questions grow longer each time because it's hard to talk to someone you don't know and even harder when you're both doing everything possible to avoid mentioning the defining moments of your life.

Thankfully, the water boils and he finishes the tea, which gives us something else to focus on.

"It's good," I lie after taking a sip.

"Nothing kills a chill faster."

I look around. "I don't think I've ever been in your house before."

He nods in agreement.

"I like it," I say. "It's minimalist but still cozy, still homely."

"Everything I need," he says, "and nothing I don't."

I sip. He sips. If this were a Western, the wind would be blowing tumbleweed past us right about now.

"It's okay," I tell him. "I'm a mess, I'm a wreck, but you can mention them. I won't burst into tears. I mean, I probably will. I almost certainly will, but I'm used to it. I have plenty of tissues on me. I promise I won't snot all over your table."

He smiles. He chuckles.

It's a deep, comforting sound. Reassuring.

"They were good people," he says. "All three of them."

My eyes moisten. "The best."

"You should be very proud of yourself."

I frown. "Why? Why would I possibly be proud of myself? Have you seen the state of me?"

"Don't talk yourself down, Amy. You've been through hell and you're still here. That's remarkable. That's more than most will ever be capable of achieving. You've had an entire life's worth of pain and suffering, and you're not even twenty-one. I don't for one second think the last few years have been anything but agony for you, yet you've come through it unscarred and unscathed."

He doesn't know about all the cutting and suicide attempts, clearly.

He says, "So you smoke some grass and wear a little too much black makeup—so what?"

I wipe my eyes with one of the tissues. I blow my nose with it afterward. "Well, when you put it like that . . ."

"Would you like some more tea?"

No, I don't want more tea. I still don't like tea.

"Yes, please."

There's still hot water on the stove, so it doesn't take long before he's refreshed my cup. "I'm sorry I didn't do more. My generation isn't good at opening up, and I didn't want to upset your parents any more than they were already upset. I told myself I didn't want to add to their suffering."

I listen.

"When my wife died I tried to grieve on the inside for the sake of my boy. I wanted to be strong for him. I thought if I could keep him busy, if I could distract him, he would get through it easier. The truth is, I was a coward. When you don't mention something, you don't have to deal with it. You can pretend it's not happening, and if no one else brings it up then the illusion holds. I was the same with your parents, to my shame. I made small talk because I was too scared to mention Maya or ask how they were coping. I wish to God I had done things differently. Because maybe if they had had someone to talk to, to share their pain with, maybe they wouldn't have—"

I shake my head. I reach out to touch his hand. "Don't take even a sliver of blame for what they did. If anyone's to blame, it's me. I was suffering so much after Maya that I didn't stop for a second to consider their pain. I needed them so much. I didn't realize they needed me too. I let them down. It's not your fault, Jefferson. It's mine. I killed them with my selfishness. I . . ."

I can't finish because I'm sobbing and my face is a mess of tears and mucus.

I'm out of tissues by the time I've finished mopping up. They form a sticky mountain on Jefferson's table.

"I'm sorry," I say.

"Don't be. You never need to be sorry at my house."

Somehow, I manage to smile. He's so sweet, so kind. I'm glad I came back here today. I'm so happy I got high in my car. I would never have seen Jefferson again otherwise. I would never have remembered him.

I notice he's looking at my wrist, and I see that the bands have ridden up to reveal the raised, pale scar tissue. I tug the bands back in the vain hope he didn't see, but I know he did.

"Day or night, summer or winter, I'm here for you. Whatever you need, I'm here for you."

I reach an arm around his shoulders to squeeze him. How can you realize you've missed someone you had forgotten?

"Can I ask you a question?" I say.

"Of course."

"Did they, Steve or Jenny, ever mention me? After Maya died, before they died, did they talk about me?"

"Of course. They were your parents."

"I don't mean small talk. I mean did they ever *really* talk about me?"

"I still don't know what you mean."

"They didn't leave a note," I tell him.

His face drops. "Oh," he utters. "Really?"

I nod. "Nothing. Not even a *see ya* on a Post-it."

"Oh, Amy."

I control my breathing to prevent more tears from coming. "I think it would have helped if I'd had a note and I could understand what was going through their heads that day. Was it me? Was it my fault for being so selfish, for being a brat, for not calling them Mom and Dad?"

"No," he insists. "You can't blame yourself, Amy."

"But if it wasn't my fault, if they didn't blame me, then why wouldn't they leave me a note? Why wouldn't they leave me that? Just a few lines would have been enough. All they had to write was that they couldn't live with the pain, and I would have understood, I would have known there was nothing I could have done. Why would they leave me alone and not even tell me why, not even say . . . sorry?"

His mouth is open, but he can't answer because he can't possibly know the answer.

When he does find some words, it's only to ask, "Can I fix you some more tea?"

I smile. "Can I be honest with you, Jefferson?"

"Of course."

"I hate tea," I admit finally. "It's coffee for pussies."

At first his eyes widen with shock at my crudeness and profanity, but then he bursts out laughing.

He's still chuckling as he makes himself another drink. "I'm afraid I don't have any coffee to offer you."

"That's fine. I need to go soon anyway."

I look around the room while Jefferson makes his tea. There's a door in the kitchen that I presume leads to the basement. There's one just like it in my own house, only this one has a bolt so it can be locked. Which is kind of odd.

Jefferson notes me looking and smiles. "To stop the ghosts creeping out at night."

I smile too. I notice a painting hanging on the wall. Amateurish, yet cute. A weird composition: a black cat, a horseshoe, and a four-leaf clover.

"I know it's odd," he says. "But I like it. You can't have too much good luck, can you?"

"I thought black cats were supposed to be unlucky?"

"That depends on your perspective."

"Are you superstitious?"

"I guess. I'll knock on wood. Does that count?"

I ask, "Do you think bad things always happen in threes?"

"Can't say I've ever put the theory to the test. Why?"

I rub the bracelet. "No reason. Forget it."

There's this look about him as he boils the water, as he refreshes his cup.

"What?" I ask.

"Excuse me?"

"You look like there's something you want to say, only you don't want to say it."

He settles into his seat, cradling his cup. He's sat perpendicular from me, close, and I can hear his breathing. His eyes are sad as they look into mine, as he continues his internal debate.

"Just say it, Jefferson, please."

"Are you sure it was suicide?"

My eyebrows shoot up so far my forehead hurts. "*What?*"

Jefferson retreats, sitting back, moving away from me. He regrets the question, but it's too late now. He's said it. He's asked. He has to continue.

"I spoke to them that day. Your dad told me about the party you were going to that night. He said he wanted to hit fast-forward until it was the next day and you were back again, safe and sound. He said he was thinking of following you to the party. Waiting outside just in case you needed him. He knew he couldn't lock you up, literally or figuratively. And he didn't want that. He wanted you to have a life of your own. He wanted nothing more than to see you better and happy again. That's what he lived for."

"Did you speak to Jenny too?"

"Not as often, but I did that morning. She asked about my grandsons, as she often did. We didn't chat long. Just a minute or two before she drove to the store. She wanted to pick up some bagels for the next morning. She predicted you'd have a hangover and she was going to be ready. We had a good laugh about it."

"You're saying because she went out for bagels that she wouldn't kill herself? That Steve wasn't suicidal because he wanted me to get better?"

He's silent for a moment. "I suppose I am. I suppose I've never been able to wrap my head around it. They were so determined to keep you alive, I can't believe they would do anything to jeopardize that, no matter their own pain."

"Then what happened to them?"

He looks into his cup for answers, for a diversion, for an escape. He tries to answer. Fails. Just shrugs.

I can feel the thump of my increased heart rate. I can feel the heat in my cheeks. My eyes are tearing up again. I need to get out of here. I need to get away.

"I've got to be somewhere," I tell him. "And I can't handle this conversation with you right now. Maybe at some point in the future I'll be able to, but it's not today."

He nods without looking at me.

By the time I'm at the door he's called out to me, but I don't stop because I don't want to hear anything further. I'm not strong enough.

Later, I'll wish I had paid attention. I'll wish I had listened, because what he said might have helped me understand. Instead, I run away because I'm not yet ready to question what happened in that garage.

Of course Steve and Jenny killed themselves.

What other explanation could there be?

SIX

When you're losing your mind, it's good to have a routine. For the last—what is it?—almost six years that routine comes in the form of seeing Llewellyn. It was a couple of weeks after Maya died that I slit my wrists. A week later, still in pain and my arms huge with dressings, I sat down in his office.

His first words: "I'm told you could use someone to talk to."

Firstly, it isn't his fault I didn't want to talk to him. I didn't want to talk to anyone. I can't remember how much I said in that initial session, but to say my answers were monosyllabic would be an insult to monosyllables. I grunted more than spoke, seeing him as an antagonist, an enemy to be defeated. It took months for me to start opening up to any real degree. It took a couple of years before I realized how much he was helping me. He was the first person I called when I found Steve and Jenny.

He's the only true constant I have now. Aside from his vacation in September, I see him every single week, so he knows me better than anyone else in my life.

"You've said that before," he tells me when I point this out.

"But this isn't a fair deal," I reply. "Because I don't know you at all."

"You've said that before too."

"I have?"

"In our eighty-first session."

"You didn't even look down at your fancy notebook."

"I have a good memory for dates."

"Which year did Anthony Hopkins win Best Actor for *The Silence of the Lambs?*"

He responds with a tight smile. I say smile because his lips barely stretch and his cheeks become no rounder, and his eyes don't change. He *smiles* like this at me a lot.

He says, "I said I'm good with dates. That doesn't mean I know every date for everything."

"Dude, it's like the only horror movie to win Best Picture."

"I'm afraid I don't watch Hollywood cinema."

Now he looks at his notebook. Writes.

Despite our age difference, he doesn't look old. He has a square, almost caveman face. In a nice way, I mean. His skin is tanned year-round, and his dark eyes are full of vigor. He looks more like a professional sportsman than an intellectual. He's always clean-shaven, and there's never a hint of razor burn. He wears reading glasses that sit low on his nose so he can meet my gaze without obstruction and still make use of them when scribbling in his notebook. It's bound in supple leather with a metal clasp and a string fastener.

Llewellyn has the most wonderful head of hair I've ever seen in my life. There's no hint of recession, no strand of gray. It's pure black from root to tip, from temple to nape. And it's thick, almost impossibly so. He wears it in a kind of sweeping quiff that has an easy swoosh to it yet somehow never moves. I've yet to see even a single hair come free, and I've spent countless hours staring at that lustrous quiff, wishing it to come undone. I don't think he so much uses product on it as raw, unfiltered sorcery.

I used to fancy Llewellyn when I was younger and my teenage hormones were a raging inferno without a more age-appropriate direction. He gave off this powerful, sexy, authoritarian vibe. I used to imagine him taking off those reading glasses of his and joining me on the armchair, leather squeaking and creaking as I ran my fingers through that glorious hair.

He styled it in the same way back then. In fact, I wonder when he first had it cut like this, or whether he popped out as a newborn with an already magical quiff.

"Why do you take so many drugs, Amy?"

"Do we really need to have this conversation again?"

"We don't need to do anything you don't want to do. But let me rephrase the question, if I may: What is it about taking illegal drugs that you enjoy?"

Shall I tell him that it's chemically impossible to feel as happy without drugs? He's probably not going to accept that, even though it's the truth. He's not asking me why I like narcotics because I've told him many times how much fun I find them. He's asking me why I need that supraphysiological amount of fun. So I sit in silence for a little while and think—really think—about what drugs mean to me, for me, and what drugs do for me that I can't do without them.

The chorus of competing thoughts and ideas answers for me:

"I get to turn down the volume inside my head."

He waits for more.

"It's just so loud," I continue, understanding myself a little better. "It's like my mind never stops. There're never any quiet moments. Not anymore. Not since . . . I can't go seven seconds without thinking about what happened, and even in those other seconds there's no peace because my mind has gone on some dark wonderings as a result of that original thought. I'm trapped in a room without doors or windows and someone is shouting in my ear through a megaphone." I look at my hands. "That person is me."

Llewellyn is making notes. The scratch of the pen on the notebook's paper is swift and fierce. He writes with a fountain pen. Blue ink. Flowing cursive, from the glimpses I've seen. Almost calligraphy.

"When I take drugs," I say, "I'm no longer in that room. I'm no longer thinking about things I don't want to think about."

The swift, fierce scratches cease. "You get to turn the volume down inside your head."

I nod that head. It feels so heavy. My neck is too weak to cope.

"Is there anything that can be done?" I ask.

"Yes," he says, and for an instant I'm uplifted and hopeful, but it's gone as soon as it arrives because then he says: "I can write you another prescription."

He makes a note in his notebook.

It's a large, dense tome that he clasps closed and ties with the string when we finish up the session. I sometimes wonder if this is a deliberate message to me—our time is over—or if it's a habit of his. Does he unfasten the string after I'm gone to review, to make more notes? Surely he must need to do this for his next patient, unless we each have our own notebook, our own set of notes. I picture the story of my life, my insanity, written out in week-by-week entries—a journal of my mind.

What does it say?

Would I recognize the girl inside?

Is she even me?

Llewellyn taps his pen against his bottom lip. "You seem distracted."

It's not a question, but there are many questions contained therein regardless.

"I've been thinking a lot lately about patterns."

"What about patterns?"

"You know, coincidences."

"I don't know. Please elaborate."

I shrug. I always feel like a little girl when I'm talking to him. I have no confidence in myself, my thoughts. Worse, though, is that I can't fake it with him. He knows me too well.

I find my voice in time: "Did you know that my parents died within three weeks of the third anniversary of Maya's death?"

He nods.

I'm surprised. "Doesn't that strike you as odd?"

"It's not uncommon for such tragedies to coincide with anniversaries."

Of course. That makes sense. And yet I'm thinking about what Jefferson said.

Are you sure it was suicide?

"Do you believe in fate?" I ask Llewellyn.

"How do you mean?"

"Is everything decided for us? How we live? How we die? Like a plan. Like it doesn't matter what we do or don't do."

"Do you think like that?"

I hesitate, toying with Maya's bracelet. "I . . . I'm not sure what I believe. Loads of people believe in fate. I don't think it's any different than believing in God. Maybe God is the name we give to fate. We don't have any control over when we're born, do we? So why should it be any different when we die?"

He makes notes.

In the silence, I say, "Are we . . . going to talk about it?"

"Hmm?"

I know he knows. He wants me to say it. He's been waiting for me to bring it up as much as I've been waiting for him to bring it up. Sometimes it feels like he's less my therapist and more like someone who is always testing me. If he is, I'm sure I'm flunking the class.

I've thought about how I'm going to say it. I've rehearsed. Settling on the specific wording isn't easy, but I think I get it right:

"The accidental overdose," I say.

A bland way to describe having my stomach pumped because I took too many pills, which is the point. Any other form of saying it might hint at the truth, and I don't want him to even suspect I meant it. He has absolute power over me. He can have me locked up again anytime he wants.

"Would you like to talk about it?" he asks me.

"Not really. But I feel we should."

"I agree that it would be healthy to talk about the experience and your feelings regarding it."

"What's so healthy about reliving pain?" My voice is quiet. "I've never understood why we need to keep articulating how we feel when we feel terrible. What possible good does that actually do?"

All these years of coming here and I still don't know.

As he makes notes, I'm looking at the magical quiff. Not looking, but staring. I'm trying to will just one hair to come astray.

"Are you having doubts about our sessions?"

"No," I say. "I know I have to come here."

"These are court-mandated sessions, yes. But you don't have to see me in particular. Would you like me to recommend someone else to talk to?"

"No way. They could have me committed."

"Only if it's deemed you are a danger to yourself or others. The judge agreed with the assessment that it was in your best interests to be out in the world under your own volition. With caveats, naturally."

"Yeah, yeah. It's seeing you once a week or it's back to the nuthouse on suicide watch."

"I wish you wouldn't refer to a psychiatric hospital like that. It's really not a helpful way to talk about mental health."

I nod to accept this. "Please pass on my humblest apologies to all the other head cases."

He does not respond. I read nothing in his expression. I never can.

I burst out laughing.

"What's so funny?" he asks.

"It just occurred to me that for as long as I've known you, your face has been stapled into that one expression. Since it never moves, I mean."

"We tend to lash out when we feel vulnerable," he tells me. "We feel more in control of a situation when we're attacking instead of reacting."

"Do *we*?"

"Tell me, in your words, what happened."

He's sneaky, right? He's not asking me about it. He wants me to open up about it. It's not purely about what I say but what I don't say. He's going to be paying attention as much to how I describe what happened as to what actually happened. I feel stressed immediately. I shift in my seat. I fidget.

I haven't said a word yet. The only sound is the scratch of the pen against paper.

"I don't really remember what happened," I say.

"Tell me what you do remember."

He's looking at his notebook as he speaks, which gives me a moment in which to compose myself. I need that moment because I've spent so long being open and honest with him that not only am I not confident in my ability to lie to him, but I realize I don't want to lie to him either. Only I must. He can't know the truth. I can't risk going back to the hospital and the constant monitoring. Always on suicide watch. Everything decided for me. A girl can go crazy in a place like that.

"It was scary," I reply, because it's an honest statement, albeit a deflection.

I can't tell if he knows I'm deflecting. He continues making notes. He makes no commentary, so I'm forced to continue.

"It really hurt. My throat . . . it's still really sore."

Scratchy, scratchy pen on paper.

My gaze focuses on the notebook that is the journal of my mind. I want to read it. I want to read about me. The scratching stops. The pen is still. I look up to find him looking at me.

Waiting.

I can see the question in his eyes. I know it's coming. I can feel it.

I talk again, fast and with increasing desperation. I talk about waking up in the hospital. The pain. The fear. The overwhelming sense of confusion, of displacement. I'm desperate to keep talking because as soon as I stop, as soon as I hesitate or even take a breath, he's going to say:

"Did you mean it?"

I'm cold. I'm silent. A paralysis grips me with incredible strength. I'm naked and alone.

I might as well have screamed *YES*.

He makes notes, then asks, "Why?"

I look down at my hands and tell him what I told Lizzy. I explain about the ad, the music, wondering what Maya had been listening to in her car.

That little box of tissues is empty by the time I'm done.

"You know I have to inform the authorities if I believe you're a danger to yourself or someone else?"

"Please don't," I beg, quiet and pathetic.

He's silent. He's not making notes.

"I won't do it again. I don't think I really meant it. I didn't cut myself. If I really wanted to die, then that's what I would do, wouldn't I?"

"But that didn't work six years ago, did it? So why would you repeat something that failed?"

"Because it almost worked then. Another few millimeters deeper at the top of my forearm would have been enough." I'm tracing the line of the scar on my left forearm with my right index finger. It's hidden by my long sleeves, and yet I know exactly where it is. "That's what they said. That's what they told me. I was so close. Just a few millimeters." I tap the end of my scar, up near my elbow pit. "All I'd have to do is press a little harder right at the top, and I'd be dead, guaranteed." I can't help but laugh. "If I want to kill myself, I literally have a map of how to do it carved right into me."

Scratch, scratch, scratch goes the pen.

"So," I say, "am I ever going to get better?"

"I can't give you a solution to your problems, because there is no definitive solution. What I promise I'll do, however, is to help you find your own."

"That's a cop-out if ever I heard one."

He closes the leather-bound notebook and ties the string. "I think that's about all we have time for."

SEVEN

ight. Lights. Blinking white light flickering over me in frightening flashes. Noise. So much noise. But no sound. How can there be noise but not sound? Pain. All the pain in the world originating from the point in my consciousness where my mind and my soul mix. I'm a cocktail. I'm a chrome shaker filled with terror liqueur and a mixer of sparkling confusion, with plenty of cold cubes of refreshing agony. Pour into an Amy-shaped glass and garnish with a slice of self-loathing and a sprig of fresh regret. Go on, take a sip. Packs quite the punch, doesn't it? Drink one for fun, two for chaos, and never, EVER drink three.

"Are you okay? Ma'am? Can you hear me? Are you okay?"

No, I'm trying to rest, and who the fuck is this? Someone too loud or too close to me. An invasion of my personal space or an assault on my ears. Either way:

"Leave me alone."

"She's talking," the voice exclaims, but not at me. "She's alive."

Of course I'm alive. I'm just tired. Why won't they let me sleep?

Hands grab me, pulling at my clothes. I try to push them away. I can't. I'm restrained somehow. What is this? A nightmare?

"I'm trying to help you," the voice tells me while the hands paw.

"Get off me," I scream in a voice as quiet as a whisper.

I feel drunk as hell. My mouth feels dry. My eyes are closed. I've passed out at a house party and someone's dad has come home early and is trying to kick me out.

"I'm going, I'm going," I tell him. "Just let me have a minute."

"No, no," the angry dad says. "You can't have a minute. You must wake up. Please."

"I am awake," I insist. "I'm just resting my eyes. Get your hands off me."

"I need to get you out of here."

"I'll be gone in a minute. Just give me a minute."

"Miss, please. I'm afraid you don't have a minute."

This dad is an utter douche. I bet his son or daughter who had this party is equally risible. Once this is over, I'm going to give them hell. I'm going to make them pay for their dad's rude awakening.

I grunt. I try to swipe away the dad's paws.

I say, "I swear to God if you don't leave me alone I'm going to smash your windows before I leave."

"My . . . windows? Please, we must hurry."

An acrid odor makes me cough. The dad's aftershave is atrocious.

"What's that awful smell?"

"The car's on fire," the dad tells me.

"What?"

"Your car," he says. "It's on fire. Please, let me help you."

My eyes open for the first time, and I see a distorted world before me. A skewed street is ahead of me, lined with crooked buildings. I blink and realize the windshield is cracked and split. I swivel my head and see the dad.

Who might be someone's dad. He's a youngish guy bent down next to my car, trying to pull me out. It's not a simple task because I'm contorted and bent over in the driver's seat. It's pushing me over, so my face is resting on the steering wheel. The seat is broken.

My car is on fire.

I can't see the flames, but I can now feel the heat and see the smoke. Thick black smoke is billowing out of the far side of the vehicle. Not from the engine block. Underneath. The fuel line. The fire is beneath me.

"Get me out of here."

"I'm trying. Can you reach your seat belt?"

"Of course I can."

"Release it."

I can't do it. I can barely keep my eyes open, and when I move my arm to the buckle, I have almost no control over the limb. As soon as I untuck it from under me it just sort of flops down. I can feel my fingertips on the clasp.

"Just release it for me, please."

He's speaking with calm, reasonable words that disguise the panic. He's more scared for me than I am. His face is blackened by smoke. He's coughing.

"You can do it," he tells me.

I've hit my head, and there's a sluggish complacency to my thoughts as well as my actions. Like when you're too drunk, and you'll happily give in to the tiredness and pass out anywhere. You'll go to sleep in places you shouldn't, in clothes you'd usually take off, in positions that aren't comfortable. You just want to sleep above all other considerations. This is me now. I want to go back to sleep and not deal with this man who won't leave me alone. I want to go back to sleep in this burning car.

"Please," he says again, "I can't reach it myself."

"Okay, okay . . ."

I want him to shut up. So I try again.

I paw with my fingertips on the hard plastic shell of the buckle. The texture feels nice. I want to stroke it some more.

"That's it," he's telling me. "You're doing great."

I don't feel great. I'd feel a lot better if he stopped yapping in my ear.

My thumb finds the rectangular button. The texture isn't as nice as the box thing.

I tap at it with my thumb, and it doesn't comply. It's all too exhausting. Maybe if I rest for a moment I can regain some strength.

"No," he says. "Don't go back to sleep. You can do it."

"I can't. It's too hard."

"You're doing so good. Just a little more. Press the button for me."

"What's so special about this fucking button?"

I feel him get closer to me. I feel his warm breath on my cheek, and I open my eyes to look at him. He's blurry and unfocused.

"Please," he says. "Can you do it? For me? Please."

His voice is soft and somewhat pathetic, almost like a child begging.

"Fine," I say, my own voice full of frustration.

I push the button down.

My seat belt unclasps with a click.

I cry out in pain because he grabs me and pulls me. I'm still bent over and folded by the seat, pressed up against the steering wheel. My legs hurt, my arms hurt, my back hurts, my head hurts. All at once, I'm overwhelmed by pain. I cry out. I scream for him to stop, to get off me, to leave me alone and stop hurting me.

"I'm sorry," he says, "I'm so sorry."

He's not sorry. I hate him. He doesn't stop. He keeps pulling at me, and the pain brings tears to my eyes, and I wail but I can't fight him. I'm so weak. I'm helpless.

I feel the cool air on my face, and it feels icy because my face is wet with sweat. I'm soaked with sweat, I realize. The jolt of coldness makes my eyes snap open, and after a moment's adjusting, I can see fully again.

I see the young man is not a young man. Without the filter of my unfocused eyes to smooth away his face, I see that he's an old man. He looks frail and weak, yet he's pulling at my jacket with all his strength, trying to drag me out of my car.

Which is crumpled after crashing into a lamppost.

Flames burn brightly beneath it; the wind is pushing the smoke away, and I realize I might have suffocated otherwise. It's so black and opaque. I've never seen anything like it. I'm soaked with sweat because the fire is an inferno. It must be an oven inside the car. The old man is seared and burnt. He's coughing up black phlegm onto the road.

Someone else rushes forward to help pull me free—a young woman about my age.

I scream another whisper.

"Help me."

The old man and the young woman drag me out of my car, and I feel the flames against my lower legs as they come free and drop to the ground. There's a brief, intense pain before I'm pulled clear of the wreckage.

Exhausted, the old man collapses down next to me, retching and coughing, and unable to move. I know how he feels.

"Oh my God, are you okay?" the young woman asks. "I need to call an ambulance. I need to find a phone booth. God, what do I do?"

"I have a cell phone," I tell her, tapping at my jacket pocket with weak fingers.

As she pulls it free and clumsily works the unfamiliar buttons, I manage to sit up. My strength and mobility are returning, little by little. I'm on the outskirts of town, on a quiet street—almost no traffic. I look around for another crashed car, but there isn't one.

"What happened?" I ask no one in particular.

The old man finishes gasping next to me. "You swerved off the road, straight into that lamppost."

"I did?"

He nods his burned head at me. "I saw it. Why did you do that?"

I look from him to my burning car and back again. His expression is not accusatory, but his face is creased in expectation of an answer. And yet there's no explanation I can give.

I can only tell him, "I don't remember."

EIGHT

I'm not hurt. Not really. The old man, Sebastian, had it worse than me. Knocking my head on the steering wheel has given me a concussion. A mild one, I'm assured. The same doctor who pumped my stomach a couple of weeks ago is the one who checks me over. His name is Aliprandi.

"We must stop meeting like this," he says, deadpan. A slight accent.

I don't bother replying.

He shines one of those little lights into my eyes, and I grimace.

"You were lucky," he tells me.

"I don't feel lucky."

"It could have been a lot worse."

"Easy for you to say."

I immediately regret these words because I overheard someone say Sebastian has second-degree burns. I can't stop thinking about what might have happened had he not dragged me against my will from the wreckage. Would my senses have returned just in time for me to realize I was burning?

I can almost hear my own screams echoing from an alternate universe.

Aliprandi says, "Do you have a headache?"

"Yes."

"On a scale of one to ten, how painful is it?"

I think for a second. "Five. It's fine."

"Any double vision?"

"Nada."

"Follow my finger."

He holds a long index finger before my face and moves it around in lines and arcs.

"Do you remember what happened?"

I look away. Shake my head.

"Nothing at all about the crash?"

"One moment I was driving along, the next I was being dragged from the wreckage."

He has a pensive look about him. I can't read his expression.

"When you were in the hospital last time it was because you had taken too many recreational drugs. Do you remember that?"

"I remember you were annoyed I didn't die."

His eyes go wide. "Excuse me?"

"Nothing. Forget it."

I look away while he looks at me. He waits until my gaze meets his again before he says, "I swore an oath." He sits forward, elbows on his knees. Something like sadness in his expression. "My job is to keep people alive, and I wanted to help people long before I studied medicine. It's just who I am. And yes, it does frustrate me when they do things that only hurt themselves. That's not because it makes my job harder but because there's only so much I can do to help someone. If they hurt themselves too much, I can't help them anymore."

"For some people, it hurts more to be alive."

"I'd like you to see a psychiatrist."

"I already see one."

I feel sorry for this doctor before me. I can see the hopelessness in his eyes. I feel bad that I ever thought he was annoyed I didn't die when I took too many pills. I mistook his frustration for anger. He wants to help me. He knows I need help. But there's nothing he can do.

"My headache is actually more like a nine," I tell him.

"I'll give you something for that."

"Thank you," I say in a rare moment of gratitude.

Aliprandi stands, defeated.

I look away so I don't have to see that defeat. He doesn't mean it as judgment, although that's how it feels to me.

He leaves and a nurse takes over for him, checking my blood pressure, pulse, and temperature and passing me the oxygen mask because my lungs are tight.

"Don't worry, sweetheart," she tells me. "You'll be fine in a couple of days."

I smile. I appreciate her kind manner.

The lovely nurse says, "Do you have anyone to come and pick you up?"

"No," I tell her. "I'll get a cab back to campus."

"That's going to cost you a fortune."

"Don't sweat it, I'm rich."

She gives me a funny look.

"When my parents died," I explain, "they left me a lot of money. Savings and life insurance. Most don't pay out with suicides, although some do after a year's exclusion. My parents chose the kind that does. Lucky me, yeah?"

"Oh," is her only reply.

Seconds later, I'm alone. No one has told me if I need to stay or can go. I decide to give Lizzy a call, but I don't have my cell. The young woman who called the ambulance must still have it. I didn't think to ask for it back. Fuck. I'm not used to having one yet, and before today I thought it was a fun toy but not a necessity. Wow, was I wrong. Everyone should get one.

This is the first time since waking up in the burning car that I've had a chance to really think about it. As I said to Sebastian: I don't remember.

I can't recall anything about the crash itself before I began coming around.

I remember leaving Llewellyn's office. I remember getting into my car and driving back toward campus. I guess I must have driven about a couple of miles, almost out of town.

What's the last thing I can picture?

I . . . don't know.

I can see the street where I crashed. I'm driving along. Hands at two and ten like a good driver. There's a little traffic. A few passing cars. Maybe one ahead of me too. Not close. Not close enough to see inside or to make out the licence plate.

Then . . . what next? I'm pinching my eyes shut to concentrate, to see, but there's nothing.

Except I can see the lamppost. I saw it. That's the last thing I remember. I was still driving. I wasn't swerving. I wasn't crashing. Everything was fine.

I think I was thinking about Maya. I can see her face. I touch the bracelet, recalling . . . not a memory, but maybe a feeling. Like a chill that races up your spine. What was that? What does that mean? Then what happened? Did I feel that chill just before I crashed? Did I see Maya just before it happened?

I wonder if someone stepped out into the road. Was it Sebastian? Maybe he didn't see me, and I had to wrench the wheel to avoid hitting him and crashed as a result. That makes sense. I can't see him in my memories, but if that's what happened, I would have seen him only the instant before I crashed.

I realize I'm breathing hard.

I try to relax. I feel like I'm going to freak out. I need a distraction, so I look around the room. There's nothing in here that can calm me. I close my eyes again and control my breathing, deliberately taking nice and slow, long breaths in followed by long breaths out. It works. A simple trick to manage stress. Pretty sure Llewellyn taught it to me years ago, but I can't be sure.

In time I feel a little calmer.

With my eyes closed, I'm paying more attention to sound.

It's quiet in this little room. I can hear the hushed noises of the hospital around me. Footsteps in the corridor outside. The faintest whisper of a conversation from the room next to mine. A scratching at the window.

Wait, what?

My eyes snap open. The blinds are drawn over the window.

Did I imagine the scratching?

No. There it is again. A quiet, faint, almost gentle sound. Like fingernails on the glass. Which makes no sense.

I stand up from the cot. I'm barefoot and have some dressings on my shins for the burns. They're only minor, I was told. Which is a bummer. I was kind of hoping I wouldn't have to shave my legs again. The floor is icy against the soles of my feet. I leave little smudges of condensation on the linoleum.

The room is small. In a few tentative steps, I'm almost within touching distance of the window. The blind is a pull-down. Some stiff fabric that's too dense to see through. I can still hear the scratching. A strange, uncomfortable sound. Is someone out there trying to get my attention?

Who? Why?

And if there isn't, what's causing the noise? Despite my efforts to control my breathing, I'm growing more and more anxious. I'm scared I imagine this noise and equally frightened that I'm not imagining it. There's only one way to find out.

Those other hushed noises from the hospital around me have deadened to nothingness. I can hear only the scratching and my own breathing. A few more steps and I'm standing right before the window. I reach my hand out to the beaded string hanging next to the blinds. I feel my heart thumping in my chest as my fingers close around it. I squeeze the string and slowly pull down on it.

The blind creeps up.

I gasp, horrified, traumatized, terrified.

My sister is on the other side of the glass, only it's not the glass of a hospital windowpane but the windshield of Maya's car. She's scratching at the glass, trying to get out. Flames blaze behind her. I thump the windshield with my fists, screaming her name.

"*Maya, Maya.*"

Smoke billows inside her car, enveloping her until I can see only her pale fingers against the glass. Those pale fingers redden with the scorching heat of the inferno and blacken with soot.

I'm screaming, crying, futilely trying to rescue her.

NINE

Jesus fuck, what happened to you?" are the first words out of Lizzy's mouth when I turn up at her door. She is shocked by my bandaged hands and head, the bruises on my face.

I don't answer right away. I wrap my arms around her for an almighty hug so for a few seconds I can feel safe. She returns the hug. Tentatively at first, because she's still taken aback by my injuries. It hurts to hold her, but I don't care. I need her.

"Maybe I'm doomed," I joke.

"Talk to me, Amy."

I do. I tell her about going home, and the run-of-the-mill visit to see Llewellyn. I tell her about driving. I tell her about waking up in my wrecked car and being dragged out by a kind old man. I tell her that I have no memory of the crash itself. I don't tell her what happened at the hospital except to skim over the various evaluations they put me through before I was allowed to go home. After they found me banging on the window and screaming, there were more scans and tests over the next day. It's hard to hold someone against their will at the best of times, thankfully, and with all my past experiences I knew exactly what to say to ensure they had no choice but to discharge me when those scans and tests showed there was nothing wrong. Physically, at least.

She's wide-eyed. Her hand goes to her mouth. She's shaking her head like she can't quite believe it.

"You're lucky to be alive."

Then the fingers fall away, and I can see nothing but smoke.

The door bursts open and the kind nurse rushes inside, eyes wide when she sees me thumping my fists against the windowpane with such ferocity the glass has cracked and is smeared with my blood.

Beyond the window is asphalt and parked cars and a couple of scared people shielding their children from the crazy girl trying to punch her way through the window.

I stumble backward from the window, and the nurse catches me as my legs give out beneath me. She yells for help, but I can't make out the words because I'm calling for my sister between unrelenting sobs.

"*Let me go*," I scream. "I need to save her, I need to save her . . ."

I'm sitting on her bed, back against the wall, knees up by my chest. She can see I'm shaken by the crash, but she doesn't know that I'm more shaken by seeing Maya on the other side of that window.

"The crash happened right after your session with Llewellyn?"

"Yeah."

"Were you thinking about his magical quiff instead of watching the road?"

"Haha," I groan.

She grins, pleased. Then asks, "I imagine after another night in the hospital you're probably not interested in getting fucked-up right now?"

"The day I willingly turn down drugs, please do me a favor and put me out of my misery."

"Deal."

I try not to think about the crash, about Maya, while Lizzy digs out her stash. She has a little decorative box that she keeps under her mattress.

We have such a blast when we're as high as satellites. We don't even need to go out. Some of the best nights of my life have been just me and Lizzy in her room, jumping on the bed or talking shit or just watching movies. So much fun you just can't comprehend it if you've never taken drugs. I hate it when people say they don't need drugs to have fun. That's like saying you don't need ice in your Coke. You don't, but it's nicer if you do. You don't need to drink coffee in the morning, but you wake up faster if you do. You don't need your food to taste good to keep you alive, but you enjoy eating more if it does. Drugs are freedom. Drugs are a release from restraints, from inherent bondage. You may be happy without taking X, only you can't be as happy. Ecstasy releases so much serotonin into your brain that it is quite literally impossible to feel as good naturally. If you've never had it, you've never felt as happy as you could feel.

Serotonin is happiness.

But this isn't a sales pitch, kids. Don't do drugs.

(Do drugs.)

Once I was so out of it that I watched powdery snowfall on a hedgerow. In that gentle white caress, I saw shapes begin to manifest in the hedge as men and women, young and old, emerging with limbs made of branches and leaves for the flesh, dusted as with an icing sugar of snow. I stared for a long time as those shapes became real, became whole and lived out short, magical lives for me alone to witness. Then I blinked, and they were gone because there was no hedge at all. Just an empty expanse of wasteland stretching into the gloom. I'm not sure it was even snowing. It was a transcendent experience, almost spiritual. My imagination created something from nothing and I watched it play out as if it were real. A movie written, produced, and directed by me, watched only by me. Mind. Blown.

What comes up must come down.

Moody Tuesdays are the worst. Someone once told me that the only time you enjoy taking drugs is the first time and every time afterward is just nostalgia, just chasing that first high, the only high. I call bullshit on that. The first time I dropped ecstasy, I didn't even come up. I was so scared, so anxious, and it didn't work. That was then, when I still cared.

Now, GIVE ME ALL THE DRUGS.

Lizzy takes a little plastic bag from her box and holds it up for me to see. Inside are maybe ten tiny white pills the size of aspirin.

"Sniff or swallow?"

"I'm insulted you need to ask."

Not many people know this, but the best way to take ecstasy is to snort it. The problem with this approach is twofold. The first and most apparent issue is turning powder pressed into a little hard pill back into powder again. The ideal way to do this is with a pestle and mortar. Don't listen to anyone who tries to tell you that an electronic grinder is better. Yes, it's quicker, but you end up heating the ecstasy with all that friction. You end up with more of a paste than a powder. Kind of like how cocaine comes when it's fresh before it's mixed with painkillers or bicarbonate of soda or dog-worming tablets. We might talk about cocaine later if it's relevant. Back to X:

Take your time grinding it down. Don't hurry. Don't generate too much friction. Slow, circular motions are best. Don't try to break the pill apart with the mortar. Trust in inevitability, and you'll be fine. Of course, how often do you have a pestle and mortar with you when you want to get off your face? Answer: never. That's where a credit card comes in useful. Hold it in a tight grip and sort of shave the pill down. It'll start breaking apart, and you'll end up with fat hard lumps, but then you can begin to crush those with the edge of the card. It's a slow, frustrating process doomed to failure. Failure because the resulting powder is about as fine as sand. Crystals more than powder. It's going to hurt like hell when you snort it. It burns enough when it's fine. Crushed with a credit card, it's going to be a sandblaster in your nostrils, your throat, your lungs. Your eyes will water. Your nose will run. You might be in real pain. It's all worth it.

It's all worth it because even in the worst-case scenario that pain is going to vanish like a smoke ring in the moonlight. One instant it's there, recognizable, tangible. The next, poof. Gone.

Now, bitch, you're high as fuck.

Drop a pill and you can expect at least half an hour before you come up, and it can take as long as an hour. Digestion works only so fast, after all. Far quicker to let your lungs push it directly into your system. And better yet: it's more powerful, more potent because it dumps into your bloodstream all at once.

It's the atomic fucking bomb of getting fucked-up.

But . . . I don't do it. I go through the whole process, and I'm looking at the little white line on the table, and I'm imagining how amazing it's going to feel to have my brain full to the brim with serotonin and how drugs make everything better, and yet somehow I can't do it.

I'm a still life.

Lizzy says, "What the fuck?"

She's not looking at me, but at my bandaged hand holding a rolled-up strip of the flyer I'm about to use to inhale the line of white powder. That hand is shaking. I stare at it, too, but even more surprised, even more concerned. The shaking intensifies under the scrutiny until my hand and wrist and forearm are flailing in some wild, uncontrollable dance. That dance is terrifying.

The flyer flies out of my grip.

I weep.

Tears soak my cheeks in seconds. Lizzy pulls me into a hug. She tries to pull me not just to her but into her, into her comfort, into her sympathy. I bury my face against her, soaking her shoulder.

"Hey, hey," she says in a quiet, calming whisper, "it's okay, it's okay. You're fine. It's over. You crashed your car but you're okay."

I try to respond, yet I can't speak. An incoherent, incomprehensible series of exhales is all I can manage, and Lizzy kisses the top of my head so I can feel her lips on my scalp where my hair parts in the center. She shushes me. She tries to reassure me.

In time, it works. In time, I can speak once more.

I pull back from her embrace, and my face pinches when I see how drenched she is with my tears. Not only tears. Great ropes of mucus drape across her chest like a gooey spiderweb.

"Fuck's sake."

She looks down. Laughs. "Don't worry your snotty little head about it."

I use the back of my hand to wipe my nose, then wipe it on my jeans. "You're going to need to change your top."

"You think?"

"Sarcastic bitch."

"Booger queen."

I can't help but smile. Lizzy can make me smile like no one ever could since Maya died.

She's not done: "Empress of Nasal Leakage . . . Duchess of the Green River . . . Princess Secretion."

"Are you done?"

"Never."

"I'm sorry," I say. "I'm so fucked-up."

"Never be sorry about that. Be sorry for your taste in music."

"House music is the future."

"Repetitive beats and a few shitty lyrics is the future? I can't live in that kind of world. It'll be the end of civilization as we know it. The apocalypse via cultural devolution. Kill me now."

My expression becomes serious again. "Me first."

She grips my shoulders and squats a little so we're eye level. She peers into my eyes, searching. "What's going on in your head? Whatever it is, it needs to come out." She steps away and gestures. "I mean, seriously, look at the state of you."

"Fuck off," I say, not in the least bit serious. But I have to become serious. She deserves that from me at the very least. "I got scared, Lizzy."

"I cracked that code, thanks. But why? What made you scared? It's just a pill. It's just ecstasy. Nothing you haven't taken before. It's from the same batch we had last time from Freddy's friend, remember? Freddy with the arms. I kind of like him, but he stinks. I kind of like the way he stinks. Is that weird?"

Yeah, it's fucking weird, so I nod with some enthusiasm. I find it hard to express myself because I don't understand why I'm so scared. I just know I am.

I tell her, "There wasn't any interest in my parents' house. I don't know why I went back there. I suppose it's the only time I feel close to them, to Maya. I love Steve and Jenny and miss them, but . . ."

When I don't continue, she says, "But?"

"But I hate them."

Lizzy waits.

"I hate them so much, Lizzy. They made me grieve for them when I already had to grieve for Maya. Fuck. Them."

Lizzy is silent.

"I know they were mentally ill. I know they weren't themselves. I know all that, and I still hate them."

"I can understand that anger," she says in a soft, quiet voice. "I think it's natural. Normal."

I continue: "That anger has helped me so much these past few years because it's better than pain. Maybe without it, I would have bought a stronger rope, cut deeper, taken more pills."

"Don't talk like that."

"Listen, earlier, after I'd left the house and was about to come back, my old neighbor saw me, and we ended up chatting. It sounds crazy, but I had forgotten all about him. He was just this nice old man who lived in the house next door. He was always around, always sweet, but up until he knocked on the car window, I don't think I've had one thought related to him since I left."

"You've kind of had more important things to think about."

I nod. "Yeah, I get that. Anyway, after we talked for a while, he asked me if I was sure Steve and Jenny really killed themselves. He spoke to them both that day and they both were talking about plans, about the future. Why would they do that if they were going to hang themselves?"

"What did you say?"

"Not a lot. I just had to get out of there. I couldn't handle it. I wasn't ready for that conversation."

"But what has that got to do with this?" She gestures at the line of ecstasy dust I'm too scared to snort.

"What if he's right? What if there is some other explanation?"

She frowns, sitting back. "Like what? Are you saying they were murdered? Because, like, how would that even work?"

"No, I'm not saying that."

"Then I don't understand."

"I don't either, Lizzy, but I've never understood why they didn't leave a note. What if they weren't in their right minds?" She's about to comment on that, and I stop her. "Yeah, yeah, I know that's what I always say. It's an illness, so by definition they weren't in their right minds. But did something happen that night I was at the party? Did someone say something? Did they take something? Were they compelled to hang themselves? Was I compelled to crash my car? Is that what happened to Maya too?"

"Whoa, whoa, whoa. Hold on a second. What do you mean by that? You said the crash was an accident."

I take a breath to steady myself and to compose my jumble of thoughts into something that makes sense. "I'm scared your premonition was right. I'm scared bad things really do happen in threes. First Maya, then Steve and Jenny, and now it's my turn. I'm going to die too. I can feel it."

TEN

Lizzy stares at me for a moment, and I begin to think that perhaps she sees what I see, but then she laughs. She shakes her head as she does so like this is all one big joke. She thinks I'm ridiculous. I never said I wasn't.

"I'm fucking *serious*," I tell her. "What if I'm right? What if bad things really do happen in threes? Had the old guy not pulled me out of the car, I'd be dead. Had he taken an extra minute to get dressed in the morning, I'd be dead. Maybe not even a minute. The car was an inferno. A few more seconds and it might have been too hot for him to endure it."

"Look," she says in the careful tone of someone who hears what you're saying but agrees with none of it. "If you really believed that, then it's already happened, hasn't it? That's what you said."

"What do you mean?"

"Your parents. Steve. Jenny. That's two people. You've already lost three people with Maya. So even if bad things do happen in threes, then it's happened. It's over."

I'm shaking my head before she's done talking. "Steve and Jenny died together. One night. One double suicide. One incident. One . . . whatever. They, together, are the second bad thing that's happened to me."

"I'm so sorry I mentioned that stupid premonition. I . . . It wasn't fair of me. I just had a weird feeling. I shouldn't have put thoughts in your head. I should have known better."

"I'm glad you did. I have a weird feeling too. I've had it ever since I woke up in the hospital from the overdose. I just didn't realize, and I'm not sure I would have understood what that feeling meant had you never said anything." I'm talking fast, so I need to catch my breath. "Maybe this is why I can't kill myself, because it's not supposed to be my choice. Perhaps the pills didn't work because I'm destined to die like the rest of my family."

She has wide eyes, wide crazy eyes, but they're wide because she thinks *I'm* crazy. "Destined?"

"Don't look at me like that. You won't walk over three drains in a row."

"That's different."

"Exactly how is that different? It's only different because nothing bad has ever happened to *you*." I rub the bracelet Maya gave me and say, "I haven't told you the worst part of the accident."

"What the fuck? How can it get any worse?"

I hold up my two bandaged hands. "This didn't happen in the car crash."

She waits.

"When I was in the hospital," I begin, throat feeling tight and tongue thick, "I was alone in this room, and I heard a noise at the window. A bizarre noise that didn't make any sense."

"What kind of a noise?"

"A scratching sound. Like someone scratching on the window."

"Creepy."

"It was. I should have ignored it. I should have left the room."

"What was it? What caused the noise?"

"It was Maya."

The smooth skin of Lizzy's forehead creases. "What do you mean, Maya? Your sister? You saw your sister?"

I nod, swallowing. My lips are sandpaper. "She was behind the glass in her wrecked car, trying to get out. It was filling up with smoke. I . . . I couldn't save her."

Gently, she holds my bandaged hands. I don't have to tell her how I hurt them.

"Lizzy, it was so real."

"You'd just had a car crash."

"I know."

"You hit your head."

"I know."

She's silent. She doesn't have a clue what to say next.

"Maya wasn't there," I tell her. "But I've never had a hallucination like that before. Not even after double-dropping the best X we've ever had. Not after the strongest skunk. Not. Ever. I could feel the heat on the glass. I could smell the smoke."

"From your own crash," she says in a soft voice.

I shake my head. "If I close my eyes and really try, I can't picture Maya's face like that. I don't remember her in that amount of detail. It was her, Lizzy. It was really her. She wasn't there, but it was really her."

"What are you trying to tell me?"

"I think she was sending me a message."

"I don't understand."

"I think I saw her just before I crashed." I'm rubbing the bracelet again. "I think Maya was warning me. I . . ."

I have to divert my eyes because I can't stand how Lizzy is looking at me any longer. I can't stand to see the concern in her gaze, the doubt, the confusion. She doesn't know the girl before her, and she's starting to realize it. I'm scared, but I'm making her afraid too. But she's not frightened for me. She's scared of me. I hate that. I hate that more than I hate myself.

If I lose her, it would be worse than dying, so I dry my eyes, fake a smile, and say, "I'm sorry, I don't know what I'm saying. It's just . . . It's just I'm so freaked out by the crash, by seeing Maya like that. I'm trying to make sense of it and failing spectacularly."

She smiles to reassure me. "I think they gave you too many drugs in the hospital."

"Not enough, you mean."

We hug and I take a deep breath to steady myself, then use the rolled-up flyer to snort that big fat line of X.

The fiery pain in my nostril is divine. There's no feeling quite like it.

Usually.

Now the pain is just that—a stinging chemical burn. My eyes water and the taste in the back of my throat makes me want to puke. I pretend I like it while Lizzy takes her line.

Ten minutes later, her pupils are bigger than the moon, and I don't feel a thing.

Just like that first time, I don't come up.

So, I pretend. I've been fucked-up so many times I know exactly how it feels. I can fake it. I know that first euphoric full-body rush so well that when I see Lizzy's initial doubt, it lasts only an instant.

"*Whoa*," I breathe.

She beams. "There it is. You're up, bitch."

"So fucking up," I tell her.

She won't start to come down for hours. I'm going to have to keep up this pretense all night. But I will. I do. My last grasp to hold on to this friendship.

SPOILER ALERT: Lizzy doesn't stick around. I push her away like I push everyone away. Backing me up in the hospital and looking after me were lovely things to do, but she did so out of pity, I know. She hangs out with me only because she always has. She doesn't like me anymore, and why should she? Having someone to share weed and pop pills with isn't worth all the drama that comes with it. When I understand this myself, I withdraw, but that's only because she'll leave me if I don't, she'll abandon me like everyone else. You will too. I can feel it. You'll give up on me before the end.

You're selfish. You're interested only in yourself, in what I can do to help you.

You don't give a fuck what happens to me.

ELEVEN

Sorry, mood swings. I don't mean to give you shit when you have enough to deal with just trying to stay alive. I suppose I could put a positive spin on things and make sure I portray myself in the best possible light, but that's no good to you, is it? You're not here to like me. You want me to be honest with you. You want me to give you the truth. No, you *need* for me to give you the truth.

Maybe just cut me some slack, okay? I'm not having the best time.

And I'm doing this for *you*, let's not forget.

Once the peak of Lizzy's ecstasy high is over, I have more time to think. I don't get a chance before that point, because she takes up all my energy. Thankfully, when you're full of happiness, you tend to tire before too long. That's where amphetamines come into things. Drop a bomb of X and speed, and not only will you be grinning like an idiot, you'll be grinning like that for hours and hours. Good speed, base, is hard to come by, and thankfully we don't have any, otherwise there'd be no way of keeping up with Lizzy.

She has a TV in her room and a VHS player, so we often zone out to whatever she has in her collection of recorded movies. While she's goggle-eyed at the flashing images, I'm staring at the wall. Was that crack always there? How long has the cobweb been there? It's amazing the little things we don't notice. What's more remarkable are the things we do see and choose to ignore. Like that couple in the café in the middle of a hushed row, only it's not a row, is it? He's hissing whispered threats, and she's quietly crying. We pretend it's just an argument, don't we? Couples fight, we tell ourselves. Best not to get in the middle of it. We'll only make it worse, won't we? Little lies we can't help but accept because we would never lie to ourselves, would we? We pretend it's just an argument so we don't have to admit it's a prelude to domestic violence. Because then we'd have to do something about it. With a bit of luck the next time we look up they'll be leaving, and then even that little voice of doubt and shame quietens.

Even if we could have done something, it's too late now.

What lies did I tell myself?

What did I think Steve was thinking about when I found him standing in the backyard in the middle of the night almost a year before he died, torrential rain soaking him to the bone? I dragged him inside and dried him off with a towel and made him a hot drink. We didn't speak about it afterward, and we barely spoke at the time. He muttered something about hearing a noise, and I knew it was bullshit, but I didn't press him for the truth. I didn't want to see the truth.

And Jenny, eyes glassy and pupils dilated in the middle of the afternoon. What did I tell myself? I knew she was high on pain-killers, antidepressants, and whatever else she could get her hands on, and yet I didn't want to believe she had a problem. Problems require solutions, don't they? If we pretend there's no problem we don't need to worry about finding the answer. I put her to bed and told Steve she had gone to lie down because of a headache once he'd returned from his tennis tournament.

Such little, little lies.

There were others, I know. Looking back, every smile was a lie, every kind word insincere. I'm glad Jefferson said what he did because it's forced me to look back and stop pretending. I knew Steve and Jenny were miserable, and I didn't want to deal with it. Maybe grief isn't selfish. Perhaps it's just me.

Yet this rare self-examination isn't enough.

I can't convince myself.

The crack in the wall widens to a void, a great tear in the fabric of time that takes me back to that night. While I'm having fun, Steve and Jenny are in the garage with the rope. Steve has a foot of height on Jenny, so he's the one tying it around the runners in the ceiling. Did they talk? Were they discussing it? What it would be like? How long it would take? How much it would hurt?

Did either of them mention me?

Or was it in silence? No words. Just a task done with Jenny's trademark efficiency and Steve's faultless practicality?

Steve used a little stool, and Jenny used a kitchen chair. The lengths of the ropes were different too. Like I said: there was a significant height difference. Weight, too, which makes me wonder how they knew for sure the runners would hold Steve. He must have been nearer three hundred pounds than two. Which makes me think he died first. All that extra weight on the rope must have closed his windpipe tighter than the one around Jenny's neck. How long was she alive after Steve had stopped thrashing? Did she change her mind?

I read the medical examiner's report back then. Not as thoroughly as I now would have liked, because I can't recall all the details. But I remember there was absolutely no doubt as to the cause of death. No ambiguity. No accident or foul play or misadventure or whatever else. Suicide. Hanging. Asphyxiation.

All there in black and white.

Although . . . I'm asking myself questions I didn't ask at the time. Such as: Was the rope a new purchase? If so, when was it bought? Did Jenny buy it or did Steve? Was there a receipt? Were there any scratch marks on their necks or frayed marks on the rope to suggest they tried to free themselves? Time of death was never specified beyond the three-hour window when I was at that party.

Which makes me wonder further. If there was no suggestion of an explanation beyond suicide from the start, if everyone was on that same page, did the police explore all avenues? I remember the faces of the cops who were at my house that night, but not their names. The detective who I spoke to a couple of days later was friendly. Lestrange, I think he called himself. He asked me a few questions for about as long as it took to drink a couple of coffees. I don't recall him even making notes. Now I'm thinking he was following protocol or whatever it is they call it. Whatever. He was going through the motions. He told me he might be in touch. He gave me a card. I probably still have it at my old house. I'm not sure I want to go back there. I don't think taking another look at their deaths will tell me anything new.

And Maya. Her crash. What could I possibly learn? I have no idea what I'm even looking to find. What do I think happened to her? What do I think is happening to me? It's just a feeling, and yet I can't shake it.

Lizzy's yawning tells me it's morning.

I've been awake the entire night.

"How long have I been out?" she asks, rubbing at her face.

"A couple of hours," I lie.

"Did you get any sleep?"

I nod. "Only just woke up."

"How are you feeling?"

"Doomed."

She thinks I'm being flippant, then realizes I'm serious. "Oh," is all she can say in response, remembering our conversation last night.

I stand up, grab my jacket. "I need to get moving."

She checks her watch. "You have ages until class."

"No, I'm not going. I need to go back to the hospital."

Lizzy clambers off her bed. "Oh God, are you okay? Is it your head?"

"I'm fine," I assure her. "I want to see the guy who saved me, Sebastian. I want to talk to him. I want to know what happened when I crashed. Maybe he can tell me something."

"Like what?"

"Like . . . if it was deliberate."

"You said it was an accident."

"That's the point. I may not know what happened when I crashed the car, but I know with absolute certainty that I didn't try to kill myself."

She nods along, understanding my train of thought even if she doesn't buy it. "So if he saw you do it deliberately, then you'll know you were . . . compelled?"

"Exactly."

She drags herself off her bed. "You must understand what this sounds like."

"I don't expect you to understand."

Her hands find my shoulders. "I want to. I promise I do. It's just so . . ."

"Insane?"

"Well, yeah. But I wasn't going to use that word. I'm just not sure you should jump to conclusions when there still might be another explanation."

"And I hope you're right," I tell her. "I really fucking do. It's just that, what I'm afraid of, is that it's like fate . . . doom . . . I don't know what to call it. I'm scared that this is what happened to Steve and Jenny, and Maya too. It's like a curse or . . ."

"You think you're cursed now?"

I sigh. "I don't know what to call it. Curse, doom, fate, destiny . . ." I stop. "No, I do know what to call this. It's like a rule. Bad things happen in threes."

She watches me zip up my jacket. "Do I have time to pee?"

"You're coming too?"

"Of course. Why wouldn't I?"

"Because you don't believe I'm right."

"You're my friend. I don't always have to believe every crazy idea that bubbles up inside your beautifully round head. But I'll always support you. Always. No matter what. No matter how insane."

My eyes moisten. "I fucking love you, Lizzy."

I wipe my teary eyes.

I have to blow my nose too.

Lizzy smiles and says, "I love you, too, Princess Secretion."

TWELVE

Sebastian is not quite as old as I remember him. When I was waking up in my car, he seemed young. Then, when I could see properly again, he seemed old. He's somewhere in between. Middle-aged, I suppose. Although that's still pretty old to me. When he was my age I didn't even exist, I realize. We find him in a ward near where I was treated. The burn unit, naturally.

It's after visiting hours by the time we get to see him, although we're not stopped. With my bandaged hands and bandaged head, no one challenges us or asks what we're doing. I look like I belong in a hospital. Maybe a nurse or two glances Lizzy's way with a raised eyebrow, but they're all too busy to interfere even if they thought it was necessary. Without the bandages, we would never have got close, I'm sure. I'm expecting Sebastian to be pretty beat-up given he's still in the hospital in the burn unit. I'm just hoping they're keeping him in purely as a precautionary measure.

I'm hopeful, but only for a moment.

He's naked from the waist up. Bandages and dressings cover half the exposed torso, one arm, and half of his face and head. He has an oxygen mask, an IV drip in his arm, a heart monitor, and other things I don't understand.

His eyes are closed.

Lizzy stalls when she sees him, and I have to drag her closer. This burn ward has several other patients. Most behind screens or otherwise unseen. It's quiet. There's an unpleasant smell in the air.

I move closer to Sebastian's bed and lean down near his head. The unhurt side. I assume he won't hear so well from the other side with the bandages covering his ear.

I don't want to startle him, so I gently whisper, "Sebastian."

He stirs a little in his sleep. He doesn't really move his body, just his head.

I repeat his name, trying to be a little louder but not loud.

He stirs again—the same subtle shift of his head.

I risk laying a hand on the skin of his shoulder, which feels hot and sweaty. I give him a little nudge.

"He's off his face on drugs," Lizzy whispers behind me. Then, "Maybe we can steal some."

"Show some respect," I snap back, still whispering. "He saved my life."

"I was joking." She pauses. "Fine, half joking."

"Sebastian," I say for the third time, no longer whispering, and give his shoulder a little shake.

He groans behind the oxygen mask, and then his one visible eye opens. It takes a moment to get a fix on me.

"Hey, there," I say in a cheery tone. "Hope I'm not disturbing you."

He gestures to the mask with a weak hand.

"You want me to take it off?"

He makes a motion with his head I interpret as a nod.

Immediately, his breathing becomes raspy and labored.

"I'm sorry," I tell him. "I didn't mean for you to get hurt."

He shakes his head. Like the nod, it's a weak imitation of the gesture. I hope it's the painkillers causing this drowsiness.

He swallows and blinks his eyes a few times.

"It's . . . okay," he says.

He's not whispering, but his voice is as thin as a whisper. He makes a sound like a groan or him clearing his throat.

"I'm glad . . . you're . . . alive," he says.

"Because of you," I tell him. "I'm so grateful."

He motions with his hand. A kind of small, lateral gesture. Like saying, *Don't mention it.*

"Sebastian," I begin, taking that hand in my own. "I don't remember why I crashed. I don't remember what happened beforehand. Can you help me understand it? Did you see it? Did you see me come off the road? Or just before?"

He shakes his head as much as he can.

My shoulders sag. I look to Lizzy. She doesn't know what to do or say, but I can see that she's disappointed for me. She wants me to get answers even if she doesn't believe the answers will back me up.

Sebastian clears his throat or groans again.

"The girl," he says.

"The girl?"

"The one who phoned the ambulance," Lizzy says. "The one who has your phone."

My pulse quickens. "The girl saw the crash?"

"Yes," Sebastian manages to say.

"Did she tell you anything? When you were helping me? Or afterward? Did she, Sebastian? I need to know what she saw."

He goes to clear his throat or groan again but begins to cough and cough and cough. Each becoming louder and more violent until he's spasming in the bed and his heart monitor is beeping warnings. The pristine white bedclothes are speckled with droplets of blood, and his mouth and chin are smeared with it.

"*Nurse*," Lizzy calls out as I back away, shocked and scared.

The heart monitor is going ballistic, and poor Sebastian is thrashing about and coughing uncontrollably. Each cough sends more blood over his sheets, his bandages. We step back instinctively to avoid being spattered.

"Holy fuck," I hear Lizzy yell. "*Nurse*."

A nurse rushes in, pushing us out of the way, telling us to get out, and we do as we're told, backing away from the horrific sight.

Before we're through the door, Sebastian is looking in my direction with his one uncovered eye. It seems as though he's trying to get my attention, maybe to tell me something more, yet his coughing is so violent and uncontrollable that he can form no words. But he's trying. I can see him trying, so I hesitate.

"What is it?" I plead.

"*Get out*," the nurse shouts.

Sebastian reaches out in my direction, and for a second I think he's managed to control the coughing enough to speak. Then he grows quiet and limp because the nurse has injected him with a sedative.

"Are you happy now?" she asks me. "Was your visit worth it?"

"No, of course not. I didn't want that to happen. I just wanted to talk to him."

"Talk to him?" she asks, incredulous. "He shouldn't say even a single word. He's lost two-thirds of his lung tissue, and his windpipe is so perforated a sip of water could kill him."

"Oh my God," I say, hand going to my mouth. "Is he going to be okay?"

Her eyebrows rise, and her forehead creases into many lines of disbelief.

"No," she says with such quiet anger it's almost a hiss. "He's not going to be okay."

My eyes well up and I open my mouth to speak, but Lizzy takes me by the hand and leads me away, and the nurse watches us the entire time until we're through a set of double doors and away from the ward.

"It's not your fault," Lizzy tells me. "Don't blame yourself. You mustn't blame yourself."

He dies in the night, I find out later.

THIRTEEN

The woman's name is Charlotte, we discover when we call my cell and she picks up. She works in the town library. Which is a building I've never set foot inside before. The campus has its own facility, after all. There's a greater range of books here. The university library is all academic texts and papers. Here, there's more fiction than not. Every genre you can imagine. I'm not sure I realized people read so much for fun. God, how is reading pleasure? Those people need to get out more. There's a section for audiobooks, although it's not large enough to be subcategorized into genres, so the tapes are listed alphabetically. A few are even on CD, separated on their own display with such prominence it's almost like they're showing off. *We're better than you,* I can feel them saying to the nearby cassettes.

The woman working behind the desk is not Charlotte.

This woman is about twice her age and twice her weight. She wears a pair of tortoiseshell glasses and a second pair, I presume for reading, hangs from her neck by a beaded cord.

Lizzy hangs back a step while I introduce myself and ask to see Charlotte.

"I'm afraid she's working right now," the woman behind the desk tells me. "What's this about?"

I hold up my bandaged hands, gesture to my bandaged head. "I was in a car crash . . ."

"Oh yes, of course." She disappears behind the desk for a moment and comes back with my phone in her hand. She lays it down on the counter, and I slide it closer. "Can't be good for the brain. All that radiation."

"I'm pretty sure they're harmless."

"How would you know? You wouldn't know it was doing you any harm until it did."

"Hmm. I suppose," I relent. "Can I see Charlotte?"

"She's working."

"Yeah, you said. But I need to speak to her. It's really important."

The woman glances up at the clock high on one wall. "She has lunch in a couple of hours. She's very busy right now."

I'm getting frustrated. I glance at the part of the library I can see. "There's about three customers in here."

"Members," she corrects. "We don't have customers. This is a library."

"A library? I thought it was Fort Knox. Only that would be easier to get into."

She doesn't appreciate my sarcasm. She may be a librarian, but she has the stern, scolding facial expression of a strict headmistress and I'm about to be expelled.

"I think it would be best if you come back here at 1 p.m. and see Charlotte when she's not working. This isn't a place to socialize."

Lizzy, having grown frustrated witnessing the woman's needless hostility, steps in front of me. "Listen, my friend here is having the worst time possible right now. You literally can't even imagine what she's going through, so why don't you just be nice to her? Why not just be nice in general? Try it. See how it feels."

"I'm afraid I don't make the rules," the woman says.

She's never going to allow me inside, so I reach a bandaged hand toward the barrier and push it. Nothing, so I pull it. Nothing. It is locked after all.

"It's locked," the woman tells me, smug and triumphant.

I'm not tall, and I'm not athletic, and my hands are tender, and I can't grip properly. However, I still manage to climb over the barrier without difficulty.

"What are you doing? Stop that."

I say without difficulty, but it's not a fast process given the afore-mentioned traits holding me back. By the time I'm over the barrier, the woman has rounded the desk and come out to block my way.

Lizzy hops over with much more ease and grace.

The woman says, "I'll call the police."

Lizzy bursts out laughing at the threat. I glance back to her desk, where the phone sits. She'll have to get out of my way to dial.

I hold up my cell. "Shame these are pointless, right?"

If looks could kill.

I pretend to thumb buttons and bring the phone to my ear. "Hi, police? Yeah, I'd like to report a hostile invasion at the local library. Yes, someone without a card came inside. Please send everyone you can spare. *Hurry.*"

Defeated, the woman stands aside and heads to the desk. "I really am going to call the police."

Lizzy says, "Whatever gets you through your day."

The library is a deceptively large space. The tall bookshelves make it seem even larger—cavernous and maze-like. I'm aware of the quiet. Every noise we make is disproportionately loud. Each breath is as loud as a sneeze. Every step is a giant's stomp.

I didn't see many people from the entrance, and now I see none. Every aisle is empty when we look down it. No one is taking books from the shelves. No one is reading. I feel like we're alone. I feel like we're somehow lost. I'm getting a little scared and I don't under-stand why. It's that weird feeling again. I can't explain it, but it's real.

Stop freaking yourself out, I tell myself.

Lizzy rests a hand on my arm. "You okay?"

I nod. I can't die in a library, can I? It's perhaps the safest place to be. A book isn't going to fall off a shelf and kill me, is it? Even if a whole bookcase tipped over, the aisles are too narrow for it to fall on me. The next shelf will stop it. Maybe a few dozen books raining over me will bruise, but we're talking paper and cardboard, aren't we? I'm not going to bleed out from a paper cut.

Still, I can't shake the unease. Convincing myself of the illogical-ity of a library-based demise is all well and good if I trust my own conclusions. No chance. I'm the queen of self-doubt. I have a crown and everything.

It seems darker than it should be at this time of day. Few ceiling lights are on, and the tall shelves create deep shadows.

Did I see someone in the next aisle?

There's a glimpse of movement here, maybe a sound there.

We're lost. I no longer have any sense of direction. All the aisles look the same. All the books are identical.

I'm breathing harder.

This was a bad idea. I need to get out of here.

"Let's just go," I tell Lizzy. "This is a stupid idea."

"Can I help you?" a voice says behind us.

I startle, then turn. I recognize Charlotte after a second, and she remembers me a second after that.

"Hey," she says.

"Hey," I say.

I'm not sure what to say, but she pulls me into a hug and then I really don't know what to say.

"I'm so glad you're okay," she tells me.

"Thanks for calling the ambulance."

"Happy to."

She releases me from the hug. Steps back suddenly as though she fears she's been overly familiar. I don't usually like strangers getting in my personal space or being touchy-feely, so I probably gave off some leave-me-alone vibes. I feel guilty about this. I don't quite know how to express to her that it was okay to hug me without making us both more awkward than we already are, so I don't.

Lizzy says, "Hi."

Charlotte does a little wave in response.

"This is my friend Lizzy," I explain. Then I just come out and say it. "Did you see what happened?"

"The crash?"

I nod. "Yeah, the crash. Before the crash as well."

"What exactly are you asking me?"

"I just want to know what you saw."

She says, "Is there a problem with the insurance?"

"What?"

"The car. Is the insurance company being funny with you?"

"I haven't even claimed," I say. "That's not really important to me right now."

"Okay."

I take a deep breath to compose myself. "I don't remember crashing the car. I think I can remember driving a few minutes before, but that's it. It's . . . Let's just say that it's freaking me out not being able to remember, and it'll really calm my nerves if you can fill in the blanks for me. Do you think you can do that? I'd be so grateful."

"Well, I did see you crash the car—you kind of swerved off the road and went right into the post. I was farther down the street, crossing. I saw you coming, but there was plenty of time to get across before you would be in any danger."

"I swerved to miss you?"

"No, no. Like I said, you weren't close to me like that. But I was looking in your direction since you were the only car on the street. I'd never just cross without looking to make sure. You . . ."

I wait. She looks away. She fidgets and pushes her hair back. She doesn't want to tell me something.

I exchange looks with Lizzy.

"What is it? What did you see?"

"Maybe I'm mistaken," she says. "You weren't far away, but you weren't super close."

"What is it? What was I doing?"

"Nothing," she says. "At first. I was at the curb and glanced down the street, saw your car. You know, nothing unusual. You weren't close, so I walked out into the road. I looked both ways as I was walking just in case. Safety first, first aid last . . . By the time I was reaching the far curb, I was close enough to see you properly for the first time. Just a girl driving her car. Then . . ."

"Then?"

She swallows. "You closed your eyes."

"I fell asleep at the wheel?"

"No, I don't know—kind of. But your head didn't nod forward or anything. You just sort of closed your eyes. Like you were blinking, but they never opened again. Which made me stop and stare. And I'm thinking, 'What is this?' and expecting you to open your eyes, but they stayed closed. I don't know how long it was for. Maybe just a few seconds. It seemed like forever. Then you crashed."

"So, I did fall asleep?"

She shakes her head. "You kept hold of the wheel for a moment. While I was watching you and you had your eyes closed, I could see your hands on the wheel like this."

She mimes ten and two o'clock.

"And then you did this."

With her arms still out to mime my driving hand position on the wheel, she jerks her hands anticlockwise.

Lizzy asks, "She turned off the road? Deliberately?"

"Yes," Charlotte answers. "That's what it looked like. It looked like you closed your eyes and then turned the wheel and you went straight into that post."

I don't know what to say. She's telling me I tried to kill myself.

"I thought you were dead."

"If it wasn't for Sebastian, I would be dead."

This is when I find out he died in the night, and I'm so overwhelmed with shock at what Charlotte has told me that I sink to the floor. My shoulders sag. I feel so dazed, so hopeless.

Charlotte lowers herself to the floor next to me, putting an arm around my shoulders and trying to comfort me. Like Lizzy before, she keeps telling me that it's not my fault because she thinks I'm like this because of Sebastian's death.

It's hard to admit it, but I'm not. At this moment, I can't spare any emotion for Sebastian. I'm so consumed with the imagery of closing my eyes and turning the wheel that poor Sebastian barely registers. Charlotte has told me that I tried to kill myself, and while I've tried before, I wasn't suicidal when I left Llewellyn's office. I wasn't exactly in a good mood, but there wasn't a single thought in my mind regarding taking my own life. And because I've tried before I know it's not a sudden, spur-of-the-moment decision. A few minutes before I crashed, I was fine. I know myself. I know suicidal thoughts. They don't just appear out of nowhere, and you act on them.

I grow cold.

I'm freezing cold with dread.

When I told Lizzy it's the rule that compels you to kill to yourself, I didn't know for sure. It was a guess, a stream-of-consciousness kind of thing. The feelings I couldn't be sure of put into words.

Now I'm certain it's the truth.

Charlotte is telling me that there are people out there who can help me. Professionals. Volunteers. Helplines. Support groups. She can put me in touch with some. Working at the library means she has lots of contacts. She can help me. She wants to help me. I nod every so often. I grunt the occasional agreement. Acquiescing, no more.

By the time I'm able to stand again, Lizzy says, "Uh-oh . . ."

"There they are," the woman from the desk says, pointing.

A grim-faced cop gestures for me and Lizzy to come with him.

FOURTEEN

Lizzy's face is pinched with concentration. I can see the tip of her tongue poking out between her lips—a hint of pink framed by the black of her lipstick. I'm not sure she's breathing, such is her focus, her intensity.

When she's finished, it's like she's free of some significant burden. So much tension flees her body; it's as if she might melt away without it. She smiles, happy. Triumphant.

Holding forth the newly rolled cigarette, she asks, "Want the first pull?"

"You do it," I say.

She's lighting up seconds later.

"I still can't believe they threw us out of the library," Lizzy says, setting the cigarette down and pouring the cheap own-brand cola into the cheap own-brand vodka she's already poured for herself.

She passes me the roll-up and I'm quick to take a drag, but no one enjoys smoking. Don't believe anyone who tells you otherwise. Nicotine is a stimulant, only it's weaker than coffee and as addictive as heroin. And that's even before we mention the lengthy list of awful, death-inducing diseases that smoking tobacco causes. It tastes like ass too.

Worst. Drug. Ever.

Also, forget what I just said, I like smoking.

I sip Lizzy's concoction. I cough. "This is dragon fire."

"You're so welcome."

"I feel welcomed."

She clinks her glass to mine. "I get the impression that cop didn't give a shit. He was just going through the motions. He didn't want to be there. It was a big waste of his time, and we all knew it. I'm pretty sure he told the librarian from hell that after he escorted us away. What a waste of resources."

"I agree."

We drink our drinks and Lizzy makes us another. She's not measuring the vodka and I can feel it already. These are large servings. Closer to quadruples than doubles. There's a telling amount of empty air in the bottle after only two drinks. We call this efficiency drinking, which we do because she has to watch her bank balance, unlike me. Efficiency drinking is really just budget drinking, which is really just drinking a lot in a short space of time. So you get drunk fast and don't have to spend too much in the process. Sipping responsibly is not something many students can afford. And when you take a lot of drugs, alcohol feels like a snail's way of getting fucked-up. Drinking the traditional way, I mean.

Lizzy wants to get me drunk. She knows what Charlotte told us is playing on my mind, and she's deliberately avoiding talking about it. When Lizzy drove us back to campus I was too numb to talk, and then she had to run—literally run—to her class, leaving me alone with my thoughts all afternoon.

I realize that while she wanted to support me as a friend, she was also convinced that Sebastian, and then Charlotte, was going to back up her rational interpretation of what's happening to me. I didn't know that she was never going to believe me. No matter what Charlotte said. No matter what anyone says.

She's going to understand the truth only after I'm dead. It's an utter waste of time to try to get Lizzy to see before then. But I'm not doing this for her.

I'm doing this for you.

Well, you and me both.

Lizzy has the privilege of being able to wait for proof. She needs all the evidence in front of her to come to the same conclusion as us.

We're not so lucky. We don't have time to convince anyone beyond a reasonable doubt.

In fact, you're the only one who doesn't doubt me. And that just so happens to be the only chance you have of beating this.

We drink.

We smoke.

We chat about anything else, and I'm really trying my best to accept the fact I have to just go it alone and not blame Lizzy for refusing to accept the truth. I'm really trying, but the elephant in the room has become a massive woolly mammoth and it's sitting on my chest and I can't take it any longer.

"Just don't fucking say it, all right?"

Lizzy is shocked. "Say . . . ?"

"I'm not suicidal, Liz. Yeah, yeah, I know I am. Usually. Some-times. But I'm not right now, and I wasn't yesterday. I wasn't even in a bad mood after I finished my session. I was as calm and in the zone as I've ever been. So don't tell me I'm something I'm not. I know myself. I know me. I've lived in this fucked-up headspace for such a long time now. I know what the buildup is like. I've been there. It's days and days of working up the courage after weeks and weeks of suicidal thoughts. It doesn't just happen. You don't just feel okay one moment and then run yourself off the road the next. You just don't."

My heart is thumping, and my face feels hot. I glug some vodka and cola to steady myself. Lizzy is looking at me with her big beau-tiful eyes that are larger than usual.

"I . . . ," she begins.

"You what?" I snap.

"I wasn't going to say that, Amy. I promise. You've told me enough to know that what happened yesterday doesn't sound like you. What Charlotte told us doesn't sound like something you would do."

"I didn't do it," I tell her. "I know I didn't."

"Then what happened?"

"It wasn't me, that's the only way I can explain it that makes any sense. The moment I closed my eyes, I wasn't in control of myself. It wasn't me at that moment. It was the rule. It was . . ."

I can't think of a way to phrase it, but Lizzy can.

"The rule of three."

I nod. "Exactly. It takes you over, compelling you until after you've kicked away the stool or crashed your car. That's why there was no note from Steve and Jenny. That's why they were their normal selves just hours earlier, happily making plans."

She listens.

"It gets worse," I continue. "Once you've done it, once the rule of three is finished with you, you come back. If that old man hadn't been there, I wouldn't just be dead. I would have woken up inside the car in time to know I was dying. This thing is sadistic. It's cruel."

"But why?"

"Why what?"

"Why you? Why your family?"

I shrug. "I don't know why. I'm going to find out, though. I have to know why. I think I'll only be able to beat it if I know why."

She sets her drink down and takes mine from my hand to do the same. She then takes my hands in hers. She smiles. "I think I may be able to help you. I mean, I have no idea if I can, but I want to try."

"I'll take any long shot you can give me."

"Okay. That's kind of what I thought. We do whatever we can. We don't know what's going to help, so there are no wrong suggestions."

"Stop milking it. I'm not a cow."

She smiles. "When I was in class earlier, we were being taught about how religion has affected the progress of language, and it got me thinking." She shuffles to fetch her bag. She unzips it. "So, afterward, I had a little idea. I went and dug out the entire list of courses they run here. Fuck me, there are so many that I cannot believe anyone would want to take."

She removes a prospectus from the bag. It has a shiny cover with smiling faces, but it's crumpled because it's from this school year. It's been well read and abused the way only students can.

The prospectus is for religious studies.

She holds it up as if it's sweet Lord baby Jesus himself.

I say, "I don't get it."

"This is why you need me on your side," she tells me as she opens up the booklet and flips through the pages. When she finds the one she's looking for, she stabs at it with her index finger. "Jackpot."

I look.

I say, "I still don't get it."

"Are you so drunk you can't see straight? Look, look. Right here where it lists the modules. What does it say?"

"Something about the occult. So what?"

"*The occult*," she says, loud and proud. "That's all about weird shit like voodoo and hexes, right?"

I don't know, so I say, "I don't know."

"But it might do?"

"I guess. But I'm not taking religious studies, and that module looks like it's next semester."

"Yeah, yeah. I know. I get that. But someone teaches it, don't they? So someone knows what they're talking about."

"Ah, I see where you're going with this. I could speak to them about what's happening to me."

"They might be able to help, right? Or they can point you in the right direction."

"Maybe."

"Maybe's better than nothing, isn't it?"

I nod.

Lizzy's so happy with herself, and I guess I'm happy, too, even if I'm not sure it will do any good. But I'm so glad she's done something to help me. I feel like she actually believes me, although I'm wrong.

It takes only a moment for our efficiency drinking to be effective, and then I'm smiling and crying in a mix of emotions. We drink more. A lot more. Combined with the painkillers I'm on, I'm soon an utter mess. Which Lizzy finds hilarious. I slur my thanks over and over again and repeat how much I love her.

I don't yet know that Lizzy is going to betray me in the worst way possible.

FIFTEEN

It's the middle of the day, yet it's dark and gloomy inside Professor Whittaker's office. There's only one small window, and the plastic venetian-style blinds have been pulled down and closed, letting just a little light inside the room. Which is small on account of all the books and folders and papers stacked up in every conceivable space. It's an organized person's idea of hell.

He's reading a paperback book when I enter. He holds up a long finger to indicate I should be quiet for a moment. I guess he wants to finish the page he's on. I can't really see the front cover, given the way he's holding the book, but I squint my eyes in an attempt to read the blurb on the back. I see it's true crime, about a killer.

Someone who murdered lots of people back in the seventies is all I can decipher before he turns over the corner of a page and sets the book down.

"Thank you for seeing me," I say.

"My pleasure."

His voice is low and booming. The kind of man who cannot whisper. He's extremely tall and walks in a stooped, awkward manner in the hallways. In his office chair, he seems contorted and uncomfortable, always fidgeting and adjusting himself. Sometimes slouched, other times bent and hunched over.

He waits for me to continue. He's busy, yet in no rush. It's his lunch hour, and he's unwrapping a sandwich from its shield of aluminum foil. He does so with careful, precise movements that make no sense to me, who would just tear my way through the foil, too impatient for any care of the process.

"What's on your mind?" he asks. "But know that it's too late to change courses."

"No, yeah. I know. I'm not."

I say this too fast, with too much certainty, and I feel as though I've offended him with my easy dismissal of his teaching.

When Whittaker scratches his head, bursts of dead skin rise up into the light in small clouds. He looks disheveled despite the smart clothes, which are too big for him, contradictory as that seems. The shoulder pads of his jacket jut out. The cuffs of his shirt are cavernous compared to the wrists that protrude from them. His trousers bunch up over his shoes.

"It's going to sound weird."

He peels away the final fold of foil, exposing the sandwich in all its compressed white bread glory. "I like weird."

His graying hair sticks up from his head in random tufts, made more unruly when he jabs his fingers into them to scratch at his scalp. Patches of psoriasis color his skin flaky pink on the back of his left hand, the left side of his neck, and the right side of his forehead.

"I'm underselling it," I say. "It's going to sound crazy. Like batshit fucking crazy."

My hand goes to my mouth too late to catch the swearing. I freeze, awaiting admonishment.

Separating one half of the sandwich from the other, he says, "Outside my class, you may speak however you wish. But be careful what you say about my sandwich."

I notice the filling for the first time. Between the two thin slices of squished white bread is a row of fat, halved gherkins, ends protruding out from the bread and glistening with bright mustard and mayonnaise.

He smiles at my grimace of distaste and takes a massive bite from one of the halves, leaving just a quarter remaining in his fingers. He's not a quiet eater.

After swallowing, he says, "Why don't you tell me what this is all about? What's so batshit fucking crazy?"

He has a patchy beard, thin here, dense there. One ear is much larger than the other, and the light behind him shines through it so that the ear glows in an otherworldly orange.

"I think I'm doomed," I say. "Well, not think. I . . . I know I am."

I tell him everything. I try to summarize and fail, so I add details and then realize I'm missing pertinent information and go back a bit, but not far enough, then too far, and then I'm jumping around all over the place and rambling and not making any sense, and as I realize I'm not making any sense I'm talking faster and faster in a damage control effort, and I'm growing hotter and redder and more and more frustrated, and Whittaker just listens and eats, and all I can hear is his loud fucking crunching on those fucking gherkins and

"*Fuck.*"

He takes out a handkerchief to wipe the corner of his mouth and his fingers. "Fuck?"

"I'm not making any sense."

"You lost your parents together in one night and your sister before that, suicides and an accident respectively, and now you believe you're going to die as well because bad things always happen in threes. Is that right?"

"Yeah. Pretty much."

"And why are you telling me all this? Until a few minutes ago, I didn't know you even existed."

"You teach religious studies. I've gone through the teaching schedule. You have a segment on the occult, paganism, all that stuff."

"All that stuff," he says, readying the second half of the sandwich for annihilation.

"Yeah. I figure you're the best person on campus to talk to about it. If anyone knows anything about what's happening to me, it's got to be you, hasn't it? Please tell me you know about this kind of thing."

"Doom?"

"Doom, the rule of three . . . whatever it is. I don't want to call it fate or destiny. I just don't. I can't . . . I can't call it that because then there's nothing I can do to stop it. If I think of it like a rule, then maybe I can do something to break it. Or if it's like a curse, maybe it can be lifted? I don't really know how they work."

"Well, with a curse one person typically puts that curse on another. I mean, it varies hugely between cultures and belief systems. Still, in essence, one person performs a ritual, and the other person receives the curse. The ritual can be anything, from saying the person's name to creating a voodoo doll to chanting to anything, really. I might take a lock of your hair and hold it up to the moon and curse you with bad luck."

"You're saying that someone did this to me?"

"No, that's not what I'm saying. I'm simply giving a very brief overview. Although even the most powerful curses don't tend to kill the person, let alone kill their entire family too."

"But a curse comes from someone else, right? You don't just catch it like the flu?"

"We're talking about superstition as though it's the reality here."

"Yeah, I get that. Can we, for the sake of argument, assume these superstitions are real?"

He regards me with a skeptic's gaze, all furrowed brow and narrowed eyes. I don't back down from this inquisition. He can think I'm weird or crazy or whatever as much as he likes. He's having a hypothetical conversation while I'm trying to learn—an amusing waste of time to him, an attempt to save my own life to me.

He concedes with a shrug. "Sure."

"Then how do you get rid of a curse?"

"I suppose that seeking out the person who gave out the curse would be the best place to start."

I sigh, because if the rule of three is a curse then someone had to have cursed Maya all those years ago. When she died, did it move to my parents, and when my parents died, it moved to me? Or was my whole family cursed? How can I possibly find out who cursed us all those years ago?

I say, "And if you couldn't find the person who gave you the curse, what do you do? Is there some sort of spell? A cure?"

"Maybe," he answers. "Depending on the belief system. Maybe a different ritual, a spell . . ."

"Would such a ritual still work if the rule isn't specifically a curse?"

"Look, I'm an academic, not a wizard." He waves his fingers as if unleashing magic and chuckles, expecting me to join in. When I don't, he finally realizes that although this discussion is an interesting diversion for him, it's deadly serious for me. "I'm sorry. I don't mean to belittle you. If I could bless you and make this all go away, I would."

"Bless me?" My eyes widen. "Like a priest would do? Could that work?"

"Sure, why not? The Catholic Church has a division that specializes in exorcism, after all."

"It does? No fucking way. So a priest could bless me and get rid of the curse or break the rule?"

"I'm really not saying that at all. You understand that this is purely a hypothetical discussion, yes?"

"Of course. Yeah. We're just spitballing here."

The sandwich is finished. He sucks the tips of his fingers, one by one, leaving the thumbs for last. He wipes them all on the handkerchief, which goes back into a pocket of his jacket. He brushes crumbs from the flattened-out square of aluminum foil and then neatly folds it back over itself until the square is a quarter of the width and depth and four times the thickness. This goes into another pocket.

"Waste not, want not," he says.

I say, "Thank you for your time and for your advice."

"I'm not sure I gave you any advice."

"No, you've given me a lot more than that, Professor. You've given me some hope."

SIXTEEN

I haven't been inside a church in years. Might even be a decade. Steve and Jenny were religious, but they were not regular church-goers. I remember going to weddings and christenings when I was a child and maybe a handful of other times too when their faith intensified for some reason or other. And then . . . nothing. I want to say they stopped going once Maya died, although I think it was before then. Trying to remember what was going on and why from back then is almost impossible. I don't even trust the things I do remember well.

While not happy after my visit with Whittaker, I'm determined. I can see the light at the end of this incredibly dark and dank tunnel I'm being pulled through.

All I have to do is find a priest to bless me.

This shouldn't be too hard, right?

I was going to borrow Lizzy's car to drive into town. I called her to ask if I could. Then I didn't ask. I don't want to get behind another wheel. It's too dangerous. Not because of the bandages on my hands. They wouldn't really impede my driving. It's the rule of three. If I try to drive into town to find a priest, I'm just going to crash again, aren't I? I don't know if that's the way I'm meant to die and that's the only way I can die, or if it's open season on Amy and anything I do carries the same risk. Either way, I'm getting the bus.

I've used the shuttle service that goes every hour between the town and the campus several times. Mostly late at night after par-tying, granted.

The driver doesn't look my way as he takes the coins. He drives off from the stop before I've taken my seat, and I have to hastily grab one of the bars to stop myself from being thrown around. The bar's too slick, however, and my grip is weakened by the cuts and bandages.

I stumble.

Fall.

For an instant, I think I'm going to hit my head, and that's how I'm going to die.

The hard plastic of the corner of the seat against my temple and crack, my neck's broken.

My fall is intercepted, though, and my temple never reaches the lethal corner of the seat. Hands grab my coat, and I'm cushioned by a man who leaps up to help me. I almost knock him over, too, but he's strong and secure. We sway and shuffle a moment, all flailing limbs and rapidly adjusting feet, until finally we have gained enough control to separate.

He's a young, handsome man. He looks a little too mature to be a student, and his clothes are a bit too clean. No three-day T-shirt or week-old jeans for this guy. He's well dressed and well presented. Clean and groomed. Nice hair. Nice teeth. A shy smile.

"Are you okay?"

I'm flustered and stumble my words into an incomprehensible jibber.

"Is that a yes?" he asks.

"Thanks," I say. "I thought I was a goner."

"Well," he says, voice full of sarcastic concern, "you might have grazed your knee."

"Yeah, that's what I meant."

He gestures. "Better sit down before it's too late." He looks in the driver's direction. "This guy is a lunatic."

I take the seat opposite him because it's the closest and I turn in, so I'm facing forward. Out of the corner of my eye, I see that he is sitting on the end of the seat, legs in the aisle, looking my way.

"What's your name?"

"Amy."

A pause.

He says, "Do you want to know my name?"

"Sure."

"Christian," he says.

"That's weird. I'm on my way to church."

"Yeah, I'm not actually a Christian. Religion is self-prescribed Prozac, if you ask me." He hesitates. "But if that's your thing, cool."

"No, it's not. I mean, I guess I used to believe or whatever, but I'm not religious."

"Then why are you riding the bus to go to church? Are you going to a meeting?"

"A meeting?"

"You know, a group. Like Alcoholics Anonymous."

"Maybe if I survive, I'll start going."

"What?"

"Nothing. Forget it. I say stupid stuff all the time. Best to ignore at least fifty percent of everything that comes out of my mouth."

"I was going to guess sixty percent."

"Funny. Do you work at the university?"

He nods. "Yes and no."

"Why both?"

"Yes, because I'm a lab assistant. No, because I'm studying for a PhD. That's why I was there. Today."

"I can't imagine how much work that takes."

"It's a lot, but it's not too bad. If you study what interests you, then it's not even studying. At least, not to me."

"What's your subject?"

"Mathematics."

I snort.

"Shut up," he says, laughing. "It's the most exciting field there is."

"I'll take your word for that," I say, my tone dripping with sarcasm.

He doesn't get the hint. He goes on about numbers and equations and theories, and before long I'm nodding and saying, "Uh-huh," and not taking anything in.

"This is my stop," I say, about three stops early.

"Oh, okay," he says as I stand. "It was nice talking to you."

"Nice meeting you," I tell him because it was nice meeting him, but it wasn't nice talking to him.

I walk the rest of the way to the church.

Why did I tell you about Christian? It's inconsequential now, but important later. I said I'd tell you everything as it happened and I am. I'm keeping things in chronological order so I don't leave anything out. That way we will both hopefully benefit.

A choir is singing when I step inside. Beautiful voices, perfect acoustics, yet it's somewhat unnerving. The effect is haunting almost. The church is old and cavernous, not well lit. I walk in shadows, my footsteps clicking on the stone floor despite the singing. I make the sign of the cross from some long-suppressed instinct. I don't really mean it because I don't really believe.

Believe, I urge myself.

I have to believe. A blessing surely can't work if I don't believe in the source, can it?

I walk along the aisle between the pews, all empty, yet somehow I can hear snippets of whispers and catch glimpses of worshippers sitting reverently. My pulse quickens.

I don't feel welcome here.

I feel like I don't belong. That the very church is judging me for this blasphemy. There's an unspoken warning in the air. I should leave. This is a mistake.

As I step slowly closer, the singing of the choir grows louder, their melodious voices crisper, the haunting acoustics even more impactful.

The ceiling rises far above my head. The walls seem to grow farther apart. I'm becoming smaller, more insignificant, less welcome.

I stop. I know when I'm not wanted.

I should never have come here.

I'm insulting God with my presence.

I turn.

A man in black startles me, my cry of alarm lost among the choir's singing.

The priest is a square-shouldered man, all stiff posture and dignity. He's old enough to have graying hair but young enough to have some of it still. He has the black clothes and the funny collar. His face is very red, like a sunburn.

"May I help you?" he asks.

"If you can't, no one can."

He takes me to a quiet back room. Not quite an office. Perhaps for meetings or group therapy. He sits me down and pours me a glass of water, and I sip and just talk at him for a good fifteen minutes straight.

He gets my life history: Maya's death, Steve's and Jenny's deaths, my suicide attempts, and everything that's happened since.

The priest is a good listener. It's easy to talk to him. Perhaps because I'm almost getting used to telling my crazy story. The more times I have to explain what's happening to me, the more succinct I am. The less waffling around I do, the more sense I make. At least, the more sense I make to myself. How others perceive me is still a mystery. I thought Whittaker believed me. I thought Lizzy believed me.

"I believe you," the priest says.

"You do?"

"Why wouldn't I?"

"Isn't this kind of thing contrary to religion?"

"Not at all. Many Christians believe only in God and discount any other forms of the supernatural, but that is to deny what the Bible tells us. We cannot believe in God and not the devil. We cannot believe there are angels but not demons."

"Yeah, sure. I hear you. What about curses? I don't know if it's technically a curse or not."

"Well, Jesus himself cursed a fig tree for not having fruit. God cursed Cain after Cain murdered Abel. Remember, faith is not the rejection of the supernatural but the absolute belief in it."

"What if it's not a curse? What if it's something else? I call it a rule. I don't really know what this is. I just know it's coming for me."

"Evil does exist in all sorts of forms we might not fully understand."

"Will you bless me?" I ask, nervous and expecting rejection.

"Of course."

I let out a massive sigh of relief and wrap my arms around him before I have time to think whether it's okay to hug a priest. I'm overwhelmed with gratitude. I start to cry.

"It's okay," he says to me softly. "It's going to be okay."

I cry for a few minutes. They're not tears of relief or happiness, as far as I can tell. They're the unloading of all the pain and fear and uncertainty I've been going through. A cleansing, if you will. The priest waits, comforting me until I have no more tears left to spill.

"Feel better?" he asks.

I nod. Smile. Wipe my eyes and my nose. "Hit me."

He's surprised. "Hit you?"

"Figure of speech," I say. "Hit me with the blessing. Please."

"Oh."

He clears his throat and stands. After a look from him of expectation, I stand as well. I don't know whether to close my eyes or bow my head, so I do both. I have my hands behind my back, sweaty palms pressed together. This is supposed to be a good thing, yet I'm anxious. Maybe even scared.

The priest begins to speak. I don't recognize the words and presume it's Latin. They speak Latin, don't they?

"*Dominus vobiscum*," he begins.

I can feel the motion of his hand near me, just the faintest change in air pressure. I can't see with my eyes closed, and I'm fighting the instinct to open them and watch. I'm curious and nervous to see what he's doing, but I'm terrified that if I do open my eyes, then the blessing won't work as it should—my face creases as I pinch my eyelids together as tight as I can.

The priest's voice is strong with purpose, yet gentle.

"*Pater Noster, qui es in caelis, sanctificetur nomen tuum. Adveniat regnum tuum. Fiat voluntas tua, sicut in caelo et in terra. Panem nostrum quotidianum da nobis hodie, et dimitte nobis debita nostra sicut et nos dimittimus debitoribus nostris. Et ne nos inducas in tentationem, sed libera nos a malo.*"

Silence. I almost open my eyes when he continues.

"*In nomine Patris, et Filii, et Spiritus Sancti. Amen.*"

I recognize the last word. Everyone knows that's what you say at the end of a prayer. Though Steve and Jenny were religious, I didn't pay too much attention to the specifics of worship.

The prayer's over. Still, I'm reluctant to open my eyes in case there's more to come. Some next part. But he's finished. I feel no different and wonder if I am supposed to.

"There," he says when I finally look up to see him again. "All done."

"That's it? That's everything?"

He smiles. "I said two prayers, just in case."

"Thank you," I say. "Thank you so much."

"It's quite all right."

"Can I buy you a beer or something?"

"That's not necessary," he assures me. "But I appreciate the kindness of your offer."

I thank him some more and hug him again. He isn't entirely comfortable with all the physical contact, although he doesn't object.

"You might just have saved my life," I tell him before I leave.

SEVENTEEN

The skies appear a little bluer when I step outside. The sun seems warmer. Colors more saturated. The breeze is crisper. I don't feel cured, if that's even a feeling, and yet I feel relief. I breathe easier. I'm less tense. My movements are smoother. It's nice to stroll along the pavement without the unbearable pressure of impending doom. There could even be a spring in my step.

Blissful ignorance, of course. But I don't know it now. This Amy gets to enjoy her little moment. She's celebrating a hard-won battle. Don't spoil it and inform her it's nowhere near over yet. Let her have this.

She needs it.

But if only I could rush back and tell her the truth. Because she's going to waste so much time thinking it's over. How many days do I lose? How much could I have learned in that time? Should I tell you about my indulgences during that wasted period? Do you need to know about the drugs and the drinks and the dicks? I'm going to make a call and omit those sordid details.

If this were a film, this scene of me walking along the pavement in the sunshine would slowly fade to black and back again to show us that some time passes before the next scene. Maybe they'll make a movie about me one day. Based on a true story, it'll say at the beginning. I hope we're both still around by then. And I hope they don't get some impossibly pretty starlet to play me. It won't be believable.

I hope whoever plays me can cry well, even though I hate that I cry so much. I've never learned how to bottle things up like other people. But I guess sooner or later we all run out of tears, don't we? That devastating sadness or pain or heartache cannot endure forever. The crying has to stop or else we would die of dehydration, wouldn't we? Do you think that's ever happened? Do you think someone has cried themselves to death?

Thankfully, as I write this, I've learned how to be stoic at last. And there are the practical considerations too. It was late in the day when I decided to write this journal. Time is short where I am now. And paper is precious. Tears and mucus dripping all over the pages would be the worst.

Can you imagine if the very thing you needed to know to survive was smudged by an unfortunately placed snot bomb? Yeah, I'd be pissed off as well.

But I still don't have the answer. Not yet.

I'm trying, I promise.

There is a way to beat this. I know there is. If I didn't, I wouldn't bother writing at all. I've never written so much in my life. I'm working at a frantic pace. My hand hurts. My shoulder aches. My back is killing me. I'm getting this down as fast as I can before I'm out of time while I'm trying to remember everything that happened.

I told you about Llewellyn and his magical quiff, didn't I?

I receive a letter because I don't show up to our next session on account of a two-day-long hangover after the celebration that came after the blessing. The letter implores me to see him as soon as I can or else he will be forced to notify the authorities. He's threatening to put me away again.

There's a certain appeal to it, I can admit. Maybe a padded cell might actually be the safest place, and yet I know it would just be a delaying tactic. Treating the symptom, not the cause. Anyway, I ignore that letter, planning to go to the next session as scheduled, only it turns out I'm going to miss that too when I realize the rule has not been broken.

What happens before that? Oh yes . . . I remember now. This is big. This is where we take it up a notch. I haven't told you about Lizzy's betrayal either, have I? We're getting to that too.

I may still be doomed, yet I'm a fighter. Just because the blessing didn't work doesn't mean I'm giving up. And best of all, I think writing this journal, this survival guide, is starting to pay off. Writing everything down gives me the chance to relive each day, to press rewind and play it through all over again. The disparate, blurry pieces of my experiences are focusing into clarity and coherence.

I have you to thank for that.

What did I do? I can hear you think. Well, you're my purpose. You're the reason I'm writing this in the first place, so you're the reason it's all beginning to make sense. Feel free to give yourself a pat on the back.

As I'm walking away from the church with that spring in my step, I feel like I've already won. It's perhaps the first feeling of victory I've ever experienced. It's like a warmth inside me. A comforting glow of contentment and safety and calm. I realize that this is what other people take for granted. This is what they get to feel on a daily basis. This is joy. I know it's joy because it's been years since I've felt this way. This is the best feeling I can remember.

I'm so happy I could die.

ILA

EIGHTEEN

"Did you hear about that girl who died?"

Alexander doesn't look up from the delicate task of rolling a joint because he takes a bizarre amount of pride in ensuring they are pencil-thin and without even a single wrinkle in the paper. I don't smoke weed, so I don't care whether he's fast or slow, but Nate is restless.

"Seriously, even Ila could roll faster."

"Perfection cannot be rushed," Alexander retorts, floppy hair flopped forward and covering half his face. He's hunched over, sat cross-legged on the beanbag in a way that makes him look half yogi, half toad. Knowing Alex, I'm sure he would take that as a compliment.

"So, did you?"

"People die all the time," I say, peering over my book to humor him. "Can't possibly hear about them all."

"Do you mean here?" Nate asks. "At this college?"

Alexander licks the paper with the tip of his tongue. He looks even more toadlike. "Uh-huh."

"No one has said anything to me," I reply. "Is it someone I knew?"

The strip of glue wetted, he proceeds to carefully make the final roll. He's so careful and precise in the way he manipulates his fingers, he might as well be moving in slow motion. "Before our time."

Nate groans. "Then how could we possibly have heard about her?"

Joint complete, Alexander holds it up between thumb and fore-finger for us to admire. I couldn't possibly care any less. Nate, how-ever, reaches for it, only for Alex to snap it away from his desperate grasp.

"Roller takes the first drag."

"Because you stack the end," Nate tells him.

Joint between lips, Alexander sparks his lighter and brings the flame closer. "Don't blame me because you can't handle your weed. If I spread it out equally, you'd only go and throw a whitey again."

"That was one time and I . . . Whatever. Anyway," he says to hide his embarrassment, "what about this girl who died is supposed to be so special?"

Alexander takes a long drag and the embers glow at the end of the joint. He holds the smoke deep in his lungs for several seconds, then purses his lips to blow it back out in a thin, pale gray cloud. It twists and swirls through the air almost like a liquid defying gravity.

"Don't forget the rule of three; it's coming for you, like it came for me."

I wait for more. When it doesn't come, I ask, "What is that sup-posed to mean?"

"It's the curse," he explains. "If you catch it, you'll die."

Nate, impatient, snatches the joint off Alexander. "That's dumb. You don't catch a curse. Someone puts it on you. Curse 101."

Alexander shrugs. "So, someone cursed her and then she died."

"Why?" I ask.

"How am I supposed to know that?"

"Because you brought it up."

"Doesn't make me an expert, does it?"

Finally enjoying his own drag, Nate relaxes. His shoulders lose their tension, and he settles back onto the couch. "Come on, just tell us the rest of the story already."

"Whatever the story is," I say, turning a page, "it never happened."

"Bad things always happen in threes," Alex continues. "Every-one knows that, right? That's the curse. That's the rule of three. If you catch it you die, and then it moves on to someone else."

"And a girl here caught it?" I ask, slowly becoming more curious as he parcels out the details.

"You don't catch a curse," Nate says again, voice already a little lower and hoarser.

"You catch this one," Alex says back. "Someone started it, but the curse didn't die when the cursed person died. It kept going. It took on a life of its own. And it'll keep going, and going, and going."

I say, "Then it sounds more like a ghost to me, like a restless evil spirit. Why's it called the rule of three anyway?"

"Because three bad things happen to you and then you die."

Nate says, "Then it should be the rule of four."

"You die because the three bad things happened to you," Alex insists, pushing back his hair in a show of agitation. "Dying isn't one of them because you're dead. You're dead because of the three bad things first, okay? If it was the rule of four, then you would die after four bad things happened."

"Whoa, whoa, just chill. I really don't give a shit."

"You will if three bad things happen to you. That's when you'll know you're going to die."

"Does this curse have a schedule?" I ask sarcastically. "Is it three bad things in one day or spread out? And how are we defining *bad* exactly? Like, does it have a universally recognized scale, or is it a matter of perspective? Because I woke up with a pimple this morning and I stubbed my toe earlier, so does that mean if I get smoke in my eye now then I'm going to die tonight?"

Nate laughs and Alex gives me the finger.

Against my better judgment I find myself asking him, "So, what three bad things actually happened to the girl who came here?"

"The worst kind. Her parents died and her sister," he answers. "One, two, three."

I take a breath to calm myself.

Nate's face drops.

Alexander hasn't noticed our reactions; his red eyes are staring at me with the intensity only a hard-core stoner can manage. "Imagine that."

"Actually, I don't have to," I tell him as calmly as I can. "I've lost three family members too. My brother and both my parents."

"Oh shit," he says, mortified despite being high. "I'm sorry, I'm sorry."

"*Dickhead*," Nate hisses at him.

I try to reassure Alex. "You weren't to know. It's not exactly something I bring up at parties." Nate shuffles closer and goes to put a comforting arm around me. "It's okay, honestly," I say, shrugging him away. "It hurts every day whether someone draws attention to it or not. No stupid rhyme can make the reality any worse."

"Even so," Alex says. "I really am sorry."

I force a smile in an effort to put him at ease, but also to deflect from the crushing sadness inside me. "I'm the one who should say sorry."

"What?"

"Because I've disproved your story. I've lost three family members, and the rule of three hasn't come for me."

He thinks for a moment, then nods and smiles too. "Yeah," he says.

Maybe it's because he's high or maybe because he's so remorseful, but when he says "yeah" it almost sounds like he's saying an entirely different word.

Yet.

NINETEEN

I visit their graves as often as I can, and I still feel guilty I don't go enough. I used to take flowers every time I went. Money's tight, though. My scholarship covers the tuition and I work for every other cent. Flowers, even those for my dear deceased family, are a luxury I can't afford.

It's temporary, I tell the three headstones. When I graduate, when I can work full-time, I'll bring them again. Be patient with me, please.

I think they understand. I know I would. Some days, however, I fear they don't. I worry they think less of me, or worse: that I think less of them.

If you cared enough, you'd find a way to afford the flowers.

I'm having one of those days today. I didn't sleep well. Alexander's words seemed to rattle around inside my unconscious, which makes no sense to me. It's not like he upset me—not really, at least—and I didn't take what he said even remotely seriously. I'm sure it's creepy when you're stoned, but to me it's just one of those stupid urban legends you hear about all the time. In fact, I might have heard it once before and then summarily dismissed it, never thinking about it twice, let alone three times.

Now, looking at the headstones of my mother, father, and little brother, I can picture Alex as he rolled his precious joint, and I can hear those words:

Did you hear about that girl who died?

My parents died in an accident. A carbon monoxide leak in the winter. They just drifted off in their sleep and never woke up again. Hunter was away at camp and I was staying over at a friend's house, otherwise we might have never woken either. I was already eighteen, so after a lot of forms and interviews I became his legal guardian. All thoughts of college had to wait because I needed to pay the bills and make sure he did his homework and take him to his therapy sessions. I'm not sure I really had time to grieve my parents when I found myself suddenly having to be one for Hunter. Perhaps that's why I visit them so much now, to make it up to them.

Don't forget the rule of three . . .

It annoys me I can't quite forget that stupid rhyme. I feel guilty being in the cemetery and my thoughts drifting elsewhere. I've never especially liked urban legends and ghost stories. I don't believe in curses, or fate, or anything else like that. But I believe in God. I think I do, I mean, because I believe in heaven. The only thing that keeps me together is knowing I'll see them all again one day. I think about that a lot. I wonder if Hunter will still be fourteen or if he'll be grown up when I join them? Regardless, I hope in heaven he showers more regularly than he did on earth. *Poo-ee*, that boy stank up the whole house.

I miss that stink so much.

Poor kid had a heart attack. Incredibly rare to have one so young, but it happens. So many of us walk around with undiagnosed conditions and get away with it. Hunter wasn't so lucky.

Why does the sky have to be so blue when I come here?

Why can't it be raining?

I'm distracted by movement. I see what looks like an entire family walking in single file between the rows of headstones. Each person carries a bouquet of flowers, bright and blooming in the sunshine. The family doesn't so much look mournful as happy, as if they're here to celebrate the life of their loved one, to remember the good times that came before all the pain. I wish I could do the same. Maybe one day I'll find a way to do so too.

Yes, I was crushed to lose my family, but it's reassuring to know they're in a better place and I'll be reunited with them at the end. My parents never tried to hide death from us. We learned when we were very young that death is a natural part of life. A sad, tragic part, granted, and yet not something that should define our lives, either through grief or fear of it. I'm so glad they did this. I know people can be consumed by grief for lost loved ones, and I know it's equally possible to waste our precious days worrying about how many we have left.

I try to tell myself I've mourned my parents and my brother and moved on with my life because it frustrates me when other people expect me to be broken. I don't want to be treated any differently than anyone else. I don't like to advertise what I've been through. Losing my parents and my brother comes up rarely, because when it does, the reaction always falls along the lines of *You poor thing . . . It must be awful . . . You must have been devastated*, yadda yadda yadda. After I assure the person that I'm okay, that I've dealt with my grief and moved on, they can't understand it. They have to challenge it. *But don't you just feel like . . . Don't bury it down . . . You don't have to pretend to be okay if you're not . . . It's unhealthy.*

Who is anyone to tell me how I should behave? I'm sure some people won't be able to understand this because we're all so utterly sure that how we think and feel is how everyone should as well. The arrogance of the human ego is boundless like that. If I've learned anything through these experiences, it's that empathy isn't all it's cracked up to be. Empathy is merely imagining ourselves in someone else's shoes. Getting someone to accept that how they would feel or react in a situation is not how everyone *should* react is almost impossible.

I tell myself I'm strong, that I can get through this one day at a time, because I know deep down I'm nowhere near strong enough. If I keep repeating it, however, eventually I'll believe my own lie.

Manifest destiny and all that.

I leave. Each footstep is hard, fighting the current of guilt that tries to sweep me back. *I'll come back soon*, I tell my family.

I take a meandering walk, heading home without any purpose.

Streets seem to blend into each other and the town becomes a blur. Noises are muted, the soundtrack to my life dialed down to white noise until:

"Did you see that?" I hear a girl say.

"See what?" another girl asks.

Two freshmen with colorful hair and black clothes. One has a face full of piercings. The other has half her head shaved down to stubble. I'm walking through the park and they're sitting on the grass, in the shade of a large oak. One is taking tobacco from a pouch and sprinkling it into a rolling paper balanced on her thigh. I don't know if she's going to add some hash or weed into it. Maybe both. They look the sorts. The second girl is texting on her flip phone.

"That dipshit just walked over those three drains," the first answers.

"So?"

"He shouldn't have done that. That's such bad luck."

They're referring to a young man on the path ahead of me and the row of three drain covers he's just walked over. From behind, he looks a bit like Nate.

The first girl is shaking her head. She's the one with all the piercings. "He should be more careful, or he'll end up like that girl."

The one with the semi-shaved head looks at the first with a questioning expression.

Piercings asks, "You don't know the rule of three?"

Semi-shaved shakes her semi-shaved head.

I slow down on the path so I don't walk away before they've finished their conversation. I realize that even doing this, I'm going to be too far away to hear within a few seconds, so I stop and unhook the bag from my shoulder. I root around in it as though I'm looking for something—a pen or a note or whatever.

"*Oh shit*," comes a high-pitched response. "It's so fucked-up, yo. The rule of three causes the girl's sister to die in an accident, and then it makes her parents hang themselves three years later, and then this girl dies three years after them. She knows it's coming for her too but she can't do anything about it, and she just drops the fuck dead."

"No way."

The grass is short and bright, dappled with spots of sunshine coming through the clouds and freckled with yellowing leaves. The girls have bags on the ground nearby. One has put down her jacket as a blanket they both sit upon.

"Because she walked over three drains?"

Semi-shaved has terrible acne. She's covered it with a thick layer of makeup, but the sun's harsh downlighting is creating noticeable shadows beneath the pustules and in the recessed scars. Rips in her faded black jeans reveal bony white knees almost glowing in the sunshine.

"It's just fate. Bad things happen in threes."

"They really do?"

Piercings is nodding with vigor. *"Don't forget the rule of three; it's coming for you, like it came for me."*

"That's not the story," I say.

The two young girls look my way, noticing me for the first time. Piercings's hair is long and dank, shielding her face as she rolls the cigarette. She peers at me through the purple strands. Her lips are black, and her lip ring catches the sunshine and reflects it as a bright white glare.

"It's a curse," I tell them. "The girl caught it because she lost three family members. It didn't kill her parents and her sister, just her."

Semi-shaved says, "So, her sister is still alive?"

Piercings shakes her head. "That's not how I heard it."

Both wear long necklaces over their tops. Semi-shaved has a silvery pentagram. Piercings has a crystal that dazzles in all the colors of the rainbow. Each has eyeliner so thick it looks as if they did it with a black marker pen.

I say, "Then you heard it wrong. Whoever told you the story didn't tell you it the right way."

They exchange looks with one another.

Piercings asks, "Like, why the fuck do you even care so much?"

"I literally don't care."

Semi-shaved says, "Then fuck off back to the eighties, perm job."

Piercings laughs and raises a palm to high-five her friend. "*Fucking perm job.*"

"My hair is naturally curly."

I shake my head and walk away from this juvenile nonsense. Though only a few years older, I feel like I'm from an entirely different generation.

They're laughing behind me.

"Ask the stylist for a refund," one shouts.

I pretend I don't hear it.

On the way home, a dog barks at me. It's a large, unkempt animal of a mixed breed. I don't give it a second glance at first. I'm walking on the other side of the street. A man in a yellow anorak is walking the dog. When we are parallel with one another, the dog begins barking. I startle a little from the sudden, loud noise. I don't know for a few moments that it's directed at me. The owner is a heavyset man, and yet he struggles to control the dog, who fights so hard against its leash that it rises up to its hind legs. The barks come at me in a relentless, machine-gun manner. Across the street, I can feel the dog's rage rippling through the air. The owner is shouting at it, and I can't hear a single word he's saying because the barking is so loud.

It makes me uncomfortable to be the cause of the dog's anxiety and scared at what it might do to me if the owner loses his grip.

I hurry onward, not brave enough to look back. I keep my gaze forward and walk at increasing speed, almost going into a run to get away.

The barks follow me all the way to the end of the street, quieter now but no less threatening. Then they stop, and I realize I'm panting from the sudden exertion and stress of it.

And in that stressed state, I fear the dog has slipped free from the owner's grasp and the reason it's ceased barking is because it's barreling along the pavement after me.

I spin around, expecting to see teeth bared and jaws salivating.

Instead, I see the owner in the distance, on his knees because the dog is on its side, lying still on the pavement.

Even far away, I can see the distress on the owner's face, and I feel the compulsion to rush to his aid. Still, my fear of the dog's sudden rage toward me is so recent and so acute I turn back and keep walking, ashamed of myself and harrowed by the owner's anguished expression.

I remember this time with great clarity. We're perceptive beings, and we're in a constant state of taking in information from our many senses and processing that information to drive our decisions and actions. It's all done for us, deep within our minds, every second, every hour. We take it for granted that we can see and hear and smell and listen and feel, yet all that has to be processed by a brain that is inherently biased toward our own well-being. I'm feeling a disruption in that processing. This splinter is beginning to work its way deeper into my subconscious, affecting my daily routine, my thoughts, my everything.

That night, I dream of the dog. Only in my dreams, it's mine, and it's me on my knees, inconsolable. But it's still me walking away, so that in my dream the person I'm walking away from is myself.

TWENTY

Our little apartment is nothing special. It's a simple one-bed on the first floor of a purpose-built building. The neighbors can be noisy, and there's a weird smell that won't seem to go away. Still, it feels like home after the year we've spent here, and it's walking distance from campus. A long walk, but I enjoy it most days.

Because I didn't sleep so well, I have to take some deep breaths to steady my nerves and my hands. I don't want to hit a vein, or worse, a nerve.

I notice Nate's reflection in the mirror above the washbasin. He's standing in the doorway, watching me. He gets closer each time he sees me do this, yet he still looks scared. Not a strapping young man but a frightened little boy. Fingers fidgeting. Chewing on his bottom lip.

Grimacing as the needle goes in.

It's reassuring to know that despite his penchant for weed—and the coke he thinks I don't know he takes—he's never going to move on to heroin.

His unease distracts me from my own. I look him dead in the eye as I depress the plunger and can't help but laugh as he has to turn away in a hurry.

"Is it over yet?" he asks.

"All done."

When he turns back around, his face pinches up in horror because I've left the needle in my thigh and taken my hands away, so the syringe is just kind of standing there, like a dart in a board.

He goes into a whole-body shudder. "*Ila.*"

I laugh from my very soul and gesture at the syringe, which is swaying back and forth from my laughter. "Do you want to tug it free for me?"

"Only if you want me to pass out. Please. I'm literally feeling faint here."

"Okay, okay."

I withdraw the needle and apply pressure with a cotton ball soaked with antiseptic ointment.

I don't remember a time when I didn't inject myself with insulin every day. My parents must have done it for me when I was too young to do it myself, and they must have taught me to self-inject when I was still small. I never had the opportunity to feel scared or confused or mad about my condition. By the time I understood just how damaging diabetes could be, I'd learned to live with it. Injecting insulin is no big deal. To me, it's like brushing my teeth. Something you do twice a day. We may not like it, but we know we need to do it. I'm supposed to check my blood glucose levels at least four times a day. In reality, this is two or three times at most. After years of this, I understand the effects of eating and exercise, so it's not necessary to do so before every meal, a couple of hours after every meal, and before bed. My numbers are pretty stable.

Discipline. It all comes down to that.

My parents made it a habit long ago, and I've never spent a whole lot of time thinking about my health. I don't worry about the long-term consequences, because I do everything I can to keep my blood glucose in check. Can I control it 100 percent? No. No one can. I can do my best. The only time I risk straying into hyper- or hypo-glycemia is when my period comes along, and nothing makes sense with my body for a week.

I pack away my things into my medical bag. It's the one I've always had. Some synthetic material with a zip and decorated with the kind of garish colors only a child can like. It's comforting to know I've always had it. Reassuring to glance up and see it in its place when I feel lightheaded or unsteady or have a sudden onset of tiredness. Nine times out of ten that's just standing up too fast or after a restless night's sleep or something otherwise benign. Only occasionally is it a fall in blood sugar that catches me by surprise, and seeing the bright bag always nearby keeps me calm.

Nate's over the injection within a few minutes and feeling horny, but I'm not in the mood, so I just jerk him off and make a snack while he cleans up.

As I slice tomatoes for our sandwiches, he rubs my shoulders. "Are you okay?"

"Yeah, why?"

"Nothing, I don't know . . . You just seem like you're miles away."

"I'm okay," I assure him. "Just . . . distracted. Too many thoughts competing for space."

Although it's midday, he hasn't been up long because of last night's shift at the bar. He leaves me alone to go play video games, and I think about what I said. It's not a lie because I do have a lot on my mind. It's that he assumes I mean studying, and I don't say anything to dissuade him from that conclusion. Is that a lie? I don't think so. It feels like deceit, nonetheless.

I finish the sandwiches. I have extra margarine on mine to slow down the rate of digestion for the carb-heavy bread. This is an automatic action. I smear a thin layer for Nate's and a thick layer for me. For some reason, I'm more aware of it this time as I lay the tomato slices on top of the sliced ham. I'm paying more attention to what I do and how I do it. Not just making sandwiches or injecting insulin. Everything. I'm more aware of the world around me and my place within it. I'm uneasy, and I don't know why. I'm overthinking everything.

There's a splinter in my brain that's irritating me more and more, little by little.

I take the sandwiches into the lounge and hand a plate to Nate. We eat our food, side by side on the sofa, in silence.

The ham is rubbery. The tomatoes too soft.

I don't finish my sandwich, so Nate does instead. Alone, I notice there's an irritation just behind the hairline above my forehead. I scratch at it, which only seems to make it worse.

I have studying to do, though I'm unfocused even when I have my books out before me. Am I still tired? Nate spends nearly all his free time playing video games. We both have jobs: Nate works at a local bar over the weekend and the occasional weeknight, whereas I error-check assignments for other students. For a few bucks, I'll correct spelling mistakes and fix grammar. Depending on the assignment, I'll sometimes make suggestions. At the start of a semester, I'm not that busy, and by the end, I'm swamped. Thank goodness for lazy rich kids, right?

"Save me, Ila," they say.

It's not a busy period for me right now, so after a few hours of inefficient study in the afternoon, I take a break. Nate isn't like me. Maybe it's because I'm a little older I see things differently, although it seems like he came to university with the express purpose of having a good time. He couldn't wait to get as far away from his family as possible. He smokes weed almost every day and does coke most weekends. I don't get how he or his friends have the money for it. Maybe it's because his brother deals drugs and Nate gets a discount. I don't ask because I don't really want to know. I try not to judge him, and I'm not always successful in that. I don't like it when he's coked up. All crazy eyes and sweat. I thought it was supposed to be a drug that made you cool. The reality doesn't quite match the image.

It's hard to be cool when you can't get hard, Nate.

He's lying across the full length of the couch, bare feet up in the air. He's in his boxers and a T-shirt, hair greasy and unruly. He won't shower all day if I don't remind him.

A cereal bowl balances on his sternum. A little milk ripples in the bowl when his chest expands to breathe. I'm pretty sure the bowl has been there since I last came over from the kitchen table, which doubles as my desk.

His head is up on the armrest, rotated to one side so he can watch the TV screen while his fingers work the console controller on his chest.

He only ever seems to play one game, which is some shooty thing that makes him angry more often than not between occasional moments of triumph, which come only after extended times of intense, stressful concentration.

I have no idea why he plays it. If I ask, he'll claim to enjoy it.

"Do you believe in fate?"

He glances at me before his gaze returns to the screen. "Sure, if you're talking about determinism."

I ask, "Do you think everything is decided for us? That we can't change our destiny?"

"I wouldn't phrase it as 'decided for,' which sounds too much like purpose to me. Like a design. That's not what I think. I believe in the certainty of randomness." He pauses. "*Fuck.*"

He's died in the game.

"What do you mean by 'the certainty of randomness'?"

He's hammering a button with a finger to respawn back into the game as fast as possible. "What's your favorite flavor of ice cream?"

"Why?"

"It's something my dad would ask people," he says. "It'll help explain what I'm talking about. Don't sweat. There's no right or wrong answer. Don't think I'm going to judge you for what you say. Just tell me which flavor you prefer."

No contest.

"Chocolate."

"A popular answer. Can you tell me why you like chocolate ice cream the best?"

"I don't know. It tastes good. Especially with the little chunks of deliciousness."

The game comes to an end, and he strains his neck to see the scoreboard that appears. I see his name highlighted near the top of the table.

He's pleased. "So what about those who prefer strawberry to chocolate?"

"They're wrong."

"Really? Could it be that their taste buds respond differently than yours or that their brain interprets the message sent by those taste buds in a different way than yours?"

"Yeah, sure. Of course. I wasn't saying I literally think they're wrong. We're all different, right?"

"Do we decide that difference?"

I pause. Think about it.

He says, "I would suggest that you didn't decide that you prefer the flavor of chocolate ice cream the best. It's that you respond best to the flavor of chocolate ice cream. Does that make sense?"

"That makes sense, but I don't understand why it matters."

"If we don't decide what we respond to best, or worst, or in between, how much control over ourselves do we really have?"

"That's a big leap from ice cream."

"Is it? Can we not apply that to every sensation we experience? I'm going beyond food flavors now. Do we decide if we don't like heights or that we love roller coasters? Do we decide if we find that person attractive or are turned off by them? Do we decide to be angry or sad? If we could decide, then we'd never be angry or sad, would we? We'd decide to be happy all the time, wouldn't we? So, if we can't decide our emotions, can we decide how we respond to them? If we don't decide everything else, it seems a stretch that we can decide that, doesn't it?"

"We have free will. We can decide how we respond. We do, all the time."

"Do we? If you get very, very angry, can you keep control of your voice and of what you say? Have you ever said something you didn't mean to say? It just comes out, doesn't it? You don't have time to stop it."

"Even if I agree to all this, and I don't, what does it have to do with fate?"

"Because if we accept we don't actually make decisions, that we only respond to stimuli, which we do in a predetermined way—our genetics, life experience, and so on—then it's comparable to say that

everything can be predicted. Hence determinism, or as you put it:
fate."

I huff. "That's the dumbest thing I've ever heard."

"You asked me about fate, and I'm telling you what I think."

"*Ah*," I exclaim, smug. "It's what you think. It's what you've
decided to think."

"Do you believe I chose to think like this? To recognize I am
a random accident of nature and nothing I will ever do is really a
choice I make?"

"Yeah," I snap. "You think it makes you different and interesting
and oh-so-superior to all us losers who believe we're in charge of
ourselves."

"Why are you getting angry with me?"

Am I? I don't mean to be angry. I'm tired. I didn't sleep well and
I can't stop thinking about what happened yesterday. About the dog.
And before that. What those two goth girls said.

Nate asks, "What's going on with you?"

I sit down on the arm of the couch, lifting his feet to one side to
make room. I can't quite look at him.

"It's okay," he says. "You can tell me anything. We're a team,
remember?"

"The best team," I say back.

I stroke one of his feet.

"Has something happened? Did you get a bad grade or . . . ?"

"No, no, no. It's nothing like that. It was these two girls. They . . ."

Why is it so hard to just express myself? I'm always scared of
people judging me. I was a geek, a nerd, a dork, a teacher's pet at
school, and I guess I've never learned how to be confident in myself
without fear that someone will try to tear me down.

Finally, I tell him about the girls: Piercings and Semi-shaved.

"They sound like a couple of freaks," he tells me with a shrug
of indifference. "Who cares what they said? I love your curly hair."

"I know. Thanks. That's not what I meant. That's not what bothered me."

"Then I don't understand. What else did they say?"

"I told you. They were talking about the rule of three."

He waits.

I stroke his shin, pushing back the hairs with the side of my thumb, imagining my hand is a lawn mower and the follicles are overgrown grass. It makes for a pleasant sound in my mind.

"They heard it a different way," I begin. "Alex said the girl caught the curse because she lost three people in her family, but these girls in the park said the rule of three killed all of them."

"So? It's just a made-up story. People change the details as they tell it. I'm sorry, I should have shut him up sooner. I knew the story, so I should have guessed where he was going with it and—"

"It's okay," I interrupt. "It was a completely innocent mistake. I've never brought it up with him, so how could he have known? If he did, he'd have to be an utter psychopath to go down that route."

"Psychopaths can be very charming," Nate says with a big smile. Then, when it doesn't get the reaction he's after, he asks, "Did it upset you to be reminded of what happened?"

"Of course it did," I tell him. "But that's not it." I pause to collect my words. "I guess what I'm trying to say is that it unnerved me that they'd heard the same story. It feels a bit too close to home, you know?"

"It's a story people tell. Others are bound to hear it, aren't they? You heard it from Alex. I heard it from someone else."

"Do you remember who told it to you?"

"Oh God," he breathes. "Could've been anyone, but maybe my big bro. I can check if you like."

"No, no. I don't . . . It's not . . . It's because I heard it from someone else it feels more real."

"Even if it did really happen, and I don't for a second think it did, then so what? Everyone loses family at some point. Everyone dies. Maybe there was some girl who lost her family and then died herself. In fact, it's got to happen all the time, hasn't it? If everyone dies ultimately, then everyone ultimately must lose their family and die, or die before the rest of their family. Given enough people, it's probably happened as it does in the story a thousand, or a million, times already."

"Maybe."

He sits up. "Not maybe. Definitely. Like the lottery. Odds are you'll never, ever win. But someone does win, week in, week out."

"One of the girls yesterday said that the girl in the story died three years after her parents, who died three years after her sister. Alex didn't tell me that part. Is that how you heard it too?"

"I'm not sure. Why is that important? Is that what's got to you?"

"My brother died about three years after my parents," I tell Nate, trying hard to mask the creeping feeling of unease in my tone. "And it's now almost three years since Hunter died."

TWENTY-ONE

I like to think of myself as a model student. I know I'm fortunate to be able to go to college, and that's not something I take lightly. My parents taught me many lessons, and perhaps the most important of those was the value of hard work. We can't ever be satisfied with our successes or learn from our failures unless we put everything we had into them. I'm no genius. I'm no smarter than the next girl. But I doubt there are many out there who will work as hard as me. Every good grade I've had is owed to diligent study.

My parents were both passionate readers, and there were books in every room of our house. They would read after dinner, before dinner, in bed, at the breakfast table. They made sure that both Hunter and I learned to read at an early age. While the other kids were still learning to spell, we were getting to know Tom Sawyer and Huckleberry Finn. It's no surprise then that I'm studying English literature. It feels so little like work I almost feel guilty. I've stopped telling Nate my grades because it makes him feel bad. Maybe go to all your classes then. Maybe don't start your essay the night before it's due.

He almost understands how motivated I am. My parents passed on to me their passion for literature, and that makes me want to do the same. Few people my age take any interest in reading, and that's such a waste. Perhaps I can help change that.

I can imagine myself like Professor Griffiths. Academic and bohemian. Teaching the Romantics and going to poetry readings in bare-brick basement bars. Sitting on the grass in the sunshine and marking papers. Penning critiques for literary journals. Perhaps even writing my own book someday. Professor Griffiths is the most passionate, inspiring teacher I've ever had. She loves the Romantics as much as my parents did, and she speaks about Coleridge with such verve and insight that I hang on her every word.

At least, usually.

I struggle to concentrate. I'm thinking about Hunter. I'm thinking about the rule of three. It has to be a coincidence, it has to be just a story, and yet I can't seem to forget it. I keep scratching at my head as though the rule of three is a splinter of doubt inside my mind and if I scratch at it enough then I can scratch it right out of me.

After class, I head straight to the campus library, a cavernous place with vaulted ceilings and endless alcoves. Typical for a library, it's a quiet place, solemn. This is the place of worship for students who fear the god of grades as much as the devil of deadlines. They pace along the aisles. They stare in reverence at the sea of knowledge they hope to sip from. I can tell just by the way they stand who is studious and who is hoping to cram at the last minute and who is missing a lecture to finish an assignment.

I'm up to date with my own work, so I don't need to be here, wandering up and down the aisles, browsing the books. I don't know what I need to find. Would it be in linguistics, anthropology, etymology . . . ? It being . . . something.

Of course, most of the texts here relate to subjects taught, and I know there is no class on urban legends. Still, I am hopeful I might find something that can help me.

I feel an odd sense of unease, like I shouldn't be here. Like I'm an imposter. Like someone is going to find out I'm not here to study and throw me out.

My neck is beginning to hurt. All that tilting my head to read the spines. I'm stretching the muscles so much I'm almost worried my head won't sit in place once I'm done.

Looking for a book you don't know the title of on a subject you don't even know how to classify in a library of tens of thousands of titles is a special kind of hell.

I must have been here for two hours when four words on the spine of a book seem larger and brighter than any I've come across until now. Maybe because this title is also a question.

How Did It Begin?

It's a slim hardcover. I slide it from the shelf and look at the cover, which is almost all words, the big title itself occupying about half the space, with its subtitle taking up the rest.

A fascinating study of superstitions, customs, and strange habits that influence our daily lives.

I don't even flick through it. I take it straight to one of the many vacant study tables and settle in for the long haul. I'm not the fastest reader in the world—I get headaches—but that is the least of my concerns.

The book has a pristine dust jacket, and the pages are free from tears. There are no cracks in the spine and no real damage to it at all. I'm amazed there is any book in this library that hasn't been savaged by the savages. I open it up, skipping the foreword, noting it's not even been stamped out once, and going straight to the contents. I run my finger over the various chapter titles.

There. Found it. I almost knew I would.

A chapter on exactly what I need, titled "Why Do Bad Things Happen in Threes?"

Pulse quickening a little, I find the chapter and read.

I learn that no one is quite sure why we think bad things happen in threes, but there are several possible explanations. The most accepted of these is that the belief originated during the Boer War— don't ask me who or what the Boers are, or were, because I haven't read a book on them—when British soldiers learned the hard way not to light three cigarettes from the same match. Because if they did, those mean enemy sharpshooters would spot the flickering light when the match was stuck, then start to aim as the second soldier lit up, before taking the shot at the third man. Makes sense, I suppose.

The other explanation is darker, older. Three is the symbol of the Holy Trinity. To make mundane use of it was to defile its sanctity and to transgress divine law. Man would invite disaster and put himself into the power of the "evil one." Therefore, a sacred rule of the Orthodox Church is not to light three candles with the same taper, for a light, trebly used, would light the fires of hell for one's own soul.

Well, I'll remember that the next time Nate is smoking weed, but I'm not sure how relevant it is to my situation. Perhaps it's more metaphorical. Maybe I'm a candle. Perhaps someone else set this jinx in motion by using the same match.

I like to think I'm a pretty logical person. I understand how we're likely to see patterns even when they're not there. That's just the way we're wired. So it's no real surprise that we think bad things happen in threes. It's not long until I'm reading about apophenia, which is the phenomenon first recognized by Klaus Conrad in 1958. Conrad was a psychologist and neuroscientist who studied the early symptoms of schizophrenia. Apophenia is when we look for patterns as a way to organize chaos. We want to make sense of the world around us even when it makes no sense. We have an overwhelming need to order disorder. Recognizing patterns has helped the human race survive and thrive. Take mathematics. We could say that an equation is nothing more than accurately depicting an outcome by the identification of a pattern. Humans are amazing at recognizing patterns because we're always looking for them.

The downside is we can't help but see patterns when there aren't any. Confirmation bias means we can't help but identify patterns that lead us to what we already know or believe to be true. We ignore, dismiss, or simply refuse to acknowledge information that doesn't reaffirm our preexisting bias.

That's the official line. Bad things don't come in threes, they say. It's just apophenia.

Why is the number three significant in our culture? Yes, some people might say it originates with the Father, the Son, and the Holy Ghost. But maybe it's because if I give you a sandwich that I made, the chances are it's not the sandwich you want to eat, and if I give you a choice of two there's still a good chance that even with the option of something else you might not be satisfied. But if you have the choice of three sandwiches, even if there isn't something perfect for your tastes, you'll be satisfied you had a real option. Three is the first number that matters. One is singular, two is a pair, but three is something else entirely. There is one of you, but you have two eyes, two ears, two hands, and so on. You don't have three of anything. Three is when life gets interesting.

Do we say bad things happen in threes because we're all so used to life getting us down we don't pay attention when it's only one or two bad things? Does it take three to get our attention? How depressing if true.

The first prime odd number? Three, of course.

Three is inexplicably linked to the human condition. We are born, we live, and we die. We are children, we are adults, and then we cease to be. It's why stories have three acts. And before you come at me and tell me that Shakespeare wrote in five acts or whatever, tell me a joke. You start the joke, you set up the punchline, then you say the punchline. A complete story in three acts. Beginning, middle, end. Three is everywhere. We can't escape that because we can't help but notice it. And that's without the fact that so many jokes begin with three characters: A priest, a rabbi, and a minister . . . We have the philosophical triad of thesis, antithesis, and synthesis.

It goes on and on and on.

But understanding where something comes from is not the same as believing in it.

I don't know what to believe.

I realize I'm scratching at that irritation on my scalp more and more. Maybe I'm developing a nervous tic, or maybe it's the little splinter of paranoia embedding itself deeper and deeper.

I thought reading up on this stuff would make me feel better. Instead, it's left me feeling a little queasy. I need a break, I realize. Some fresh air and sunshine to set my head straight.

I go sit on the grass in the quad to make the most of the sunshine. I lay out my books before me so I don't look crazy. I don't read any of them. I sit. It's not as dull as you might think.

There's plenty to do when you're people watching. I feel like a narrator in a nature documentary with the two species of students and university staff under observation. It's fascinating to see them in their natural habitats. The campus is its own biosphere bursting with life. The new day brings forth new opportunities for two distinct yet similar species. Both receive nourishment from the campus biosphere as both predator and prey.

I see Professor Griffiths. She's walking fast because it's only a couple of minutes until the hour, so I guess she's running late. I wonder if the very tall, older professor who is walking a good way behind her has anything to do with it. They both appear to have come from the same direction. He's looking a bit tired, yawning between sips of his takeout coffee. Did she cause his tiredness, and is he the reason why she's late?

I don't know his name or even what he teaches. His long limbs make him look gangly and awkward, as though he might trip over himself at any moment.

I must watch hundreds of students walk by. There's something entrancing about crowds: so many individual faces making up an anonymous whole.

My gaze is drawn to one of those faces. At first I don't know why, and then I notice little glints of light on piercings. She's wearing different clothes and has changed her hair color again. It's now a shocking pink tone.

I'm not sure what makes me stand, but I do.

Piercings is on the far side of the grass and heading toward the main building, so I have to be quick.

"Hey," I call out when I'm near enough to be heard, although I don't yet know why I'm calling out to her at all.

She doesn't hear me, else assumes the call is for someone else. I walk fast to get a little ahead of her so she can't be mistaken when I say "hey" again.

Her lip ring now has a little ring of its own, with a metal spike dangling from it. I know she recognizes me because she shoots me an annoyed glare and keeps walking.

I take hold of her closest arm to stop her walking away, to let her know I need to speak to her. She spins my way in response, fast and aggressive.

"Fuck is with you?"

I'm a passive and unconfrontational person, and I let go of her arm and instinctively retreat. All the careful words I'd composed in advance disappear from my mind. I struggle to speak.

"Do you . . . like cake?"

"Of course I like cake," Piercings says. "Who doesn't?"

"I'll buy you a slice," I tell her. "I'd really like to talk to you."

"I've got class."

"Afterward, then. I'll wait right here. It won't take long."

She reads my eagerness and says, "I'll do it for two slices."

"Deal."

TWENTY-TWO

It's no surprise to find out Piercings is not her real name. It's a few minutes into our conversation at the coffee shop before I realize I haven't introduced myself. I mean, I call it a conversation. It's more of the two of us sitting in silence. Her eating cake or slurping milkshake and me staring into my coffee cup for help it's refusing to give me.

I'm thinking far too much, I know. I'm paralyzing myself with indecision.

Piercings soon understands she's going to have to make the first move or we might end up sitting here forever.

"I'm Mack," she tells me.

"I'm Ila," I say, so relieved and grateful I thrust my hand across the table in an awkwardly formal way, my arm stretching at full length into space, fingers neatly pressed together.

She looks at it over the rim of her milkshake. Raises her eyebrows into tall arches. Then grips my fingers from the top down to shake my hand.

"Did you say your name was Mack?" I ask her.

"Mackenzie, but I don't like it."

"Okay. Nice to meet you, Mack."

She lets go of my fingers. "Sure. It's a pleasure or whatever."

I've been thinking carefully about what I would say to her since she went into her class, and now my mind is a void. More empty than it was when I tried to talk to her earlier. Is it her or is it me?

She's seemingly patient with me because she has two slices of chocolate cake to devour and the largest chocolate milkshake on the menu to slurp her way through. I wonder what Nate would say about her free will right now.

I have a regular coffee, but I don't want to drink it. Maybe I did when I ordered it, yet it's just a prop now—something to fiddle with and distract us both from how weird and awkward I'm being.

Once the first slice of chocolate cake is nothing but crumbs on the plate, Mack says, "Do you want me to start?"

"You know what I'm going to say?"

"Not at all."

"Then I don't understand."

Mack uses her fork to cut off a little of the next slice. "I'm trying to throw you a bone here."

I manage a shy smile. "I'm a bad catch." She almost smiles back, and this is enough to put me at ease, so I can take a deep breath, pull my chair forward, and say, "How did you hear about the rule of three?"

She swallows some cake away. "I don't know. Why? Is that want you wanted to ask me?"

"Do you think it's true?"

"What? I don't know. Maybe. Who knows?"

I toy with the spoon in my coffee cup.

Mack asks, "Why do you care?"

Should I tell her? It's an impossible choice. Chances are she's going to think I'm crazy, right? No one in their right mind is going to take me seriously the second after I admit what I think. If my own boyfriend doesn't believe me, then why should Mack, a stranger?

I feel the scrutiny of her gaze as I do everything I can to avoid looking her in the eye. I'm trying to summon the courage to look like a fool. All those insecurities about what people might think of me are coming back in wave after wave of self-doubt. I'm a child again, embarrassed about my curly hair when all my friends have perfectly straight locks. I'm a teenager again, ashamed of my good grades because others in my class call me a nerd.

Mack says, "Oh my God, it's happening to you too."

Not a question.

"I . . . I don't know," is all I can manage for a moment.

"*Fuck*," she whispers, drawing out the word into one long, quiet exclamation.

"I don't believe in the rule of three," I'm quick to state. Maybe too quick. "It's just that there are similarities between the girl in the story and me, and it's creeping me out."

"You lost your parents too? And your sister?"

"Brother," I tell her. "But after my parents, not before like the girl in the story."

She listens to this without disbelief or challenge.

"I didn't hear it the way you told it to your friend. I didn't know the deaths all happened three years apart."

"When did your brother die?" she asks.

"Almost three years ago."

"That sucks. What are you going to do?"

My mouth opens, but no words come out. I shrug. I shake my head. I think.

"I want to know if the story is true," I tell her eventually.

"How? I told you I didn't know if it's true or not."

"I need to find out about the girl in the story. See if she existed. See if she's real. Was real, I mean."

Mack asks, "What's her name?"

"I was hoping you could tell me that."

"Shit," she says. "Sorry."

I kind of expected this. My old defeatism is bubbling back to the surface, and I assume nothing is going to go my way.

"Are you sure you don't remember who told you the story in the first place?"

She apologizes with her expression.

"No clue at all?" I ask in a way that's almost a beg. "Even if you don't remember who it was, do you remember anything else?"

"Like what?"

"I don't know. I . . . like, maybe it was a friend or someone you didn't know? Or someone in your family?"

"Definitely not my family," she's quick to answer. "They're so fucking annoying I cannot even stand them. Why do you think I came here? I'm no academic, but it was the quickest way to get out of that hellhole." She stops. Hesitates. "Sorry."

"What for?"

"I didn't mean to . . . I mean, I should be grateful to still have a family, right?"

"Oh. I didn't even make the connection. You don't have to worry about me. I'm not going to get upset if you tell me you hate your parents or your brother makes you crazy."

"Sure, okay. I'm still sorry, though. It must suck to lose them."

I nod. "Oh yeah, totally. There's so much I miss about them, but I try to remember all the good things. The way my dad would read me stories when I was a kid or my mom would cut my sandwiches into different shapes each day, or just watching stupid movies with my brother. I try not to think about them dying. It happens to everyone at some point, doesn't it? And I know I'll see them again one day, so why be miserable about it? It won't help me, and it won't bring them back. I don't want them looking down on me crying all the time."

She's stabbing at the slice of cake with her fork, a little awkward and uncomfortable with such an honest, intimate admission. She probably thinks she's an adult at twenty, and here she is unable to respond with anything more meaningful than:

"Good for you."

I spare her more discomfort by bringing the conversation back round to my inevitable death.

"You said that you were sure your family didn't tell you the rule of three," I begin. "What about friends?"

"I guess it must have been a friend."

"From back home?"

She stares off into space over my shoulder for a moment. "No, no. It was more recent than that."

"While you were here?"

She nods. "Yeah. Probably."

"Me, too," I say.

Mack asks, "What does it mean?"

"The guy who told me said the girl went here, so if you heard the story here too then it feels to me like if it's true then it must have happened here."

"You really think the girl went to this college?"

"It would make sense, wouldn't it? We heard it here as an urban legend because it started here as a true story. If it's actually real, I mean."

"But when?"

I think. "A few years ago, maybe. If it was a recent thing, then we'd have heard more details. If it was a really long time ago, then no one would still talk about it."

"Makes sense," she agrees. "Do you have a plan?"

"A what? A plan?"

"Yeah, you know. Do you know how you're going to find out?"

"I guess the university must have records of everyone who came here, yeah?"

"Sure."

"And they would have a record even if they dropped out?"

"It must happen dozens of times every semester."

"True," I say, thinking. "They might record the reason why the student dropped out."

"Assuming they would actually know."

I sigh. "Yeah, you're right. Unless they specifically record student deaths, then it won't matter."

"Because even if you get a list of every student who died, it's not going to tell you if they're the girl from the story."

"But it's a start," I counter, as much to her as to my self-doubt. "If I start with a list of students who died in, say . . . the last ten years, then I have a chance, don't I? I can't possibly look into every female student who came here. That's going to be thousands. Tens of thousands, probably. But those who died? That's got to be a tiny fraction. Not even one percent. I might be looking at one hundred. I could be looking at ten."

"Do you remember at the start of the year? That German student died. Pneumonia, right?"

"That . . . I . . . I think I do."

Mack is nodding, sure of herself. "There was a thing in the student newspaper about it, wasn't there?"

"I don't read it."

"I don't either. Not really. I flick through it sometimes. They have coupons . . . They did a thing. What's it called? You know, when someone dies? They do a thing in newspapers. What is it called?"

"An obituary."

"Yeah. That's it. They had one of those for him."

My eyes widen. "Which means they could have obituaries for other students who died."

"Could do," Mack says, slurping at her milkshake. "Although . . . say they do . . . how's it going to help you? If you find out who the girl in the story was . . . how does that help you?"

Good question. I haven't thought that far ahead.

"I need to know if it started somewhere, if it's based in reality," I tell her. "If I find nothing, then I'll know it *is* just a story."

"And if it's true?"

"It can't be true," I say, as much to myself as to Mack. "It doesn't make any sense. Bad things happen all the time. Sure, there are going to be patterns. That doesn't mean there's a rule, does it? Just because three bad things have happened to me three years apart doesn't mean it's anything more than coincidence."

"Right," she says, sitting back. "So, you don't think it really happened to that girl?"

"No."

"Then I don't get why you want to find out if it's true. Do you see what I mean? You don't believe it's true, but you want to find out if it's true."

"I don't just want to think it, I want to know for sure," I say, realizing I have hairs trapped under my fingernails from all the scratching at my scalp. "I need to prove for certain that it's only a story, or I just know I'm going to drive myself crazy thinking about it."

In a sheepish tone, she adds, "Or die too."

TWENTY-THREE

How do you find a girl who may or may not have existed, whose name you don't know? Yeah, I don't know either. But someone must. I try the admissions office and get nowhere. Under the smallest scrutiny, my cover story about why I want a list of students who died falls apart, and the woman I speak to looks at me like I'm the worst human being alive.

"It's inevitable we'll move to digital," the helpful young man at the university paper tells me. "Now people are moving to smartphones, I mean. They're going to change the world. Print is going to dwindle and die. It just doesn't know it yet."

His name is Zach. He looks like he's too young to be here. Acne. Glasses. Braces. His T-shirt has a comic book character. He's short and skinny—all bony elbows and jutting Adam's apple. Greasy hair is pulled back tight into a short ponytail that looks almost stiff. To my eye, he doesn't look old enough to be at college. I don't imagine he's any kind of savant. I think I'm just at that point when someone younger than me seems too young.

"Doesn't that scare you?"

"Why would it?"

"Because you're writing for a student newspaper."

Zach has one of those chains on his belt that suggests he's a skater or wants to look like one.

He says, "It's something you have to do if you want to be a proper journalist someday."

"You want to break the big stories of the twenty-first century? Be the next Bernstein?"

"Maybe. I mean, I could if I want to."

I feel I have to ask, "What do you want to do instead?"

"I want to write movie reviews."

"Okay . . ."

"Getting paid to watch movies would be the best job ever." He beams as he talks. He's thought about this a lot. "Get invited to all the premieres and after-parties. Meet all the stars. I hear they treat you like *you're* the star so you give them a good review. Can you imagine that?"

"I almost can."

He bites his nails a lot. At random intervals, a hand will jerk up to his mouth and he'll gnaw for a few seconds. Could be a nervous tic or some obsessive trait.

"Everything's going to be digital," he tells me. "Even movie reviews. You'll read them on your smartphone."

"Sure," I say, having no idea if he's right or not. "I don't even have a smartphone."

"You will," he says, convinced.

"They're so expensive."

"Cell phones were once a luxury item; now everyone has one. In a few years, everyone will *need* a smartphone. They won't be able to live without them. The world will never be the same again."

"Wow," I say, like he's blowing my mind with his visionary insight. I don't care either way, but he does, and I want to keep him sweet.

"Electronic readers will be the next big thing," Zach continues. "All the big tech companies are working on them, I hear."

"You mean a device to read books on?"

"That you can carry around with you and has dozens, maybe even hundreds of books on it."

"So, like a computer?"

"I guess."

"That only lets you read books?"

He notes the skepticism in my tone. "Just you wait."

I nod a few times so I don't offend him. I say nothing, so he doesn't continue.

After a couple of seconds of silence, I ask, "You were saying that you keep old issues for posterity, but not all of them?"

"Paper just doesn't last. The same substance that makes trees able to stand up will get oxidized sooner or later and weaken and yellow. It's called lig-something. Ligtin, lingbin, ding-a-ling. Whatever. Kind of like a glue. The more of it, the stiffer the paper. Cardboard has lots of it. Bet you thought cardboard was just thick paper, didn't you?"

"Uh-huh."

"And then they're going to stink. Newspapers smell musty fast. It's because the paper is so porous. Mold and mildew use them like a petri dish. You can't stop it unless you keep them in the Arctic."

"The Arctic?"

"Because of the humidity," he explains. "The lack of it."

"Wouldn't a desert be better?"

"What do you think the Arctic is?"

I take a breath. Force a smile. "How many years' worth of old issues do you have?"

"I don't even know. They're in the library."

"Of course they are." I back away. "Thank you for your help."

"Wait," he says, catching me up. "They're just in old boxes that are stacked up floor to ceiling." He raises a hand high over his head to emphasize this. "It'll take you forever to go through them."

"I don't have much choice."

"Use the fiches instead. You'll save a boatload of time."

"Sorry, what? Fishes? Boats?"

"*Duh.*" Zach taps his forehead with his palm. "The microfiches. Use them."

"I'm still confused."

Now he puts both palms together for a little bow. "Forgive me." He pauses. Starts again. "The old newspapers have been photographed onto a special film. But not one of those microfilm reels. A microfiche is a rectangular card thing of film, like a big floppy disk. The library has a machine to read them on. You stick a fiche into the machine, and it magnifies it up so you can see it."

He comes with me to the library to show me where the microfiche reader is located. I don't think I've noticed it before. It kind of looks like an old computer from a distance. Like something out of prehistory. I'm not sure I've seen anyone use it.

"They're going to get rid of it," Zach tells me. "They want to put another work desk here instead. I think that's a shame. It's like throwing away history."

He spends a few minutes demonstrating how to work the machine and shows me where to find the newspaper microfiches. They're in a metal cabinet nearby. He slides open the drawer, and I see it is filled with small cardboard boxes about the size of one of those big compilation double-CD cases. They're not labeled.

"Each box is about a month of fiches," he explains. "But there's some runover. Please put them back in the order you take them out."

"Will do."

Zach thrusts a triumphant fist into the air. "*Lignin*," he proclaims, proud and pleased. "That's what the glue stuff in paper is called. Thank goodness I remembered before I left you."

He's so happy with himself he doesn't notice my sarcasm when I say, "Phew, I couldn't have coped otherwise."

"Have fun," he tells me as he leaves.

The drawers are subdivided into sections with the dividers denoting the school year. There must be thousands and thousands of microfiches in the drawer, going back all the way to the early nineties.

I take out a few boxes and set them on the table next to the machine. I'm starting with last year's issues. I've decided to work backward since I have no idea when the girl from the story would have died. Could be last year for all I know.

Looking at all the fiches, I'm overwhelmed by the enormity of the task before me yet also excited at the prospect of getting some answers.

What I'm going to do with those answers, I don't know.

TWENTY-FOUR

The machine isn't straightforward to use, even after I've been shown what to do. The first thing is to set the lens. Zach gave me two, each in its own frayed cardboard box that seems incredibly flimsy. This cardboard clearly doesn't contain much ding-a-ling. Each lens is a different magnification. He told me I'd almost certainly need only the stronger of the two for the oldest of the editions, so I take the weaker one out of its box and set it next to the machine.

I hear his words in my head, *Turn it on, pull the slide to the left*, and I do that.

Whirring, clunking, the machine comes to life. The viewer is like a monitor screen and is set above the glass slide, onto which a bright light now shines before I move it clear.

There's an apparatus underneath the monitor and beneath where the light shines. I have to move that forward. It has a holder for the reels of microfilm, but I'm not using that part. In the center of the apparatus is a gap for the lens, which I insert.

It'll just click into place, Zach's voice in my head tells me. *You don't need to force it.*

The voice is right. The lens fits where it's supposed to fit with no effort at all. I don't hear any actual click, so I'm hoping I didn't do something wrong.

The lens is a chunky piece of glass and plastic. The latter surrounds the glass and is shaped like two gears, one on the top and one beneath. After a bit of fiddling around, I get the hang of how it works. Turn the bottom one left, and it zooms in, right, and it zooms out. The upper gear adjusts the focus.

There's a lever for opening up the glass slide, which lets me slip a microfiche underneath. The fiches are rectangles of flexible, plastic-like material. They're dark, almost black. The glass slide is pushed back down to hold the fiche in place, and then I position it under the bright light.

Instantaneously, the fiche appears on the viewer screen, magnified so now I can see transparent borders subdividing the dark areas into uniform segments. Each almost-black rectangle is a negative of a newspaper page, the text now white, or is it clear? I'm not really sure how it works. I didn't know these things even existed until today.

A dial on the viewer can be twisted to orientate the fiche. Well, the image of it on the screen, which is helpful because I didn't quite put it squarely under the glass slide.

I play with the zoom gear and the focus gear until I can clearly read the text. There's a lever on the apparatus that holds the lens. I can move it to position the lens and the light around the fiche so I can see different pages. It's too fiddly to use, so I improvise and move the piece of the machine where the glass slide sits instead. This is much easier to control. There might be another way to adjust which part of the fiche appears on the screen, but Zach didn't tell me, and I don't want to risk breaking anything. It all seems so old and delicate.

At first, I'm dismayed to find there are dozens of pages on each fiche. The student paper is a weightier publication than I imagined. It takes me a long time to scan through each page looking for an obituary and longer still to operate the clumsy machine.

Three fiches in and I'm wondering if this is going to be a hugely frustrating waste of precious time.

But then I find my first obituary.

It's for a former chemistry professor who sadly died last year. He lived to the ripe old age of ninety, though. Good for him.

I make a mental note of the page it appeared on in case the student paper has a system for placing them. Although I expect it must vary. It's not as though there will be a consistent number of staff, students, or alumni dying every week. The chemistry professor's obituary is near the back of the paper, so I'm hoping that this is the system.

I decide to start at the back of the editions and work my way toward the front.

This pays off fast when I find another obituary a few fiches later. A former student this time, and another retiree. As soon as I see the negative of his aged face, I skip ahead. I feel guilty for this disrespect, and I hope he forgives me from beyond the grave. Sorry, but I just don't have the luxury of reading about your life, Granddad. I wish I did.

Soon into my research I recognize one of the faces in the obituaries. The German guy from my sophomore year who Mack said died of pneumonia. I didn't know him that well, but it's still hard to see his face. I guess when it happened I assumed he had been here for only a semester or two and had gone back home. Maybe this kind of thing happens all the time. Someone dies, and we don't even notice.

I've never had any interest in the school newspaper before this. I don't really have the time to read anything that isn't on my study list, and I don't care if the basketball team has made it to the playoffs. The various sports teams get a lot of attention in the paper, I find. So much so that I wonder if there would even be a newspaper without sports to report on. And not just actual games either. There are interviews and team sheets and practice reports and injury reports and articles about the opposition teams—pages upon pages of it. Then half a single column for an obituary. An entire life reduced to a couple of hundred words.

Society is an absolute joke.

Maybe that's unfair. We should celebrate life and all its nuances, even if it is just a way to help us cope with the inevitability of death.

I take a few steadying breaths. I have to concentrate.

I don't remember what time I began this. Hours and minutes don't matter anymore. I miss texts from Nate. Well, I ignore them. I switch my phone to silent when he tries calling. He knows I'm not in class right now, and I wonder what he thinks I'm doing. He's just going to have to wait.

I realize I'm feeling a little tired and lightheaded, which is a big no-no. I've been too focused on the rule of three, so I reach into my bag for some candy to quickly boost my blood sugar. Within a few minutes, the moment has gone and I get back to work.

I don't notice when it gets dark outside.

Only when I have to stand to take a bathroom break do I see the sun has set. The library is quiet, with a scattering of users. I'm the only one in the bathroom, which feels so chilly I wish I had brought my coat. I sit on the cold seat, hugging myself for a little precious warmth.

There's some graffiti on the stall walls.

I have nothing interesting to say, reads one line in thick black ink.

Do you always bring a marker with you when you pee? someone else wrote beneath.

I smile at that one, then I notice three short lines in small blue letters.

Don't forget the rule of three, reads the first.

The fluorescent lights begin to flicker overhead.

I hear footsteps in the corridor outside, growing closer. A slow walk, a steady rhythm. Heavy footfalls made louder by the near silence of the library, so booming they're audible over the sound of my urination.

They seem to stop at what feels like the other side of the bathroom door, which is odd because they have to belong to a man and the sign is clear as day.

I squeeze with everything I've got to cease peeing so I can listen better, waiting for those footsteps to continue on their way. The men's room is at the other end of the hallway. I passed it on my way here.

I wait. I can hear nothing. The compulsion to keep peeing builds and builds. The fluorescent light flickers more and more.

I don't like this. Something feels wrong. Why has a man stopped on the other side of the ladies' room?

When I hear the quiet creak of the door opening, I almost expected it.

I should have expected it.

A rigid shoe heel strikes the tiled floor.

Oh God, he's coming inside.

What the hell is this?

A stupid student prank? A dare?

Something worse?

There are only five stalls. I'm in the fourth-farthest away from the door. I didn't choose it for any particular reason.

I notice the catch isn't engaged, but I *know* I locked it. Who doesn't lock the door? I always do, so why didn't I lock *this* door? I'm sure I did. Yet the door is now open. Can they come free on their own?

It's not wide open—just a crack. But definitely not locked.

When I reach forward to push it shut and engage the catch, I see the mechanism is broken. The door can't be locked. I would have noticed, I know, and yet I didn't.

Slowly, I lift my feet from the floor.

I raise my knees a few inches so my feet are higher than the gap beneath the stall walls and doors, which is more challenging than I would have expected. The urge to urinate again grows to an incredible intensity.

The fluorescent lights flicker and flicker.

I try not to breathe.

This doesn't make sense, I tell myself. Nothing makes sense.

One of the overhead lights flickers out, plunging my part of the bathroom into darkness.

I stifle a gasp of alarm.

The bathroom door swings shut with a clunk. I heard no more footsteps, so he's still here. But not moving. Standing still and making no sound while I sit still making no sound. The strain of holding in my pee and holding up my legs is deepening into pain.

I'm grimacing.

My legs are shaking.

Maybe he went out when the door swung shut. Maybe he left, and I didn't hear it. The noise of the door shutting might have hidden his footsteps, right?

Not likely.

Which means he's just standing there in front of the door. Doing nothing. Or . . . ?

Is he trying to peer beneath the stalls?

No. Footsteps again. Not outside. Two slow steps. Loud on the floor tiles.

Silence.

The remaining lights flicker and flicker.

They go out, one by one.

The whole bathroom falls into darkness.

Why is this happening?

It can't be real.

To keep my feet off the floor, I wrap my fingers under my thighs to help take some of the weight. I'm squeezing my pelvic floor muscles so hard they're going into spasm.

A quiet creak of hinges.

Then silence.

Then a shuffle of footsteps.

Then another quiet creak of hinges.

More silence.

The door to my stall begins to open . . .

Wake up, Ila, I yell at myself.

TWENTY-FIVE

I jolt from unconsciousness with a dry mouth and racing heart, immediately feeling lost and confused and still feeling the chill of the bathroom. The fluorescent lights above me flicker in the exact same way as they did in my dream before they went out.

I'm still at the desk, and I throw a quick look over my shoulder to make sure no one's there. I twist too fast and hurt my neck. It seems late, as if I've been asleep for hours, and yet I feel as though it was no more than a few minutes. I'm in a place where time is incalculable. The laws of the universe do not apply here.

I shut my eyes and pinch the skin at the top of my nose. My pulse is still hammering from the nightmare, but it's slowing down.

I can't remember having a dream so real, nor with such a lasting physical effect. I'm trembling.

It wasn't real, I remind myself. It's over. I didn't know I was so on edge, that my anxieties were having such an impact. For a moment, I consider just giving up and forgetting the stupid rule of three. I know it can't be real. I know it. Yet I can't shake the unease.

Stick to the plan, Ila.

Don't just tell yourself it's not real.

Prove it.

Another look over my shoulder to make absolutely sure no one is watching, and I go back to my research. It's a slow process made slower by fatigue. I won't stop until they throw me out of here. I realize I don't know when the library closes. I'm sure there are a hundred messages from Nate by now on my phone that remain unanswered. I'm not going to let myself get distracted. I think the world of Nate, but I know I don't love him. Maybe I did once. Maybe he's always been someone I care about and that's all. Someone to have so I'm not alone. Regardless, I don't want to lie to him about what I'm doing. I can't tell him the truth either. I don't want a lecture. I don't want him to put me down. I'll make it up to him when this is over.

Where was I?

I've gone through almost nine years' worth of issues now. There are fifteen editions per semester, thirty issues per year. Each edition is on one fiche. The number of pages varies per issue, but thankfully the obituaries are consistently within six pages from the last. I've gone through four hundred editions by now. Maybe more.

I'm about to take out the fiche from beneath the glass slide when I realize that I haven't checked it or I don't remember checking it. I must have fallen asleep at some point during the process. I adjust the slide to begin at the end of the edition and stop.

I see something toward the start of the issue. A word. A phrase. Something caught my eye.

When I'm adjusting the slide to find the back page, I'm zoomed quite far out, so there are multiple pages presented on the viewer at one time. It makes it much quicker to move around the fiche the farther I'm zoomed out. Then when I have the last page centered, I zoom in, focus, and then move the slide along in small increments so there is one full page in the viewer at a time.

I zoom in a bit more and more the slide around, trying to catch whatever caught my eye.

There. Got it.

Memorial

Part of a subheading.

I adjust the slide until that particular page is in the center of the viewer, and then I turn the gear to zoom in and increase the size of the image until it fills the screen. It's now a blur I can't read, so I turn the second gear to focus the lens and bring the negative into clarity.

Memorial for Popular Student

There's a photograph accompanying it. A candlelight vigil in negative. Dark figures and a light sky. Glowing black candles. A young woman is addressing a small crowd of young people. Students from almost a decade ago.

Tragedies beset her short life

I read on, expectation growing with every word. Excitement and fear and dread and impatience all rolled into one. I feel like I've had too much caffeine. I'm incredibly alert and not in a good way. I'm breathing too shallowly and too fast.

I want to take this all in, yet I'm desperate to get to the information that will tell me what I need to know. It doesn't matter what class she took or what her friends said about her. I don't care about the effect she had on people and what she liked to do in her spare time. A friend wrote the piece about her, and it's expectedly sentimental. No one wants to say anything bad about the dead, do they? Even the worst, most disliked people are canonized in their obituaries. Only the positives are worth remembering, it always seems. Terrible parent? Adulterous? Cruel? We can forget all that because you once won a swimming race.

Halfway through this rambling love letter to the departed and I'm thinking it's going to tell me nothing of substance at all. Platitudes abound between sickly sweet anecdotes of friendship. Quotes from students and faculty staff are littered throughout.

Come on, come on. Tell me about the tragedies. Stop writing about "bittersweet joy" and "cutting sense of humor."

"We're closing now," says a voice behind me.

I startle, palm going to chest.

Looking over my shoulder, I see it's not Zach. An older man I don't recognize at first. Thin. Very tall.

"Just a few minutes."

"It's 10 p.m."

"You're joking."

"Why would I joke?"

I shuffle the boxes of fiches on my desk so it looks like I'm beginning to pack up. The man walks away, and I realize I saw him with Professor Griffiths earlier today.

I go back to the screen. I know it's coming. I can feel it.

She lost her sister at a young age.

I'm staring at the screen so hard my eyes hurt. There's not a drop of moisture in my mouth. I'm reading as fast as I can without missing a single word. I find myself leaning closer to the viewer, my elbows up on the desk.

I have to adjust the fiche to continue the piece as it runs onto the next page, which is on the row below.

My manual dexterity has gone to hell in my adrenaline overload. I can barely work the slide to get the next page centered. The zoom and focus gears become impossible to operate in small increments. I zoom out too far, then in too far, then I focus too far and make the words even blurrier than they were the first time. I'm trying to go as fast as I can because I know the stickler is going to come back at any moment to tell me to leave.

The lights above me go out, as they did in my dream, and as they do everywhere else in the library, plunging the interior into darkness. The glow from the viewer screen and the glare of the bright light illuminating the fiche become more intense.

I'm so focused I barely react. The lights going out isn't going to stop me.

With dry lips and shaking fingers, I finally get the text clear and readable on the screen.

I've found her.

Amy's parents took their own lives.

Amy. Her name was Amy.

Oh God, the rule of three isn't just a story.

TWENTY-SIX

All week, I'm a zombie. I seem the same, albeit with a faraway look in my eyes. When people talk to me, I don't listen. When they ask me questions, I don't answer. Every word out of the mouths of my lecturers might as well be a buzzing white noise.

In my favorite class, I'm not even making notes. I don't raise my hand to join in the discussions, which are sometimes heated. Professor Griffiths looks my way a few times. She's noticed I'm not getting involved like I usually do, and there's a puzzled look on her face. I don't so much avoid eye contact with her as look straight through her when I'm not looking at the empty page of my notebook.

The whole lecture, the page remains blank. The notebook is of good quality, more expensive than I can really afford. Still, I find there's a correlation between the quality of the notebook and the quality of the notes within. The pages are thin paper, not quite yellow, not quite white. The thin lines are brown. Thirty-two in total. I know this because I can't help but count them while I ignore what's going on around me. It's all my mind is good for right now.

I'm tired, yet I'm wide awake.

I'm not sure how much I slept last night. I was awake long after Nate fell asleep next to me. He didn't attempt sex. Even he could see it would be a waste of time. He spent a long time in the bathroom before coming to bed.

He did his best to reassure me I was worrying over nothing.

I can't ignore the question. It follows me around like my shadow, always there even if I can't see it, sometimes clear and obvious, other times faint and insubstantial, but they're both the same. Inescapable.

Do bad things always happen in threes?

Just because the rule of three isn't totally made up, doesn't mean I'm going to die, too, does it?

My parents died in an accident, while Amy's committed suicide. Her sister crashed her car, while my brother had a heart attack.

Similar, but not the same.

Finally, I use my pen.

I write out two columns. In the first, I write *sibling/accident* on the first line, *parents/suicide* on the second, then *Amy/???* on the third. I don't know how she died, as the obituary didn't mention the cause of death. Mack talked about her dropping dead, which could mean anything.

In the second column, I write *parents/accident* on the first line, then *sibling/natural causes*.

It takes me a long time to write anything on the third line.

The pen quivers in my shaking hand.

I know the person closest to me is looking my way. Maybe they've seen the page and what I've written. They might think I'm weird or crazy.

It's quite amazing how something that we cared so much about yesterday can be irrelevant today.

I take a breath and write the third line.

me/???

Did I make some noise? Did I make a loud sigh or mutter some words of anguish?

Everyone's looking at me.

It takes a moment to realize it's not just the person closest to me, who is a weedy guy with a pathetic soul patch of peach fuzz. The pretty girl in front of me has turned around and is creasing her face with confusion. The jocks in the row beyond are all turned around in their seats. One smacks gum.

A glance over my shoulder, and I see the rest of the lecture hall has eyes only for me.

Which must mean:

"Ila?" Professor Griffiths asks.

Like everyone else, she is looking straight at me.

I realize that's why I have so much attention. She's singled me out, and I didn't even notice.

"Sorry, what?" I ask.

A few murmurs. Many smiles. Sniggering.

I feel my cheeks grow warm.

I'm not in on the joke, because the joke is me.

"Are we interrupting you?"

Professor Griffiths, once my favorite-ever teacher, is enjoying this cruelty. She's the mama cat, and the class is full of her kittens. I'm the mouse she's torturing for their amusement.

She asks me, oh so innocent of tone, "Why don't you tell us what you've written down?"

My heart thumps. I'm embarrassed to be caught not paying attention. Worse, I'm terrified of anyone seeing what I'm doing.

"Don't be shy, Ila," Professor Griffiths tells me. "Why don't you read out what's so important? We're all curious."

My face is expressionless, and I make no noise, yet my eyes betray me. They moisten with tears that I beg to remain stationary. I'm trying not to blink so much that I start to tremble.

Professor Griffiths realizes she's gone too far. What she thought was playful admonishment was, in fact, unbearable humiliation. My notebook and those two columns are now smudged with teardrops, blue ink spread to mottled blotches.

She stumbles over her words, mumbling and stammering a change of subject and then clapping to refocus all her gleefully bloodthirsty kittens to the rest of the lecture.

I don't move.

I don't look back down at my notebook.

I don't look at the other students, some still glancing my way to understand what just transpired.

Instead, I look at Professor Griffiths.

I sit statue-still, my cheeks glistening and my eyes red, staring at her. She thinks she went too far. She doesn't know the truth. She doesn't know that I'm terrified. But I want her to suffer. I want her guilt to eat her up from the inside out. I want this cruel kitten mama to choke on her regret.

I don't know how much longer the lecture lasts. It doesn't matter. Thirty seconds or thirty minutes, I don't care. I stare for every single moment that remains.

She pretends not to notice. She pretends not to look my way.

But I know.

She knows too.

I project all my fear and humiliation and anger onto her.

Lightning bolts of revenge streak across the airspace, blasting her into atoms.

I will her head to explode.

No, I want her to suffer first.

I want her to feel her demise, to know she brought it on herself. I'm amazed by my own capacity to desire harm upon another.

I'm a savage. I'm an animal.

Who knows what I'm capable of?

Professor Griffiths looks at the clock, then addresses the class. "Finally, I'd like you to think about a question: Does poetry have to be about something? Should it be about something? Are words alone enough? Is a beautiful rhythm of language not worthy in itself? Should Coleridge's 'Kubla Khan' hold less value than Thomas's 'Do Not Go Gentle into That Good Night'? I still don't know the answer to this question, so don't expect to learn either by the time you graduate." She smiles. "But if you do, please come educate me."

The class is over.

I'm slow to pack away my things. Slow to stand. Slower to shimmy out of the hall.

I ignore the rest of the class. Maybe some look my way. Maybe some wonder.

I feel her watching me as I descend the broad steps. The carpet is frayed. I think it might have been green once. A long time ago. Now it's some nondescript earth tone. That green has been polluted by dirt until nothing remains of any vibrancy. It's a forest stripped bare.

"Ila."

I want to ignore her. I try to ignore her.

I don't realize how much I fail the simplest things.

I'm the winner at failure.

I can see her coming closer as I slow toward the exit. Students outside are congregating in the hallway, and those of us left inside crowd before the doorway.

"Ila," Professor Griffiths says once more.

My gaze is on the bleached hair of the girl in front of me. I focus on the individual strands. I see all her split ends.

Professor Griffiths is close enough now that I can smell her perfume.

"Ila."

I lose it. "*What?*"

Split Ends startles.

Professor Griffiths steps back and gestures for me to follow. Split Ends is looking my way, as do several others waiting for their turn to get through the door.

I can't stand the scrutiny, so I step out of line and move over to where Professor Griffiths is waiting.

She's young for a professor. I'm thinking she's around thirty. Her skin is smooth, and her hair is a glorious rusted red color. Looks natural too. She wears it bunched up, and it doesn't suit her. Like she's trying to seem more mature. I know a lot of the guys on my course think she's hot. I guess I do too. But now I hate her.

"Are you okay?" she asks me.

A redundant question. We both know I'm not.

I don't answer.

"You haven't been yourself all week."

"You don't even know me."

She's taken aback. Frowns. Shuffles. "I know enough. I see you in class, making notes constantly, and I sometimes wonder if you're writing down every single thing I say. All the *ums* and *ahs* too."

"So?"

"Today I'm not sure you heard a word I said."

"Is that why you decided to pick on me?"

"I don't think I'd call it that."

"How would you prefer me to describe it?" I'm all sneers and cynicism. "Making fun of me? Humiliating me? Bullying me?"

"If that's how you felt, then I apologize."

"You saw me crying," I tell her. "And yet you wait until everyone else is gone before apologizing?"

She nods. "You're right. What I did was wrong, and I should have said sorry right there and then."

"May I go now?"

I'm not sure why she looks sad, but she does. "Yeah, sure. Of course. Feel free."

I move toward the door.

"I'm worried about you," Professor Griffiths says as I go. "You're not yourself. Has something happened to you?"

"No," I tell her. "Not yet."

TWENTY-SEVEN

Nate has been yelling at me since the moment I arrived back home around midnight. Where have I been? Why didn't I answer him? Why didn't I call him back? Why couldn't I even text? He's been sick with worry. He's been scared to death something happened to me. He started calling hospitals around nine. This is so irresponsible of me. So disrespectful. Doesn't he matter to me? Isn't he worth just a little consideration? Am I mad at him? Don't I care about him anymore? Who was I with all this time? What were we doing?

I tell him I was at the library again, as I have been every day, every night this week, poring through the student paper, trying to find more mentions of Amy, or any indication that the rule of three happened to anyone else.

The simple truth is I lost track of time.

He can't quite work out if I'm lying to him to cover up something else. And if I was at the library all day and night, why did that stop me from replying to his texts?

Now I have to start lying. I'm not going to tell him in that moment, for those few hours, he didn't matter to me. Does that mean he's never really mattered to me? If I can ignore him for a whole day, not consider his feelings at all, does that mean I don't really care about him at all?

I tell him I was lost in my research.

It's a version of the truth. It is technically true.

He can't believe I would prioritize some stupid urban legend over our relationship. He would never let anything else come before me. Shame he doesn't carry that philosophy into the bedroom.

He has a light bulb moment. The library closes at 10 p.m. Campus is only a mile away. What have I been doing for the last two hours?

Good question.

I went for a walk and just kept walking, heading nowhere in particular, thinking about my family, thinking about Amy, thinking about the rule of three.

I was in a daze. Conscious but not in control of myself.

I think I found a bench under a streetlight and sat down to read Amy's obituary for the hundredth time.

Nate tells me I'm stupid for being out by myself for so long. That's how girls get themselves into trouble.

It's not a girl's responsibly to avoid danger, Nate.

That's not what he means; he stammers to make his point again, and this dilutes his anger.

He hugs me.

He's glad I'm safe and home.

I'm only one of those things. I don't tell him.

Am I hungry?

No, but I should eat something. It's been so long since I've eaten, I'm putting myself at risk of a hypo.

I nod, and Nate makes us a midnight snack.

I tell him all about microfiches, and he's as surprised to find out what they are as I had been. I tell him how they work and how the machine operates and that the library has cabinet after cabinet full of them.

He asks what else they have stored on them, and I can't tell him. I didn't pay any attention.

When we've finished eating, he says, "Come on, show me what you found."

I hesitate. "What's the point? You won't believe it."

"Just show me."

I have the printouts in my bag, and I fetch them and hand them to him. He spends a few minutes reading. He glances up from the pages a few times. I guess it's when he gets to the parts about tragedies and Amy's sister and her parents.

"What did I say?" he asks. "With enough people, the odds that the same tragedies will affect . . ."

"Yeah, yeah. I remember. I also remember you telling me all about how you don't believe in free will and how you wish you did."

"So?"

"So, I don't want to believe in the rule of three. Only it's hard to ignore when it's staring me right in the fucking face."

"I don't think I've ever heard you say *fuck* before."

"You haven't," I confirm. "But I feel circumstances now warrant it."

"*Circumstances.*"

He says the word in a mocking tone. He's shaking his head.

"You said we were a team."

"The best team."

"Then why does it feel like I'm on my own?"

"You want to go to the police? I'll give you a ride."

"Why would I want to go to the police?"

"If you believe something's going to happen to you, why wouldn't you go?"

"They're not going to believe me."

"Why not?"

I stare at him. "Because my own boyfriend doesn't even believe me."

"I'm not going to believe that just because some girl died almost a decade ago, it means you're going to die too. That's ridiculous. That's nuts. It's just a stupid urban myth. None of them are real. They're stories. Nothing more."

I'm silent.

He continues: "You're the most logical person I've ever met. The smartest person I've ever known. If I came to you with something like this, you would tear it all to pieces within seconds. The first thing you would say is: Where's the evidence? You'd tell me that you can't make a conclusion from an unsubstantiated hypothesis. You'd make me feel like a fool."

"You're making *me* feel like a fool right now."

"Because you're allowing yourself to believe that there's something real about what amounts to little more than a coincidence."

I know he's right. In a way. It *is* a coincidence, and there's no evidence it's anything more, but it's such a huge coincidence that I can feel it at a cellular level.

"No," I say. "That's not why I feel like a fool. I feel like this because I expected my boyfriend to actually support me when I need him to."

"What you need is to wake the hell up."

"You're right that if you brought this up with me, I would want to see the evidence. I'm going to find it," I tell him. "I'm going to find out what happened to Amy. The article doesn't say how she died."

"Does it matter?"

I take my notebook from my bag and open it on the kitchen table.

"Look," I say, pointing. "Amy's sister died in an accident, and so did my parents. My brother died of natural causes. Amy's parents killed themselves."

"Exactly. It doesn't match."

"Not yet," I say, pointing to *Amy/???* and *me/???*. "If Amy died of natural causes, then it does match. Accident, suicide, natural causes." I point to my column, first at *sibling/natural causes*, then moving my fingertip down to *parents/accident*. "Natural causes, accident . . ." I stop at *me/???*.

"You're telling me you're going to kill yourself? What the fuck?"

"I'm saying that's the pattern. The order changes, but the causes of death are always the same."

He rubs the back of his head, frowning. "This is the most fucked-up, ridiculous load of crap I've ever heard in my life."

"I'm not saying any of this makes any sense. It doesn't. I know it doesn't. I don't need you to tell me that. I'm saying how it appears to me because that's what my gut is telling me." I scratch at my scalp.

"I've felt like there's a splinter in my mind for days. Something's been wrong and I couldn't explain it. So, for once, I'm actually going to listen to my instincts. I'm going to act as if this is true, as if the rule of three is real. And if not, then I look forward to you telling me that you told me so. It'll mean I'm still alive."

He takes a breath, shakes his head, then humors me. "Okay, what's the plan? How are you going to find out how a girl died years and years ago?"

"There are death records, aren't there? I must be able to check. I don't know how to go about doing that the official route, but there's a far simpler way."

"Oh yeah, what's that?"

I gesture to the printed-out newspaper article I've kept with me all week. "I didn't notice at first because I only cared about what was in the piece about Amy's memorial, not who wrote it. Her best friend did. Elizabeth. She's the one in the photograph."

He leans closer to the table to look at the byline. "Is this . . . ?"

"Yeah," I say, nodding. "Amy's best friend, Elizabeth, is now my English professor."

TWENTY-EIGHT

She doesn't look like how she does in the photograph. I guess that isn't surprising. It's been nine years, after all. She's put on weight. Twenty pounds, maybe. Her hair is a different color. Though the photograph is black and white, her hair is darker. Now it's lighter—lots of highlights. I must have been wrong when I thought it was natural. Without the byline, I would never have recognized that my professor was the girl in the picture leading the candlelight vigil.

She smiles when she sees me in class. I've missed the last one—the one before that was the one where she made me cry.

Again, I'm not paying attention.

I'm thinking about her and Amy and what I'm going to say when the class is over.

Can I ask you about your friend who died?

There must be a better way of putting it. A softer way. A gentle approach seems like the right one. Tell her I really need to speak to her. A quiet chat somewhere private. Take a meandering route to the point. Tell her about my life. My brother. My parents. Watch her reaction. Say I've been thinking a lot about this urban myth I heard. That I wanted to prove it wasn't true. But I found the opposite.

Maybe she'll refuse to speak about it. I'm sure I'm going to bring up a lot of old feelings of sadness and grief. I don't want to hurt her, but there might not be any choice. I need to ask her about Amy. I have to know how she died.

She notices me looking her way one too many times and mouths a quick, *You okay?*

I nod.

She continues teaching, and I watch her, wondering where she used to sit when she was studying here. She must have been a good student if she ended up getting her doctorate. She must have fallen in love with the university, even despite the death of her best friend.

Has she heard of the rule of three?

It strikes me as the kind of thing students tell one another, but not faculty. She could have overheard it, of course. Perhaps she's the only one from that time who hears the rule of three and knows where it began.

The class is the longest of my life. The seconds tick by in slow motion. It's as though the hands of the clock refuse to turn. There's an incredible exertion just sitting here and waiting. I always thought of myself as a patient person, but I was wrong. I'm so anxious for the class to end to get the chance to talk to Professor Griffiths that I'm sweating by the end of it.

My armpits are damp, and my palms are clammy as I stand up from my seat. I make sure to take my time as I gather my things. I don't want to speak to her with an audience.

She's sitting at her desk, looking at something on her laptop, as I approach.

"Ila." She smiles when she notices me near. "Good to see you back in class."

I'm shuffling closer, and I'm nervous, and I'm unsure of myself.

She can't fail to notice my anxiety. "What's wrong?"

"I really need to speak to you," is about as good as I'm able to do at the moment.

"Uh, sure. Okay. Do you mean now?"

I nod. "Please. If you can. It's important."

"Can you give me five minutes to finish these emails?"

I nod again, then go a take a seat at the end of the front row. I stare at the floor and wait.

However, a minute later, I notice Professor Griffiths is standing over me. I look up.

"From the look of you, it can't wait, can it?"

I can't bring myself to answer.

She takes the seat next to me. "What's wrong, Ila?"

My preplanned softly-softly approach goes out of the window because the first thing I say is, "Have you heard of the rule of three?"

There's a moment in which I think she's going to say no. Her face is stone. Not a hint of recognition. Then her whole posture changes as a stiffness takes over her. She nods.

She has to clear her throat before she can ask, "Why?"

"I lost my parents first," I begin.

She must guess where this is going, because she says, "First?"

"An accident. Carbon monoxide leak. They were in bed and just never woke up."

She waits for more. She knows what's coming.

"Hunter, my brother, had a heart attack when he was fourteen. Just died out of nowhere."

"Oh, Ila. I'm so sorry."

"There's no need to be," I tell her with a sad smile. "He's in a better place. He's with Mom and Dad."

She puts a hand on my shoulder. If we knew each other better, she would hug me.

"Who told you about the rule of three?" she asks in a quiet voice.

"We had a friend over. He mentioned it, thinking it was something fun and creepy to share. I didn't take it seriously."

"But you take it seriously now?"

"I guess I do. I wanted to ignore it. I wanted to believe it was just a story. I hoped it was all made up, that the girl in the story wasn't real."

"There's a specific reason you're telling me this, isn't there?"

"I went through the archives of the university paper. I figured if the story was true, it probably started here, since I'd been told it here and so had the girl I overheard."

"You read my piece about Amy's memorial?"

"You must have cared about her very much."

"I did. So much. She was so joyful and so fun. Just out-and-out reckless, wild fun. But so sad beneath it all. We did everything together. We hit it off that first week and were inseparable after." She pauses, looking away. "It's weird. Losing her felt like losing a part of me too. With her I felt utterly, completely free. After she was gone, I don't think I ever felt that way again." She manages a sad smile of her own. "But my grades improved."

"Is it true what they say in the story?" I ask. "Did Amy know she was going to die?"

There's a horrendously long pause while Professor Griffiths stares off into space, and then her eyes mist and she nods.

"She thought she was doomed. I didn't believe her, but I tried to be there for her as much as I could. She was . . . erratic and emotional, and her mood could flip in a second. She made it very hard to be her friend in those weeks leading up to her death."

Her eyes are no longer misty, because they're glassy with a dam of tears. When she blinks, twin rivulets, dark with mascara, snake down her cheeks.

"I'm sorry," she says. "I haven't talked about her in a long time. I haven't even thought about her, which makes me angry with myself. I only knew her a short time, but I did love her."

She fetches a tissue to clean up her face.

"The article you wrote didn't mention how she died. I have a . . . theory. If I'm right, I think her death was natural causes."

She shoots me a look of surprise that confirms my theory.

"Aneurysm. Bleeding on the brain. She just died . . . Amy thought she was going to kill herself, which made a certain kind of sense because she had tried before. She was utterly broken losing her parents after losing her sister. She tried a couple of times. She used to joke that she was too weak to overcome her own strength."

"Why did she think she was going to kill herself?"

"She was getting more and more . . . erratic, I guess you'd call it, the closer it got to the anniversary of her parents' death. She was in a car crash, and she didn't remember it. A witness said she closed her eyes and then deliberately drove off the road into a lamppost. Amy swore she wouldn't have done it willingly."

"So, what was her explanation?"

Professor Griffiths opens her mouth to speak and then stops. Stands up. "Listen, I'm not sure how comfortable I am discussing Amy like this."

"Please." I stand up too. "I get what you're saying, but I have to know everything you know. I intended to prove it was just a story, and yet now I'm scared that this is all too much of a coincidence. It's getting close to the third anniversary of my brother's death . . . You're the best and only hope I have of getting answers. I know it must be hard for you to relive all this. It must eat you up to admit that you didn't believe her when she thought she was going to die. And then she did. Please, I need to know everything you know. Tell me this is all just some weird coincidence. Please don't tell me that what happened to Amy and her family wasn't anything more than just bad luck."

She takes a moment to compose herself. "I could try to tell you what Amy went through, but I think it's better if she tells you herself."

"Hold on . . . tell me herself? How?"

"She kept a journal," Professor Griffiths tells me. "You can read it and make up your own mind."

TWENTY-NINE

I now know why people call it the rule of three.

It literally says it on the black cover of the notebook. Amy scratched it into the surface with a Biro. I can just about see the faint sheen of blue in the scratches, which are deep and ragged.

The years have not been kind to it. It smells musty. The paper has yellowed. All that ding-a-ling has oxidized. The once-stiff cardboard cover is a little soft. The whole notebook is bendy. I could probably roll it up into a cylinder and shove it into the back pocket of my jeans. Maybe Amy did just that nine long years ago.

A day has gone by between Elizabeth telling me about the journal and me actually getting my hands on it. I spent every waking moment in between imagining reading it, anticipating reading it, and being desperate to read it. Yet for maybe an hour, I can't bring myself to pull free the faded, frayed elastic ribbon and open the damned thing up.

It's like getting exam results or getting the admissions letter from college. The desperation for good news is tempered by the terror of the bad.

No, it's not like that, because I don't believe this journal will give me any good news. I get why Elizabeth wanted to share this with me, but I wish she had told me more about its contents. I'm scared about what I'm going to find.

Am I holding a curse in my hands?

Only one way to find out.

I take a deep breath to steady myself and open up the journal.

I wasn't always crazy, but I was never sane.

I don't know exactly how long I'm sitting there on the grass. I do know that I don't look up until I'm finished. I'm not a fast reader, and I'm not a slow reader. Average, I guess. I read Amy's journal both fast and slow. Every line read makes me more anxious to read the next, yet I know I have to take my time to absorb everything she tells me.

Elizabeth told me that Amy kept a journal. That's inaccurate. She didn't fill it in day by day. This reads to me like she wrote it all down in a handful of sittings. Maybe all in one go. I can imagine her writing away nonstop, frantic to get everything she knew on the pages.

Her writing fills about a third of the notebook, and I know the end is coming well before I reach it. Just holding the book in my hand, I can tell the first third of it has been used while the rest remains fresh in comparison. Knowing the end is coming makes me more and more desperate for answers. I'm reading the last few chapters of her words, knowing her time is running out faster than she realizes herself.

I'm so happy I could die.

What is she going to write next? I wonder. Did she know more about the rule of three? I think she did. She knew a lot more, only didn't get the chance to write it down. She wrote it for a reason, to share what she had learned, only her survival guide is incomplete.

And who is it for?

Who did she think would need to read it? She evidently felt someone else would go through what was happening to her. I feel like she was speaking directly to me, yet she couldn't have known back then I would be reading it all these years later. She writes with such certainty, however, like she was sure I would need to read it one day.

What was she trying to tell me?

Why did she think what she felt was happening to her would also happen to someone else? I don't know at this moment that I'm going to continue her story. Writing down what's happening to me is not even a consideration. But, like Amy, I'm going to realize it's my duty eventually. I owe it to her as I owe it to you.

Who was it who said that those who ignore history are doomed to repeat it?

That's not going to be me, I swear to myself.

Amy convinced herself that she was doomed to die, whether fate, destiny, or a curse was behind what she was going through. I think about my own experiences in comparison to her own. I've had no blackout moments like her crash. I've not seen any of my dead family members in hallucinations.

Do I believe she did? All those drugs she took could have messed with her mind. I was once told that the mind is like liquids of different densities, all sitting on top of one another, layer upon layer. They don't mix. Until we take drugs. Imagine all those layers of liquids in a bowl, a doctor once told me, and then imagine putting your hand into that bowl and stirring it around. That's the effect of drugs. Those layers are all jumbled up together until they eventually settle back into order. Take too many drugs too often, and those layers never settle back together again.

I don't think it's a stretch to imagine years of drug abuse damaged Amy beyond repair.

Does that mean her death, the aneurysm, was connected to her drug use? Because then it wouldn't exactly be natural causes, would it?

But does that even matter? How is finding out one way or the other going to help me? It's not going to make me believe I'm next any more than it would convince me to forget all about it.

Regardless, I refuse to be like Amy and resign myself to the fact that I'm doomed. Even if the rule of three is a real thing, I won't give up and accept my fate. Who makes these rules, anyway? Who gets to decide when we live and when we die? Because I sure as hell didn't give them permission to decide on my behalf.

If there's fate, I'm going to make my own.

I don't tell Nate what I'm doing. I know what he'll say, and I don't want to hear it. If he asks me straight, I'll tell the truth. Until then, he can stay in the dark. I realize that it's not his admonishment that I want to avoid, but how that will make me feel about him in return. I never before thought of him as someone whose support I could not rely upon. This realization is causing me to question my feelings toward him more than ever. I can look past his lack of focus and ambition. I can't look past his inability to be by my side no matter what.

I can't imagine the pain Amy went through after her parents killed themselves. I don't think I could have coped with that. She clearly couldn't. Could anyone, I wonder?

Amy thought the rule of three meant she was doomed to die.

What if the reality is even more sinister?

THIRTY

I meet Elizabeth in the early afternoon. She has her lunch with her in a paper bag. I present the journal to her, and she shakes her head.

"Keep it," she says. "At least for a while. I'm sure it's more use to you than me right now."

"Then you, too, believe in the rule of three?"

"I believe that Amy believed in it," she answers in a careful tone. "What I think now doesn't really matter."

"Amy wrote that you and she stopped being friends. She said you betrayed her. In the worst possible way, I think is how she described it."

Elizabeth looks away. "That was tough to read. As I said before, I felt very close to Amy, and her death hit me hard. Reading that made it a lot harder. I didn't know she felt that way."

"So . . . there was no, to use her own words, betrayal?"

"I thought I was always there for her, and she never said anything that made me feel I wasn't. Sure, we had a few heated discussions. I didn't just accept all the crazy things she would tell me sometimes. I don't believe in curses or anything else like that. I never wanted to lie to her, and I always wanted to be there for her. Did I strike the right balance? I don't know. I was very young and immature, and Amy wasn't always the most stable person. Did I do anything that might remotely be considered a betrayal? If I did, I didn't know I had."

I'm surprised to hear this. I had expected Elizabeth would show some reluctance to talk about the more painful aspects of her depiction in Amy's journal. I hadn't expected her to deny outright what Amy wrote.

So, which is the truth? Did Elizabeth betray Amy, or is the journal inaccurate? If it's the former, why is Elizabeth lying to me? And if it's the latter, why did Amy write untruths?

"What about the car crash?" I ask. "The girl who saw it take place, Charlotte, said Amy closed her eyes and swerved off the road. That's what really triggered Amy into thinking she was doomed, like she had been compelled to crash her car, like her parents had been compelled to hang themselves."

"Charlotte never said that explicitly," she tells me. "She saw the crash, but she didn't see why it happened. Amy asked her if she closed her eyes before the crash, and Charlotte told her she couldn't be sure."

"You're saying Amy lied in the journal?"

"I'm saying she was trying to make sense of the crash. She wrote her interpretation of events, as told through her own biases. She didn't remember the crash and Charlotte didn't see exactly what happened, but Amy really believed she was compelled."

I think of Amy smoking weed in her car before speaking with Jefferson. Maybe she smoked some more after seeing her therapist. Or maybe she smoked even more before she crashed her car.

With the drugs, with the grief, with her evident desperation, I can believe that she wrote down what she perceived to be accurate, yet wasn't. We all tell our lives through our own lens, don't we? None of us can be expected to be impartial when it comes to ourselves. Amy was no different. I've tried to be as dispassionate as possible in my own writings. I've been attempting to separate fact from feeling. Amy blends the two so much that I'm wondering how much of it actually happened the way she wrote it.

I say, "Amy mentioned meeting a young man named Christian on the bus when she went to the church that day to receive a blessing. Did she say anything more about him when she returned? She notes that there's a reason why she's writing about him and that she'll come back to him later. Obviously, she doesn't get to continue the journal. I know it's a long time ago now, but do you remember her mentioning him?"

I can tell something is wrong while I am still speaking. A bemused expression creeps into Elizabeth's face that then becomes almost like a sad resignation. I give her a moment to collect her thoughts. It can't be easy trying to remember specifics about what happened nearly a decade before.

"No," she answers, scratching at her forehead. "Amy never mentioned the Christian she writes about in her journal."

"Not once? Can you be certain? Maybe you forgot."

"I haven't forgotten, because I remember that day with absolute clarity. As Amy writes, it felt like a victory. It felt like the curse, her obsession with it, was finally over. And we did as she said and celebrated. She was celebrating her survival, and I was celebrating having my best friend back."

"You think she forgot to mention him because he didn't seem important then? And only later, when she realized the curse wasn't broken, he became important? Perhaps they reencountered one another, and you didn't know?"

She's shaking her head before I'm finished. "Listen," she tells me, resolute and confident. "Christian isn't real. He didn't exist."

"What?"

"I drove Amy to the church that day."

I'm speechless, my mouth open and my eyes wide.

"I drove her back too. She didn't take any bus."

"She made him up? That doesn't make any sense. It's her journal, so why write down something that isn't true?"

Elizabeth continues, "Amy was out of her mind with grief and with worry. Maybe she misremembered, and she met him another day for a different reason. I don't know when she wrote the journal, but it was close to the end. She was probably high as a kite on pills or weed or alcohol or all three."

"Then how am I supposed to believe *anything* she wrote?"

"I can't tell you that. I gave you her journal so you could make up your own mind."

"But I'm as lost now as I was before I read it."

"In which case I'm sorry."

I now understand why Amy felt so doomed.

But did she really have no memory of her car crash? Did she actually *see* her sister behind the window outside the hospital, or was it *like* she saw her? I'm going to drive myself crazy second-guessing her, I know. But I have to remove my empathy for her and treat what she wrote as biased. It's witness testimony, not irrefutable evidence.

Or is there something else going on here? I'm starting to worry Elizabeth knows something she's not telling me. Did she, in fact, betray Amy? Is that betrayal so unforgivable Elizabeth won't even admit it nine years later? Is she trying to distract me from the truth?

"Do you know when she started working on the journal? Just a guess? A clue?"

"I have no idea. She never mentioned it to me. I didn't know it even existed until after she died."

"Did she really die three years after her parents died? Which would make it her twenty-first birthday, I think."

"No, she didn't die on her birthday. It was after that."

My mouth falls open. I feel a rush of relief. "Then it's not true, is it? The rule of three isn't real."

"Amy's sister didn't die exactly three years before her parents either. I'm sure you noticed Amy doesn't mention in her journal that Maya died on Amy's fifteenth birthday."

"I . . . I didn't. No. When did Maya die?"

"I'm not wholly sure, but it was close to that date. A few weeks beforehand."

"*Three* weeks before?"

"Maybe."

"Do you remember when Amy died? How close it was after her twenty-first birthday?"

"I do remember," she says. "I remember exactly. It was nineteen days after her birthday."

"Which puts it within three weeks," I say.

Elizabeth nods.

That relief was delicious but shorter-lived than I could ever have imagined.

"I wish I could say something to make you feel better," Elizabeth says, patting my thigh.

"Tell me what Amy was going to write next," I say back. "Tell me what she knew but didn't have time to write in the journal."

"I can't, because I don't know."

"She said she omitted the time after she went to the church when she had been blessed and thought it had stopped the curse. Or cured it, or whatever. It read like she had been celebrating. Drink, drugs, and . . ."

"Ah yes. For someone who wasn't all that fond of living, she had a way of making the best of it. I'm not sure there's anything in that time to share. I don't remember most of it. We were partying even harder than normal, and that comes with a price for the old gray matter." She taps her skull. "Oh, and I'd prefer it if you would keep my past indiscretions to yourself. The faculty's pretty open-minded, but still."

"Of course," I'm quick to say. "Nothing from the journal will go any further, I swear."

"Thank you. I appreciate you have a lot on your mind right now without having to also worry about my reputation."

"Can I ask you a question?"

"Anything."

"If you were me," I begin, "what would you think?"

She spends a long time considering how to answer. I've noticed before that she looks into the middle distance to help her think, and she's doing that a lot now.

"I think that life and death are complicated phenomena that we don't fully understand. And I think that Amy tried to make sense of the tragedies she experienced."

"So you're telling me what happened to her family and what happened to mine is just coincidence?"

"In my opinion, yes. Of course. But it doesn't really matter what I think. It only matters what you believe."

"I don't know what to believe at this point. At first, I thought it was just an urban legend. Then I thought it was an eerie coincidence that made me uncomfortable. I wanted to prove the rule of three was just a story, and all I've done is make myself frightened that it's actually real."

"And that's why you're the only one who can make up your own mind. But when we're in the middle of something we can't also see the bigger picture. We can't see the thing we're inside, can we? So what I'm saying is to imagine I'm coming to you for advice, and you're advising me from a position of authority because you know what I'm going through. What do you tell me? What should I think? What should I do?"

She looks at me with a kind smile on her kind face, full of respect and expectation, as though our roles really are reversed and I'm the older, wiser person ready and able to offer sound advice.

I can imagine this working in other circumstances, with simpler problems, but I'm so full of doubt and uncertainty that all I can manage is, "I have absolutely no idea."

THIRTY-ONE

The rest of the day passes in a haze. I go to the campus library after classes have finished. I have an assignment to do, and the library beats the kitchen table. I'm there two whole hours, and I just about get the title page done. I was hoping Elizabeth would give me some answers, and all I took away were more questions.

I can't shake the feeling of unease that's been building day after day. The last thing my logical brain should believe in is the veracity of an urban legend or the journal of a disturbed mind.

I don't believe in it.

Yet I can't ignore it.

I look at the page in my notebook—the two columns. My eyes are drawn to the third line of the second column.

me/???

I feel like a whole other person. I'm frustrated with myself because this is not me. I believe facts, I believe the evidence, I believe in logic. I tell myself I shouldn't have looked into the rule of three in the first place because I never believed in it then.

I refuse to believe in it now.

Do you? a voice in my head responds.

I drift slowly home.

There's no sunshine today—only gray cloud above gray buildings that flank a gray road.

Nate's on the sofa playing video games.

We exchange a few words. He's busy protecting his precious kill/death ratio, and I have nothing worth saying.

In the bathroom, I stare at myself in the mirror to see who will blink first: me or my reflection.

Was I always this washed-out?

How long has my hair been so dull?

When did the color leach from my eyes?

I check my teeth, expecting to find irreversible decay.

The splinter of unease in my mind has taken root. It's growing. Not actually a splinter of unease, but a seed of dread. I can feel it inside me. Irritating. Frustrating. Impossible to reach.

I scratch at my head and find temporary relief.

No dread now, only contentment through pain.

I keep scratching at my head until hairs fall free and my nails are caked in dead skin, scraped away.

The pain feels good. It overrides all else.

I keep scratching, slowly stripping skin that is not dead. My fingertips become moist, and the scratching sound is muffled to something wet.

The first drop of blood snakes its way through my hair. It follows the line of my skull until it escapes my hairline behind my ear. It's cool on my neck, tickling as it continues all the way to the shallow behind my collarbone. There it rests as a tiny dot of orangey red until it is joined by another that follows the exact same path.

My nails dig deep into my scalp, carving grooves that squelch beneath my fingertips. The blood no longer leaks away in single drops. The little pool in the crook of my collarbone fills. Then the red lake bursts its dam over my chest. More blood runs down my back, along my spine. More still patters my shoulders.

I keep scratching away the flesh beneath my scalp until I reach bone.

My skull is too resilient to scratch away with nails alone, and I have no screwdriver handy. Instead, I push my fingers beneath my scalp, prizing away its hold on the skull. This makes for a sound like tearing apart Velcro.

My fingertips feel along the smooth bone until I find the jagged depression where the plates fused as a child. Here I dig in my nails, thankfully strong and robust, and then I pull.

I'm not strong, and those plates are fused hard.

I grunt and grimace, my hand almost entirely hidden beneath my scalp, blood drenching my arm and head and running down over my face.

I grunt and grimace some more and pry apart those plates through sheer will, the bone seal giving way in cracks of protest I refuse to recognize.

I've ripped open my scalp to the base of my neck with my searching fingers and extended wrist. A piece of torn scalp flops down over my eyes, and I push it to one side with my free hand so I can continue to see in the mirror what I'm doing.

I tilt my head to look upon the gap between the plates, which is wide enough to get my fingers into. Fluids spill out from the cranial cavity, and an unpleasant smell reaches my nose.

My fingers squelch their way into my brain, digging deep into the jellied tissues.

It feels disgusting. *Squelch, squelch, squelch.*

But I've come this far. I'm not going to stop now.

Soon, only my knuckles remain outside the skull, held back by the narrow gap between the plates.

My fingers search.

It's all slimy and gelatinous and far warmer than I expected. Like the steaming water you wash your dishes in.

There, I've got it.

I withdraw my fingers from my skull and hold them before my face. My hand is entirely red with blood. Fragments of skin and brain are glued to my fist in many places.

Between the tips of my index finger and thumb is the seed.

There's a small shoot poking out of one end and tiny roots out of the other. I rub the roots between my fingers to wipe away the blood and brain matter. They're pale white. I clean the shoot too until its black leaves are revealed.

I brush my flopping scalp to one side so I have an uninterrupted view of this little growing seed in my fingers.

It has an unexpected beauty.

"Are you going to be long?"

Nate's peeking through the doorway behind me. I didn't realize I hadn't properly closed the door. He's edged it open just enough to poke his head through in case I'm doing something in here he doesn't want to see.

"No," I tell him, still staring at the sprouting seed. "I'm pretty much done."

"Great," he says, pushing the door open farther. "I'm bursting for a piss. You've been ages." He gestures at the toilet bowl. "Do you mind?"

I shake my head to tell him it's okay, my scalp flopping this way and that.

He makes a huge sigh of relief once he's whipped his dick out and started urinating next to me.

We won't do the other thing in each other's presence. Pissing's okay as long as we ask first. Unless one of us has had asparagus.

"You okay?" he asks, mid-stream. "You're looking a little . . ."

Bloody? Critically injured? Insane?

"Pale," he finishes.

"I haven't slept well this week."

"I wish you'd let it go."

I open my fingertips to let the tiny sprouting seed fall from my fingertips and into the washbasin. It lies precariously across the plughole grate.

I've let it go, Nate.

I step back to let him wash his hands, which is just a quick rinse under the tap. Not even worth the effort if you ask me.

The black leaves and white roots are washed away.

"It's just a stupid story," he tells me for the thousandth time.

He gives me a quick hug and kisses my head.

"I know," I say, forcing a smile so we don't have to go into it again.

Reassured, he smiles back, lips smeared and glistening with my blood and textured with little scraps of my skin.

He leaves me alone in the bathroom.

Just me and my gory reflection.

In silence, I smooth the flap of scalp back into place and start to clean up all the mess I've made.

THIRTY-TWO

Colors have weight. You dress yourself in black, and you'll hunch, you'll plod. Black will weigh you down. You'll bury yourself in it. Dress in white, and you're light as a feather. You'll bounce, you'll glide. Dress in white, you might even fly.

I'm wearing gray, which is appropriate. I'm neither plodding nor flying. I'm drifting. I'm a paper sailboat in a pond. There's no current to pull me and no wind to catch my paper sails.

I can't sail away, and I can't make it back to the shore.

Sooner or later, I'll sink.

I feel like an outsider, like I don't belong here. Not just because it's becoming increasingly obvious I have so little in common with the other, younger students. Now I sit through my classes and I take nothing in, my mind elsewhere, thinking of Amy, thinking of Hunter, thinking of my parents.

Thinking of myself.

When I walk the hallways between classes, I do so alone. I don't discuss what we've just been taught with my classmates. I don't comment on the latest gossip. I only walk at a slow, shuffling pace, the world around me racing along while I'm in slow motion.

It's only when I see the very tall man from the library that my speed catches up with reality.

He's even taller now that he's closer, growing taller than anyone needs to be as he approaches, as though he were a normal-size person stretched out by some unnatural means. He walks in a stoop, trying not to stand out any more than is unavoidable. I find myself pausing in the corridor and standing to one side to allow him to pass unimpeded. He's thin, however, too thin as he's too tall. I feel as though I take up more space. As he nears, I notice a dusting of dandruff on his shoulders and the reddish discoloration of psoriasis on his neck.

I'm not sure if I gasp out loud in my realization I've read about this man in Amy's journal. He is:

"Professor Whittaker."

He stops at the mention of his name, turns his head, and angles it downward to look at me. He seems confused, as though he misheard me.

"I'm sorry, what?"

I try to compose myself. "You're Professor Whittaker."

He seems even more confused, his eyebrows pinching closer and the lines between them deepening. "I'm afraid you must be mistaken. Have a pleasant afternoon."

He walks away from me as I echo his confused expression. While stooped in posture, his strides are so long that within a few seconds he's almost gone.

"*Wait*," I call after him, hurrying to catch up.

He doesn't hear at first, and it's only when I'm reaching out to take his arm that he stops.

"I'm really quite busy," he says.

"You teach religious studies?"

"One of my many sins, yes."

"But your name isn't Whittaker?"

"Why would it be?" He sees how perplexed I am, and it amuses him. "It's not often I'm mistaken for someone else."

My mind is racing to understand what is happening here. I'm not sure what to say. I don't know what this means.

"What is your name?" I find myself asking.

"Whitfield."

"Definitely not Whittaker?"

He shows a smile: part amused, part confused. "I think I'm best placed to know for sure."

He may be partly confused, but I'm utterly bamboozled. I'm not sure what to say, because I'm wondering why the hell Amy referred to him as Whittaker in her journal when that's not his name. I'm missing something. I have no clue what, but I hope she was just high or misheard since they're kind of similar names.

In my silence, he says, "Hmm, I . . . Well, I need to get to my office now. So . . ."

He shrugs and nods, as unsure of what to say as I am of this encounter. I do the same.

I watch as he walks away for the second time, growing smaller the farther he walks down the corridor until he seems like a man of regular height.

Again, I chase after him.

He hears my hurrying footsteps, and I see his shoulders rise in a sigh of frustration. Maybe he even rolls his eyes as well. He doesn't stop this time, however. He doesn't turn around.

As soon as I've caught up with Whittaker—no, Whitfield—I have to walk fast just to maintain pace with his long legs.

"I really need to be getting on," he says.

"I understand," I say, my voice coming out a little flustered from the quick pace. "I'll walk with you to your office. That's okay, isn't it? I'm not keeping you that way."

"Then I'd say you have approximately three minutes, but I have no idea what good they'll do. I'm afraid you're not going to convince me I've been going about with the wrong name and didn't realize."

"Do you remember a girl named Amy?" I ask. "You would have met her something like nine years ago."

"I taught her?"

"No. As far as I understand it, she spoke to you in your office one time."

"You'll appreciate it if that isn't a lot to go on."

"She died soon afterward."

He looks down at me. "I'm very sorry to hear that. And I'm even sorrier to say that it doesn't refresh my memory. Perhaps she spoke to someone else? The actual man named Whittaker maybe?"

"No, no, it has to be you. She came to this college. She spoke to a tall man who taught religious studies."

"Perhaps she confused Whittaker and myself, then. Describing me and meaning him? With similar names I can see how that might happen."

I want to shake my head, yet I can see his point. "She thought she was doomed or cursed," I begin. "She came to you for help, to try to understand. You told her to see a priest to get blessed and—"

"I'll stop you right there," he interrupts, no polite accommodating smiles now. "There is no possibility that I would recommend to anyone, ever, to receive a blessing from a priest. If anything, I would advise someone thinking they were cursed to see a psychiatrist." He's impatient now. "You really do have me confused with someone else, or this is all part of an elaborate joke that I don't like one bit. Considering a young woman died, I find this to be in very bad taste."

He stops. We're at his office door. He takes the handle, opens it. Begins stepping inside, when . . .

"Your sandwiches," I blurt out, speaking fast in a barrage of thoughts made into sound. "Pickles and mayonnaise or something like that . . . You bring them wrapped in tinfoil, which you then fold up and take away with you to use again."

In a quiet voice, almost to himself, he says, "Waste not, want not."

"Please," I say, because I can think of no other plea.

He sighs and nods. "Come in. Let's see if we can't get to the bottom of this."

He holds the door open for me, and I step into his office. It's small and box-shaped, with a bookcase against one wall and a desk in the center of the room. There's a laptop on the desk and a neat pile of paperwork. The files, textbooks, and folders on the bookcase are just as neat. Everything in its proper place and nothing he doesn't need.

After sitting back in his chair, he gestures for me to take a seat. I decline with a shake of my head. I want to stand.

It's hard to know what to tell him. I don't want to sound insane, so I stick to the more mundane facts about Amy. "She was going through a tough time. She wasn't herself. But she mentioned speaking with you about curses."

"How long ago are we talking about?"

"About nine years."

He grimaces at the prospect of remembering a conversation from almost a decade ago. "And she wasn't a student of mine?"

I shake my head.

"Then I'm afraid this is a lost cause. I teach hundreds of young men and women every year. I see thousands of them, all thinking they're so very unique, and yet I couldn't even tell you the names of my best students from nine years ago. Maybe not even from last year."

My shoulders slump.

"Look, either the young woman you're talking about misremembered, or I've understandably forgotten a single conversation that took place a very long time ago. Or," he says with a pause, "it simply never happened in the first place."

"It must have happened," I insist. "She was right about your weird sandwiches."

I'm saying it almost as much for my own benefit, trying to convince myself as much as him, because I don't want this to be another figment of Amy's imagination like Christian on the bus or Charlotte's eyewitness testimony.

"I don't think there is anything especially weird about them . . . Regardless, a single accurate detail does not a conversation about curses make." He glances up to a clock on the wall. "I'm afraid I really must be getting on. I am sorry I couldn't be of any help, but what's this about exactly? Maybe if I understood, I could be of more assistance. I know you're interested in this poor Amy, but why? Who is she to you?"

"There's no point trying to explain." I look back as I reach for the door handle. "You'd never understand."

"Have you considered the possibility that you don't understand yourself?"

I laugh. Not intentionally. It just comes out. "I absolutely don't understand, I assure you. I'm trying to, though. I'm really trying."

"Perhaps you're going about things in the wrong order," he suggests, doing his best to help a strange girl who is making no sense; he can see I'm upset. "In my experience, sometimes the faster way to a conclusion is to first conclude the antithesis."

"I'm not sure that helps me," I say.

He shrugs his narrow shoulders. "I'm not sure anything will until you try."

"Thank you for your time," I tell him as I leave.

My pace is slow as I walk down the corridor. Students and faculty members pass me, moving so fast in comparison they seem to motion-blur into swooshes of light. I feel so alone. So helpless.

I think about what Whittaker—Whitfield—told me: sometimes the fastest way to a conclusion is to first conclude the antithesis. Is that possible with the rule of three? What is the opposite of an urban legend?

The truth.

That doesn't help. I try breaking it down into smaller chunks. Amy died, her family died, as did my own. The opposite of death is life, so again that's no use to me.

I think of Amy's aneurysm and her sister's car crash, and I think of my brother's heart attack and the gas leak that killed my parents. I think of Amy's parents hanging themselves. Accidents and natural causes and suicides. What is the antithesis of all those? I'm not sure there's an antonym for suicide, but I realize I don't need one because I don't need an antithesis for every individual death.

I began this thinking it's all a coincidence, and the opposite of a coincidence is design.

I stop.

If the rule of three is not a coincidence, then it must be by design.

It's so ridiculously simple. I can't believe it hasn't occurred to me until now. It's been there the entire time, right in front of my face. A design. A pattern.

A series.

What if it's not a curse or fate or anything like that killing entire families, but a person?

THIRTY-THREE

Could it be true? Could it be that Amy wasn't doomed, but murdered? That the rule of three is a killer instead of a curse?

If the rule of three is real, then I don't think Amy was doomed. I think instead she must have been murdered. It's the only way I can explain the similarities between what happened to Amy and her family and what happened to mine. And if I'm right, then I'm next. If I'm right, there's someone out there at this very moment planning to kill me.

I'm too late to save my family, but I can still find their killer. A killer who has murdered seven people so far in ways no one knew were murder. A killer who has gone unnoticed since Amy's sister died fifteen years ago.

And that's assuming there aren't more victims out there. Maybe Amy was the first to realize something wasn't right, and I'm just the first to think a killer is out there. Doesn't mean we're the only ones.

Until I know for sure, I'm going to work on the assumption I'm correct. If I'm wrong, I lose nothing.

If I'm right, then someone murdered my brother, and my parents before him, which fills me with rage and despair. All the grief and pain I dealt with comes rushing back, and I can't control my emotions. I scream. I wail. I yell.

But not for long.

I can't get overwhelmed, because there's a murderer out there, and he's already closing in on me. He took my whole family from me. I hate him as much as I'm scared of him. I'll never find peace again until he's brought to justice. Could be a she, of course. Most killers are male, though, as we all know, but that doesn't mean women can't kill too.

And at this point it's just a theory. I can't just walk into a police station with no evidence. In fact, I have less than no evidence, because the deaths I'm attributing to a killer have already been labeled as accidents, natural causes, and suicide. All I have is a hypothesis. I have to test it. I need to find . . . something.

I don't know what. Yet. But there has to be something to prove it one way or the other. There just has to be. I have seven deaths over five incidents to look into. There's going to be something in one of those that isn't right. Something that didn't fit the narrative. Discarded or ignored because it made no sense at the time.

I need just one.

One of those deaths. If I can cast doubt on one, maybe that's enough to cast doubt on them all.

No one's going to do that for me. No detective is going to drop everything to look into a case that isn't even a case. I can't waste time trying, and I don't want to be seen as a nut before I can show that I'm not.

Ignore her, she came in before talking nonsense. Don't waste your time.

I'll have one shot to get someone's attention—a single, unrepeatable chance to be taken seriously. I'll go to that policeman Amy mentioned . . . Lestrange. Maybe he remembers. Maybe he always felt something wasn't right.

I'm not made for all this, I know. I work so hard because I don't want the pressure to succeed. Spending two weeks on an assignment that can be done in a day spreads that pressure. I can handle it that way. I won't get overwhelmed.

Knowing that so much hangs on my ability to convince some overworked, pragmatic officer who has nothing to lose by sending me on my way is terrifying. I've never felt pressure like it.

And that's without acknowledging the fact that I'm on a deadline.

I don't have all the time in the world to prove my theory. I might not even have time to prove it's worthy of consideration.

Focus, Ila. Focus.

I need a plan.

I need reports. Death certificates, police files, or whatever else is compiled when a person dies. A medical examiner's report? I'm so ill-equipped.

No, I'm not.

A sudden wave of hope washes over me. If there's anything I can do well, it's studying. I'll read my way to finding something: every report, every file, every note. Whatever has been written, I'll absorb all the information until I'm a walking library of knowledge. Any investigative technique, every decision made, I'm going to understand. If there's a hole in the reasoning, I'm going to find it.

I know it's there because it has to be there. No one can murder seven people without leaving evidence behind. That evidence has been missed because no one ever looked for it. They were led to believe what the killer wanted them to believe.

I'll have to tell Nate, of course. I won't be able to hide what I'm doing from him. Plus, I'll need help. He won't believe me, and I'm ready for that, and it doesn't matter. I just need him to play along. Someone to bounce ideas off and someone to lie next to and feel safe.

The more I think about my theory, the angrier I am. Not only at the person who took my family from me but at the investigators who might have failed to notice. Too lazy, too incompetent, too easily led . . . I don't care why they screwed up. If they hadn't just accepted my parents died in an accident, my brother would be alive today. Did they spend any time at all checking if the carbon monoxide leak could have been deliberate? I accept that I don't have any idea how someone could induce a heart attack in another person, let alone an otherwise healthy boy, but do I think that it might be possible with drugs or another way I don't yet understand? Yes, although whatever method would need to stay hidden from a postmortem.

And if a heart attack can be induced, then maybe so can an aneurysm. Two people could be forced to hang themselves, couldn't they? A gun in your face and you'll do anything to avoid that bullet. A car crashing off the road? Please. A laser pointer shining in your eye would do it.

Whoever is out there is cunning, and worst of all, they're patient. They've got it all worked out, I'm sure. They already know exactly how they're going to kill me.

Only they're not quite as smart as they think, because now I know they're coming.

The killer, on the other hand, has absolutely no idea I know they're out there.

EVE

THIRTY-FOUR

Lestrange has lovely eyes. They're kind, baby blue, and hold my gaze in an intense grip that I don't want to escape. He's thick at the shoulders and even thicker at the waist. He's the type of man you might call robust or fat, depending on your mood that day. He's lost most of his hair, and the sparse strands left seem to have a mind of their own—little wisps of rebellion. A hint of color remains, hiding among the gray and white. Doomed yet proud. When he looks at me with those baby-blue eyes, I feel like the rest of the world has ceased to exist for him. Not in a creepy way. When he looks at me, he's paying attention to nothing else. When he's listening to me, he's really listening.

Of course, he doesn't believe me.

"Tell me, Eve, are you thinking of hurting yourself?"

"Yeah," I say. "I'm so scared I'm going to die, I'm going to skip to the end and blow my own head off." I push pistol fingertips into my temple. "*Kapow.*"

"Do you own a firearm?"

"I was being sarcastic. Seriously, why would I come to you if I was going to hurt myself? But yeah, I've got a gun. That's the first thing I did when I realized it was happening to me too."

Lestrange is stone-faced.

"Listen," I tell him. "My parents died just over two years ago now. My sister died three years before them. Which means in less than twelve months' time, it's going to be my turn. That's how it works. That's the rule of three. Bad things always happen in threes. It happened to Amy and her family, and then it happened to Ila and hers. This is not just some wild theory of mine. It's all over the internet. Don't you ever see what's trending?"

"Trending? Like fashion?"

"Like social media." I start tugging out my phone. "I'll show you."

"That's not necessary," he says with the veneer of patience. He's as frustrated as me. He's just better at hiding it. Practice, I suppose. If you can't keep your cool when you're in law enforcement, then you're not going to go far. He adjusts the way he's sitting, which is a decent distance from the desk between us. I can see how his trousers bunch up at his hips. His arms are folded and resting on the huge shelf of his belly. Shirtsleeves rolled up. Hairy forearms. Thick wrists. Dense fingers.

I sigh. "If it weren't so tragic, I would laugh. Ila wanted to go to the police, but only after she had found some proof. She knew she wouldn't be believed otherwise. And here I am living out her thoughts, only I was dumb enough to assume the police might care that by now there are eleven murders committed by the same serial killer."

"They're not as commonplace as TV would like you to believe."

"Yeah," I say. "Because the cops don't bother investigating them even when the evidence is staring them in their fat faces."

Lestrange takes that on his fleshy chin.

He examines the folder between us that summarizes everything I know. It's about four inches thick. Pages and pages of notes and lists. "You've obviously put a lot of effort into this."

"I've put my entire life on hold to get this far."

"You have an understanding boss?"

"I live in my dead parents' house and I eat a lot of canned beans," I tell him. "I don't have time to have a job."

Lestrange turns the pages of the folder, and paper and plastic rustle. "White male," he reads aloud, "forty to seventy years old . . . organized . . . three-year cooldown between killings . . . meticulous . . . patient . . . possible medical background . . ."

"It would explain some of the deaths . . . the knowledge of drugs and their interactions with various conditions, whether they would show up in an autopsy, and so on. But he could quite as easily just have read up on it all. That's what I did."

"Why forty? Why not any younger?"

"I think he's older, actually. Middle-aged by now, with forty as the minimum as far as I'm concerned, given a forty-year-old would have been a teenager when Maya crashed her car. Which is a stretch, but it's possible. Could have been crossing the road on his way home from school and she swerved to miss him. Maybe he did it deliberately. Or could have been an accident. But he liked it. Then—"

"Don't forget the rule of three," Lestrange reads. "It's coming for you, like it came for me . . . What does that mean?"

"It's the rhyme everyone knows. Bad things always happen in threes. It's an urban legend. Only it's real."

"Real," he repeats. He takes a deep breath. "I wasn't always crazy, but I was never sane . . ."

"Amy's journal," I explain. "I have it printed out so you can read it. Ila's is in there too."

He turns pages. "You're saying these were written by the alleged victims?"

"That's right. They're—"

"Where did you get them from?"

"Online. This forum . . . That's why I know about this stuff in the first place. That's why I knew it was happening to me."

"If you got these from the internet, how do you know they're genuine?"

I stare at him with wide eyes. "That's why I'm talking to you." I lean across the table to flip pages. "You're in here. Amy mentioned you by name . . . There. Underlined."

"Lestrange," Lestrange reads.

"That's you."

"Must be dozens of police officers with that surname."

"There's another eight," I tell him. "In total . . . across the entire country. I know where each and every one is stationed. I know their ranks. I know how they like their coffee. Like I said: I don't have time to have a sympathetic boss."

He turns more pages, browsing summaries of everyone Amy and Ila mentioned in their journals, along with any details that might help identify them.

"Keep the folder," I say. "Read through it. You'll see."

"With the greatest of respect, this is all hearsay."

I take a deep breath to stay calm. "If you don't want to look into it, then help me. Just tell me Amy's last name or her old address. Something . . . real. I need only one actual, verifiable fact and I can take it and use it to turn everything else I have into facts. That one starting point, and I know, I *know*, it will take me the rest of the way. I'll be able to come back to you with some hard evidence."

"A thorough girl like you must know I can't do that. Even if I believed you, there are privacy issues."

"Whose privacy issues? Everyone I want to know about is *dead*."

I'm breathing hard. Angry, frustrated. Failing.

He flips over more pages. "And the dates you've given me don't add up. You say the deaths all happened three years apart, but that's an . . . interpretation. This one here occurs a month before what would be considered three years."

"Twenty-one days," I say. "Not a month. Three weeks on the nose. Okay. Forget the other girls. Let's look at what happened to my family. My sister killed herself, if we believe the ruling. Jumped off a bridge."

My eyes are wet just thinking about it. Poor, sweet Josey. I miss her so much, and I fight hard to maintain my composure. I owe it to her not to break down and cry. I owe it to her to get justice. "Hard to prove or disprove, I get that. But my parents just happened to have heart attacks on the same night. I mean, really?"

"One induced the other," he states matter-of-factly. "They were both in poor health, and your father finding your mother collapsed would have been a huge shock."

"Maybe. My parents were unwell, but they had different conditions. My mother suffered from low blood pressure. My dad had arrhythmia and angina. He had a pacemaker almost all his life. Did you know that the nitrates they give to relieve the symptoms of angina can cause a severe drop in blood pressure?" He waits for more. "Which means the medication my father used on a regular basis would be fatal if taken by my mother. And the midodrine my mother popped daily to raise her blood pressure would put an unbearable strain on my dad's heart if he took them."

"Are you suggesting they deliberately took each other's meds?"

"No, that's the opposite of what I'm saying. I'm saying that someone made sure they did."

"You think this killer broke into your parents' house and switched the labels on their meds?"

I'm shaking my head. "No, I don't. I think he turned up at their door, polite and respectful, and gave them a good reason to let him in. They almost certainly knew him somehow, so letting him in wasn't a big deal. Then I think he used a gun or some other threat to convince them to take the wrong medication. He spends three whole years getting to know his victims inside and out so that when the time comes, he knows exactly how best to kill them."

"Not everyone has a heart condition."

"My sister didn't, but he still killed her. Whether he pushed her off that bridge or pointed a gun at her and told her to jump, I don't know. Either way it looks like suicide. I don't have a heart condition either. But I'm an accident. He can kill me a thousand ways. He didn't arbitrarily pick heart attacks for my parents. He used their bad hearts against them."

"There was nothing in the toxicology report."

"Quick chemistry lesson: Nitrates combine with oxygen in the blood to form nitric oxide. Which we produce naturally to relax smooth muscles. The toxicologist didn't test for nitric oxide in the blood because no one tests for it because it's there anyway. It would be like testing for blood in the blood. And midodrine is a prodrug, okay? That means it does nothing by itself and needs to be metabolized by the body before it actually acts. It becomes desglymidodrine.

Then desglymidodrine is bound to alpha-adrenergic receptors to increase arterial resistance and—"

He frowns and squints. "I'm sorry, what?"

"The drug Mom took is metabolized into something else, and that something else binds to receptors in the arterial walls. So it's gone. You can't test for it because it isn't floating in the blood, and even if you could test for it, what you'd test for isn't the actual drug that was taken in the first place."

"Let's pretend I'm stupid." He shows a self-deprecating smile. "Give me a summary."

"To induce a heart attack in both of my parents at the same time, all you would need to do is swap their meds, neither of which will show up in the blood after death. That's how he did it. Two murders that look exactly like natural causes."

"How do you know all this stuff about these medications and how they—?"

"Because my life depends on it."

He closes the folder. "Do you have any evidence?"

I growl. "I literally just said that there won't be any evidence."

"People die all the time—accidents and natural causes and suicides—every single day. Take a large enough—"

"Are you going to do anything?" I interrupt.

"I want you to know that if you experience anything suspicious, if you see anyone following you, if anyone makes you uncomfortable, I'm here. I'll listen. Okay?"

"So, that's a no. You're going to do nothing."

"I'm sorry you feel that way, but I'm not sure I can do anything at this point. All you have are theories and no evidence."

"If you could, would you?"

"In a heartbeat," he answers. "In half a heartbeat."

There's no point continuing this conversation, so I stand. He gives me his business card and walks me out, which is nice of him. I know that he cares about my fears even if he doesn't believe they are founded, which is a pretty gigantic problem. I don't need sympathy.

I don't need a hug.

Just before I leave, I smile at him.

There's confusion in his baby blues, and he has to ask, "Why are you smiling like that?"

"Because I will convince you, after all."

Curious, he listens.

"When you see my pale corpse on the mortuary table, you'll realize you should have listened. When it's ruled my death was accidental, you'll remember this conversation. I'll be dead, and you'll have to live the rest of your life in the knowledge you did absolutely nothing to help me."

He's a tough man, but he's not impervious. He breaks eye contact.

"That's why I'm smiling. Because I have convinced you. You just don't know it yet."

I see this sad resignation in his eyes, and it strips away my frustration with him. Now I feel bad, like kicking someone when they're down. So, before I walk away, I tell him, "Hey, don't beat yourself up. I should have known this would be too much to swallow. No hard feelings, okay? I'll do it alone."

"Do what alone?"

"Solve my own murder before it happens."

No one helped Amy, and no one helped Ila. I'm not going to waste any more time expecting the opposite for me. Yet I have the head start Amy and Ila never had. Eleven people have been murdered so far, and I'm not going to be the twelfth.

No way.

Hi, I'm Eve, and I'm the one who beats the rule of three.

Let me tell you how I do it.

THIRTY-FIVE

I pour myself a cup of coffee from the dispenser. It's a giant machine that looks older than I am. It seems like there's an equal chance of it tipping over or exploding. The coffee is instant, so it tastes terrible, but I'm not going to give anyone a hard time about the quality of the beverages. The fact is it's free, as are the cookies and cake. I grab a paper plate and pick the best-looking of the cookies that remain. Options are slim because I'm always late because I make sure never to get here on time.

I've overfilled the corrugated plastic cup, so I have to walk with slow, careful steps.

"Ten says she spills some," a voice says.

A second adds, "I'll take that bet."

I don't look up. My eyes are fixed on the cup and the black coffee that clings to the rim. When I reach the circle of chairs and people, I have to take my gaze away so I can squeeze through the narrow gap between an unoccupied chair and the person in the next seat. It's going to take all my balance to avoid making a mess.

"Let me help you," I hear him say as he shuffles laterally, chair legs scraping on the hard floor.

"Not fair," the first voice complains. "She's not allowed any help."

"You didn't stipulate the terms."

"This is a fix."

Now that the gap is wider, I can step through without trouble, and I sit down on the chair. It's an uncomfortable hunk of orange plastic. Maybe they're donated rejects from a school. I'm sure the chairs, like the coffee dispenser, are older than I am.

The guy who shuffled to make room shuffles back.

"Hi," he says. "I'm Johnathan."

I glance his way. "Eve. Thanks for helping me out."

Johnathan looks like he's come straight from the office. He's wearing a suit. A raincoat is folded and hanging over the back of his chair. Folded because the chairs are low, another reason I think they came from a school. A coat of any length hanging from the back might as well have been thrown on the floor. He's pale and clean-shaven. Groomed, but not overly so. I can see no gray in his hair. and yet there are obvious crow's feet around his eyes and deep frown lines bisecting his forehead.

I raise the plastic cup to take a sip. Like with walking, I do this slowly and carefully.

"Is the bet still on?"

"Only if it's double or nothing."

I shoot a glance to where Alejandro and Sal are sitting. "Does it count if I throw my coffee at you both?"

Alejandro rolls his eyes. "Look who's in a feisty mood."

Sal agrees with him. "She's just acting tough for the new guy."

I take the first sip of coffee and don't spill any.

"You owe me twenty," Sal tells Alejandro.

"I didn't agree to double or nothing. You still owe me the original ten. Tell him, Eve."

There are others sitting on the orange plastic chairs arranged in a rough circle. It always starts off pretty regular, and then the shape deteriorates as people get up for coffee, snacks, or bathroom breaks. By the time the room empties, there's nothing left that could even remotely be considered a circle.

We have nine today, including me, which is about right. Most of us are regulars even if we don't come every week. New people like Johnathan either come for one or two sessions and then drop out, or they're here for the long haul. It's mostly the former.

The sessions are held in the community room of the local church. It's a large space with the walls covered in children's drawings and paintings. Most are painful to look at, although some are cute. These change from time to time, depending on what activities the church is running.

At the start of this process, I had the misconception that group therapy was like sharing a therapist—a wait-your-turn kind of thing. I quickly learned that the other people are as much the therapists as the designated group leader. Some sessions, the therapist is the one who speaks the least. We're all encouraged to support the others and offer our takes on a member's specific problems. Group therapy is all about symbiosis. Everyone benefits, or no one benefits.

Besides support and advice, it's all about hope. When someone you know is a broken mess achieves something they had believed to be impossible, it's inspiring. Not only do they win, but you do too. You're so pleased when Sal gets the promotion he deserves despite his terror of rejection, and you're also given hope. If he can do it, so can you.

"One of the things I find so difficult," Alejandro is saying, crossing one leg over the other, "is that the same level of care and consideration I have for the rest of the office is not reciprocated. I don't make myself a coffee without first asking who else wants one. But I can't tell you how many times I see other people coming out of the kitchen with a cup for themselves and no one else."

Sal is quick to give his opinion. "You're under no obligation always to make other people coffee. Just stop doing it."

"Oh please, honey. I've thought about it a billion and one times. But I know what will happen. They're going to be like, *Look at her, who put a bee in her bonnet?*"

"You wear a bonnet to work?"

Alejandro lays a hand on Sal's knee. "If that's how you picture me, lover, I'm not going to shatter the illusion."

"You don't want to know how I picture you."

Alejandro's eyes light up. "Oh, I do."

I say, "I feel like I need to sit between you before you start rutting."

Alejandro smiles my way. "He's a rut tease, nothing more." He lets out a wistful sigh. "Salvatore's so straight they use him to quality-control rulers."

Stephanie says to Sal, "Is 'just stop doing it' your honest advice?"

"It sure is."

Stephanie is lovely. She has one of those round, kind faces. Cheeks like a baby. Maybe I see her as a mother figure, and in some ways she is just that. I know she has a job to do, and I know she wouldn't be here otherwise. Despite that, I know she really does care about us. She tries to maintain a certain professional distance, and maybe if you've been to only a few sessions that's all you'll ever see. I've been coming long enough to have caught the crack in the facade. I've seen her dab her eyes when she thinks no one is watching. Sometimes after a session she seems unsteady getting up and not just because she has a cane to help her walk. I think she has a problem with her hip, although she's not old.

She says, "I think it's important when we give advice that we take a moment to realize why we think telling someone what we think is a good idea." Stephanie lets this idea settle into our minds. "Could it be, Sal, that you wish you had more often stopped doing things for people who didn't appreciate it?"

I have a sneaking suspicion Stephanie bakes the cake and the cookies, although she always denies it if someone asks her.

She's always sweet, but she's not afraid to strip your defensive layers one by one, until you're naked in your utter lack of emotional protection. She'll push you to a sobbing wreck if she thinks it will finally mean you're honest with yourself. Group therapy isn't about easy solutions, because there are none. This is a long road to travel, and emotional stamina is as important as anything else. To feel better, you have to be ready to feel worse.

"What I will never understand about my parents," I find myself saying, "is why neither of them did anything to fix their problems. Virtually all my friends had parents who had divorced or split up. I'm sure that was tough at first, but then things get better, don't they? It never got better at home for us. We just remained in this perpetual state of unhappiness. Surely if you're miserable, then you want out? If you don't and things suck, then why wouldn't you at least try to make things better?"

"Some people define themselves by their misery," Alejandro says in a sympathetic tone.

To hear Mom tell it, Dad was the devil incarnate. She cut up all their wedding photographs long before I was old enough to see them. I don't think there was a day that went by when she didn't tell us how much she hated him. She almost reveled in telling us how unhappy she was, how her life had been wasted, how she had once been happy long ago, before she met Dad. I grew up filled with guilt for her situation until I understood how self-destructive she was and how cruel she was to Josey and me in the process.

Dad wasn't cruel, but he was a scary man. He hit us only a couple of times, and never more than a slap on the butt, but I understand now that abuse is more than just actual violence. He had a face etched into a permanent scowl. Like he was as miserable as Mom, only he didn't say the words. It leaked out in anger. Like everything everyone did was wrong. We didn't so much walk on eggshells, but tiptoe. We trembled on the tightrope of his temper at all times. Those eruptions were there, albeit rarely, yet we lived in a perpetual state of fear of them. The unceasing dread of pain was a thousand times worse than occasional pain.

There were a few good times, I think. I remember some trips weren't so bad. Until they were. Then four of us in a car no one could escape might as well have been a cage slowly flooding. When Mom stopped coming away with us, it didn't help. Then there was always that empty space in the car to remind us all that while there was no screaming, that respite only existed because there was so much hatred.

When I was old enough to realize that no sane person would live such a life and asked Mom why she didn't leave, why they didn't just get a divorce like countless others, she told me she stayed so one day she could dance on Dad's grave. That was the closest I ever got to an explanation beyond vague terms like "having no choice" and that it was "too late to start again." I'll never know why Dad never walked away from it all. I suspect it didn't occur to him.

Then Josey died.

And for a time, seeing their pain, I forgot how miserable all our lives had been because we were united in our grief. Yet little by little, I saw their selfishness still, because they never cared about my grief in the way I cared about theirs. They didn't stop to think how I had lost the only member of my family who ever bothered to get to know me. There were still three of us in that house, and yet I may as well have been all alone.

I didn't cry once when Mom and Dad died. It was almost a relief.

"Suffering can become like a badge of honor," Alejandro adds, seeing me tear up. "Without it, they have nothing left."

I wipe my nose with my sleeve. "And if your suffering makes people you supposedly care about suffer too?"

He shrugs. Out of ideas.

Johnathan says to me, "Can you not just ask them?"

"I have done," I reply.

"And what did they say?"

"I can't hear the answers." He's confused until I add, "Six feet of earth between them and me makes communication difficult."

"Oh," he says, eyes dropping. "Sorry."

I smile to show him he's done nothing wrong.

In fact, so far Johnathan has done everything right.

THIRTY-SIX

There is plenty of chitchat afterward. Cookies to finish. A last slice of cake to wrap for the journey home. Plus chairs to stack. And many have only group in their lives beyond work. They don't want to go home. Whereas I'm dying for a smoke, so I'm always first to leave. I like those few minutes of quiet reflection. Just me and the cigarette and the night sky. It's the only time I smoke.

Sometimes I can finish a whole cigarette before the next person even exits. It's like a game. I'm not trying to smoke it fast just so I can finish first and win, but I like it when I do. Stephanie is always last to hobble away as there is some clearing up to do, although Alejandro and Sal stack the chairs for her. I feel bad for not helping, too, but I have to get away and have a moment by myself after a session.

Bad luck, Eve, but you don't win tonight's game, because a voice behind me says, "I'm trying to quit."

When I look over, Johnathan is eyeing my cigarette with the longing only a smoker knows. I tap my jacket pocket and the pack of cigarettes inside. "Want one?"

"I shouldn't. But yeah."

"Are you sure? I don't want to be the one that knocks you off the wagon."

"I've already had three today."

I smile. "In which case . . ." I fish out the pack by the lid with a finger and thumb.

I present it to him, but he shakes his head. He has his own, which is a shame.

Johnathan takes his time exhaling. "Why does it have to feel so good?"

"No one likes to get kicked in the shin."

"Excuse me, what?"

I point down to my leg and make a kicking action. "I read it in a book. When you're addicted to nicotine, it's like someone is kicking you in the shin, and when you get some nicotine, it's like they stop kicking you. So what you're really feeling isn't pleasure, it's the absence of pain."

He takes a long drag. "I do love me some absence of pain."

"Don't we all." I'm almost finished with my cigarette, so I'm savoring the last few millimeters of smokable tobacco. "How did you find it in there?"

He holds out a hand and makes a so-so gesture.

"You can't expect to get much out of it from the get-go," I tell him. "It's kind of like smoking in that way."

He shrugs. Nods.

I finish the cigarette and stamp it out under my heel. "Well, maybe see you again sometime. If not, have a nice life."

I begin walking away. I'm taking my time walking because I'm giving him the chance to . . .

"*Hey*," he calls, rushing to catch up with me. "Do you want to go get a drink?"

"Dude, you're like old enough to be my dad."

"Oh, uh, I . . . I didn't mean anything by it. Sorry. I mean . . . sorry."

"Chill, Grandpa," I say with a smile. "And sure, I could use a beer. There's a bar just around the corner. But we aren't supposed to fraternize with one another outside the group."

"How come?"

"We need to remain strangers so we can be honest with one another."

"We can only be honest if we're strangers?"

"That's the theory."

I gesture for him to follow me.

The bar we go to is not that nice, and it's not that bad either. It's a weeknight, so it's quiet. We have our pick of the place and choose a table in a corner. Johnathan offers to get the beers, so I go and sit down. A TV shows a sports game. Could be anything. One bunch of guys running around is the same as any other to me. The other patrons disagree. They're enraptured by it. Good for them, I guess. Must be kind of nice to care about something so pointless. I'm not even being sarcastic. I can't bring myself to care about anything not directly related to my current life situation. Maybe I'll get into sports when this is over.

Johnathan is taking his time with the beers. He's having a conversation with the bartender. From the way he's smiling, I guess an interesting anecdote shared or a piece of trivia learned, perhaps.

He sets the two glasses on the table. "There's a microbrewery in the neighborhood. These are local beers. How funny is that?"

"Hilarious," I say with sarcasm he doesn't notice. I shift my glass closer, hiding my annoyance that it's not a bottle.

The beer is one of those craft beer things, full of extraneous flavors and with a dark, suspicious color.

"Wow, that's good," Johnathan says, wiping his lips with the back of his hand to get rid of the foam.

"It tastes like ass to me."

"Oh," he says, disappointed. "You . . . you are old enough, aren't you?"

"I think you're leaving it a little late to check."

"The bartender asked, and I told him you definitely were."

"It's breaking the law to supply alcohol to a minor."

He's looking anxious now. "Tell me you aren't, please."

"Chill, Grandpa. I'm a major."

"You're a what?"

"A major," I repeat. "It's literally what you are when you're not a minor."

He goes to take another sip, then notices something and leans a little closer. He raises a finger to point. "Is that a cut in your eye-brow?"

"It's actually a scar. Kinda still fresh and juicy."

"Ouch," he says. "Must've hurt."

"Didn't feel it until the blood got in my eye."

He has a wide-eyed look of disbelief.

"MMA," I explain.

"Wow," he says. "You don't look like . . ."

I shrug. "I wanted to find a fun way to keep fit."

"Fun," he echoes.

"Better than a treadmill."

He prods his stomach. "I've been dodging that treadmill re-cently."

"Really? I figured you'd have a perfect six-pack under there."

He's flattered. "You did? Wow, thanks. I . . . I look like I work out?"

"Sure," I say. "Like one of those guys who hit the gym every lunchtime and refuse to eat until it gets dark."

He's almost blushing now. "I . . . Well, you know, I try . . . I mean, I guess the shirt helps. It's tailored. All shirts should be, really. They never fit right otherwise."

"Come on," I say. "It's not just the cut of your shirt. No need to be modest. Take the compliment."

Another two beers later and we're outside saying goodbye. He's going one way, and I'm going the other.

Only he's not making a move. Literally or figuratively.

He has the reluctance of a man who knows he shouldn't be doing something and yet can't bring himself to stop. His hesitation is a little off-putting. It's not hot to want someone more than they want you.

Thankfully, I'm not shy.

I step into his personal space, hands taking his lapels, and I tilt my head back as he comes lower and our lips meet.

No tongues, but it's a lingering kiss.

As his hands move from my waist to my hips and then start to

slide around to my behind, I break away. I give him a big smile, turn
around, and head along the pavement.

I give it a few moments and look back.

He's staring after me, obviously, and raises a hand. "Uh . . . Bye
then, I guess."

I say nothing in return.

It's a ten-minute stroll through the neighborhood back to the
house, and I make it in six. Mom and Dad's house sits at the end of
a quiet lane, set back from the road at the end of a long, broad drive.
That house is just a building. Walls and a roof. Rooms. I can't call
it a home. It never felt like one even when all four of us lived there.
I used to joke with Josey that while so many of the kids at school
were scared their parents would get divorced, we were scared ours
would stay together. My earliest memories of childhood are sitting
at the top of the stairs, crying alongside Josey while we listened to
Mom and Dad scream at one another downstairs. Had I not needed
a place to stay while I conduct my investigation, I would have sold
it a long time ago.

As soon as I've applied both dead bolts and the chain behind me
and entered the code to deactivate the alarm system, I'm rushing to
the dining room that has become my study.

I haven't opened my mouth since I left Johnathan standing confused outside the bar.

I sit down at my desk, pulling out a drawer to get at my sample
kit. I open up the box and remove the cotton swabs. I wet one with
a drop of distilled water from a dropper bottle. I shake the swab to
make sure the cotton is not too wet, and then I pass it across my
lips. This is a very light touch, as little pressure as I can manage. I
go from left to right in a gentle, sweeping motion. I do this several
times, bottom lip and top, rotating the swab as I do. Then I put the
swab inside a sterile test tube, sealing it, and then repeat the process
with the dry swab. This goes into a separate test tube.

I label both so I don't confuse them later.

THIRTY-SEVEN

I call him Three.

Not his real name, naturally, but I think it's an appropriate moniker. It's his rule, after all. I find it helps to give him a name because it makes him real. Not an all-powerful curse or some shadowy entity. He's a real, flesh-and-blood human being. Just like me. Just like you. He's just a person.

While I can't be positive he's a he, the statistics say it's most likely. Yes, 50 percent of female killers exclusively use poison, which we know Three likes, and most commit their crimes in the home or workplace, so again Three ticks those boxes. However, my amateur studies in criminology also tell me that only one in twenty serial murderers are women. And more often than not, a female serial killer is motivated by money, murdering spouses, relatives, and such. They don't tend to go for strangers to fuel bizarre fantasies and obsessions. So I have to be realistic, sensible with my time and efforts, when it's almost certain Three is a man. The only doubt in my mind is because women are more likely to keep killing over greater lengths of time. If my assumptions are wrong and Three turns out to be a woman, then I'm going to feel foolish, sure, but I won't have to worry about her lifting me from my feet and throwing me into the back of a truck. Every cloud . . . as they say.

Prior to seeing Lestrange, I'd spent over a year trying to find people mentioned in the journals. I've spent thousands of hours attempting to make connections between what happened to Amy and what happened to Ila. The only person who was written as being in both their lives is Elizabeth. Amy's best friend and Ila's English professor. So it made the most sense to start with the one guaranteed connection between both girls. I thought she would be easy to track down, and I was wrong. The college where she studied and then taught shut permanently a few years ago. Something to do with too much debt and the primary lender not extending the line of credit. I couldn't find her in the phone book. She's not on social media either. At least, the Elizabeth Griffithses I found were not her. Maybe she moved far away. Maybe she's married now. I don't know. I haven't been able to find the professor of religious studies either. Plenty of men with the surname Whittaker, plenty of Whitfields out there too. None who match Amy's description, as far as I can tell. No shrink called Llewellyn I could locate. No doctor named Aliprandi. No part-time barman who goes by Nate. No Jefferson, Freddy, Cath, Christian, Zach, or Mack. Without full names or addresses or other identifying details, they might as well have not existed even without the fact that Amy or Ila spelled the names incorrectly, misremembered, or made a mistake.

I wasted so much time trying to join the dots. I've made hundreds of cold calls and sent endless DMs and emails on the off chance that Mr. Zachariah L. Porter once worked in a college library, or that MackDaBest81 remembers having chocolate cake with a girl with curly hair. I've lost count of the priests I've made uncomfortable asking if they blessed a girl who thought she was doomed almost twenty years ago. I spend a huge amount of time trying—I chase every lead I can—but even if I can't find those people, I know Three is going to find me. That's the one thing I can be absolutely positive about. He's going to come into my life like he did into Amy's and Ila's. If he's not here already, that is.

Amy wasn't even looking out for him, and Ila realized he was out there only when it was too late. Which means he could have been in their lives and they didn't notice. They could have met him and not thought to mention it. Neither was paying attention when they should have been. Neither was analyzing the people they came across. Ila realized what she was up against only right at the end. And she didn't expect anyone from Amy's journal to be in her own until she found out about Elizabeth. Of course, either may have come across Three and not thought it noteworthy. They might have crossed paths with him dozens of times and not realized.

Which is why I pay attention to every man I come across. Three isn't just going to show up one day and kill me. That's not how he rolls. To fake a natural death, suicide, or accident must require an incredible amount of diligent preparation. He needs to be close; he's always close. Watching me or following me to learn my routines, to formulate my weakness, to know me. There's a good chance I've met Three already. Maybe more than once. Three might use disguises. I'm not talking prosthetic noses and glue-on mustaches. A change of clothes, a haircut, a shave, or a combination thereof would be enough. How often do we really pay attention to the people we walk past or queue behind or say "excuse me" to?

Maybe I even smiled at Three once, having no idea that he was planning to kill me. Did I think he was cute?

We live in a society, yet so much of the time we go out of our way to avoid interacting with others. We're too busy, we tell ourselves, when the truth is we just don't care. We'd rather look at a featureless pavement than meet a homeless person's gaze. Three could be my doctor or my neighbor or the guy who runs the deli or the bus driver or the man who trims the trees or anyone in their forties and up.

I dream about Three often. The faceless man planning to kill me. I try to form his features in my mind. As I told Lestrange, I think Three has a minimum age of about forty. Chances are he's older, which seems like it would help me, but do you realize how many middle-aged and older men there are out there? Absolutely loads of them. They're all Three until I'm sure they're not.

I can't recall precisely when I first read about the girls who came before me. I had gone through a phase in my mid-teens wherein I was obsessed with mysteries, unsolved crimes, ghost stories, UFOs. Everything weird or unexplained, I was into it. I spent a whole summer reading about that medieval map of the Antarctic that shows the landmass beneath the ice. As a kid I loved that old TV show where the two agents investigated aliens and the paranormal. I couldn't get enough. I loved looking into the origins of sayings and folklore. Where history blends with fantasy. I love a good mystery, and I love a good creepy story too. Naturally, urban myths were a passion of mine also. There are whole internet sites devoted to them.

At one point there was an entire forum devoted to the rule of three alone. Someone had scanned in pages from the journal, both Amy's section and Ila's follow-up. Someone even more obsessed than I had transcribed it, word for word. I must have read it a dozen times. I spent countless hours discussing and arguing and debating with the other members of the forum. Which bits were true? Which were distorted? Which were outright lies? We all knew that Amy and Ila couldn't both be right about their experience. I spent a whole night discussing Amy's trip to the church to get blessed and meeting the guy on the bus, Christian. Ila found out that wasn't true, but maybe Amy did meet Christian and Ila wrote it down wrong.

The biggest question was always: Is the rule of three real?

Could the journal simply be an elaborate hoax? A practical joke for the internet age. Set a mystery that can't be solved and throw it out there to see if it could go viral. I didn't believe that. At least, I didn't want to believe it. I wanted to prove it was true. Lots of us did.

But sooner or later, everything loses its shine. Every so often a new theory would surface when someone spotted something in the text that hadn't been noticed before. That would add a top-up of polish that would fade all too soon. At one point, I was logging into the forum several times a day. I felt I was part of a real online community.

That was years ago now. What felt so important became forgotten. As I grew up, I drifted away from UFOs and urban myths. Regular teenage pursuits of getting hold of cigarettes and alcohol and spending time in the back seats of cars took over.

Do you even notice when you stop caring about something? You don't, do you? It just sort of fades unnoticed, little by little, and then one day you're reminded and taken by surprise by how much that thing, or that person, could ever have mattered to you.

To me, that's proof we're ever-evolving creatures even when we're fully grown. I've always been me, but I'm not *that* me anymore. You're not *that* you either.

How has Three changed? I wonder.

Even when I'm not actively hunting him, I'm thinking about him. It's impossible not to do so. I write entire biographies for him based on the scraps I know and imagining the rest. Of course, he thinks he's so very special. After two decades of remaining undetected, I bet his ego is the size of a mountain. He's out there right now. Going about his regular life, interacting with ordinary people, seemingly no different from them. Yet inside he has a massive grin. He's perpetually smug. He's not some sexual sadist psychopath getting off on deviant fantasies. No, that's beneath him. He's playing a game of his own making, and he wants to win. He doesn't need recognition or infamy. He's doing this for himself and no one else.

Three has the patience of a saint. Three years between kills is an insanely long cooldown, even though he spends that time planning how to get away with the next murder. He must be meticulous in his research. He knows everything about his victims. He would have to, wouldn't he? He's always watching, always learning. He's no spree killer, no disorganized murderer.

I'm constantly trying to answer the biggest question . . . why? It's a fruitless endeavor. I can't possibly understand him. Not really. But I try. I imagine what might drive me to murder. What would I get out of it? Why would I do it the way I do? There's a sadomasochistic element to this, I know. I'm torturing myself, and I can't stop.

I'm going to get justice for Josey, and I'm going to protect myself in the process. While I wasn't close to my parents, it still hurts to know they're gone and that we'll never be able to reconcile. That pain is still raw and fresh and different from the powerful sadness I feel for Josey. I'm angry too. I'm so angry at what he did and how smug he feels for getting away with it.

Enjoy that smugness while you can.

If I want to stay alive, it's up to me. No one is going to get to the bottom of this for me. At least, not while I'm still alive. I can imagine what will happen once I'm dead. Lestrange, the skeptic, is going to doubt his skepticism, is going to doubt himself. He will be full of guilt, and those baby-blue eyes might never look so blue again. He's going to investigate the shit out of my death, I know, but that's a little too late for me. I don't hate him. I wish I did. It would be easier that way.

I'm not scared like Amy, and I'm not trying to prove myself wrong like Ila. Just like Three, I'm in this to win it. I'm going to wipe that smirk from his face.

Three thinks he's one step away from completing his trilogy. He doesn't realize this is his last act.

It's almost funny, isn't it?

I've now spent more than two years looking for Three. It is my single purpose in life to catch him. Nothing else matters to me, and yet . . .

To find him, all I have to do is sit back and wait.

THIRTY-EIGHT

There's something immensely satisfying about putting holes through paper. In this way, my .38 is like a big, shiny hole punch. Heavy. Noisy. Lots of fun to use. It's a small gun, but still large in my little hand. Why not a sleek semiautomatic instead? Because I could bury my revolver in the ground for a whole year, and it would still fire the first time when I dug it up again. Automatics can jam if you look at one the wrong way. If I ever need to squeeze the trigger for real, I want to hear an almighty bang, not an impotent click.

I go to the club at least once a month to keep the muscle memory toned. I'm a little ashamed that I like my gun so much and that I enjoy going to the range. It's a much-needed way of relieving the constant stress that is my life right now. Mostly, I find firearms inherently terrifying, and it took a long time to get over the fear of shooting one. I don't want to relapse if the time comes when I need to use it for real. I succeed in overcoming my fear only by constantly challenging it.

I spend too long shredding targets, so I have to rush home to meet Yoshi, who is already at the front door. She's cute and chubby. She has her hair short and swept to the side. Streaks of bleached blond interrupt the otherwise pure black strands. She's smiling when she sees me arrive, smiling wider when I get out of my car and approach. She has a clear plastic container in her hands, which she moves out of the way as I come in for a hug. I can just about get my arms around her. She squeezes me like her life depends on it and kisses me on the top of my head.

"I love your new glasses," I tell her.

They're like old-fashioned wing tips made from wood and branded, literally, with the maker's mark.

"Reclaimed timber," she says. "I think it's from an old shipwreck or something. They're so hippie I could die."

I let us inside and take her coat. "Thanks again for those brownies. Each bite gave me a mouthgasm." I act out a full-body shudder.

She's grinning like a schoolgirl. "They were mostly made with sweet potato."

"No way," I say, remembering what a delicious, sticky mess my mouth had been eating them.

She beams. "I knew you wouldn't have tried them if I'd told you first."

I gesture to the container. "Whatcha got for me this time?"

Yoshi is giddy with excitement. "White chocolate truffles under a solid coconut cream outer layer and a raspberry coulis liquid core."

"I've just cum."

"They're vegan," she tells me, as she always does.

I put a hand to my chest, feigning incredible shock. "You're kidding me."

She gently backhands my arm and rolls her eyes.

"They're going to roll right out of your head if you keep doing that."

"Then stop making me," Yoshi says as she pushes the container into my hands. "Try one, try one."

"Okay," I say, with a heavily sarcastic sigh. "If I absolutely must."

"You absolutely must."

I pop open the lid, pluck out one of the truffles, and examine it closely. "How do you get them so perfectly spherical?"

"*Just eat one*," she cries.

"Oh. My. Zeus," I say, biting through the thin but crunchy outer layer and into the soft truffle.

She grins and claps her hands in unfiltered excitement. "It gets better, it gets better."

I reach the liquid coulis center and stumble back a step. "I'm done."

"I know, right?"

She's so pleased with herself.

I chew the truffle in slow, savoring motions. "It's like it's making tender love to my tongue."

"You really like it?" Yoshi asks, still insecure despite all my praise. "Do you promise?"

"Cross my heart and hope to . . ."

She backhands my arm again before I can finish.

"*Ow*," I say. "That actually hurt."

"I'm sorry," she's quick to say, looking mortified. "Don't hate me."

"Never, ever." I push the lid back onto the container. "You need to stop making these things for me. I feel guilty enough as it is."

"Don't be silly. The more you eat, the less I have around to eat." She places both hands on her belly and gives it a jiggle. "You're doing me a favor, not the other way around."

"So you're saying that by eating these, I'm like your diet coach?"

Still jiggling her belly, Yoshi says, "You're not doing a very good job."

She wanders into the dining room while I fix us both some wine. When I join her, she doesn't notice me for a moment. She's too engrossed in looking at the walls covered in my work: photographs of men I've come across, police reports, autopsy reports, newspaper articles, maps, and more. The dining table is similarly covered with stacks of papers and folders and countless notebooks.

She takes her wine. "You're going to run out of room, you know."

"I'm going to run out of room or run out of time." I clink her glass. "Let's hope for the former."

"I'll never get my head around it," she says. "Why write a journal for the benefit of someone else and leave out so much information? You'd have thought there would be the odd address or a date at least."

I gesture at my research. "It's like putting together a jigsaw, only most of the pieces are missing from the box."

"Are you sure that's not deliberate?"

"How so?"

"Maybe those pieces were left out of the box for a reason."

"What kind of reason?"

My tone is unintentionally challenging, snapping almost. She shrugs in response, uncomfortable with the sudden scrutiny. "I don't know. I'm just trying to look at it from a different perspective."

"Okay. Sure. It's good to get another take on things."

She nods and says nothing. I feel bad. Yoshi is a good friend, and although I think her theory doesn't make sense, I'm glad to have someone to talk to about all this.

She glances at a map on the table. There are red circles dotted across it. Most circles have a red X through them. "What's this one show?"

"Care homes and retirement villages," I explain.

Her finger moves back and forth between the circles. "The X means it's no good?"

I sip some wine. "Yeah. I cross it out once I'm sure there is no one named Jefferson there."

She notices something. "This circle is underlined."

I nod. "They have a resident named Jefferson."

"*Exciting.* Do you think it's him?"

"I won't know until I speak with him. I'm not quite ready to do that yet."

"I can't believe he's still alive. How old did Amy say he was back then?"

"She doesn't. I'm hoping he was younger than she made out. If when she wrote *old* she meant sixty, then it could be him. If she meant eighty, the odds aren't looking good that this Jefferson is *the* Jefferson."

Yoshi spies a thick envelope with her name on it. "How long were you going to keep me in suspense?"

"I always feel bad."

She puts down her wine and taps her palms together in little, excited claps. "It's like Christmas morning. What's Santa brought good little baby Yoshimasa this time?"

"Saliva, from skin," I tell her, handing over the envelope containing the test tubes.

"And you've double swabbed," she says, feeling there are two tubes inside. "I'm so very touched."

"You taught me well."

"I did, didn't I?" She holds up the envelope so it's close to her face and whispers to it, "I'm going to phenol-chloroform the hell out of you."

"I love it when you talk dirty."

Yoshi is a scientist in a research laboratory focusing on genome sequencing. This means she has access to all the equipment necessary to extract DNA from a saliva sample, or anything else for that matter. I'm not going to say this is the only reason I'm friends with her—because I do love her dearly—but I wouldn't have had the chance to become her friend otherwise. It still breaks my heart to carry around that initial deception.

Yoshi is a scientist, and yet she still reads her horoscope, still believes in the healing power of crystals. She accepts there are things that science can't explain and is happy to trust to belief until science catches up and works out the mechanism. Maybe that's why she helps me, or perhaps it would be more accurate to say she's giving me support. She sees this as an experiment. As a scientist, she can be both skeptical of an assumed result without the proof and still happy to test the hypothesis.

"You've got that look about you," she tells me. "Do you think he's the one?"

I pick at my lip. "Maybe. I've thought of all the ways in which Three might enter my life, and as a romantic partner has got to be the best. What better way of getting close to me? This guy's at the young end of the spectrum, but any older and he would be too old to hit on me. Plus the timing is perfect. He walks into my group therapy with a few months to go? Asks me for a beer? Just so happens to smoke. What are the odds?"

"Maybe he just likes you."

I huff.

"I'm serious," she says. "Not every man out there is a serial killer."

"They are until I prove otherwise."

"That's quite the unconventional dating philosophy. Don't you feel like you've missed out these last couple of years? Not just on guys. On life?"

"Sometimes," I admit. "But not really. It's the hand I was dealt, so that's what I play. I'll start living again when this is over."

She comes closer. "I wish I'd spent less time studying and working so hard and more time having fun."

"You're doing what you've always wanted, right?"

"Do what you love, they tell us. So we do. But then once we have to get up at early o'clock to do what we love five days a week for the rest of our lives . . . the love dies an awful, painful death."

I squeeze her arm. "Poor baby Yoshi."

She pouts out her bottom lip. "The real world sucks. Why does no one warn you about that?"

"I think they do. We just don't listen."

She thinks of something and gives me a suspicious look. "Saliva from . . . skin, yeah? Do I even want to know more?"

Now it's my turn to backhand her on the arm. "It was only a kiss."

"That's totally gross. What's wrong with the rim of a bottle?"

"I didn't have a choice," I tell her. "He bought some stupid craft beer in glasses. I could hardly slip one into my bag without him noticing."

"Yeah, yeah," she says. "Or maybe you secretly wanted some disgusting hetero action."

She makes a circle with a thumb and index finger. The index finger of her other hand makes aggressive stabbing motions into the ring.

"*You're* disgusting."

"If even miming the act disgusts you, then I hate to break it to you but you might be teetering on the cusp of joining the sisterhood."

"Keep referring to it like that and the sisters will be handing in their membership cards."

Motioning to the test tubes in the envelope, she says, "This might take a little longer than usual. Lab's busy right now."

"No worries," I tell her. "I'm guaranteed immortal for"—I do a quick calculation—"another one month, two weeks, and four days."

"Which has to be one of the strangest proclamations I've ever heard said with utmost sincerity."

I do a little flourish with my arms. "I try my best."

I joke with Yoshi about my immortality, but the cracks in that bulletproof armor of mine are widening day by day. When I started this I had seemingly all the time in the world.

Now the deadline is so close I can almost touch it.

THIRTY-NINE

S peed it up a little bit," Guill tells me.

I nod. My heart rate is over 180, so I can't talk back. Guill extends the pads toward me at a faster pace, so I have to hit them quicker. The punches become a little shorter, crisper.

The pace kills me, but in a good way.

It's all about the hips. The power comes all the way from the floor, from how your feet are positioned. You want to swivel from the ball of your rear foot, driving the energy up your leg so it can be accelerated by the twist of your hips, shooting it through your torso and down your arm and into your fist. Which you want to connect at the apex of that power curve. Ideally, that's your opponent's face.

"Faster," Guill says.

Bam, bam. Bam, bam.

"That's it," he tells me. "Not too shabby."

Despite the exertion, I smile. When Guill says that, it's like getting a hug from a proud parent. And given that this particular parent doesn't actually hug, it also makes sense that he doesn't give out these metaphorical hugs very often either. Which, naturally, makes it more meaningful when you do receive one.

I wanted to find a fun way to keep fit, is what I told Johnathan and is what I tell other people who ask about my MMA training. It's kind of the truth because I love it. Only I didn't know that was going to be the case when I started. I wanted to learn how to defend myself in case I fail to find Three before my time's up.

So I started attending MMA classes in a local gym. They had me sparring in my very first session. Not full contact. Mostly just getting hit around the head with a pad while I tried to execute the technique I'd just been shown. I had never experienced anything like it. The shock and pain and disorientation were off the charts. I got mad at the girl I was training with for striking me so hard. I was pissed at the instructor for allowing me to be brutalized like that. I didn't say thanks when I left. I had no intention of going back. How dare they?

And then it . . . uh, *hit* me that I had never been hit before. Now I had. Albeit with a great big pad instead of a fist, yet I had found what it felt like. The shock of it was worse than the pain. It hurt a lot, sure. But I could handle it. I was disoriented. But I still managed to pull myself together. I realized that when it happened again, it wouldn't come as such a shock. Learning to get hit was just as important as learning how to hit.

I couldn't wait to get back and get hit again.

These days, I love to spar. Gloves, headgear, and full contact. I'm proud of my bruises. A bloody nose is a badge of honor. A cut to the cheek or eyebrow might as well be a trophy to show the world I'm not going down without a fight. I made Guill tap out once from a rear naked choke. Maybe my proudest moment.

After class, I go straight to the park to meet Yoshi, although she messages me to say she's going to be a few minutes late. It's a sunny day, so I decide to use the calisthenics equipment. I do some chin-ups on the horizontal bar. I have to leap straight up to reach the bar because I'm tiny. I couldn't do one a year ago, and now I can do twelve in a row. Struggling with motivation to get to the gym? Pretend someone's trying to kill you and you might need to fight or run for your life. Then see how you do.

After MMA earlier, I'm exhausted by nine reps and have to grind out the last three with some grunts and swinging.

I release the bar and drop into a crouch because I'm so fatigued. As I get my breath back, I gaze out across the park. People are walking. Some are jogging. Others are having picnics.

Then I see him.

A man sitting on a bench nearby.

He's about forty-five. He wears glasses. He's not tall, and he's not short. He's of medium build. A little soft at the waist. His hair is short. Like an outgrown buzz cut. He's clean-shaven.

I can't see his eye color at this distance. I guess brown. It fits with his skin tone and common brown hair. He's wearing blue jeans and a green synthetic jacket. A zip-up, open. A dark T-shirt underneath. He's reading a newspaper. Or is he?

Maybe it's just an act.

Maybe he's watching me.

When I have recovered a little, I stand and go over to my sports bag that's sitting on the grass nearby. I have my water bottle and towel and bag and phone and other things inside it, including a notebook and pen. My gun is in there too. I never go anywhere without it.

I withdraw my notebook and pen.

I look up at the bar and screw my face up in thought. I count on my fingers.

In the notebook, I write down the time, the location, and words that include *bench*, *newspaper*, *glasses*, *forties*, *shaved*, *short hair*, *average height*, *medium build*.

Then I drop the notebook and pen back into the bag and reach for my cell. I have an expensive phone. It's all about the camera, you see. I hold up the phone, smile, and pretend I'm messaging someone back. A guy, probably. Based on my grin.

In fact, I'm taking a snap of the guy on the bench. I'm taking many pics. I've developed a natural-looking pose when holding my phone. My arms are out a little farther than necessary. They're a little straighter. People tend to look down at their screens, which is no good if you want to take a photograph of someone in the distance. They also tend to hold up their phones in front of their faces when they're taking someone else's picture. That's the giveaway. So I've learned to keep my phone well below my face and to keep the screen close to vertical to maximize the distance. I have one thumb operating the camera while the other is moving about at random. Together it looks like I'm typing on the screen.

The guy on the bench gets up and leaves before I've finished my next set of chin-ups. I make a note of the time he goes, and tonight I'll file this Three away with all the others.

It's been over a week since I gave Yoshi the test tubes. For her, this is an unforgivably long wait, even though she had warned me the lab was especially busy and even though she's doing me a favor and I'd never expect her to work to a deadline. When she meets me at the calisthenic equipment, she's brought me some cupcakes by way of apology.

We take a seat on the same bench where the guy was sitting. I glance around to see if he's left anything behind and find nothing.

"Red velvet," she tells me with a glint in her eyes. "Cream cheese icing, dark chocolate pieces, and a special red velvet crumb."

I take them from her. "I'm going to drown in my own drool."

She's happy to hear this. "The cream cheese is vegan."

"No. Way."

She rolls her eyes and hands me the folder containing the DNA profile, report, and commentary. "I really am sorry it took so long."

"Then I'm guessing these cupcakes are going to be especially good as a result?"

Her insecurity comes back with a vengeance. "I hope so. Let me know if you don't like them, and I'll bake something different."

"Are you kidding me? They're going to be amazing. I'm assuming you've tried one already."

She looks sheepish and holds up some fingers.

"Four?"

"Don't," she says with her trademark light backhand to the arm. "It was a new recipe, so I had to make extra sure they were delish."

"Are these the last of them, or do you have some more waiting for you when you get home?"

She looks sheepish again.

"You deserve them," I tell her. "You're the best."

I wish there were some way I could adequately repay her for all she does. I've offered her money, drinks, (vegan) pizza, and plenty more. She's always a little offended that I would try to "pay for her friendship," as she puts it. I can't help it. The more she does for me, the guiltier I feel. I'm hoping to one day set her up with a nice girl I meet. So far, no dice.

I give her a hug and a kiss on the cheek. She turns her head in and kisses me on the cheek at the same time. Our lips almost touch. I don't think this is an accident.

We made out once. Maybe twice. Nothing serious, at least for me. I suspect Yoshi was hoping it would turn into something more, although she's never said anything to that end. It's not a new experience for her. She's told me many times about fumbles with curious, or drunk, straight women. They seldom go any further, and Yoshi has said more than once that her heart is "a minimum fifty percent scar tissue."

"Do you realize you stink?" She wrinkles her nose. "I hope it's your own BO and not soaked up from rolling around on the floor with sweaty men."

"You make it sound so sordid."

She shudders. "Because it is sordid in a revolting, horrible way. I don't know how you stand it. All that body hair and those awful dangly bits."

She pretends to vomit.

"You forget that girls train, too," I remind her.

Her eyes light up. "Tell me everything."

"They're more handsy than the guys. The men are terrified of grabbing you in the wrong place. It's kind of pathetic. Like, dude, we're here to fight. You gotta touch. The girls don't give a damn. My tits are black-and-blue sometimes."

She makes a throaty moan, and I laugh.

"Found anything more about the guy at the retirement home? Is he *the* Jefferson?"

"I don't know." I shrug, then shake my head. "I've done all I can remotely. I'm going to have to go there and speak with him in person."

"Is that safe?"

"He's not a suspect. I can't believe he's Three even if he's in amazing condition for his age. Unless he's planning on boring me to death."

"Hey, be nice. I love old people. They've lived lives we can't even imagine. My great-grandmother is over a hundred years old. When she was a kid, television hadn't been invented. That blows my mind. Literal living history. We should appreciate them more. They've already learned all the lessons we're going to struggle to find by ourselves. Be nice to them."

"I was joking."

I change the subject to something more mundane. I try to limit how much I talk about Three with Yoshi. I'm never quite sure if she believes me. I guess she must if she's helping me. But the willingness to help is not the same as belief, is it? If Yoshi were in trouble, I'd bend over backward to help her out, no questions asked. I guess it shouldn't matter really, and yet it still does. I want her to believe me because I don't want to feel so isolated.

Of course, she's told me she believes me, which is no reassurance. She could be lying, couldn't she? She could be telling me what I want to hear. All this time on constant alert means I have a hard time trusting people, which is not surprising given the position I'm in. I don't mean only men of a certain age either. The reluctance to trust is the fear of vulnerability, I know. We've discussed it at length in group, and being able to identify the root cause of my problem sadly doesn't mean I'm able to fix it. I think a part of me doesn't see the point in getting close to anyone. I can't be entirely honest with them, so why bother? No relationship can work if the other person has no idea who you really are, can it? And if you refuse to open up to someone, they're never going to be able to care about the real you, are they?

Plus, there's the other reason.

When I don't know for certain I'm going to be around for long, is it worth the investment? It's hard enough saying goodbye. I'm terrified of someone getting too close to me if they're only going to lose me one day soon. I know what losing people is like. I can't in good conscience put anyone else through that.

I have to do this alone.

FORTY

The man I meet is ancient. His skin is as thin as paper, translucent where it's not mottled with dark brown age spots. He has almost no hair aside from a few wisps above each ear. His eyes are gray and milky. The bags beneath them are large and puffy. He has enormous, gnarled hands. His fingernails look thick as talons. He seems both thin and frail, yet somehow still threatening. I'm not scared of *him*, I remind myself, it's that the aged frighten us with a glimpse into our future.

He takes his time to stand from the armchair, although he needs no assistance. He leans forward and braces with his hands on his knees. Like most people do when they stand up, just slower, more deliberate movements. Careful balancing and even more careful application of force.

I make the mistake of moving to assist. But he shoots me a look that stops me in my tracks, and I just have to stand there and watch him struggle until he's standing up. The effort puts a redness in his cheeks. Otherwise, he is so pale he is almost colorless.

Reading glasses hang from a beaded string around his neck. He wears a collared shirt and tie beneath a red sweater. His slacks are ironed and his shoes well polished. He sees me notice.

"When you have nowhere to go," he tells me, "you must always look your best."

I respond with a polite smile. I don't remember the last time I put any effort into my appearance. Maybe he's dropping me a hint.

We take a slow walk through the halls of the nursing home and into the gardens, which are bright with colorful flowers. I see some of the more able residents tending to them. Others sit on benches. It's both a beautiful space and a heartbreaking one. There are so many people yet so much loneliness.

"How was the drive?" he asks. "Not too long, I hope."

"It was fine. Nice scenery around here."

"I've never been a big fan of driving. It always seems to bring out the worst in people. When we're out for a walk, we don't shout at pedestrians walking too slowly, do we?"

"I guess not."

I'm not sure what to say. How to start. I'm thinking about Yoshi's urge for caution. The old man gives me a look of interest, or maybe suspicion.

"How do I know you again? I'm afraid I'm not so good with faces, and the staff were a little imprecise with the details."

"That's because I was deliberately vague with them," I admit.

He looks at me with interest. "I don't know you, do I?"

"You don't. But I'm hoping you can help me."

"How might I help you exactly?"

"Did you once live next door to a couple named Steve and Jenny?" I'm not sure if I see recognition in his eyes or merely interest in why I'm asking. "They had two daughters, Maya and—"

"Amy," he finishes.

I nod, swallowing hard. He *is* Jefferson.

"They died," I continue. "All of them."

"It was very sad. So much misfortune happening to a single family. They were all so lovely."

"You remember them well?"

"The eldest girl, not so much. We didn't really speak to one another beyond a good morning. I spoke to her parents a lot. We were not exactly friends, but we were friendly."

"Amy?"

"When she was young, she was very talkative. She would help me in the garden, offer to clean my car. Things like that. Then she was a teenager, and you know how teenagers are to their seniors. I didn't take it personally."

"She wrote about you," I tell him. "In her journal."

"That's nice."

"She came back to the house once, and you had tea with her in your kitchen. Do you remember that?"

He nods, sighs. "I upset her. I didn't mean to, and yet . . ."

He can't finish.

"You suggested her parents might not have killed themselves."

"It was just so unlike them. They loved Amy so much and were so worried about her that I can't believe they would leave her alone."

"She was never the same after Maya died."

"It was all those pills she was taking," Jefferson tells me. "They made her worse, not better."

"Amy thought she was doomed," I explain. "She called it the rule of three. Her sister died, then her parents, so she would be next. Like fate." He listens, intrigued and unnerved. "But I think someone murdered her and murdered her family. I think he made it look like her parents committed suicide."

"But how?"

"I don't know for sure. I think it's possible someone forced them to do it. If he had a gun, if he said he would kill Amy if they didn't . . . As you just said, they were too worried about her to leave her alone."

"My God," he breathes.

"Maybe that same person caused Maya to crash her car, and maybe he gave Amy some kind of drug that killed her. When she took so many others, it might not have shown up in her system. I'm trying to find him, Jefferson. I think he killed another girl, too, as well as her family before her. Every three years he kills. I think he killed my sister and my parents, too, and now I think he wants to kill me."

Jefferson doesn't know how to respond. He looks shaky and takes a seat at the nearest bench. He falls into it more than sits. I didn't think it was possible, but he seems paler. His gaze is far away. I'm not sure if there are tears in his eyes or not.

"I'm hoping you can help me," I continue. "I'm trying to find the killer. I don't have much time left . . . Anything you can tell me, anything at all, will help. I think he was in Amy's life somehow. I think she might have met him. At the very least, I think he was there, watching her, learning about her and her family beforehand. I think he was in Ila's too. He's in mine, or at least will be. I want to be ready for him. I want to see him coming."

"I . . . I don't know what I can tell you. It was over twenty years ago. No one treated those deaths as suspicious. I'm sorry, I don't think I can be of any help."

"You asked Amy if she thought it really was suicide," I say, the words from her journal clear in my mind. "What did you mean by that?"

"I'm not sure I remember."

He looks away as he says this, and I wonder if he's holding something back. I decide not to press him on it just yet. I think about what Yoshi told me about being nice. Besides, I don't want to go too heavy too fast and cause him to shut down.

"Can you tell me your old address at least? That would really help me. I've been looking into this for a long time and don't have some of the most basic facts."

He's nodding along. "Do you have a pen?"

I take out my phone and open up an app, writing down the address he gives me for the house he used to live in, and beside it, Amy's old house: the house in which her parents committed suicide.

"Thank you," I say. "Thank you so much." I'm thinking of all the possible lines of inquiry that were out of reach for me before. Now I have something concrete to build upon. My heart is racing with excitement. "This could change everything."

He's looking at a bee flying from flower to flower. He seems lost in thought, and I'm not sure he's still paying attention until I see he's fumbling to take out a handkerchief to wipe his eyes. They're red and teary. He tries to hide this show of emotion.

I pretend I don't notice and say, "Would you like a glass of water?" as an excuse to give him a moment.

He nods. "Thank you, I would."

The look he gives me makes me think he has something else to tell me, so I hurry as I head back into the nursing home to fix Jefferson a drink. We passed several water dispensers on the way from his room to the gardens, so it doesn't take me long before I'm tugging on the little valve and a plastic cup is rapidly filling with water. I'm willing the cup to fill even faster because I'm eager to get back and find out what he might have remembered in case it slips his mind in the interval.

When the cup is at maybe two-thirds capacity, I decide that's good enough, release the valve, spin around, and almost spill the water all over myself because there's an old lady standing right in front of me.

She's barefoot, short, and wizened, with frizzy white hair exploding out of her head in every direction. Surrounded by heavily sagging, wrinkled skin are the greenest eyes I've ever seen.

I must have been distracted in my hurry and didn't hear her padding up behind me.

After I control my surprise as well as the cup of water, I say, "Excuse me," and try to move past.

"He's mean."

"I'm sorry, what?"

She hasn't yet blinked. "The man you're speaking with in the garden. He's mean. You need to be careful."

I think I've misheard her at first. "Jefferson? Seems harmless to me."

"That's what he wants you to think," she insists, eyes wide and staring. "But he's mean. He's cruel if he thinks no one is watching."

"Cruel? You're kidding. In what way?"

"He takes things he knows you like, and then he laughs when you can't find them."

This doesn't seem cruel to me until I think of vulnerable people, perhaps with dementia or Alzheimer's, growing frustrated and upset looking for precious belongings deliberately hidden from them.

"That's pretty shitty if it's true," I tell her. "I'll keep my bag close, thanks."

She's not done. "He locks us up too."

"He . . . locks you up? How?"

"He steals keys when they're not looking." I imagine she's referring to the staff. "If you don't watch out, he'll lock you in your room. You can't get out. You have to ring the buzzer for help, but he unlocks it before they arrive. Then they think you're senile, and no one believes you when he takes your things or locks you in a cupboard."

Something stirs in my mind, like a memory I know is there, and yet I can't quite make it whole. "He locks you in cupboards?"

She opens her mouth to answer, or perhaps say more, only she's aware of a member of the staff nearing, and locks her lips closed, pinching them between thumb and index finger in case they might open without permission and betray her.

A robust woman with a big smile says, "There you are, Priscilla." She looks down. "Did you forget to put on your slippers again?"

"They're stolen."

"Is that so?" Her tone is skeptical. "I hope you haven't been accusing this young lady of taking them."

"No, no, she hasn't," I'm quick to say, feeling the need to defend Priscilla's integrity.

The woman places a gentle palm on Priscilla's back. "Come on," she says with a heavy sigh. "I'll help you look for those slippers of yours."

"We won't find them."

"I'm sure they're right where they're supposed to be."

I receive a knowing look from the member of the staff, like she's telling me to dismiss what Priscilla is saying because she's old and confused.

"Told you," Priscilla says to me as she's guided away.

For a moment, I'm tempted to say something, to intervene, but what can I realistically do? Besides, if Jefferson is playing cruel tricks on the other residents, then I'm going to give him a piece of my mind directly. When I return to the bench where he's sitting, ready to do just that, there's another man next to him. He's a lot younger, and there's a vague similarity in their facial features. Same nose. Same chin.

"Eve," Jefferson says to me. "This is my grandson, Nathan."

"Why are you upsetting my grandpa?"

I stumble over my words as I hand Jefferson his water. "I . . . uh . . . no, I'm . . . I didn't . . . I'm sorry. I wasn't trying to upset him."

Jefferson says, "We were just talking," but Nathan isn't having it.

He stands up from the bench and positions himself between Jefferson and me. Nathan is a big guy, early thirties, with a short dark beard flecked with gray. His hair is receding, and up close, I can see he has the same eyes as his grandfather, albeit without the same milkiness to them.

"I think you should go," he tells me.

I glance between him and Jefferson, hoping for a sign that Jefferson wants me to stay.

Nathan says, "What are you even doing here in the first place?"

"I just wanted to talk to your grandfather."

"Why? About what?"

"Some people he used to know."

Nathan gives a mocking smile. "He's ninety years old. He's known a lot of people."

Jefferson reaches out to him. "It's okay. It's—"

"No," Nathan interrupts, coming closer into my personal space, index finger extended and stabbing the air as makes his point. "It's not okay for a complete stranger to show up and start interrogating an old man."

I've had enough of this douche. "You know what's also not okay? Him hiding the belongings of other residents and locking them in their rooms."

Nathan is momentarily shocked into silence, finger paused in space. I'm not finished, however.

"What's also not okay is some guy getting all in my personal space and giving me shit for no reason. So, ease off or I'll take that finger and snap it in two."

He's taken aback. He wasn't expecting a young woman half his size to stand her ground. But I've sparred enough not to be intimidated by some guy like Nathan.

"Uh . . . you don't get to tell me what to do. No one asked you to come here. No one wants you to stay. When it comes to my grandpa's well-being, what I say goes."

"Nathan," Jefferson says in a soft tone. "She mentioned Ila."

"Hold on," I say. "You knew Ila as well as Amy?"

Nathan is confused. "Wait, what? You knew Ila too? You couldn't have. You're what, twenty? You would have been just a kid back when I dated her."

I'm open-mouthed. I take a step back, looking at him with new eyes. It takes me a long, torturous moment before I can speak.

"You're Nate."

"It's actually Nathaniel," he corrects. "I go by Nathan these days."

"You were Ila's boyfriend in college."

He steps forward, closing the distance I created. Despite Jefferson and the other residents in the garden, I feel alone and vulnerable.

"So? What's that to you? Why do you keep talking about Ila?"

I don't answer because I can't answer because I'm shaking my head and walking backward, scared and shocked and overwhelmed. Nathan watches me go. Jefferson watches me go.

This isn't part of my plan. I don't know what this means.

I turn.

I run.

FORTY-ONE

I'm distracted in group. I barely hear Stephanie or Alejandro or Sal or anyone else talking. Their voices are quiet compared to those of Jefferson and Nate repeating inside my mind. I realize I'm pushing my thumbnail hard into my bottom lip, seeking stress relief through pain. Sal is sitting next to me and nudges my knee with his knee.

Are you okay? he mouths, and I nod.

I see Stephanie notices this silent exchange as well as my general lack of interaction as she addresses the group:

"Think of it like this," she's saying. "Everything we do, and say, services a need. When we give advice, it could be because we want to help that person, and it could be because we need to feel like we have grown and understood our mistakes. When we ask a question, we're interested in the answer, but why do we want that answer? In this group, I want everyone to consider themselves because in doing so, you consider the other people here. The more we can relate to one another in here, the better we will understand the people out there." She points to the door. "And then we understand ourselves even better."

In a way, that's what I'm trying to do. I'm trying to understand. I wanted to find connections between the journals beyond Elizabeth, but I didn't expect Ila's boyfriend to be the grandson of Amy's next-door neighbor. One of the grandsons, I mean. Amy wrote that her sister had a crush on one of those boys. Nate would have been too young, so that crush was on the elder boy. *Maya had the hots for one of the boys next door, Jefferson's grandkids, only he was at* *college and not interested in someone still in high school.* In Ila's journal, she mentions that Nate's brother deals drugs. Nate even mentions his *big bro* might have been the one who told him about the rule of three. In both journals, he's mentioned but not encountered. He has no name.

Alejandro, sitting on the other side of me, whispers, "Your lip is bleeding."

"MMA," I whisper back.

It's not, though. I used to have this awful habit of scratching at and picking my lips. I couldn't stop. It's an endless cycle because the skin on your lips doesn't scab in the same way as normal skin. The skin on your lips will grow back hard over the piece you've picked away. Which makes you want to pick at it more. I'll bite down on it, too, where it's sore. There's a strange pleasure in the pain. I can bite down just hard enough to get the exact right amount. It's addictively satisfying. I can give myself a steady, controlled increase in that pain. It feels good all the way up to the point it doesn't. And then, even when it no longer feels good, when it is actually painful, there's like a crescendo of pain, an orgasm if you will, then I stop biting down and it's over, and there is nothing left but incredible relief.

I used to dream of scratching off my lips, one layer of skin at a time until my mouth was nothing but a rimless oval opening in my face.

Alejandro hands me a tissue, and I hold it to my bottom lip.

"You can keep it," he whispers with a smile. "My treat."

I don't know when I first started doing this. Almost certainly in those awkward teen years. Probably one winter when my lips were dry and chapped. Probably when I was super stressed about Mom and Dad arguing and scratching and picking and biting my lip relieved that stress because it distracted me from it. And because it worked, I kept on doing it throughout all those horrible years, and now it's back.

I thought I was handling the whole hunted-by-a-serial-killer thing pretty well. Guess not.

Stephanie glances at the clock, then says, "That's about all we have time for, I'm afraid. But before you go, I want you to remember that sometimes it's easy to forget that who we are comes with practice. Being the best version of yourself is never a given. Think of it like learning a new language. It's a skill that takes time to master. If no one taught us, we have to teach ourselves. And when we're used to being a lesser version of ourselves, it can seem an impossible mountain to climb to be any better. We don't climb the mountain because we're afraid of falling. So let's keep on practicing in here. This group is the climbing wall, and while you climb, everyone else is holding the safety ropes." She stands to signify the session is over, using her walking stick as a support, and smiles. "Even if you fall, the rest of us are going to make sure you land softly."

I'm thinking about Nate's brother as I head to the exit. If he was college-age when Maya liked him, then he would probably be in his mid-forties at least by now.

Why didn't Ila mention that Nate is Jefferson's grandson? She must not have found that out. I can't quite work out how long she was with Nate and there is no reference to the rest of his family, so she must not have met any of them.

As I push through the exit, I see Johnathan under an awning. The glow from his cigarette illuminates his features with an uplight that turns the smile he makes when he sees me into a devilish grin.

He takes one last pull and throws the cigarette away to join the other stubs. "I thought about what you said last week. About us not fraternizing with members of the group. Given the choice, I think I'd rather fraternize."

"You don't go to a group unless you need it. In the grand old scheme of things, a kiss ranks about here on the importance scale." I bend down and hold my hand out horizontally near my ankle. "While personal growth, mental health, and recovery"—I stand straight and extend my hand far above my head—"rank somewhere around here." I stretch up onto my tiptoes for extra emphasis. "Capeesh?"

"You make a compelling point," he says in return. "And I figured you might do exactly that." He smiles, a little smug. "Which is why I've joined another group." He points off into the distance. There's nothing over there, but that's what people do. "A Presbyterian church. It's a great little place. Really nice people. They run a surprisingly extensive range of community programs. I've been to a couple already to test them out. Slightly different approach, but I don't think that's any kind of bad thing. Anyway, there's no impropriety now. We go to different groups. We can be honest with different strangers." He smiles. "Wanna get a drink? Doesn't have to be the same bar. Or we can take a walk. It's a nice night. See where it takes us."

"I'm not in the mood."

"Sure, sure. Wanna do it tomorrow night instead? Later in the week? I'm going to this thing on Friday. An open-mic . . . event. But not comedy. Well, some comedy. It's like a free-for-all. People do whatever they want. Jokes, poetry, a reading . . . I'll be honest, it's kind of a lottery. One guy might make your cheeks hurt you laugh so much, the next then bores you to tears by reading from their achingly serious unpublished novel. But that's kind of the fun of it. What do you think? We could—"

I stop him. "Listen. It was just a kiss. No biggie. Let's not make it into a whole thing. Okay? Look, I gotta make a move. Have a nice life."

He's hurt, and he can see I'm a completely different person from the one he had beers with, the one he kissed a week or so ago. "What's really going on?"

I tell him the truth. "You're too young for me."

"Too young? You told me last time I was old enough to be your dad."

"Let me guess: the only thing next to your sink is your toothbrush. Skincare doesn't make you less of a man. It just means you don't look forty when you're in fact thirty-three."

He's offended now as well as confused and hurt. "Wait, what? How do you know I'm thirty-three? I didn't tell you that."

"You didn't have to. I swabbed my lips after we kissed to get your skin cells and then had my biochemist friend extract the DNA so I could feed the information into an online ancestry checker. Once I'd done that, finding out the rest was easy."

"What? Why? Why would you do that? You're joking, right? You must be joking."

"I'm serious as it gets," I tell him. "I know all about you. I know your age, I know where you were born, I know you were a kid on the far side of the country when a certain car crashed twenty years ago. I know you couldn't have murdered Ila because you weren't even on the same continent when it happened."

"Of course I haven't murdered her. Or anyone. Who is she, anyway? What is this? I . . . I don't understand."

"You're not supposed to," I explain. "But I wish you did."

"You wish I'd killed this Ila?"

"That's literally what I've just said. Would have made my life a hell of a lot simpler."

His eyes are wide and his mouth is open, and his forehead is all creased up. He pushes fingers through his hair. Confused. Hurt. Angry.

"I don't understand. I—"

He reaches out to put his hand on me as I start to walk. I see it coming and pivot into a fighting stance, grabbing his outstretched wrist and wrenching him off-balance.

He stumbles forward, all his weight on his front foot, and can't correct himself before he's doubled over and I've taken hold of his hand too and rotated his whole arm into a vicious lock. Just like I've trained for a thousand times.

It takes all my willpower not to then drive my knee into his face. Guill would be horrified to find I don't follow through as he always teaches.

"*Don't ever touch me, okay?*" I release him with a shove, and he takes a few backward steps before he's regained his balance. "I'm not interested."

He rubs at his wrist. "Thanks for making that absolutely clear."

"I tried letting you down gently and you didn't bite. Next time: take the hint."

Johnathan nods, finally accepting reality. He points toward the church. "You know what? I'm glad I quit the group because it obviously isn't doing you any good. You don't need therapy, you need to be locked up."

It makes him feel better to get in a final blow, and I can admit that it's a pretty good jab. He might even be right. I could throw a comeback his way . . . remind him he's trying to pick up someone over a decade younger, or whatever. But I don't. I let him leave with the last word. He needs it more than me.

I feel bad—I do kind of like him—and yet I have to keep myself free and single, just in case that's the game Three wants to play. Maybe Johnathan would be useful to have around from a protective perspective, but then there's no chance for Three to try to slide into my life as a potential suitor. I want to leave opportunities open to Three that I can control. I don't want to leave him with no other option but to keep at a distance. The closer he is to me, the more chance I have of spotting him.

I remember something, only I'm not yet sure what. I can hear Johnathan's parting words: *you need to be locked up* . . . Locked up.

I think of the old lady with the greenest eyes and our conversation by the water cooler. She told me about Jefferson locking residents in their rooms or in cupboards. At the time, it sparked a memory too.

From the journals, I know it. I get on my phone and open up the digital file. I scroll back and forth as I scan pages, first looking through for mentions of Nate to see if he's the reason. Nothing. I go back to the start, to Amy and her conversation with Jefferson at his home.

There it is.

Amy notices the door to the basement is locked from the outside with a sliding bolt. Son of a bitch.

Was Jefferson locking people up almost twenty years ago? And if so, who? Nate?

Or Nate's brother?

FORTY-TWO

In a way, Amy's old house is a lot like mine. They're both on quiet streets in quiet parts of quiet suburbs. It's a handsome building, two stories of pale gray bricks and a roof of dark shingles. The lawn is immaculate. So green it almost glows. Until I've crossed the street, I can't be sure it's real.

Jefferson's old house is pretty much the same except the grass is overgrown and there's a For Sale sign outside. I get a sense of déjà vu looking at the sign, picturing Amy when she visited her own home that hadn't sold. I wonder why this house isn't selling. No one hung themselves in the garage like next door. At least, as far as I know.

I'm coming, Three. You had better believe it.

The young man on the lawn of Amy's old house looks my way. He's playing with a little girl who is sitting on the grass with her fat little belly out for all to see. She's wearing a yellow hat to keep the sun from her face. There isn't any sun to speak of, but he's a parent.

I don't look like any kind of threat. I'm a slight, young woman. He still watches me, though. Not in a direct way. He's not eyeballing me or anything. He's playing with his little girl, making faces for her and peekaboos, and she loves every second of it. Every now and again, his eyes flick my way.

He knows I don't belong here.

I walk along the opposite pavement at a slow pace, dragging each step so I can look at the house for longer. By the time I've stopped and summoned the courage to approach, the young father is tense.

He stands to his full height, which is not exactly tall, yet the message is inarguable. He steps forward, putting himself between his child and me.

Maybe he worries I'll try to take her.

I raise my hands to show I come in peace. It doesn't help. I'm too keen to prove I'm not the kidnapper he fears, and I thrust my hands up far too fast.

He flinches.

"*I'm sorry, I'm sorry,*" I blurt out. "It's chill, I'm chill."

He says nothing in return. He's full of protective suspicion and confusion.

"I was hoping to have a chat."

"What about?"

His voice is deadpan.

"Your neighbor."

He glances at the For Sale sign next door. "He doesn't live here any longer."

"Yeah, I know that. I've already spoken to Jefferson in the care home."

He scratches his head. "Then I don't understand."

"I guess I didn't just mean Jefferson. I'm curious about his grandkids too. Did they ever visit while you've been living here?"

"I'm not sure that's any of your business."

I'm chewing at my lip as I'm trying to carefully tread closer. I glance past him, looking over his immaculate lawn and at the house beyond.

He sees this look. He understands now.

"I saw you earlier today, didn't I?" he asks me, and I'm not sure what to say. "You didn't come this close that time. You just stood on the opposite side of the street and stared. I saw you from the window." I'm silent. I look down. "It's creepy. It's not okay."

"I'm sorry, it's just that—"

"Do I need to get a restraining order?"

"What? A restraining . . . No, no. Of course you don't. I'm not dangerous. I'm not a stalker. I only want some information. I—"

"The answer is no."

"Excuse me?"

"Anything you want to ask me," he explains, the deadpan tone enlivening with building anger, "the answer is no."

"You don't know what I'm going to ask."

"Doesn't matter. The answer is no." He shuffles backward until he's next to his child, whom he scoops up into his arms. "Don't come back here."

"Please," I say. "It's important."

"Are you writing an article about it?"

"About what?"

"About what happened here twenty years ago. Ah, no, I suppose it's a podcast. You want to go viral digging up the pain of others, of course. You people are vermin, you know that?"

"Please." I'm begging now. "It's not like that. I swear. I need your help. Please, I just need information."

He's backing away from me. Turning around.

I see a shape in the shadows of the open front door.

"I'm in danger," I call to his back. "Please."

He's speeding up to a fast walk. The door opens as he nears it. A woman with dark hair stands looking out at him, at her baby, at me. She's confused. Unnerved.

In seconds he's going to join her and be gone.

"*Please*," I yell at him. "I need your help."

"I already told you," he calls back without looking my way. "The answer is no."

I watch the front door slam shut.

I'm so distraught I almost collapse to my knees. I consider unleashing my disappointment as rage and shouting something crude. I don't. Had our roles been reversed, I'm sure I would have acted the same.

I walk away, head down and eyes on the pavement until I notice there's a car parked along the curb farther down the street. A man is in the driver's seat, facing my way, although I cannot see his face. He's just a silhouette. The car is gray and anonymous. I look down at the license and can't read it. It's smeared with mud. The bumper isn't.

I slow. I can feel my heart hammering. I remind myself I still have time. I'm not going to die today. It's too early. So this is just a man in a car with a dirty plate. My heart doesn't listen to me. It's still thumping hard, still afraid.

Just because it's not my time to die right now doesn't mean the guy in the car isn't Three, does it?

Breathing hard, I'm a little slow off the mark to reach for my phone as I walk toward the car and the figure behind the wheel. My hands are shaking and my fingers have no dexterity. I struggle to enter my passcode and open up the camera app.

The car is turning around to drive away by the time I have it zoomed in and lined up in the center of the screen. Walking fast, I snap a burst of photographs of the rear before the car has gone.

Breathing even harder, heart pounding even harder, I thumb through the pictures, dismissing the many that are blurred or missing the license plate altogether. I find a clear shot of the back of the vehicle, but the plate is unreadable. Too dirty and too pixelated. I zoom in to see if it helps, and it only makes it worse as the pixelation becomes more extreme and all I see are blurs where letters and numbers should be instead. Why does it always seem so easy in the movies?

Frustrating, but it's not why I'm here.

I step off the pavement and onto the driveway of Jefferson's old house. The lawn is overgrown and dotted with weeds. The trees framing the lawn have become so untamed and wild they are almost threatening. The For Sale sign has been stuck in the ground so long it might now be alive, having grown roots, becoming one with the earth on which this house sits. The wind blows harder. I hear it whistling in a low monotone.

I don't know if the guy next door is watching me. I don't care if he is, because he's too young by far to be Three.

Jefferson's house seems to swell and grow as I near. The walls rear up, and windows expand. Those windows are unblinking in their stares. I feel small. I feel afraid.

The trees bend in the wind, branches rattling above me, leaves chanting in a chorus of rustling. Dead leaves follow me along the driveway. They swirl around my ankles as if trying to surround and ensnare me.

A branch groans high above, and I peer upward into the black mass of leaves shifting and rippling as a single, living entity. I back away, the wind now in my face, debris peppering me, aiming for my eyes.

A shingle from the roof explodes on the ground where I had been standing a second before.

Hand on my chest, I catch my breath.

Undeterred, I reach Jefferson's front door, which has faded and cracked paint. I notice the overgrown lawn again. I see the leaves strewn across the property, dancing in the wind. I'm thinking no one's home and hasn't been home for a long time. I ring the doorbell just in case.

Not that I really expect anyone to let me inside to take a look at the basement. I don't know how I'd even ask without them calling the police.

When the doorbell goes unanswered and I hear nothing from inside, I take a walk. There's no gate blocking the way between the garage and the fence, so I circle the house. I'm careful to stay on a strip of grass and avoid the gravel path to stay quiet. Behind the garage, I come to a door to the kitchen. It has transparent glass panels that I cup my hands to peer through.

It's hard to see into the unlit interior with any clarity, but the kitchen table is obvious enough. Some eighteen years ago Amy sat there or at a table just like it. I imagine where she might have sat and where she might have glanced. I reposition myself to get different angles, to see different parts of the space, until I see a closed door along one interior wall. It's painted in a dark color, although in the gloom, it could be any shade. I can't see enough to tell if there's a bolt or not.

The rear garden is as overgrown as the front. I pay it little attention as I look for small windows around ground level. Leaves and other detritus have blown against the house and collected there, so I have to bend down and sweep them aside with my palm.

They're dry as ash and disintegrate, becoming swirling spirals of dust in the wind.

A few swipes are all it takes before I see glass. I lower myself to my knees to clear away all the leaves and twigs until the entire window is revealed. It's not much bigger than a mailbox, the glass green and brown with grime. I use the sleeve of my jacket to rub it clean.

Lying on my belly, I get low enough to look through the window and into the basement beyond.

There are boxes and storage shelving. I see glimpses of dust sheets and maybe a ladder. It's very dark, and I can't get an angle that shows me anything. Anything that happened here was a long time ago. And that's if Jefferson actually locked anyone up in here in the first place. Maybe there's nothing worth seeing. Maybe this is just a basement.

Only I'm leaving nothing to chance.

I find a stone. One that fills my palm. I clutch it hard as I approach the kitchen door. I see no signs of an alarm system, so I focus on one of the panes of glass just above the door handle.

I'm hesitant because I'm about to commit a crime. I have to tell myself what I'm doing is right, that I have to do what I must to survive. Lestrange didn't want to help, so what am I supposed to do if the law doesn't care what happens to me?

I take a deep breath as I pull back my hand, ready to throw it through the glass.

Only then do I realize I'm not alone.

"I don't think that's something you really want to do, is it?"

FORTY-THREE

The voice is soft, the question asked with care and thought so as not to startle or frighten. And I don't.

I turn. It's the woman from Amy's old home. The wife I saw in the doorway. Although she must have left the baby with the father. She's come around the side of the house as I had just done. Her expression is full of concern for me instead of what I'm doing.

"What's your name?" she asks in her soft voice.

"I'm . . . I'm Eve."

"That's a pretty name," she says. "I'm Aubrielle."

"No, *that's* a pretty name."

"Please call me Aubrey."

"Only if you call me Eve."

She steps a little closer in a deliberate and obvious move, like I'm a deer that might bolt if she doesn't. "What are you doing here, Eve?"

I look at the door and the rock in my palm. "Becoming a criminal."

"At this precise moment you've done nothing wrong," she says. "Besides trespassing, I mean."

"I was going to break into this house."

She smiles politely. "I can see that. But why?"

"It's a long story."

"I'm sure. Why were you at my house, Eve? You told my husband you were in danger. Are you?"

I toss the stone away. "You could say that."

"Are you okay?" she asks.

"No," I say, almost laughing. "I'm the farthest thing from okay."

"What's wrong? Why are you in danger?"

"I can't tell you why, Aubrey. I mean, I can. You won't believe me. You'll think I'm crazy. It'll take forever to explain why I came to your house, why I was about to break into this one, and you won't believe a single thing I say." I push my palms against my forehead to relieve some of the tension. "That's the most maddening part. It doesn't matter what I know. No one else believes it."

"Why don't you try me?"

"How come you came out?" I ask her. "Hubby must have told you not to."

"He doesn't tell me what I can or can't do."

"He didn't want you to come to me, though."

She nods. Smiles a little. "You're right. You scared him."

"How? I'm tiny."

"He doesn't like to think about what happened in our home, however long ago it was. Even if that's the only reason we could afford to buy it when we did. He doesn't want our daughter to know. He's terrified of the day she comes home crying from school because some little shit told her all the gory details."

"I get that. I'm sorry. I was trying to take a meandering route to the truth and screwed it up. I'm not very good at this kind of thing."

"What kind of thing?"

"Good question. I'm not fully sure. I guess I mean I'm not very good at playing detective."

"You're not making a podcast?"

"God, no. I don't know why your husband said that. I don't even listen to them. Aren't they just like a documentary made without a camera? What's the point?"

"Are you a distant relation, then, or something?"

"Okay, I'll try to give you the shortest possible version." I take a deep breath. "I think the people who died in your house all those years ago are connected to other people who've died over the years since. People who include my own family."

"I'm very sorry for your loss."

"Me too."

"When you say the deaths are connected . . . ?"

"I think they were all murdered by the same person. I think he spends a long time, like three years long, working out ways to make the murders seem like accidents, suicides, or natural causes. He kills a whole family. Then moves on to the next to do it all again. I think the people who lived in your house were the first victims."

Her brow furrows and her mouth opens, and I cut her off first.

"As I said, it's going to take forever to explain why I think all that. But I do. I absolutely, one hundred percent believe it. The cops don't. No one else does. It's just me. I'm trying to find out who killed all those people because he's still out there, and if I don't find him in time then I'm going to be his next victim."

She absorbs this for a moment, and I can see she has a thousand and more questions to ask, but she stops herself. She takes a breath and says, "What do you need from me?"

I'm so thankful I could cry. I leap at her and hug her. She returns it after a few seconds.

When I step back, I say, "You believe me?"

"No," she says, and I'm confused, until she adds, "but I can see that you believe it and that's enough for me. When we're scared we don't always make the best choices." She glances at the glass I was about to break. "And I can see you're scared."

"So you're not going to call the cops on me?"

"If you tell me what you being scared has to do with my neighbor's house, then I think we'll let the police deal with actual criminals."

"Good enough for me. The old guy who used to live here, Jefferson, is involved. Not literally in the murders, because he's ancient, but he knew the family who died. One of his grandsons dated another of the victims."

"Jefferson's not lived here for years. I miss him. Lovely man."

"I'm not fully sure about that," I say in a careful tone. "That was kind of why I wanted to take a look inside."

"As I said, he moved out. Jefferson kept falling over, sadly. The family are asking a high price for the house and it needs a lot of work, which is why I believe it hasn't sold. It's sat like this for a long time, so I don't see how looking around inside would help you."

"If it's been empty all this time, then any clues might be untouched."

Her eyebrows arch. "Clues? Like what?"

"I'll know them if I see them."

She gives me a look like she's debating something. There's some question she's trying to answer. Perhaps whether I'm insane.

Jury's still out on that one.

"Okay," she says with a nod, answering her question in the affirmative.

"Okay, what?" I ask, curious.

She's wearing jeans and reaches to a hip pocket. Producing a set of keys, she selects the one she needs and then opens up the kitchen door I had been prepared to enter through illegally.

"I have a spare," she explains. "I said I'd keep an eye on the place for the family. Well, for Jefferson." She gestures for me to enter. "Let's see if you know those clues when you see them."

I smile at her, as grateful as I am surprised by this uncommon kindness, and step into Jefferson's house.

It's a surreal experience to stand inside his kitchen. The room is neat and clean, almost unnaturally so. Like a showroom.

Aubrey notices my expression. "When Jefferson moved out, they packed up most of his belongings. Only left out a few bits so it wasn't so stark and empty for potential buyers."

I'm already approaching the basement door.

Inside now, I see that it's a dark green color. I see no bolt on the outside, but I see holes in the wood of the door and in the frame where a bolt used to be screwed in place. I run my thumb over the holes. They're smooth instead of rough against my skin, covered in paint.

I ask, "Do you know when the lock was removed?"

"I couldn't tell you. I'm not sure if I ever saw one."

"Are all Jefferson's things in the basement now?"

"Far as I know."

Beyond the door, there's a set of wooden stairs leading down. I descend a few steps and pull the string hanging from the ceiling to turn on the light. Even before my feet are on the basement floor I can tell it's an entirely different space than it would have been back then. It's so full of boxes and stored belongings that any semblance of what it once looked like has long gone. There's barely enough room to move about, let alone see or find anything noteworthy.

What am I expecting to find here?

I don't actually know. I'm here on instinct alone and I'm at a loss. Nothing in the basement suggests anyone was ever locked down here. I lift a lid off one of the storage boxes, finding ornaments secured with bubble wrap. I can just make out the face of a carriage clock through the plastic. There are dozens of boxes like this one. It would take weeks to go through everything even if I thought it would help, and I don't have that kind of time to spare.

"Do you want any help?" Aubrey calls down from the top of the stairs.

"Thanks, but no," I say as I run my fingertips across the frame of a painting lying on a shelf. "I'm done."

"Already?"

I head back up the stairs toward her. "This is a waste of time. Sorry for being a nuisance." I sigh, frustrated and resigned. "It's not down there. It's just boxes."

"What's not down there?"

"The smoking gun."

"Oh," she says.

"I was hoping I'd find something to confirm Jefferson locked someone up."

She's curious and uncomfortable with the thought. "Whyever would he do that?"

"Great question," I answer. "I have no idea. But I thought it might be one of his grandkids."

"Nathan?"

"No, the older one. Although Nathan is such a tool, I actually hope he was locked down there too."

She has no idea how to respond. I'm creeping her out.

"What I mean," I say, trying again, "is that Nathan is just too young to fit my profile. I'm talking about his older brother. Maybe Jefferson used to lock him in the basement."

"I know he was something of a problem child, but why would he lock him up in the basement?"

"Because Jefferson is an abuser who enjoys controlling people."

"I don't believe that for a second."

"It's only one theory," I admit. "Maybe it wasn't deliberate abuse, and it was the only way to control the grandson when he became *too* much of a problem child. Maybe that happened a lot for the same reason. Maybe his grandson was traumatized. Maybe that grandson is the one-in-a-hundred person who doesn't have proper functioning in the anterior insula, anterior midcingulate cortex, somatosensory cortex, or right amygdala."

Her eyes widen. "Excuse me?"

"They're the parts of the brain where we experience empathy," I explain. "The types of people who lack proper functioning there are usually called psychopaths. Who are mostly harmless, thankfully, but if you lack empathy and are also abused when you're young, then there's a chance when you grow up you become a—"

"Serial killer." Aubrey's face is ashen.

"I was going to say someone who enjoys hurting people, but yeah. I know this is a lot to take in. I'm no expert on psychopaths, although I've done a lot of research. I'm almost certainly wrong with this theory, but I need to know for sure. I need to find the other grandson. Anything you know about him will be a great help. You've helped me plenty already, obviously, so I appreciate this is asking a lot."

She's still processing what I've told her and her mouth hangs open for a few seconds before she says, "I haven't even seen Chris for several years now. Not since before Jefferson went to the nursing home."

"Chris?" I stare at her lips, first in curiosity, then anticipation. "Is that short for Christian by any chance?"

"That's how Jefferson referred to him, although he introduced himself as Chris to me. Aside from a few minutes' worth of small talk, I've never had a conversation with him, so I don't think I can offer any great insights. "

I think of Amy on the bus into town and a young man named Christian and the words she wrote about him. *Why did I tell you about Christian? It's inconsequential now, but important later.*

She never had the chance to write why she mentioned him, why it was important. But then Elizabeth told Ila that Christian didn't exist. If he did, then why didn't Amy include the fact he happened to be her next-door neighbor's grandson?

Ah, maybe she didn't realize it on the bus. Perhaps she worked it out only at a later point.

"Poor Jefferson," she continues. "Such a lovely old man. I know you don't really believe it, but I do. Broke his heart to talk about how his grandson turned out."

"Turned out?"

She purses his lips. "He's a real bad apple."

I swallow. I say, "Do you know how I can find Christian . . . Chris? Or can you find out?"

Based on what she's said so far, I don't expect so, so I'm surprised when she says:

"I know exactly how to find Chris. Like I said: a bad apple. Far as I know, he's still rotting in prison, where he belongs."

FORTY-FOUR

It's a tiring drive. Far out of town, along a road I've never traveled before. I leave civilization behind as the scenery becomes wilder and the weather savage. Rain lashes the windshield, and I sit hunched forward in my seat to peer through the patches of clear glass that become distorted an instant later. The radio can't find a signal for more than a few seconds at a time. Old songs with melodies that should be warm and soulful are jagged in my ears. Sweet lyrics become an alien tongue of fragmented words and staccato syllables.

The rain is a curtain separating my reality from this other dimension. Here is a shadow world without sun or hope. It is the rain that tells me I don't belong here, and yet I won't listen to the warning. I won't turn back.

I'm hunting Three.

Nothing's going to stop me.

Not the drive, not the weather. Not the walls of the prison that rise so high I feel like I'm an ant as I approach them.

I'm disoriented from the moment I step through the entrance. Corridors seem identical. All guards look the same. I squint against the overwhelming fluorescence. Cold light beats down without relent, reflected by pale walls and floors. The waiting room is loud, with a baby's cries and adults yelling. There is despair all around me, and these are the free people.

I keep my gaze on my feet because so many eyes are turned my way. They know I'm not one of them, and they don't want my pity.

Everyone is standing and moving and louder before I understand we're going elsewhere. Maybe I didn't hear the instruction, or a sign could have flashed. I follow along, too small to see beyond those in front of me. I don't know where we're going, but I go anyway.

The next room is larger. A high school cafeteria with no food. Many tables all spread out, a man in an orange jumpsuit sat at each. The visitors disperse, threading their way between the tables, seeking out their respective husbands or fathers or brothers or sons. The baby's cries intensify.

I swivel my head to find a stranger I've never met. All could be him.

A spread hand touches my back, and I startle. Turn.

A guard looms over me. He gestures to a far corner, and I see a man waiting, slumped in a chair, legs outstretched, and I can see the soles of his cheap prison shoes. His chin is near his chest, so I can't see his face.

Is this him?

I sense the guard moving to usher me again with a touch, and I don't want him to touch me. I make my legs work against their will and approach the man in the corner.

The baby is silent now amid the noise of greetings and chastisements and arguments.

My eyes are fixed on the man in the corner, on his slouched form, on the soles of his cheap shoes, and on the top of his head. His hair is clipped, and I see the cold fluorescent light pooling on his scalp.

I only blink when I stop before his table and say, "Christian?"

The head tilts up only enough for him to meet my gaze. His eyes are pale blue and bloodshot. He does not answer my question.

Christian has that emaciated look. I can see the veins in his forearms bulging beneath his skin. His under-eyes are dark and sunken. His hair is patchy and gray. He doesn't fit the image I had in my head from Amy's description. Which I should have expected. It's been twenty years. He's no longer the young, handsome man she wrote about. He's middle-aged now. Worn down. Beaten by his life choices.

"I'm Eve," I say because I can think of nothing else.

"That's what it says on the form," he replies. "I don't know any Eve, but I figure I've got nothing else to do."

The thousand questions I need to ask have dematerialized from my mind. I just stand before him.

"Chair's not there for decoration."

I see it for the first time. I drag it out, and its metal legs shudder and flex, sending unpleasant vibrations up my arm. I lower myself into the chair, slow and awkward as if I'm not sure it will hold my weight.

Christian watches me without expression.

I begin to fidget with my hands. Feeling self-conscious for this, I lean forward and set my elbows on the table, tucking my fingers into the pits of my elbows to keep them still.

"You gonna talk at all?" he asks. "I'm only in here for another nine months."

"Thank you for agreeing to see me. I appreciate it."

"Why do you?"

"This is going to sound strange."

"No, it won't. You're already strange. What you say is gonna sound real normal for a strange girl."

I swallow. "Do you remember a girl named Amy who lived next door to your grandpa a long time ago?"

"How long ago are we talking about?"

"Over twenty years ago."

He's thin, and when he grins his face creases into many folds. "I don't remember what I did this morning, let alone twenty years ago, and I do the same thing every morning."

"She had a sister, Maya, who had a crush on you. She died in a car crash."

He gives me a look that makes me think he's starting to remember. Maybe not the details, but this might be something buried deep inside his mind.

"Go on," he says.

"Amy and Maya's parents killed themselves a few years later. Amy went away to college. Your grandfather, Jefferson, was fond of her, of the whole family."

"I ain't seen that old fuck in forever."

"But you used to, right? You and Nate used to visit when you were younger."

"Sure. Why does any of this matter?"

"Was he a good grandfather? Was he kind to you or . . . ?"

"What? Was he kind? The fuck you talking about?"

"Someone at his nursing home told me he was cruel, that he locks up residents in their rooms, in cupboards."

I'm watching his eyes for any sign of recognition. All I see is confusion. Then amusement.

Christian says, "Who told you that? Some senile octogenarian? Keep going with this shit. What else you got for me?"

I decide to move on, not sure whether I believe him or whether I paid too much attention to that wizened lady with the green eyes. Christian is just old enough to be Three, yet he's in prison, so I ask him, "How long have you been in here?"

"Eight years and change. Why?"

I let out a long exhale. Not a sigh, but a release of pressure. He isn't Three. He couldn't have killed my parents or my sister. He won't be able to kill me either when my time is up in a few weeks.

"Do you remember Amy and Maya?"

He hunches his shoulders in an exaggerated shrug. "Maybe there were a couple of girls who lived next door. Maybe I knew them. Maybe I didn't."

"Please," I say. "I really need to know."

"Why? Why should I care if you need to know?"

He's looking around to see where the closest guard is located. They're doing circuits through the aisles between desks.

I say, "Because you've got nothing better to do."

"Whatever," he says. "Yeah. I remember. Sure. There were a pair of cute sisters who lived next door to my grandpa. Amy and Maya,

Maya and Amy. So what? Was a kid back then. Hadn't even got my dick wet yet. Not for want of trying, obviously."

I let out a breath of relief. "Did you go to the local university?"

His face creases again in a smile. "Yeah, I did. Hard to believe it now, but I was smart once. Back then, you couldn't see me without a book in my hand. *Fuck*, that was forever ago. I can't even believe it. Like I'm watching a documentary about someone else. Almost an alternate dimension, you know? A mirror image."

I don't know. I nod anyway.

"I wasn't a nerd, though." He's smiling. Reminiscing. "That wasn't my thing. I was cool and smart. I was cool *because* I was smart. I was cocky. I was so fucking cocky because I was so fucking smart . . . Like a superpower. So smart I could do anything I wanted. So smart I could take drugs and not ruin my life like all the dumb junkies. Ha, ha. Idiots. I wouldn't be one of them." He leans forward, and I lean closer in response. "Between you and me," he says in a quiet voice, gesturing to his surroundings, "I'd suggest I may have overvalued my intelligence. Serves me right for always trying to prove to my old man I wasn't such a loser."

"Did you ever meet Amy again? Specifically, when you were studying for your PhD?"

"I didn't even make it a year." He shakes his head and diverts his eyes. No more happy memories to relive. "I was selling by then. I thought I was doing it to fund my studies. I wasn't. I sold shit so I could take it. I ruled that campus. Whether they sold grass or pills, every dealer there got their product from me." He scratches at his scalp with all ten fingers in a sudden, frenzied action. He growls. "I used to think numbers were so cool. *Fuck*, who was I? Genuine question because I don't know who I am anymore. I can't even complete a page of sudoku these days. It's like that part of me is locked away somewhere inside my mind I can't reach."

He pauses. I don't know what to say.

He isn't finished. "I don't mind being stupid now. I know I poisoned myself. That's the trade, paid in full. No refunds. It's that I know that the smart part of me is still there locked away. It's not gone. I just can't bring it back." He looks away. "I wish I could forget who I was so I don't have to spend every day for the rest of my life knowing I can never be him again."

He blinks and wipes his eyes on a sleeve. It takes a moment before he can look my way again.

"I'm sorry," I tell him.

"Why the fuck are you sorry? You didn't give me the pipe."

I don't respond. I give him a moment to get himself together, and he sits himself upright in the chair. Stares at me. He looks angry. I realize he's embarrassed to have cried in front of me. Maybe he doesn't like showing weakness inside the prison, where strength must be the most valuable asset. Whatever the reason, it's my fault. I did this to him. Everything about him projects dislike, and I'm scared he might attack me. I try not to show my fear. I try to hold my ground.

He doesn't blink. "Are we done?"

"I'd like to ask you a couple of other questions. Please. It's really important."

"Why? Why? Why? What's so important about who I was or who I knew twenty years ago? Shit, who gives a fuck? What is it with you people digging up the past?"

"I'm sorry, what? Who is 'you people'? Has someone else come to see you? Asking about Amy? Who was it?"

I have too much sudden energy in my voice. He sees my urgency and that he can play with it. "Maybe someone just like you."

"What? Who?"

He fixes me with an unblinking stare. "Maybe someone who almost had it worked out."

"The rule of three," I manage to say. "Who else asked you about it? Why?"

He opens his mouth to answer, and I'm so eager for the answer I can't help but lean closer in expectation.

He closes his mouth, slowly and deliberately clicking his teeth together, as if sealing the truth away from me for no other reason than spite. He leans back in his chair to look over his shoulder toward the closest guard.

"*Yo, yo,*" he calls to the guard. "We're done here. This bitch don't know me. She's played you all."

The guard eyes me with suspicion and approaches. Some prisoners nearby find this amusing. He's playing for the crowd.

"No," I say to Christian. "Please. I didn't mean to make you angry. I didn't—"

"Nah, you didn't make me anything. You don't have that kind of power over me." He's all arrogant posture now. Overcompensating. "I'm just bored of this conversation."

The guard is closer. I feel my chance slipping away with every step he takes toward me.

"I'll give you anything you want," I say to Christian. "Please, just tell me if you ever met Amy on the bus into town from the university. Did you bump into her?"

The arrogance lessens. Curiosity in his gaze.

"She fell into you, didn't she? She told you she was going to church. Neither of you thought anything about meeting at the time because you didn't recognize each other. But you did later, didn't you?"

He hisses out a mocking exhale. "Who gives a shit?"

"I do," I yell at him. "I give a fucking shit. Tell me. Tell me. Why won't you tell me? *Tell me.*"

Everyone around our table hears me. The guard hurries. Seconds away.

"You're crazy," Christian says with a smile. He kisses his teeth. "In fact, you're even crazier than Amy turned out to be. I don't know anything about a bus, but once we synced up again. *Wow.* She. Went. Wild."

My mouth hangs open.

There's a glimmer in his eyes. Smugness. He's reclaimed the power he lost through tears.

"You did know her." I'm not shouting now. I'm shocked into whispers.

The guard's shadow falls over me. "Ma'am, it's time to go."

Christian makes another exaggerated shrug. "I never forget my best customers."

He winks at me—the bastard winks.

I launch myself across the table before I know what I'm doing. "What do you know about her death?" My fingers grab his jumpsuit even as the guard grabs me from behind. "What do you know? What do you know? WHAT DO YOU KNOW?"

He laughs the entire time it takes for the guard to pull me off him and answers only when I'm dragged away, screaming and fighting every step. He doesn't speak, however. He says no words. But he mouths them so only I understand.

He mouths, *I know you're next.*

FORTY-FIVE

I'm escorted all the way out of the prison to my car. Only when I'm behind the wheel am I left alone. I find I can't bring myself to turn the ignition key. I just sit in the seat, hands on the wheel, staring into space. I'm recalling everything I said, everything Christian said. I'm terrified I might forget some tiny detail of what just took place. I wish I'd been able to record the conversation with my phone, but they take them away from you.

I'm trying so hard to focus and remember because the inevitable questions are screaming inside my mind. How does Christian know I'm next? Who else came to see him? Who else asked about Amy? Why did Elizabeth tell Ila that she had driven Amy to church that day? I know I won't be able to answer them if I forget anything Christian said. Or didn't say.

An a-hole but not Three if he's in prison, so how does he know I'm next? Was it just a lucky guess? Maybe he worked it out on his own, seeing my fear and desperation, and wanted to mess with me out of spite? What did Amy tell him all those years ago?

It's dark by the time I drive away. The rain is following me home. Opaque clouds try to drown me.

It's only when I'm almost back at the house that I realize what I need to do. I pull over on the outskirts of town and find my cell.

He answers on the first ring.

"This is Lestrange."

"Two years ago you told me that if you could help me, you would."

"Who is this?"

"In a heartbeat, you said. In half a heartbeat. Do you remember telling me that?"

A pause. "I do."

"Now's the time," I tell him. "I need a list of visitors to a prison who went to see a certain prisoner. Is that something you can get hold of?"

"If it's relevant to a case I'm working on, sure. Otherwise, no. Not really."

"It is relevant to several cases."

"Closed cases."

"That shouldn't be closed. Cases that are closed because no one bothered to look beyond the surface to find out what actually happened."

"I think we've been over this."

It's subtle condescension. I suppose I should be grateful he didn't hang up.

"Are you going to help me or not?"

"What's this about?"

"Are you going to keep your promise or not?"

"I'm a man of my word." There's a tiredness in his voice. I'm not sure whether he's tired of me or the day in general. "That doesn't mean I jump just because someone tells me to."

"I'm not telling you to do anything. I'm asking you. I'm asking for the little help you promised to give me when you refused actually to help me."

"I know you've been through a lot and—"

"I've not *been* through a lot. I'm *still* going through it."

"You're going through a lot," he says. "I appreciate that. I get used as a punching bag for the world's problems daily. Doesn't mean I like it. Doesn't mean I do my job better for it."

"You want me to be nicer to you? You want me to get on my knees? You can't see me, but I will if that's what it takes."

He doesn't answer.

I'm infuriated. Why won't he just help me?

"You want me to do something for you in return, don't you?

I get it." My anger makes me cruel. "You want me to suck your shriveled-up old-man dick? Is that it? Fine. I'll do it. I'll drive straight over. We can use my car. No one ever has to know. If getting you off is what it's going to take for you to keep your word, tell me and let's get this over with."

No response. Just breathing. Maybe a swallow. Shuffling, perhaps.

At first, I'm even angrier that he's not yelling at me. I want him to meet my rage with a rage of his own so I can hate him like I hate Christian, Johnathan, my bastard father, and every other man who has let me down.

And then, I'm scared.

He might hang up. He should hang up. I would if our roles were reversed. He might never answer my calls again.

I start to shake.

"Please," I say down the phone, trying to keep my voice from breaking apart into sobs. "This is the only thing I've asked of you in all this time. It's one little thing. A list. Names. That's it. Case or not, you can call the prison, you can ask. You must know people there who can give you that list with a couple of clicks of a mouse. And if you don't, you're a cop. They'll fall over themselves to help—a thirty-second favor. No biggie. Kind of thing that must happen a thousand times a day. You could have done it already in the time it's taken me to beg you. *Please.*"

I'm staring at my reflection in the rearview mirror. I hate the face that looks back at me. Her eyes are red. Her cheeks are wet. She's weak. She's desperate. She's pathetic. She thought she could do this all by herself.

She's a failure.

I hate her more than I hate him.

"Okay," Lestrange says after an eternity. "Give me the details."

I do. But I don't thank him.

"I'll get back to you tonight on this number."

He hangs up.

I scream.

Not in fear or rage or pain. I scream for release, to let out all the stress that's been building up inside me for the past two years. The pressure I've pretended I could cope with, could bury down and lock away until this was over. I scream and bang my fists on the steering wheel. I punch the horn. I elbow the door. I slam my palms against the ceiling. I hit the headrest with the back of my skull. I kick at the pedals.

I'm not sure how long I'm screaming. By the time I stop, my throat is hoarse, and my hands are sore.

The windows are all steamed up.

I'm sitting there for a long time. Not thinking. Just sitting. Breathing. I check that my phone has enough charge left. I make sure it's not set to silent. I make sure the vibration is on, and the ringer volume is at maximum. I see smudge marks on the screen, so I clean it on my sleeve. I know I have to put it away, and yet I can't do it. I'm worried I'll miss Lestrange's call. If I don't let the phone out of my sight, he'll call. If I can't see it because it's in my pocket, he won't.

I rest it on my left thigh, screen up, visible with just a glance down.

I drive to the only place where I feel safe.

I drive to the church and to my destiny.

FORTY-SIX

I don't participate. I don't even listen. I sit on the uncomfortable plastic chair, phone in hand. My other hand is busy tearing up my lips. I'm using the pain to manage the stress, which is so high only agony works. I push a sharp thumbnail into my bottom lip with such force that my eyes water. It's excruciating. I need it. Nothing less can help me.

I know people are watching, and for once I don't care. Lips that are all cracked and raw and bright with blood are disgusting. I used to hate people seeing me like that. Not just because I didn't want to look repulsive to anyone, but more than that I didn't want anyone to know that I do something so disgusting.

We lip-pickers are always pariahs. Society finds self-harm perfectly tolerable only as long as no one has to look at it. We're taught from a young age to hide our pain, to be ashamed of our suffering. *Don't cry, you're okay. You're a big girl.* As if we don't have enough other problems to endure as a species, we're expected to endure with a minimum of fuss. Heaven forbid our agony or sorrow or poverty causes someone else to feel awkward and uncomfortable.

Die quietly, behind closed doors.

Don't upset the neighbors.

There's no one new here tonight. No Johnathan. No man of the right age. No Three.

Here is the only place I'm safe, and yet I'm still scared.

I'm so close to Three, it's like he's breathing down the back of my neck. I'm worried he knows my every move. I'm thinking about that car parked down the street from Amy's house. I'm wondering if Three knew the steps I would be taking.

I know you're next, Christian mouthed to me.

Did Ila speak to him about what she was going through? I wonder. Maybe she worked out his connection with Amy and never had the chance to write it down. Ila's the one who worked out Three was behind the deaths that came before her.

He, on the other hand, has absolutely no idea I know he's out there.

What else did she learn that she never had the chance to pass on? Just like Amy, there's more to her story than she told us. Which is odd, now that I'm thinking about it. Both their journal entries ended just when they had more to tell. That doesn't feel right to me. That's too symmetrical.

Oh God, are there pages to their journals that I never read? Did they write more that was never found?

Did they tell Christian more than they've told me?

I can believe that Amy revealed to him about what she was going through and then Ila could have done the same, or he learned about her from Nate after she died. Maybe Christian guessed the next girl would eventually seek him out.

No, there was too much certainty in his taunt. He knows a lot more about the rule of three than he let on. Maybe one of the other people who visited can help me.

What did he say? Someone else thought they had it figured out too? Does that mean that there's another person like me who has been investigating Three? What have they worked out that I don't yet know?

I just hope when Lestrange gets back to me, the list isn't huge. I don't have much time left to solve this riddle.

I replay my conversation with Christian in my head, trying to pick apart everything he said. He told me about his PhD, about getting into drugs, about enjoying being smart, and knowing that part of him has gone now and won't come back.

Serves me right for always trying to prove to my old man I wasn't such a loser.

Who is his old man? Who is the father of Christian and Nathan? Who is Jefferson's son?

"*Shit*," I hiss as my nail digs into my lip so hard the pain makes me cry out.

All eyes on me.

Stephanie asks, "Is everything okay, Eve?"

I nod, too enthusiastically. She doesn't believe me.

"Why don't you tell us what's on your mind?"

"I'm not finished," Alejandro says.

Sal snorts. "Let me guess; someone at the office is making you feel unappreciated, and you don't know how to express your feelings. We'll discuss this in full for forty minutes before you come to realize that all you have to do is talk to them."

He's grinning like an idiot.

"Screw you," Alejandro says, nudging him on the arm. "Don't take your blue balls out on me. It's not my fault your girlfriend won't peg you anymore."

Sal laughs and gives Alejandro a playful slap in return.

Everyone in the group enjoys their boisterous flirting except Stephanie and me. She's still looking at me. It's clear something is wrong. She notices how I'm clutching my phone as if my life depends on it, because it does.

"It's nothing," I say before she can ask. "I'm expecting a call. I really can't miss it."

She smiles to reassure me. "We're here whenever you're ready to talk."

I wasn't going to, but the words come out anyway.

"Have you ever been so deep in something that you've lost all perspective?"

"Only if I'm really lucky," Alejandro says.

Stephanie casts him a look that tells him it's not the time for jokes.

I continue: "I've been doing this thing . . . a project. A long-term thing. Over two years now. And it's coming to an end. Almost done. I've worked my ass off on it. I'm not exaggerating when I say that I've put my entire life into it." My fingernail is back at my lip, pressing hard. "And now I'm doubting everything I've done. I think there's a good chance I've backed the wrong horse. I'm like a cosmologist whose entire life's work has been studying the planet Pluto, only to discover that Pluto isn't even a planet after all." I'm almost laughing at myself. "You know? I think I've fucked up so badly that I could have just sat on my ass for two years and ended up in the exact same place."

"Self-doubt is natural," Stephanie says after a moment's silence. "We all have it. The more we invest in something, the more we care, the greater our fear of loss becomes. Confidence isn't the absence of self-doubt. It's the acknowledgment of that doubt and the refusal to be deterred by it."

"That's me," I reply. "That is exactly me. I mean, it was me. I have been so determined for all this time. I refused to second-guess myself. I've never been deterred until now."

Stephanie nods. "Perhaps we can help you better if you tell us what's wrong. What is this project you've been working on all this time?"

"I can't. It will sound ridiculous. You'll think I'm crazy."

"We won't," Alejandro says.

"No way," Sal adds. "There's no judgment in here. You should know that by now."

Should I do it? Should I tell them?

I look at the group, at the unfamiliar faces and the faces I recognize, and then at Stephanie's face, and Alejandro and Sal, and I feel guilty keeping such a massive part of who I am from them. These people are like family to me, and indeed have cared more for me than my own parents ever did, and I've lied to them. Not directly, but I have willingly kept them from ever really getting to know me when all they've done is try to help me.

They want to help me now.

"Okay," I say. "Have you ever heard of something known as the rule—"

I don't get a chance to finish, because my phone rings in my hand and I'm so startled I almost drop it on the floor.

Lestrange is calling.

"I'm sorry," I tell the group, standing up. "I've got to take this."

The chair legs scrape and judder on the flooring as I pull it to one side. My actions are jerky and uncoordinated as I'm rushing.

"I'm sorry," I say again, heading for the door. "Carry on without me."

I notice Stephanie is standing up, and I feel guilty since she struggles to do so quickly with her walking stick. It looks like she's going to say something, to call after me, but I don't stop. I push through the doors and into the hallway outside and answer the call that my life depends upon.

"Yeah," is all I can say.

"Eve? This is Lestrange."

"Yeah, yeah. Thanks for calling me back. What did you find out? Did you get the list?"

I'm heading to the exit, to my car outside. My mouth is dry. I notice there's blood crusted under the thumbnail I kept digging into my bottom lip.

"Yeah, so I spoke to someone at the prison. They're going to send me a list of names. I'm not sure how useful that's going to be for you. Christian has never had many visitors, even when he first went inside. This isn't his first stay behind bars for drug offenses . . . Aside from his lawyer, he's only ever been visited by one other person apart from you."

I'm expecting him to say Nathan. I push open the exit and step out into the rain. My car's a minute away.

"So," he continues. "The only other person to visit Christian is a woman. Dougherty, Elizabeth S."

I stop. Rain patters my head.

Elizabeth . . . That has to be Amy's best friend. Ila's professor. Of course, she would be connected to my story too. Dougherty must be her husband's name. Or she changed it. Irrelevant details right now, because all I care about is:

"When?"

"Let me see. I figured you wouldn't be happy waiting for the record to arrive, so I scribbled some notes . . . I'm afraid I didn't write down every detail. I'm sorry. But she was last there three days ago."

So recent. Just before I found out about Christian.

"Is she still a college professor? Where does she teach?"

"That's not the kind of thing they make a note of for visitors."

"I know," I tell him. "You can find out, though. You're working late, yeah? I can hear you tapping on a keyboard while you talk to me."

"I'm not sure that's entirely ethical. She's a private citizen, same as you."

"Look her up, and I swear I'll never phone you again. I'll never ask you for anything else. I swear."

"This is the last thing I do," he says with a resigned sigh.

"Thank you," I tell him as I listen to him typing.

"No," he says after a moment. "She doesn't teach as far as I can see. She's a counselor now. She runs group therapy sessions."

Trembling, I say, "What does the S stand for?"

FORTY-SEVEN

Elizabeth *Stephanie* Dougherty.

In Amy's life, in Ila's . . . and in mine too. I suppose that was inevitable. Elizabeth is the one who set Amy on her course of self-destruction. She had the premonition. She told Amy that bad things always happen in threes. She even refused to believe that Amy was cursed because she knew she wasn't. It was Elizabeth who gave Ila the journal. Elizabeth was the last person Ila spoke to in her own journal entry. It was Elizabeth who lied to Ila about taking Amy to the church that day. It was Elizabeth who visited Christian.

What else has she been doing?

Getting to know me, of course. I've been opening up to her every week. I've never told the group about my situation. However, I've been transparent and open about my mental state, my inability to trust, my paranoia, my obsessive nature, my painful family history, my grief. I have to give her credit. She knows all about me. There was no better way to get into my confidence.

No better way for Three to get close to me.

I was wrong that Three would be a man. But as I said: I feel foolish, and yet I don't have to worry about her overpowering me. She can't even walk without her cane.

I wonder now if she even needs the walking stick or if it's purely for show? To make her seem frail and unthreatening. If so, it worked like a charm.

I'm soaked by the time I step back inside.

Each footstep leaves a watery sole print on the linoleum.

When I push open the swing door to reenter the hall, only Stephanie looks my way. It's a glance—a look of surprise and concern for my sodden appearance. At least, that's the act. I smile and shake my head as if I buy it. As if I'm touched by the fake concern of the woman who plans to murder me.

I take my chair.

I listen to the conversation, and yet I don't hear a single word anyone says. I ask generic questions, offer platitudes, nod, and look interested and sympathetic. It's an effortless display. I realize that these recent years have turned me into an incredible liar. My whole life is one big act, so I guess I shouldn't be surprised.

When group ends, I'm not the first to leave for once. I'm the last. I hang around to chat, eat a cookie, and have a coffee. Alejandro makes fun of my hair, all stringy from the rain. I laugh and pinch his stomach, telling him he's put on weight. That puts him in his place and makes Sal get in on the action. Alejandro grows annoyed with Sal trying to poke and pinch his love handles. Stephanie watches us, smiling. Her act is almost as good as my own.

Sal and Alejandro leave together.

I'm alone with Stephanie.

Face-to-face with Three at last.

"I'm glad you're still here," she tells me. "I was hoping we could talk."

All this time hunting Three, and I've never stopped to think what I would say when I finally found him. Her.

"Sure," I say, still acting without effort. "How come?"

"Has something happened?"

Stephanie's all innocence and concern. Her tone is gentle. Her expression is caring. No wonder she's managed to fool me all this time.

She can't fool me any longer.

"Yes," I say. "It has."

"The phone call?"

"That's only part of it."

"Bad news?"

I shake my head. "No, not bad. Not bad at all. It's the best news I've had in years."

"Oh," she says. "I'm so pleased to hear that. Let me get you a tissue." She wedges her walking stick under her arm while she reaches for her bag.

"What for?"

"Your lip," she says.

She fetches a packet of tissues, takes one out. and hands it to me. I dab it against my bottom lip and hold it there for a second.

When I take the tissue away, we both look at the dot of blood soaked into the fibers.

"Thank you," I say. Then, "For everything."

"My pleasure. I do hope these sessions are proving useful."

I smile. "Likewise."

She does an excellent job of acting confused.

"Buy you a beer?" I ask. "Or a coffee?"

I know she's genuine in her surprise. No murderer expects the victim to take them out for drinks.

"That's a lovely offer," she responds. "I'm afraid I have somewhere I need to be. A personal matter . . ."

"This late?"

"It's okay, I'm a night owl," she explains with a smile.

Oh, I bet you are.

I shrug and act disappointed. "Another time then. See you next week."

"Take care of yourself, Eve."

That's precisely what I am doing, Three.

Outside, I wait in my car. I keep the lights off. I sit hunkered down in my seat. In the dark, in the rain, she doesn't see me when she leaves a few minutes later, walking with the aid of her stick to her car.

She doesn't see me when she climbs into the vehicle.

She doesn't see me when she drives away.

She doesn't see me when I follow her.

FORTY-EIGHT

I 'm aware of my fuel gauge. The tank is low. I wasn't expecting another long drive today. To the prison, then back. Now . . . I'm not sure where I'm going. All I know is there are two blurry taillights in the distance, and I'm going where they're going.

Out of town, into darkness.

This is not a route I know. She takes a turn where I see a faded sign for a psychiatric hospital. Is this where Amy went all those years ago? I wonder.

And then I hear Amy's words in my head: *I've known her a long time, since we were both wayward teens* . . . How wayward was Elizabeth? Did she come here too? Is that how they knew one another?

I don't take the turn. When I'm close enough to see the sign, I realize there's a long drive leading to the hospital, which sits in its own grounds. Trees shield it from the highway, which I guess is why I can't see any lights. I keep going until I can turn around and head back, figuring Stephanie must have reached the hospital by now or at least be so far along the drive she won't see my headlights following.

I soon realize I'm wrong. Though shielded by trees, they're not the reason why I could see nothing of the building from the highway.

It's abandoned.

I kill my headlights so I don't announce my presence. I stop my car while I'm still on the long drive. I don't want to give myself away.

I take a deep breath and climb out.

The hospital grounds are overgrown. Where there should be a lawn are waist-high shrubs and tall grass. The wind makes the grass ripple like water. A scratchy swooshing sound accompanies each flowing wave. Flanking trees tower above me, thin, crooked branches reaching out into the sky like arms, naked fingers spread wide, long nails casting jagged shadows on the rippling grasses below. Shriveled brown leaves swirl about the path.

Time has assailed the hospital without mercy. Windows are broken. Climbing plants snake and slither over the brickwork. Paint is stripped and curled on windowsills. Wood stain is faded on doors.

I make no noise as I approach. The screeching wind swallows my footsteps. My eyes are half-closed as my hair is whipped across my face. A leaf strikes my cheek and disintegrates to dust.

The wind is behind me, compelling me forward.

It thinks I will resist. It's wrong. I want this.

I don't need the wind to push me toward my destiny. I take each step with relish.

Stephanie's car is parked outside.

What is she doing here?

The rain has stopped, and many puddles reflect the moonlight. I glance at my distorted reflections as I near the building.

How long has it been since anyone else was here? Impossible to know, but the windows didn't break themselves. The wind alone could not force the door.

Inside, it's no quieter.

The wind slips through those broken panes and whistles a high-pitched keen. My heart hammers even louder.

Dust and grime disguise the lobby's floor. Leaves gather in the corners and along the skirting as might insects. They share these spaces with crushed cans, cigarette butts, snack packaging, and syringes.

The walls are a wild pattern of colors, dark in the shadows. Blood-red and midnight blue overlap with soulless black and crazed green. No urban art here. Only the incoherent scrawling of the intoxicated and enraged. How many graffitists contributed, I wonder? Or is this the work of just one hand?

On the wall above a mighty staircase, a dribbling stain of red reads, Take Me Home.

Perhaps a plea from the hospital itself, which is forever bound to this place, yet which no longer belongs.

I see many avenues to take; hallways and doors, and the staircase leading up. I search the floor with my eyes, seeking any sign of Elizabeth's passage. A scuff here. A bare patch of tiling there. Nothing that can only be newly done.

This place will not help me.

I'm alone.

I've always been alone.

I listen, focusing, letting the hissing wind quiet, and the echoes of the hospital become louder. Faint, yet I hear it nonetheless. A sharp sound from the bowels of the building. Footsteps.

I follow, my own steps light and careful. My tennis shoes are soft-soled and quiet. Though I am an intruder here, I belong. I do not disturb this disturbed place.

Away from the open door and windows, the shadows deepen. The keening wind diminishes to faraway whispers and murmurs.

Abandoned buildings are never truly abandoned. They are never silent. Other sounds take over from the wind: the walls groan, and the floor creaks. I will my heart to cease its thump, and it takes no notice. It knows what I refuse to accept.

I creep down a long hallway that stretches off into blackness. Dim shafts of light bisect the dark and reveal floating motes of dust. I sense a weak scent of perfume lingering in the air.

A rusted gurney interrupts my path. With only three wheels, it's canted in a mocking bow. There is no padding, only stark metal, yet leather straps remain to tell of long-ago thrashes and screams.

My gaze is fixed on the gurney as I step around. I look upon it as if it might rise up against me, brought to life by malevolent spirits bound in place when the last vestiges of hope finally died upon it.

Dust irritates my nose, and I feel that irresistible tingle. I try to fight it regardless and yield only when I can muffle my face with my sleeve.

The sneeze seems to rumble through the hallway, rattling the walls and spreading the booming concussive wave to every corner of the hospital. Anything sleeping here has now arisen. Anyone alone now knows otherwise.

I push on into the darkness, picking out the hint of doorways and traces of fixtures. Silence accompanies the gloom. I'm forced to decide the route I take on nothing but intuition. My fearlessness is slipping away with every step, every blind stumble. My fingers inch along the wall ahead of me, feeling the way forward. I dare not look back. I don't want to see the impenetrable blackness behind me when it's all I can see before me.

The hospital has become a labyrinth, and I don't know my way back out of it.

I tell myself the strange noises I hear are only in my head. There's no scuttling around my feet. No one is laughing at me unseen.

When my fingers touch something wet and slimy, I startle, and my hand goes straight to my chest, feeling the thumping heart behind. And there it is against my rib cage. The solution. My phone.

I didn't want to use it before and give myself away, although now it's obvious I need to see more than I need to stay hidden. I fumble my phone out of my jacket pocket and turn on the flashlight.

My reflection stares back at me from a mirror, and I just manage to catch the terrified yelp before it escapes my lips. My uplit face looks haunted.

The moisture on my fingers is from dampness only. The wall here is rotten. The plaster is caked and crumbled; water leaks from a hole in the ceiling above.

I shine the light all around me. The ruinous hallway opens up to a ward. Empty beds line the walls. Like the crooked gurney, they have no bedding. Their frames are bare. Comfort stripped away to reveal tortured skeletons.

The light reveals the rot and decay all around me. I'm no longer stumbling in the dark, yet what I now see offers no relief.

A door nearby has a little square window, and I position my phone to see into the padded cell behind. Black mold has infested the cushioned walls. I take an instinctive step away.

The swath of flashlight moves from the window, and the random movement of my hand means for a moment I brighten the hallway that brought me here.

I glimpse a more organic shape among the right angles.

Was that movement?

I regain my footing and redirect my phone down the hallway. No one is there, and yet I don't believe it. The hallway does not exist in isolation. There are doors and doorways and other hallways leading from it—a dozen places to hide, at least.

I hold the phone out before me and retrace my steps.

I don't get far. The light from my phone illuminates the hallway and shines through an open doorway. I see the room beyond. An office once, perhaps. Now an almost empty box. Yet along the far wall are a desk and chair. Simple, featureless furniture that attracts no interest.

Atop the desk is . . . something.

My throat feels stripped raw as I enter the room. I walk with short, slow steps. Somehow I know I am making a terrible mistake and can do nothing to stop it. I am compelled forward by an irresistible force.

Closer, more details come into focus. I see the vinyl padding on the chair is cracked and split. I see the varnish is worn and thin on the desktop.

I see a notebook and the scratches in the black cover.

The Rule of Three.

FORTY-NINE

I've never seen it before, and yet it looks exactly as I expected. Amy never described it, but Ila did. A regular notebook with a black cover. A handwritten title scored with a Biro. Over twenty years old at this point. The corners curl up and the pages are unfurled. It sits on the desktop bent into a shallow U shape.

I read the journals online, on the forum. I downloaded them into a document so I could read them whenever I wanted, so I could print them out if I wanted to. At some point I knew them so well I didn't need to read them anymore.

Here, now, I begin reading once more.

My hands are trembling, making it hard to turn the pages. I think I'm worried they might crumble to dust at my touch, like an ancient scroll found in a forgotten tomb.

On the first page is the rhyme.

I've always hated it. The casual finality of those few words. The implicit doom. I turn the page.

I almost don't want to read this. I'm holding the last testament of the two girls who came before me. The two girls who laid the foundation for everything I achieved. Without them, without their words, I would be living my life oblivious to the peril I'm in. I owe them so much. And that's why I don't want to read any more. Because I don't want them to die. Because I know them. I've lived their lives. If I don't turn the page, then I can spare them their fear and pain.

I wipe my eyes on the back of my sleeve.

Something occurs to me.

I turn the pages in clumps, glancing over Amy's mad scrawls and Ila's beautiful cursive. Ila continued where Amy left off, adding her own story into the notebook for the next girl.

Me.

The last third of the notebook is empty.

Ila's journal ends halfway down the page.

The killer, on the other hand, has absolutely no idea I know they're out there.

Just like Amy, she ended her journal on a high note, at a point where she felt positive. Victorious even. Amy began her journal when she knew she had made a mistake, when she realized the curse, as she called it, was not yet over. I don't know when Ila began writing.

I thumb through the pages in the last third of the notebook. I'm not sure what I'm looking for in those empty pieces of paper. I can't help but wonder when I'll begin filling in my own pages.

Hold on, why is this notebook even here? Amy's and Ila's original handwritten journals just lying around in an abandoned psychiatric hospital.

I'm not sure what instinct drives me to pull open the top drawer of the desk; I can't possibly know what I think I'll find there, and yet I do know. There's a pen in the drawer. Nothing else.

A pen so I can begin writing.

Realization crashes over me in a foaming wave. That's why I'm here, why I've been lured here.

This is Three's trap for me.

I'm fast to my feet. All that training, all that exercise, paying off in an instant of explosiveness.

Fast to my feet and fast to spin around.

Straight into the clubbing blow of Stephanie's walking stick.

FIFTY

The cane hits me on the forehead, and I crumple straight down to the floor. I don't feel pain at first, because I don't feel anything at all. My vision darkens and sounds become disembodied and far-away, as though the floor opens up and swallows me whole.

I sink deep into the ground, through the tiles and concrete and earth. I'm too tired to slow my fall.

This isn't me, I know. I'm no quitter. Yet my hands find no purchase. There is nothing to grab.

I am a helpless passenger on this descent.

Down, down I go. So deep that the only light is a bright pinprick high above me, surrounded by night.

Then I'm floating instead of sinking. The ground around me has no mass. My limbs are liquid in this empty space.

The pinprick of light begins to flicker as a distant star, only that star is burning itself out.

I don't know how I know, but if that star ceases to shine then I'll never again see light.

Please, little star, keep shining. Shine just for me.

I'm not ready.

I'm not ready for the blackness.

I won't give up if you don't give up on me.

The merciful star hears my pleas and ceases to flicker.

Slowly, it burns brighter. That pinprick grows in size, fighting back the night, and I feel myself floating up toward it. This beacon calls me back.

I blink, and the glaring light from my phone shines into my eyes.

I'm lying on the floor of the little office where I fell. My phone is next to me.

Now comes the pain.

A white-hot searing pneumatic drill of agony at the front of my skull. It's relentless, intensifying by the second as my faculties return. But soundless. I can't hear.

All sounds are drowned out by a tinnitus whine that accompanies the pain, volume rising as the agony increases.

Three is near. I cannot hear or see, and yet I sense her presence. I feel like Stephanie is speaking down to me, explaining her madness, instructing me on what I am to do in this prison that is to be my home until I've completed my journal and her life's work. Her trilogy.

I try to turn my head away from the blinding light. With enormous effort and enormous pain, I do. I still see little. My vision is a firework display of flashes and blurs.

They overlay the darkness beyond, the darkness that is the room outside the reach of my phone's light.

A shape moves on the far side of the fireworks.

Moving away from me.

At first, I don't understand. My mind is working too slowly, and it's then my instincts that understand. Three is leaving, is going to exit this cell and lock the door behind her, entombing me for the rest of my short life.

I want to shout to her, to ask a question, if only my lips would work on my command.

My hands need no such orders. Long hours of practice, of repetition, mean muscle memory takes over for me. Into my pocket my hand reaches, grips, withdraws, and rises.

Do you know what the difference is between life and death, Three?

About six pounds of pressure.

I don't see the flash of the gunshot among the other flashes.

I hear no bang above the incessant whine.

However, I know I hit because I feel the thud as she joins me on the floor.

Cordite irritates my nose. I've never liked the smell. I wonder if this is the last time I'll ever smell it.

Could be a minute before I can stand. It might be ten.

I'm unsteady, I'm in pain, but my vision is clear enough to see where Stephanie lies so close to the door. So close to sealing my fate.

I don't know if my deafness is because of the blow to the head or the gunshot. In either case, I don't get to hear Three's final gasps.

I shot her dead center, just like I practiced at the range. I squeezed the trigger only once. In the dim light, I can't even see the bullet hole.

Her mouth is opening and closing in jerking, spasm-like movements. There's a slight, stuttering tremor to her whole body. Like in those really old black-and-white movies where the frame can't keep still.

I don't think she's aware of the situation until I step closer to where she lies. I keep the .38 pointed at her the entire time. I stop out of reach. I'm taking no chances. When her eyes focus on me, I know she's still there. I'm pretty sure the bullet is in her spine. She can't move. She can't speak. She just lies there shuddering, her goldfish mouth doing its thing.

The opening and closing slows down.

The stuttering tremors of her body stop.

I can't think of anything to say to her.

Six pounds of pressure doesn't seem enough, does it? Life should be heavier than that. Death should be more challenging to reach than applying less pressure than you do when you use a pencil. How can we truly be extraordinary if that's all it requires to take that specialness away?

I keep the pistol pointed at her for so long my shoulder begins to ache.

When I finally lower it, I let out a massive release of panting breath.

Three is dead.

I've killed her.

I feel dizzy. I lower to a squat because I feel unstable on my feet. My mind is racing at a hundred miles an hour. There's so much to feel, so much to think. One thought is strangely more important than the others. It's a question.

How much does a single bullet cost?

I suppose I could break it down. Divide the price tag of the box by the number of rounds within. Do the ones I fired at paper targets count too? I don't know the answer. I'm not a philosopher. But I do know if I add up the cost of all the bullets to the value of the gun to the cost of using the firing range, it's still not a lot of money.

Although something of a bargain for justice.

For Amy and Ila, for their families, for my own.

All those lives lost, avenged.

I've saved the system a fortune.

Sounds to me like I'm trying to rationalize what I've done when the truth is I justified it a long time ago.

How was I expecting to end this story?

Show the rest of my findings to Lestrange? Sit back and wait for the swift competency of law enforcement to correct so many wrongs? Wait for the justice system to find Stephanie guilty, to sentence her, send her away?

I never even thought that far ahead.

It was always purely about finding Three before my time came. Maybe I was protecting myself by refusing to think about what would happen next. Which I would do only if I needed to defend myself because I knew what I would have to do. I was destined to kill.

Is becoming a murderer to stop a murderer still murder?

That's a question for smarter people to answer.

It's funny. As I retrieve my phone to aim the light over her dead face, she's the one who looks afraid.

Maybe we all do at the end.

I've spent most of my time with Stephanie when we're both sitting down in a circle in group. I've never sat next to her. Maybe that's random chance, and that first time I sat where there was an empty chair and then always gravitated to that area of the circle, or maybe my trepidation kept me clear. Anyway, I guess I didn't notice I'm taller than her, by quite a bit. And I'm short as it is.

Cunning and patience were Three's strengths, and now I realize why. She was never going to overpower anyone if she couldn't strike them from behind.

I want to know why, of course. I've always wanted to know why. What makes a person kill? Sadly, that's a question to which a corpse can have no answer. Yet I know there's nothing you can be told that will really make sense, that will really make you understand. I've read and seen enough interviews with killers to know that.

I stare at her body for a long time. I've never seen a dead body before. It's ironic to say it looks so lifelike. Aside from a tiny hole in her clothes, she could be simply lying down. Her eyes are open, and it's like she's on mute. She's a character on the TV screen I can see, yet can't hear. The remote's out of reach. I can only read the visuals.

I'm not sure how long I stare. I feel . . . I don't know how I feel. I just know I don't want it to end.

There's a rush, yes. Physical, though. A jolt of pure adrenaline from all that's happened. Knowing she's dead and I killed her is a sense of incredible power. But I'm feeling something even greater than that. It's a sense of intense satisfaction. I'm not sure if this is pride, but I've never known anything like it.

For these few moments, I am as Three.

Now I understand why.

FIFTY-ONE

Group taught me a lot about myself in ways I didn't realize were worth learning. It's like training for life, to be yourself in a place where there are no setbacks for failing like out in the real world. So few of us are utterly alone in this life, so most of our problems are, let's face it, other people and how we relate to them, and how they relate to us in return. Group is all about relationships.

If you need change and haven't changed, you need therapy. Could be a chronic behavioral pattern or something acute. Sometimes change can come from the simple fact that in a group, you get lots of different perspectives. When someone solves a problem, and we hear how and why whatever they did worked, we might think about doing the same. Especially if they did something we had never considered before. I've changed. For a while, I wore my hair in a different way to disguise the bruise and swelling. Now I wear glasses too. My eyesight never quite recovered.

This new me sees three empty chairs tonight. Which is an improvement. Several of the regulars left when Stephanie stopped showing up.

No one likes the new counselor. Alejandro rolls his eyes at me during a long, monotone monologue about coping with grief. I try not to giggle. Sal pretends to fall asleep, then pretends to jolt awake again at random intervals. It's all I can do to keep on the chair.

We're schoolkids again, playing up for the substitute teacher.

When the new group leader announced that he was taking over from Stephanie, I pretended to be surprised like everyone else. I speculated after the session with the others. Why would Stephanie leave us without saying goodbye? Has she moved away? Is she sick? The new group leader didn't tell us anything during the session. He announced he would be running the group from now on, and while he appreciated this would not suit everyone, Stephanie wouldn't be coming back. He wouldn't take it personally if people wanted to drop out or join another group.

I kept my eye on the news. I kept waiting for a knock on my door that never came. I was sure Lestrange would call me. I was convinced I would be the prime suspect.

I practiced so hard for the inevitable questions. I can only guess that by the time they found Stephanie's body, Lestrange had forgotten the favor he did for me. Thank goodness he never believed me about the rule of three. If he had, there's no way he wouldn't make the connection.

I suppose I shouldn't be surprised. The cops failed to notice there was a serial killer out there for over twenty years.

It doesn't take long before we stop speculating why Stephanie is no longer taking the sessions. In time, we get used to the new guy and his new ways. In time, we can get used to anything, can't we? Human beings are clay that never hardens. Always malleable. Always ready to be reshaped by our experience. We feel vulnerable because we're so easy to dent. We need to understand that's not a vulnerability, not weakness, but strength in adaptability.

The dent that defines me as a murderer is smoothed over almost before it even registers. There's no cross to bear for me. I don't so much as have a nightmare. In fact, I've never slept better.

I have good dreams now. My memories are happy ones.

"What are you smiling about?" Alejandro asks me when we take a break to refill our drinks and grab another cookie. Which aren't so great now that Stephanie isn't around to bake and bring them.

I shrug. "Just having nice thoughts for once."

"Get you," Sal says.

He's not really listening. Playing with his phone and slurping coffee.

Alejandro frowns. "You'd better not get all well-adjusted and leave us." He stabs me in the shoulder with a pointy finger. "Don't you dare become a normie just happily going about your life without a care in the world."

I swat him away. "Fear not, I'm never leaving. Seriously, where else would I go?"

Alejandro doesn't look convinced. "Humph. Maybe. I mean, no one will put up with you like we do."

"*Bullshit*," Sal growls.

"Aww shucks," I say, acting touched. "That's so sweet of you."

"Huh?"

"You really think there are people out there who will put up with me like you and Alejandro?"

"What? No . . . Yeah. Whatever. I wasn't referring to you." He gestures at his phone. "I just . . ."

Alejandro nudges me with an elbow. "Not enough likes. This boy lives for the validation of strangers. He can't get enough of it. That's the real reason he comes here."

Sal is smiling and shaking his head at the same time. "I only live for your validation."

Alejandro's eyes narrow to slits, and his lips purse into an angry pout. "Then try harder, sweetheart."

I feel like I want to leave them to it, but there was something in Sal's exclamation that intrigues me. I want to know more.

"Come on," I say to him. "What's going on." I gesture to his phone. "What is it?"

"Ah, just some troll winding me up," he says with a dismissive gesture, as though he knows he shouldn't care and yet still does. "I always fall for it."

Alejandro sees a chance to jab a flirty taunt. "Someone accuse you of stuffing socks into your gym shorts again?"

Sal rises above it, instead says to me, "I'm a member of all these forums. It's kind of geeky, I know. Nerds talking nerd stuff. On this one site, this one poster . . . they're trolling. Saying shit for shit's sake, you know? It pisses me off. We're just people trying to connect with a shared interest. There's no need to be a dick about it."

"What's the forum?" Alejandro asks. "Closets Anonymous?"

"I'm too old for this shit," Sal begins, refusing to bite. "But I love an unsolved mystery. Something weird. Especially if it's weird. Aliens, paranormal . . . serial killers. All that scary, dark side of reality."

"Go on," I say. "What's the troll doing?"

"I'll give them a lot of credit," Sal says, holding up his phone to show what's on his screen. "They've put their back into it. Look at all this shit. It's not so much a post as an essay." He thumbs the screen to scroll down to what looks like thousands of words of text. "See?"

Alejandro rolls his eyes. "I won't even read an email if it can't fit on one screen. Brevity is the most underrated of qualities. Seriously, the human race needs to learn how to say more with less. Why do people feel the need to use a hundred words when three will do?"

"Funny you should say three," Sal says.

"Why is it funny he said three?" I ask.

"That's how many holes he wishes he had," Alejandro interjects. "Two's just not enough."

"You know what, I'm starting to think you're not actually gay," Sal tells him. "And this is all an elaborate act to fool us into thinking you're not so utterly vanilla. It's the only explanation. You're trying too hard to be interesting, straight boy."

"Why is it funny he said three?" I ask.

"*Honey*," Alejandro says to Sal, "they had to jab my mama full of every chemical in that hospital to induce my birth. Because I tell you, even in the womb I knew there was no way I wanted to touch a vagina willingly."

Sal laughs, and Alejandro is very pleased with himself.

"*Why is it funny he said three?*"

They both stare at me. Other group members nearby sent shocked glances my way.

"Are you okay?" Sal asks me.

"Please, just tell me."

"Okay. Okay. It's no big deal. I didn't mean to keep you in suspense. It's just . . . There's this story. A rhyme. The rule of three. Like a creepy, mysterious . . . thing."

"I know it."

"Sure, yeah. Lots of people have heard it. Anyway, I've been looking into it for a long time. That's what the forum is. We talk about the rule of three. There are these diary entries. Journals written by these girls. Like telling their stories. But they're incomplete. We don't know what happens to them. We just know they're dead."

I nod along. "Yeah, yeah. I used to go on it all the time when I was younger."

"You did? Awesome. Whoever came up with this stuff is nuts, right? I love that bit where one of the girls pulls a little black shoot from her brain . . ." He scratches at his head as he speaks. "She just claws her way into her skull with scalp flapping over her face and—"

Alejandro exhales. "Ohmygod, why won't this fade away? Every few years someone hears this one stupid rhyme, and then *boom*, the same old theories come back, and everyone thinks they're so very clever for spotting a minor detail and spinning it into an elaborate theory. It's not even real, so why bother? Let. It. Go."

I feel that I should be removing myself from this conversation so as not to incriminate myself. And yet I can't. I'm a part of this story. I need to know what other people think of it.

"That's what I'm saying," Sal says to Alejandro. "This troll on the forum is trying to claim theirs is the final journal entry."

I can only say, "Is that so?"

"It's kind of pathetic," Sal continues. "Listen to this," Sal says. "The arrogance of the troll is off the charts. *I'm the one who solves the rule of three. Let me tell you how I do it.*"

I say, "They do sound pretty full of themselves."

Sal nods. "I know, right? As if."

It's an odd experience having my own words read back to me.

I hadn't logged into the forum for years. I was too busy living it to read what a bunch of geeks were saying. It's kind of funny that

Three wanted to force me into writing my own journal, and yet there I was doing it anyway. Why? Good question.

I guess because this is my story to tell.

I debated how to do it, of course. I'm not exactly going to upload a full confession onto the internet, am I? But I needed to tell the world it was over. My duty to honor Amy and Ila. I could never have done this without them, after all. And I can't stand the thought that people might think their deaths are meaningless. People need to know they didn't die in vain.

So, here we are.

I left out a few specifics, naturally. Doctored some details. Names changed to protect those involved. The truth, yet shone through a prism.

Besides, perspective is everything. What matters to Sal and what matters to me are never going to align.

Sal says to me, "I wish you'd have said before now you were into this. We could have chatted about it. But . . . you know, you don't really talk about yourself. Not really. Not like me or Mister Anti-Vagina here."

Alejandro says, "I have nothing against them, I assure you. I'm actually very pro-vagina. In fact, I'm all for protecting the sanctity of the vagina. I mean it. I think we should lock them all up and keep them safe . . . Somewhere far, far away from me so I don't have to touch one or look at one. Present vagina excepted, naturally."

I do a mocking bow of gratitude, then ask him, "Why did you say before the rule of three is not real?"

Sal answers instead, excited to talk about one of his interests. "Oh, it definitely is. But what the troll is missing is that the whole point of it is that it's a puzzle you're not meant to solve. There are no dates; only one character has a full name in the whole thing. Where does it even take place?"

"That's how you know it's not real," Alejandro answers with a shrug.

Sal shakes his head. "No, it has to be the killer himself hiding facts and changing names to stop anyone figuring out the truth."

"I think that's a little on the nose, don't you?"

Sal says, "Nah, creepy AF. I really shouldn't still care, but I can't help it. Once you notice one thing like that, then it sort of cascades. I can't quite decide whether the journals are entirely written by the killer himself or if he actually instructs them what to write."

"How would that even be possible?" Alejandro asks.

"When he finally gets them," Sal begins, "he has them write down their story. That's his kink. It's all about control, dominance. He creates the world as he would like it to be, nice and organized, and then releases his work out into the real world and we all obsess over it and he moves on to stalking the next girl. He simultaneously gets to show off and stay anonymous."

Alejandro says, "I don't buy it. Who's going to write a massive journal for a psychopath?"

I say, "If they lock you in a room with a pen and a notebook, what else are you going to do?"

"Maybe." He strokes his chin. "But wouldn't it be better with a supernatural explanation? Like that one girl thought. Like a curse . . . only you catch it if you read the journals. Once you read them, the rule of three has you. Like some ancient evil entity trapped in words. We could be dealing with something that transcends human understanding. Even the very conversation we're having now could be dictated by it."

"So meta." Sal laughs. "And it means we're sadly all doomed now. Regardless, this is the literal point. We drive ourselves crazy trying to figure out what everything means."

I say, "You're both failing to account for the obvious."

"Which is?"

I smile. "That she's not a troll. It's both real and it really is over. So, you already have the conclusion, but you're refusing to accept it."

"Well, it's no fun if it's over," Sal admits. "Especially not when this girl even calls the bad guy Three."

Alejandro rolls his eyes. "She's so basic."

Sal nods. "If she really wanted to sound credible, then she should have just called him Nine."

They share a little fist bump, each so very pleased with himself.

"Excuse me, what?" is the only way I can respond for a moment. "Why Nine?"

They both look at me as if I'm speaking a foreign language.

"Are you serious?" Alejandro asks.

Sal says, "You're not joking?"

"I'm literally not joking. Why Nine? Why would a troll call the killer Nine? What does that have to do with the rule of three? It's about the number three. He's called Three, right? Nine doesn't make any sense."

"Well, it's because three multiplied by three is nine," Alejandro says in a dismissive tone. "That's why. If someone is obsessed with the number three, it's only natural they'd fetishize three threes even more."

"Well, I don't know about these days," I say, shaking my head, "but you're totally overthinking it. It's the rule of three, not the rule of nine."

"You didn't notice that all the characters but the victims have a nine-letter name?"

I hesitate. "They do?"

"Literally every single one. Oh, I'm sorry. I feel like I've just spoiled the story for you."

"No, no. I mean, yeah. I did notice. I just don't care. It doesn't change anything."

"I'm not so sure," Sal says. "It's only when you really get into it that this kind of stuff stands out. You're not meant to take it all in the first time. If you could spot all the codes in the text, then there would be no mystery, would there?"

"Not to toot my own horn," Alejandro says with a cocky head sway, "but I saw the codes straightaway. Third word of every third paragraph of every third chapter."

"Bullshit you did," Sal says in disbelief.

"You're literally told at the start it's about the number three. Don't hate me because I actually paid attention like it stated."

"So," Sal begins, "I suppose since you're of such a superior intelligence, you also knew to check the ninth word of the ninth paragraph of the ninth chapter?"

He hesitates for a second. "Yeah, sure. Of course I did. I'm not a noob." He quickly changes the subject. "So, what else is the troll saying? About their *journal*?"

"Oh, you know . . . Works out who the baddie is. Kills them. Same old, same old."

"If I had a penny for every girl who figures it all out, I'd be able to afford real therapy. Does she not get the fact that every girl thinks she's on to the truth just before she dies?"

Sal only shrugs.

Alejandro groans. "I literally hate you two. I thought I was done with all this, but now I want to read some more of the journals. How many legit ones are there by now? I don't care about these fan fiction efforts."

"I've read both of the originals," I say. "I'll have to catch up with this new one from the *troll*."

I kind of like referring to myself as a troll, as if I've made the whole thing up to feed the machine. I feel like a celebrity acting incognito, hanging out and shooting the breeze with her fans. I picture myself with a wide-brimmed hat and oversize shades. In fact, now that I have time for a life, I need a new look. Go glam for a change.

"Both?" Sal asks, a little confused.

Alejandro shares a similar look of confusion.

They both stare at me, so full of intrigue and expectation I'm not sure what to say, as if this is some kind of weird trick question.

Am I the butt of some joke I'm not aware of?

"Uh-huh," I say, tentatively, expecting a cream-pie punchline in the face at any moment. "I've read the two journals already out there . . . Why, haven't you read both of them?"

The back of Alejandro's hand goes to his brow as he staggers back a step in some deliberately overacted expression of shock and admonishment. One eye on his future Tony Award.

"I hate to break it to you," Sal says, "but there's like five of them we're all currently obsessing over."

"We're way ahead of you, girl," Alejandro adds.

"If this new one turns out to be genuine, then it'll make six," Sal says, thoughtful. "Which means only three to go if Nine is aiming for nine girls as some of us think."

Alejandro pokes me with a rigid finger. "You need to keep up with the seasons if you wanna hang with the true fandom. What have you been doing all this time?"

I shrug. I'm not sure what to say, so I say, "Had more important things to do, like living my life."

Alejandro tuts in disapproval.

Sal leans closer. "We better take our seats before the silver fox starts tapping his watch again."

The silver fox being the new counselor.

Alejandro says, "Do you think it's real?"

I say, "Do I think what is real?"

"The hair."

"The hair?"

"Do you think the hair is real?"

"Do I think the hair is real?"

He says, "Is there a parrot in here or something?"

I smile because it's funny to annoy him. "Looks pretty real to me."

Alejandro purses his lips. "I'm not convinced. That quiff is just too luscious. Yet it doesn't even move. Like magic, like it's breaking the immutable laws of the physical world as we speak."

"*Immutable?* Have you started reading a dictionary before bed?"

"Been doing it for years, honey." He winks at me, and we head back to the circle of chairs.

When we're all sitting down and paying attention, the new counselor unties and unclasps his leather notebook and continues where he left off:

"They say there are five stages of grief. Yet such a complex combination of emotions cannot be so easily quantified. If no two sets of fingerprints are the same, then why could we ever assume two people act and think and feel in the same way? How you grieve and I grieve are never going to match up. What's right for you and what will work for me can't possibly align. But that's okay. You like chocolate ice cream and I like strawberry. We don't choose what we like best, so neither of us is wrong." He pauses. Shows a tight smile. "I can't give you a solution to your problems, because there is no definitive solution. What I promise I'll do, however, is to help you find your own."

I get a weird sense of déjà vu, like I've heard these words before somewhere.

Alejandro nudges me with an elbow, interrupting my thoughts before they can fully form, and whispers, "You know what? I think I'm going to write a journal too and continue the story. Call myself Fay . . . or something. Show that troll she doesn't get to decide when the story ends."

I whisper back, "Can't wait to read it."

I don't look at him, because my gaze is drawn to the floor. The linoleum has had a recent buff, I notice. I can see my reflection.

Only it's Stephanie looking back at me. She's smiling, like she's proud of me.

I feel proud too.

I've completed my life's work and handed it in early. Top marks. Extra credit. Maybe a ribbon. Regardless of what I uploaded to the site, this is a trophy I must display in secret. It sits in a cabinet inside my mind, shiny and glorious, and invisible to everyone else.

I admire it now and again. It's okay to feel pleased with myself, isn't it? It's not smug to celebrate, surely? I'm alive.

I've solved the rule of three.

But with no more samples to take, no more evidence to pore over, and no need to update my spreadsheet, there's one unexpected yet inevitable downside.

What am I supposed to do with all this free time?

ELIZABETH

FIFTY-TWO

Amy meant too much to me in so many ways. She was the sister I never had. Growing up in foster care created a desire to have a family of my own that was so strong it almost consumed me. Every time I was moved to a new set of childless parents, every time I was deemed too much to handle, I prayed that it would be the last time. I willed this new set of parents to keep me, to decide not simply to be my foster parents, but my actual parents. I prayed they would adopt me so we could become a happy little family of three.

Eventually, I woke up.

No one wanted me. Not my father, who walked out on me before I was old enough to even know him. Not my mother, who gave me up when she could not forgive me for driving her true love away.

Family meant pain to me. It meant being let down. It meant realizing I was not good enough to be loved.

In the absence of love all I had left was hate.

Hate for my father for leaving me, hate for my mother for abandoning me, and hate for each and every pair of foster parents who tricked me into believing I had at last found a home.

I first met Amy when we were both patients in a psychiatric home. Her for her suicide attempt and me for torching my foster father's new car after he climbed into my bed one night.

We bonded instantly. Amy had lost her sister, leaving her family fragmented in three pieces that could never be whole again, and me knowing I would be sent to form another family of three that would break my heart all over again. Just as soon as I had my rage issues under control, of course.

The doctors were happy that Amy and I got along so well. We helped one another's recovery. We did what meds alone could not. Soon Amy wasn't deemed a danger to herself, and before too long the orderlies didn't need to watch me so closely when I was out of my padded cell.

Amy was released first. Her smiling parents came to collect her, and I had never before felt such envy. I smiled and waved her goodbye while inside I was boiling with anger at the sight of the three of them together.

Why did she get to have this family who loved her so very much when I had never even had one who could tolerate me for long?

Without her, my anger returned. I was restrained and sedated and evaluated more and more.

If I hated families before, now that hatred rose to new heights. I hated Amy for being part of a family. I hated her parents for taking her away from me.

Why couldn't Amy have been abandoned like me? Then we could be a family of our own. Just the two of us to make one another whole.

I didn't need parents if I had Amy. Amy didn't need parents if she had me.

I found myself wondering what it would be like if it really was just the two of us.

Which could never happen if I spent every day in a straitjacket. I needed to get out. I needed my friend.

I began hiding my rage. I kept my anger deep inside me, locked away in a fiery cage that filled little by little, day after day. But it worked. I burned from the inside, and on the outside I was calm as any pond.

It was only a matter of time before I was released and I could find Amy and show her that we needed only each other and no one else. I knew I could convince her that we were meant to be a family of our own. She didn't need her parents. It was their fault she had cut herself, after all. If they truly cared, she should never have felt she had no reason to live.

And then something happened I had not expected.

Amy came back to the hospital.

My best friend, my sister, had returned to me.

She had tried to kill herself once again, I overheard while she was kept in isolation under continued observation. It was all the proof I could ever need that I had been right. Her parents didn't deserve her. They had failed her a second time.

It was only when she was allowed to mingle with the other patients that I found out the awful truth.

Her parents had hung themselves.

She had found them on her eighteenth birthday, dangling by their necks in the garage. Amy had tried to do the same a few weeks later.

I had wanted nothing more than to be with my sister again, but not like this. Never like this. She was devastated all over again, and I could see in the eyes of the doctors and nurses that no one expected her to get through her grief a second time.

I was determined to make sure she did.

Her recovery became my mission in life. All my prior hatred toward her parents was forgotten, all the rage inside me had to take a back seat because I had something more important than myself to worry about.

Slowly, little by little, she improved. I spent every single day by her side. If she wanted to cry all the time, then she did so on my shoulder. If she wanted to scream in grief and injustice, I let her do so at me. When she was ready to talk, I listened. When she was able to find joy again, I made sure she found as much as she could take.

We were released within weeks of one another, and no one was surprised when we went to college together.

Since I'd grown up in the system, my fees were paid on my behalf. I'm not sure if I really wanted to go, but I wanted to be with Amy. She was all the family I had ever known.

I never got over it when she died.

But my rage never returned. In that way, Amy saved me in a way I couldn't save her.

It was hard to read her journal, to get that glimpse into her state of mind in those final weeks of her life, to know she felt I betrayed her. Maybe she realized I never believed her about being doomed to die, about bad things always happening in threes. I didn't. I went along with it because I would have done anything for her. I didn't do enough, I eventually realized.

Years later, when one of my students approached me to discuss Amy, to tell me about something the kids called the rule of three, I was stunned. I had thought about Amy a thousand times since her death, but I had never thought that death had been suspicious. Some of us just aren't long for this world.

Then Ila died too.

I convinced myself it had to be a coincidence. She had diabetes, after all. Even with the best will in the world, bad things can and will happen.

That's what I kept telling myself, although there was always that doubt, that *what if?*

And beyond that, there was the guilt. I didn't save Amy, and I didn't help Ila nearly enough. I should have done more for my best friend and for my student.

Eventually, I retrained. I became a counselor. Perhaps that was to manage my guilt, but I like to think I wanted to be there for people who needed help. And I did help them. In individual sessions and in groups, with addiction and self-esteem and especially with grief.

I got married. I got divorced.

I discovered I had perimenopausal osteoporosis when I broke my hip by bumping it on the corner of a desk. Having to use a cane is no kind of fun, and yet I feel lucky I can still walk at all.

The guilt never went away. Or the doubt.

I found myself on forums late at night discussing an urban legend called the rule of three.

Somehow the journal I gave Ila ended up online. Not only that, Ila had written her own before she died like Amy had done. There were other journals too that I couldn't be sure were real or merely fan fiction. I read all sorts of wild speculation by internet sleuths who had it figured out. Some were convinced that there had never been an Amy or Ila or any other girl, some certain that Amy was still alive and killing other families because her own had been taken from her.

Some believe the rule of three was a curse.

Others that death himself was playing a cruel joke.

But a serial killer made sense to most.

I don't necessarily believe that, but I definitely don't believe in anything supernatural. Until I'm certain otherwise, this is all a bizarre coincidence.

It was surreal reading posts and comments from strangers online discussing people I had known. They didn't realize that I had firsthand knowledge of many of the events they argued passionately about. They didn't know that some of what Amy wrote as fact was her interpretation or her speculation. They couldn't know she sometimes changed people's names or forgot specifics. I could almost laugh at elaborate theories that were furiously argued by those who had built them on foundations of sand.

Then I understood that if anyone could find out the truth, it was me.

I reached out to people I had known who had known Amy. No one could really help me, because no one really had known her as I had known her. The only missing connection was Christian. Amy wrote she met him on the bus, which I know didn't happen, but what if she met him another time? Why was he so important to her story?

I didn't realize back then that he was supplying us with the pills we took and the weed we smoked. Not directly, though the students we bought drugs from obtained them from him. He had ended up selling drugs full-time when he flunked out of school. A truly sad case of a smart young man destroyed by bad choices. He was still in prison when I finally tracked him down.

At first, he didn't want to engage with me. He was mean. He was cruel. I almost gave up until I saw why he had ended up that way, that he had been abused. He reminded me of myself when I had been young and full of anger.

I didn't ask who had hurt him, but I've been a counselor long enough to know that it would be a family member. Most likely his father.

The meanness, the cruelty, is a shield with which to protect himself. Slowly, I get him to lower it, little by little. He doesn't really tell me anything useful until I discover that Christian is the older brother of Ila's college boyfriend. If only I had paid more attention to Ila while I had the chance, who knows what else I could have learned? When we're told our time is up, I ask if I can visit Christian again. He agrees. He likes the idea of playing detective with me to crack the rule of three. He tells me he'll call his dad to see what he remembers. I don't say anything to this, as I know survivors aren't always estranged from their abusers. If Christian is still in touch with his father, that's his choice to make.

At that point, I know I'm getting close to the truth.

It's not long before someone on the forum claims to have the original journal I gave to Ila, which Ila herself continued. There is another entry in the journal that was never uploaded to the internet, they claim.

I'm almost breathless with anticipation. This could be the final piece to the puzzle that will make the whole clear to me.

They won't upload it, however. I have to collect it in person. They want to sell it to me, of course.

That's fine with me. I don't care about money. I care about getting answers for Amy and for Ila. I couldn't help them when they were alive, but I can help them now.

I'll admit I'm a little frightened to meet a stranger, but if I want the truth then I have to do it their way.

Besides, if this is some kind of ambush, I'm not as frail as I look. If someone is up to no good, they're going to find themselves on the wrong end of my cane.

LESTRANGE

FIFTY-THREE

I find myself tired these days. I ask myself if I was always this way, or if the sudden freedom of responsibilities has left me without energy. Maybe if we have nothing we need to do, we waste away.

At first, I'm not really listening. I don't want to be here, and yet here I am anyway. I don't want to be rude, so I pretend to listen. I sit in an attentive posture and narrow my eyes into a focused gaze. I make sure to nod at regular intervals.

You need this, my wife told me. *If you don't want to do it for yourself, then you can at least do it for me.*

Which is fair. I'm driving her up the wall now that I'm at home all the time. I'm not used to twiddling my thumbs, and I'm no good at it. My digits are far too thick to even attempt a twiddle.

She suggested I get myself a hobby. It's important to have a hobby, she insisted. In life we have family and partners and friends and work and responsibilities, so it can be too easy to neglect ourselves. We need to dedicate time just for us. It's not selfish to put yourself first every now and again.

All of which made perfect sense. Only one small caveat: nothing interests me when I have so much on my mind. I can't willfully distract myself.

Llewellyn sees I'm distracted. "I think I've said enough about the process, so why don't we dive right in. What is it about your recent case you find so troubling?"

"That's the thing," I tell him. "It's not even a case."

"I'm not sure I understand."

"A young woman drowned in the bay."

"How terrible."

"Yeah," I manage. "Nothing to suggest it was anything other than an unfortunate accident. And yet I've thought about little else for weeks."

"Go on."

"She told me she was going to die," I begin. "A while back, I mean. She was convinced she would have an accident. I didn't believe her, of course. She told me I would be convinced when I finally saw her corpse in the morgue."

"She sounds troubled."

"You got that right."

"You think you should have taken her more seriously?"

"Yes, I mean no, not really. She was a fantasist, I'm sure. But being sure doesn't mean I can forget. Besides, she murdered someone, which became apparent in the aftermath of her own death only when we found her . . . research, as she called it."

"I see."

"It was my fault. I helped, stupidly. I bought her bullshit. Only for a single moment, granted, but in that moment I shared confidential information with her that led to a shooting."

"The reason for your suspension?"

I have to break eye contact. I can't bring myself to answer, so I merely nod. "I'm going out of my mind with nothing to do."

"I often recommend my patients keep a record of their thoughts."

"Like a journal?"

"Exactly. Keeping one can help make sense of the world around us. It's about taking control," he explains. "When life doesn't make sense, we make sense of it however we can. For some of us, we turn to drink or drugs to cope. Others make sense of the world with hobbies. Simply writing down our thoughts can be of tremendous benefit. And it will give you something to do."

"I'll think about it."

"What made you believe her?" he asks. "In that moment you mentioned."

"She was desperate, scared, pleading," I answer, remembering that phone call when I was working late. "She had no family of her own, and I thought of what would happen to my own daughter if I wasn't around to help her."

He scribbles notes as I talk. "Family is important to you, I take it?"

"Family is everything to me. Been married thirty years and still going strong. Two kids. Boy and a girl. Still young enough to be at home but old enough to no longer want to."

He shows a tight smile. "Tell me more."

"Neither was planned," I admit. "Which I think was best, as I might never have pulled that trigger willingly. What about you? Assuming you're allowed to tell me about yourself."

"I'm not going to tell you my deepest, darkest secrets," he says with another tight smile. "But it's perfectly fine for you to ask me questions if it helps you open up. I have two sons, Nathaniel and Christian. Do you like being a father?"

"Best thing in the world was watching James grow up. At least until Sia came along. Then I had the same experience all over again. I don't know how I got so lucky, I really don't."

"Sia," he repeats, then again, "Sia," and again, "Sia," as if trying the word out for size. "What a lovely name." Llewellyn smiles. "Tell me about her."

First thing: take a deep breath.

I can't overstate how important it is to breathe. Do it now. Inhale, long and slow. Hold it in. Exhale even slower. See, you're calmer already, aren't you? I need you calm because you need to listen.

I know you. I know you're terrified and overwhelmed. I know no one believes you and you're desperate and going out of your mind. I know you because I *was* you. I thought I had it all figured out. I thought I knew it all. I was so very, very wrong.

I'll tell you everything that happened. Every little detail. As it happened, how it happened. Because maybe you'll see something I failed to notice. I know the answer is here somewhere. I just couldn't find it myself.

So pay attention. Pay attention to every single detail.

Before we start, you must remember one important fact.

What you'll read didn't save me.

But perhaps, together, we can save you.

Good luck,
Sia.

ACKNOWLEDGMENTS

My wholehearted thanks goes to everyone who helped make this book possible, with particular gratitude to my brilliant agent who believed in the concept from the very start; James Wills and the team at Watson, Little; my amazing and talented editors, Katherine Armstrong and Emily Bestler, whose ideas and attention to detail have been invaluable; the lovely people at Simon & Schuster on both sides of the Atlantic who include Craig Fraser, Maudee Genao, Paige Lytle, Judith Long, Libby McGuire, Morgan Pager, Hydia Scott-Riley, Karin Seifried, Sierra Swanson, Dana Trocker, Rich Vlietstra, and the S&S sales team; the many people who read early drafts and provided feedback or merely allowed me to waffle and vent were Liz Barnsley, Alexandra Benedict, Emily Field Griffin, Saskia Kantsinger, Bodo Pfündl, Mary Sweeney, Rebecca Tinnelly, Chris Whittaker, and Kevin Wignall.